"Lauren Royal knows how to make history come alive."
—Patricia Gaffney, *New York Times* bestselling author

Tempting Juliana

"A light, adorable *Emma*-style romance destined to delight anyone looking for a witty, engaging plotline and utterly delightful characters who get caught in meddling, madness, and mayhem on the way to a happy ending."
—*Romantic Times*

"Delightful from first page to last, full of superb characters, clever dialogue, and laugh-out-loud situations. This is a fun-tastic Regency romp you won't want to miss."
—Reader to Reader Reviews

"Very funny and extremely romantic. I loved all the characters and especially adored Juliana and James. I highly recommend this book." —Fresh Fiction

"This book has everything a great romance should have: a delightful historical setting, humor at all the right places, and a host of memorable characters."
—Fallen Angel Reviews

"Ms. Royal has penned a wonderful tale. . . . New readers will not be disappointed, and fans are probably waiting anxiously to get their hands on this title."
—The Romance Readers Connection

Lost in Temptation

"After brilliantly evoking the splendor of Restoration England in her six previous books, Royal brings her flair for mixing richly detailed historical settings with sinfully sexy romance to the Regency world in the beguiling start to a new trilogy featuring the Chase sisters."
—*Booklist*

continued . . .

"A deeply satisfying and original read."
—Historical Romance Writers

"This deliciously humorous, tender, touching romance, with a dash of recipes from the era that you can try, is a delight for the heart, soul, and stomach. Royal takes history out of the doldrums and gives the era brightness and color that draws readers straight into the story."
—*Romantic Times*

Praise for Lauren Royal's Flower trilogy

Rose

"Bringing her Ashcroft sisters trilogy to a delightful close, Royal vividly details the seductively glamorous court of Charles II." —*Booklist*

"A rip-roaring tale." —Romance Reviews Today

Lily

"Another triumph of deliciously sensual romance played against the fascinating world of Restoration England."
—*Booklist*

"A refreshing story, told with much humor . . . a real joy to read." —Romance Reviews Today

Violet

"A delightful story starring two . . . endearing, brilliant eccentrics." —*Midwest Book Review*

"[Royal] entertains. . . . This breezy summer read will satisfy her rapidly growing fan base."
—*Publishers Weekly*

Praise for Lauren Royal's Jewel trilogy

Amber

"Lively . . . energetic . . . filled with likable characters."
—*Publishers Weekly*

"The glitter of Restoration England is expertly evoked in Royal's latest romance." —*Booklist*

Emerald

"A passionate tale that brings late seventeenth-century England vividly alive . . . fast-paced and filled with action from the very first page to the climax."
—*Midwest Book Review*

"With strong characters and an action-filled plot, *Emerald* is a Royal flush." —*Affaire de Coeur*

"Brimming with action, adventure [and] love. Ms. Royal brings Restoration England to life right before the reader's eyes. I highly recommend *Emerald*."
—Romance Reviews Today

Amethyst

"An accomplished debut." —Patricia Gaffney

"All of these characters are so well drawn and developed. . . . A promising debut."
—*The Romance Reader*

Also by Lauren Royal

Lost in Temptation

Tempting Juliana

The Art of Temptation

Lauren Royal

A SIGNET ECLIPSE BOOK

SIGNET ECLIPSE
Published by New American Library, a division of
Penguin Group (USA) Inc., 375 Hudson Street,
New York, New York 10014, USA
Penguin Group (Canada), 90 Eglinton Avenue East, Suite 700, Toronto,
Ontario M4P 2Y3, Canada (a division of Pearson Penguin Canada Inc.)
Penguin Books Ltd., 80 Strand, London WC2R 0RL, England
Penguin Ireland, 25 St. Stephen's Green, Dublin 2,
Ireland (a division of Penguin Books Ltd.)
Penguin Group (Australia), 250 Camberwell Road, Camberwell, Victoria 3124,
Australia (a division of Pearson Australia Group Pty. Ltd.)
Penguin Books India Pvt. Ltd., 11 Community Centre, Panchsheel Park,
New Delhi - 110 017, India
Penguin Group (NZ), 67 Apollo Drive, Rosedale, North Shore 0745,
Auckland, New Zealand (a division of Pearson New Zealand Ltd.)
Penguin Books (South Africa) (Pty.) Ltd., 24 Sturdee Avenue,
Rosebank, Johannesburg 2196, South Africa

Penguin Books Ltd., Registered Offices:
80 Strand, London WC2R 0RL, England

First published by Signet Eclipse, an imprint of New American Library,
a division of Penguin Group (USA) Inc.

First Printing, October 2007
10 9 8 7 6 5 4 3 2 1

Printed in the United States of America

For June Jørgensen Schelde-Mollerup,
who has been part of my family
for more than (gulp!) eighteen years.

I cannot believe you have
three children of your own now!

Acknowledgments

I wish to thank:

My editor, Laura Cifelli, for her unfailing insight; my critique partner, Terri Castoro, for her patience and talent; Deborah Alexander, MD, for helping me choose an appropriate illness and spending much precious time describing all the pertinent details; Andrew Potter, research assistant at the Royal Academy Library, for the list of Academicians on the 1817 Selection Committee and historical information on the selection process; Devonie Royal-Gordon (best daughter in the world), for reading bunches of old Minerva Press novels and pulling out quotes for me; Brent Royal-Gordon (tied for best son in the world), for designing and maintaining my Web site; Ann and Andrew Scott, for hosting wonderful book signings at Highland festivals; Jack, Brent, Blake, and Devonie, for putting up with hearing, "Not now, I'm writing," way too many times; my official First Readers—Ken and Dawn Royal, Herb and Joan Royal, Taire Martyn, and Karen Nesbitt—for invaluable feedback; my incredible, hardworking Street Team (many more names than I can list, but they're all on the Street Team page on my Web site), for their ongoing enthusiasm and support . . . and, once again, my readers, because I do this for you.

Thank you, one and all!

Prologue

IRISH WHISKEY CAKE

Take butter with sugar and put in this eggs and flour and a bit o' coffee to make a nice flavour. Put in your pan and bake in your oven. Make a syrup of coffee with much sugar and a wee dram o' whiskey and pour this into your cake. Bring to table with sweet whiskey cream and a sprinkle of nuts.

My mother used to caution, "Who gossips with you will gossip of you." Nonetheless, she surely did love to gossip. She used to serve this cake when the womenfolk came for tea. She claimed it loosened ladies' tongues.

—Deirdre Delaney Raleigh, 1819

Kilburton, Ireland
November 1807

On a damp Tuesday shortly after he turned eighteen, life as Sean Delaney had known it ceased to exist.

First he received a letter, an event in itself. All of Sean's acquaintances lived in the village of Kilburton—nobody ever had reason to write him a letter. A very official letter it looked, too. As he watched the lad who had delivered it retreat down the lane, Sean's mother came in from the sitting room, where she'd been serving tea to some womenfolk from the parish.

"Was it not Mary McBride, then?" she asked. "She's late."

"It wasn't Mrs. McBride, no." Sean shut the door and turned to her, the single folded sheet clutched in one hand. "It's a letter. For me."

"For you?" Her pleasant, guileless face looked as surprised as he felt. "Well, open it, then, will you?"

He nodded and broke the seal.

"Who is it from?" she asked impatiently.

"A solicitor." Below the imposing engraved letterhead, he scanned down the page. " 'On behalf of Mr. Patrick Delaney—' "

"Who is that?"

He shrugged. "One of Da's relations, I expect."

"Your father has no living relations." She frowned. "What is he wanting, then?"

"He's wanting . . ." He read further and gasped. "He's not wanting anything. He's dead. And he left ten thousand pounds. To me."

"Ten *thousand* pounds?"

To a vicar's wife like Ma, the number was all but incomprehensible—enough to support a villager and his family and a servant or two for fifty years. Staring at Sean, she slowly lowered herself to a plain oak chair. Muffled feminine voices tumbled from the sitting room—her guests were gossiping, no doubt. Uncharacteristically, she ignored them.

"Ten thousand pounds, Sean. Whatever will you do with so much money?"

"I don't know," he said.

But he did know. He'd known instantly. He just didn't want to tell her.

He didn't want to disappoint her, not yet.

"I'm after going for a walk." He grabbed a heavy wool cloak from the peg by the door. "I shan't be gone long," he promised softly before slipping outside.

It was raining, as was usual this time of year. As was usual all year, for that matter. Tucking the letter under the cloak where it would stay dry, he hurried down the lane.

Such a vast amount of money—more than Ma had seen in her entire life. She would want him to do good with it. Charitable works or some such. She was a vicar's wife, after all, and a very kindly one at that.

But Sean didn't want to do good. Oh, he'd pay the expected tithe. He was a vicar's son, perhaps not as devout as his father would wish, but no rebel, either. The tithe would be an unprecedented boon for the parish, one Sean would be pleased to provide. He'd been raised with all of these folks—spent his entire life surrounded by them, cocooned in their comfortable familiarity—and it seemed right that they should share a tenth of his good fortune.

But after that, he was going to leave Ireland.

He was going to London.

He was going to make a life for himself, something better than he'd ever imagined growing up in wee Kilburton.

It wasn't going to be easy leaving kinfolk and friends, striking out on his own. He knew that. His heart seemed both heavy and light as he turned away from the village, crossed the harvested fields, wandered the age-old riverbank. Touching the precious letter beneath his cloak, he alternately laughed, pondering his immense luck, and trembled, wondering what lay ahead.

Three hours passed—three tense, exhilarating hours—before he took a deep breath and started home. It had stopped raining. When he reentered the village, the sun was setting low on the horizon, its last rays fighting through the cloud cover as he trod the lane toward the vicarage. Just before he reached the squat house, two figures came out of it, dark shadows against the silvery glow.

"You have no choice." The Honorable Mr. William Hamilton's voice came low and angry through the gloom. An imposing man if not a tall one, he was the same height as the son he pulled toward their fancy carriage. "Not this time."

Wondering what was going on but not wanting to be seen, Sean hid himself behind a tree.

"You paid off that village girl without any repercussions." Young John Hamilton sounded sullen, furious. "And that maid—"

"Two. Two lowly maids." His father pushed him up the carriage's steps. "She's not some servant's get, you idiot," he muttered, following his son inside. "I'd lose face should you not—"

The door shut, and Sean heard nothing else. As the carriage rumbled off, he stepped from behind the tree and hurried into the house.

It was warm, welcoming, filled with the soft light of oil lamps and redolent with the scent of the whiskey cake his mother had baked earlier for her guests. A good home, simple but clean and cared for. Sean had a fine family, a sister three years his junior and parents who had always been there for both of them, giving of their hearts although they'd never had much to give materially.

He felt sad, knowing he'd soon be leaving all of this, and also excited about his new life. But mostly, he was mighty curious to learn what had made the Hamiltons leave their huge manor house to pay a call at the modest vicarage.

Hearing voices from the sitting room, he headed there. And stopped short when his sister turned to him with a grin. "I'm marrying John Hamilton."

Sean stared at fifteen-year-old Deirdre. He couldn't have heard her right. "What did you just say?"

Her golden hair gleaming in the firelight, she lifted her chin. "Mr. Hamilton told John he'd have to marry me."

"But why?" His gaze shot from his father's bloodless face to his mother's eyes, swollen from weeping. There could be only one reason they looked like that, one reason John Hamilton might be forced to wed Deirdre. "You're not . . ." As he looked back to his sister, the rest of the sentence stuck in his throat.

Her grin widened as she folded her hands over her deceivingly flat middle. "I'm with child, aye. And I'll be the wife of John Hamilton, the handsomest, richest unmarried man in all of Kilburton."

In all of the county, more like. The Hamiltons' lofty new manor house sat in the shadow of their ancestral home, centuries-old Kilburton Castle. John Hamilton's father was the younger brother of the Earl of Lincolnshire, sent years ago to oversee Kilburton, one of the earl's many lesser estates.

Growing up, Sean and Deirdre had been educated in a chilly one-room schoolhouse, while John had a parade of private English tutors. The boy had always been temperamental, and Sean had thought him haughty, unfeeling, and selfish. But the two had been born the same year, and since there were no other lads their age in Kilburton, Sean's mother had told him to play with John anyway. After all, she'd often said—all *too* often, in Sean's estimation—it was the Christian thing to do.

Being a biddable sort of son, Sean had done what he was told and played with the fellow more times than he could count. But Hamilton had always wanted to stay inside and fiddle with paste and paint, while Sean preferred outdoor pursuits like fishing and building forts. He'd never really liked John Hamilton.

Deirdre, on the other hand, a rather wild girl and the bane of her parents' existence, obviously liked John Hamilton just fine.

Fine enough to let John ruin her.

Still and all, Sean loved his sister. She was pretty and fun, the best of companions, always ready with a smile and a plan for mischief. Looking at her now, her eyes dancing, Sean clenched his fists.

He no longer disliked John Hamilton . . . he hated the rotter. For life.

Chapter One

Ten years later
The British Museum, London
April 1817

"We want to see the Rosetta Stone," two feminine voices chorused.

For the third time in the last quarter hour.

"Just a few more minutes," Lady Corinna Chase promised her sisters, her gaze focused on her sketchbook.

"A few is three," Alexandra, the oldest, pointed out. "Or maybe five. But certainly not thirty. You said 'a few more minutes' half an hour ago."

"And half an hour before that," Juliana, the middle sister, added.

The squeak of wheels threatened Corinna's concentration. Alexandra was rolling a perambulator back and forth in hopes of soothing Harold, her infant son. It was all but unheard-of for ladies to cart their babies around town—most aristocratic mothers happily left their children in the care of wet nurses and nannies. But Alexandra had insisted on buying one of the new contraptions, because she rarely let little Harry out of her sight.

Squeak. Squeak. Squeak. "How can you stare at statues for so long?"

"I'm not staring. I'm drawing." Corinna sketched

another line, following the curve of a muscled male thigh. "And in case you haven't noticed, the Elgin Marbles aren't all statues. This particular panel is part of a frieze from the illustrious Parthenon in Greece. Even more important, the figures are anatomically correct."

Which was why she was here, of course. Why she'd been willing to drag herself out of bed at an ungodly hour to sketch. Corinna wanted nothing more than to study human anatomy. Unfortunately, the anatomy classes at the Royal Academy of Arts were entirely forbidden to women.

Entirely.

Forbidden.

It was infuriating. Corinna's fondest wish was to be elected to the Royal Academy, an honor no woman had attained since 1768. Though she harbored no dreams of accomplishing this goal at her current age of twenty-two—for one thing, Academicians had to be at least twenty-four years old—getting nominated and eventually elected was a long, involved process, and she hoped to take her first step within a matter of weeks, by getting one of her paintings accepted for the Royal Academy's Summer Exhibition.

That was something women *did* accomplish on a regular basis, although not usually with portraits. Traditionally, ladies painted only landscapes and still lifes—painting people was considered fast and unseemly. However, Corinna's heart lay in painting portraits. She was drawn to the human form, compelled to render personalities in oil on canvas.

But how was a woman supposed to accurately paint people if she wasn't allowed to attend anatomy classes?

"We cannot stay much longer," Juliana said. "I need to make sure everything's in place for Cornelia's wedding." Cornelia, Juliana's mother-in-law, was marrying Lord Cavanaugh at her home later that evening. "And I want to see the Rosetta Stone," she added for the fourth time.

"So go see it."

"And I want to see the gems and minerals," Alexandra said. "And the jeweled—"

"Go see it all. Go see everything in the museum." Corinna flipped a page, refocusing on the nude form of the gorgeous Greek god before her. "I'll be right here."

"That would take an hour or more." *Squeak. Squeak.* "We cannot leave you here in the Elgin Gallery alone."

"I'm not alone. There are people everywhere." Too many people, constantly jostling her and blocking her view.

"The Rosetta Stone is in the main building."

"It is perfectly proper for two married ladies to cross the museum grounds together." Unlike Corinna, who was known as a bit of a rebel, her sisters were always concerned with being proper. "I knew I should have brought Aunt Frances along instead. She's more patient than either of you."

"She's also nine months gone with child." Alexandra sighed. "We'll be back in an hour."

"Make that two or three," Corinna muttered, but they had already left. Hearing the pram *squeak-squeak* toward the door, she smiled and licked her lips. She and the Greek god were alone at last.

Holy Hannah, he was magnificent.

Major changes in Sean Delaney's life always seemed to be heralded by a letter.

The first had been the letter informing him of his unexpected inheritance, of course, but more letters had followed. A year later, a letter had told him his parents had perished of smallpox. He'd received numerous letters each time he'd established a new company, each time he'd bought an ongoing concern, each time he'd purchased a piece of property. More recently, six short months ago, a letter had arrived from his sister, Deirdre, confessing the failure of her marriage and advising Sean she would soon arrive to move in with him.

Nevertheless, when his butler brought him a letter this fine spring morning in Hampstead, he broke the seal without a second thought. Opened it. Scanned the scrawled message quickly.

Then crumpled it into a ball and hurled it into his library's fancy white marble-manteled fireplace.

"Who was it from?" Deirdre asked from the plush blue velvet chair where she sat reading a book.

He turned to her, thinking she looked prettier than ever. He wouldn't have said the same when she'd first arrived. Following a decade of trying her best to make her ill-fated marriage work, Deirdre had looked haggard when she'd shown up on Sean's doorstep. Only twenty-five years old, she'd appeared middle-aged, run-down, and desperate.

After being forced to marry her, John Hamilton had treated her like dirt. Or less than dirt, considering one usually noticed dirt and did something about it. In contrast, Hamilton had completely ignored her while he'd concentrated on one painting after another, coming up for air only to indulge himself with a series of paramours, some of whom he carried on with right under Deirdre's nose. Tragically, Deirdre had miscarried three months into their marriage, and the two hadn't shared a bed in all the years since. Deirdre remained childless, while Hamilton, now a highly acclaimed landscape artist, had bastards all over Great Britain.

Sean glanced at the paper ball in the empty fireplace, wishing it weren't such a warm, sunny day. Had there been a proper blaze burning on the hearth, the damn letter would have been ashes by now. "It was from Hamilton. Your husband." He all but choked on the final word.

"From John? What did he say?" She shook her head and sighed. "Never mind. I really don't want to know. I'm done with him."

Sean *wished* she were done with him. The reason Deirdre looked so much better these days was she'd met another man and fallen head-over-heels in love. She wanted nothing more than to marry Daniel Raleigh, and Raleigh—a respectable merchant Sean sometimes did business with—wished to marry her. But despite many impassioned pleas, Hamilton had denied her the divorce she sought.

Unfortunately, it was impossible for a woman to sue for divorce. Only a man could do that, and Hamilton had never been the cooperative type.

"He wants me to meet with him at noon," Sean told her. "At the British Museum. He claims he has 'something important' to discuss."

Hope leapt into her eyes. "My divorce?"

"I doubt it." Hamilton was too selfish to set Deirdre free. "It sounded more like a favor. What makes him think I'd do him a favor? Me, of all people?"

She squared her shoulders. "It doesn't signify. I've no need of a divorce. Daniel wants me to come live in his home, and I have told him I will."

Raleigh had a fine house and could provide well for Deirdre. He was a steady man of good character. Sean liked him, and he treated Deirdre like a queen.

But all of that was beside the point. "Without the benefit of marriage?"

"I made a mistake, Sean. I'll be the first to admit that. But should I suffer for it forever? John's had a hold on me long enough. I'd prefer to marry Daniel than live with him unwed, but sadly that isn't an option. He's willing to take me anyway, and it's time I lived again."

"What would Ma say? And Da?" For the first time ever, Sean was almost happy they'd died. They'd both have been mortified. Though Deirdre had always been a wild one, this went beyond improper. It was all but unthinkable. "At some point, you have to grow up. You've got a chance for a fresh start here in London. If you want to be well thought of, you need to stop defying society's expectations."

"I'm not part of *society*, Sean."

"I'm not meaning in the sense of the upper crust, and well you know it. The public in general, Deirdre, the respectable people. Someday you'll have children. Don't you want them to be accepted?"

"You're one to speak! As though you've never shared a woman's bed even though you've yet to wed. You've had mistresses yourself, if you don't remember."

"It's different for men." She opened her mouth to protest, but he rushed on. "That may not be fair, but it's a fact. And I've never taken a woman's innocence, nor slept with one who expected marriage. Who expected anything more than some pretty baubles and fancy new clothes."

His mistresses—and he'd indeed kept a few of them—had been actresses and opera dancers all. He'd admit to having gone a wee bit wild himself after escaping Kilburton and his upbringing, but he'd been young, after all, and randy, and there were only so many hours a man could spend building his fortune. He'd often worked late and on a Sunday, but past a certain hour there was really nothing much he could accomplish, no one around with whom to accomplish it.

London had proved dazzling those first few years. Huge and vital and seductive. He'd enjoyed the theater, and yes, he'd found himself attracted to some women up on the stage. Since he wasn't a man who liked to share, he'd provided them housing, made them his mistresses in exchange for temporary fidelity. But it had been years—two years or more, he suddenly realized—since he'd had that sort of arrangement. He'd lost his taste for that life, for those shallow, unemotional relationships.

He'd grown up. And it was time Deirdre did, too.

Rising, he strode to the fireplace, snatched out the crumpled paper, and smoothed it on his rosewood desk. "I'll meet with Hamilton. We'll work this out. I just have time to get to the British Museum by noon—"

"No. Don't." His sister leapt from her chair to grab his arm. "You've other plans for today."

"Nothing that matters as much as this."

"I'll not have you begging on my behalf. It's pointless and humiliating."

"While your living in sin won't be?" Sean shook his arm to dislodge her hand. "I'm going, Deirdre. You cannot stop me."

Gritting his teeth, he summoned his curricle and headed for the city . . . praying that, instead of a favor, "something important" would turn out to be the divorce that would solve his sister's problem.

Chapter Two

"I have a problem," Hamilton announced without preamble when Sean stepped into the museum's lobby. "I wish your help with it. I wish to view the newly arrived Elgin Marbles."

"That presents no problem at all," Sean said dryly, gesturing toward the back of Montagu House. "We need only to walk through here and outside toward the new temporary Elgin Gallery."

Never one to respond to humor, the artist slanted him a peeved glance as he fell into step beside him. "My uncle, Samuel Hamilton, the Earl of Lincolnshire, is dying."

"My condolences," Sean said automatically before wondering if the man even cared. Hamilton looked cheerful enough, considering his usual bad temper. In contrast to Sean's own black suit and white shirt, he was dressed in colorful, flamboyant style. Though his cravat appeared brown, Sean suspected it was bright red or green. "And your problem is?"

"I'm Lincolnshire's heir, and he's not seen me for many years. Not since I was a babe in arms, in fact. He wishes to get to know the man who is about to inherit his title and estates."

"I find that unsurprising," Sean said as they stepped outdoors.

Hamilton's failure to see his uncle despite regular visits to London was no surprise, either. Deirdre's husband was nothing if not reclusive.

Although the man's paintings commanded outrageous sums, few collectors had actually met him. Once a year he slipped into town, served as a judge on the Royal Academy committee that chose the pieces to be displayed in the annual Summer Exhibition, renewed his ties with colleagues, and slipped out again—without ever pandering to his patrons.

He claimed that keeping to himself—with the exception of female companionship, one should understand—was necessary in order to maintain his artistic vision. Sean, however, had always attributed this behavior more to temperament: a combination of sheer orneriness and a twisted delight the man took in concealing himself from the public.

"And the problem with that is?" he repeated as they trod the path toward the new building, which Sean's experienced eye told him was nothing but a large, prefabricated shed. "Go see the man, if that's what he wants."

"He doesn't want to just *see* me. He's demanded I come stay with him through his final days. He claims that should I fail to arrive posthaste, I should expect to inherit the title and entailed estate and nothing else. He will leave the rest of his holdings to charity."

"Sounds fair enough to me. How long is he expected to live?"

Before the door to the Elgin Gallery, Hamilton stopped. "A week or two," he spat.

A week or two during which the selfish cur would be deprived of his hedonistic lifestyle. "So go stay with him. Sweet Jesus, Hamilton, it won't kill you." Disgusted, and knowing this was not a good time to bring up his sister's divorce yet again, Sean turned on a heel to leave.

"No." Hamilton moved to block his way, stopping him with an outstretched hand against his shoulder. "I've a once-in-a-lifetime chance to paint the legendary waterfall on Lord Llewelyn's estate in the Tanat Valley. Lady

Llewelyn has extended an invitation. It came in the same mail with the demand from Lincolnshire. I'm leaving before nightfall."

Sean glared down at his brother-in-law's hand until the man dropped it. It was common knowledge that Lady Llewelyn was Hamilton's latest paramour. The nerve of the rotter, abandoning his dying uncle for a sexual liaison when he refused to sleep with his own lovely wife. "I suppose Lord Llewelyn will be conveniently absent."

"Abroad," Hamilton confirmed. "And neither he nor his ancestors have ever allowed any artist to paint the falls. Furthermore, it's spring, the season when their volume is greatest. This very month of April, in fact, is said to be when the monk and the lady are most likely to appear. If I can capture them in paint, it will prove the coup of a lifetime."

"The monk and the lady?"

"A monk in his long robes, the Guardian of the Falls, said to materialize in the pattern of rushing water. And the Lady of the Waterfall. She's said to peek out from behind the towering gush, her body concealed in flowing skirts, her face hidden by her long hair—"

"You believe this blarney?" Sean interrupted. "This utter nonsense, the stuff of fairy tales?"

"You don't? You're Irish, for God's sake. You have to believe in the fairies."

Sean snorted. Hamilton didn't want to see fairies appear in waterfalls. He wanted to see Lady Llewelyn's clothes *dis*appear in his bed. "Your uncle needs you, Hamilton. Paint the falls another time."

"There won't *be* another time. Llewelyn refuses to grant access, and he hasn't left the country in years."

Why the hell was the man coming to *him* with this damned problem? Sean had a knack for making money, not plucking solutions out of thin air. "If that's the way you feel, you'll have to forgo Lincolnshire's unentailed holdings."

"Lincolnshire's unentailed holdings comprise the bulk of his substantial fortune."

"And doubtless you intend to keep every penny. There's nothing I can do for you, Hamilton. You'll have to postpone your journey to the Tanat Valley." *And live without your ladylove for up to fourteen long days*, Sean added silently. "Your uncle's expected to survive only a week or two. If Llewelyn's abroad, he'll be gone much longer than that."

"But there are a mere six days left in April, and even traveling without pause, it will take two of them for me to get to Wales. Maybe three. And there *is* something you can do for me." Hamilton fixed him with a cold stare. "I want you to go to the old man, introduce yourself as John Hamilton, and live with him until his death."

Aghast, Sean gaped at him for a few moments, mainly because it took him that long to force closed his slack jaw. "I suggest you find someone else to do you this favor. Perhaps someone who actually likes you. Why the devil should I, of all people, do this—or anything—for the man who ruined my sister's life?"

"Why?" A sly glint came into Hamilton's lazy-lidded eyes. "I'll tell you why: because if you cooperate, I'll grant Deirdre her precious divorce. And because if you don't, I won't. Ever."

It took a while for Sean to reclaim his breath. Hamilton was offering him exactly what he wanted . . . if only he'd do something he found absolutely abhorrent.

Since pointing that out would likely strengthen the cur's resolve, Sean chose another tack. "You'll soon be an earl," he said coolly. "You're going to need a legitimate heir to carry on the line. With or without my cooperation, you'd best divorce Deirdre and remarry."

"Siring an heir will prove no problem." Hamilton waved one smooth, pale hand. "I shall simply make your sister move back in with me until she bears me a male child."

Though that would be devastating for Deirdre, Sean

knew she'd have to comply. The law was clear: A man had the right to compel his wife to live wherever he pleased. And forcing a woman to do her "wifely duty" . . . well, the term said it all.

Duty would never be considered rape.

"Only you can pull off this deception," Hamilton continued, pressing his advantage. "You're the one man on earth who not only looks somewhat like me but also knew my father, my mother, our estate in Ireland . . . in short, everything my uncle would expect you to know."

The man did have a point. Although Sean was taller, they both had dark hair and green eyes. And Lincolnshire hadn't seen Hamilton in twenty-seven years. No doubt Sean *could* pull it off.

Except he couldn't.

"Regardless that I know all those things, your uncle will never believe me. He'll never believe I'm an artist. I'm color-blind, which you seem to have conveniently forgotten."

Hamilton laughed. "People don't question such details. The old man will believe whatever you tell him. He's ill and dying—and hell, even another *artist* will believe you're an artist. I'll bet you," he challenged, opening the flimsy door to the Elgin Gallery. "I'll bet you I can convince another artist that you're an artist, and if I can, your forfeit will be to carry out my plan and thereby secure your sister's divorce. If I fail, I'll grant Deirdre the divorce as my forfeit. Take it or leave it, Delaney."

Before Sean could protest any further, Hamilton pushed him toward a young woman busily sketching.

Chapter Three

If only she could find a real man who looked like *this*, Corinna mused as she sketched another Greek god, life would be downright blissful.

Not that she was interested in wedding anytime soon, much to her brother Griffin's chagrin. He wanted nothing more than to marry her off, to have her—his last unwed sister—out of his house and off of his hands. To make her someone else's responsibility.

To that end, he'd insisted on shoving her toward eligible men at all the balls this year. He'd also been dragging her to Almack's and every other social event on the calendar. The Season had been under way but a few weeks, yet she felt as though she'd met more men this month than the rest of her life combined.

It was annoying, to say the least.

She did enjoy balls, and she also liked men, of course. She'd especially liked kissing the few who had managed to get her alone. Although artists were supposed to be passion-filled creatures, she'd sadly lacked passion in her life until recently. Her grandmother, father, mother, and eldest brother had died in succession, keeping her from socializing for four long years. Now that she'd finally experienced some passion, she'd found men's lips to be softer and warmer than she'd expected, and the closeness had proved positively exhilarating. Enjoyable, indeed. But right now her art was more important than any search for love.

Unless she were to find one of these Greek gods . . .

Catching her lower lip between her teeth, she used her pencil to shade the fascinating muscles on the god's perfect, bare, toned chest. Then she looked up, suddenly spotting two gentlemen heading in her direction. As though some higher power had read her mind and sent him to fulfill her fantasy, the taller one seemed to her a Greek god come to life.

Flipping to a new page, she started sketching the real man instead of the stone replica. Quickly, before he disappeared from view.

His angular, sculpted face was framed by crisp black curls that grew long at the back of his neck . . . long enough to make a woman's fingers itch to comb through them. His eyes were the greenest she'd ever seen. Unfortunately, he was rather more clothed than the marble gods, but having sketched quite a few of them, she fancied she could imagine what he looked like beneath his well-made but conservative trousers, waistcoat, and tailcoat. Her pencil outlined broad shoulders tapering to narrow hips—

She froze midsketch as the two men walked right up to her.

"Good afternoon," the shorter one said.

Like the taller man, he was dark-haired and green-eyed and good-looking. And he was much more fashionably dressed. But all in all, she decided, not nearly of the same Greek-god caliber.

Still, she swallowed hard. She wasn't accustomed to handsome gentlemen introducing themselves. Good manners dictated they ask permission of a young lady's chaperone, who would then provide the introduction.

She might have kissed a few men, but none who hadn't gone through the proper channels to meet her first.

"Good afternoon," she returned guardedly. "Mr. . . . ?"

"Delaney," he said smoothly. "Sean Delaney, at your service. And this," he added, indicating the taller man, "is my good friend Mr. John Hamilton. Having noticed you sketching, he wished to be introduced to a fellow artist. You've heard of him, I presume?"

Had she heard of him? Corinna's sketchbook and pencil fell to the floor as her jaw dropped open. *Everyone* had heard of John Hamilton, the renowned, reclusive painter of landscapes. She turned to him, positively stunned. Her Greek god was John Hamilton—John Hamilton!—and he'd requested an introduction. To *her*, Corinna Chase, possibly the most *un*renowned artist in all of London.

"Mr. Hamilton," she gushed, "I cannot tell you how much I admire—"

"Please stop," he interrupted, bending to scoop up her supplies. He straightened and, with a roll of his gorgeous emerald eyes toward Mr. Delaney, handed the items to her. "I'm sorry, but I'm not John Hamilton." His lilting accent was distracting. The deep, melodious Irish voice didn't quite mesh with the Greek physique. "I'm Sean Delaney. And I'm afraid my brother-in-law here—the *real* John Hamilton—has a horrible sense of humor."

"Now, Hamilton." The other man dolefully shook his head. "There's no need to hide your identity from this charming young lady."

"It's your identity in question, and you hide it from everyone." The Greek god drew a line in the air that traced the other man from head to toe. "You'll note he's the one dressed in artistic style," he pointed out to Corinna before brushing at his own, much plainer clothes. "I am merely a common man of business."

"Please forgive Mr. Hamilton." Mr. Delaney—or perhaps he was Mr. Hamilton—raised a brow toward Corinna. "He's much too self-effacing."

"Blarney!" the Greek god shot back. "You're a dunce, Hamilton."

Corinna had observed a tennis match once, and she

now felt like that little ball bouncing back and forth between the two men. She didn't know which one to believe. But since she didn't expect to see either of them ever again, she figured it didn't signify.

While they'd volleyed, she'd regained her senses enough to remember Mr. Hamilton was a member of the committee that chose artwork for the Summer Exhibition. *That* was what truly mattered.

She clutched her art supplies to her chest. "I'm an oil painter myself," she told both of them, praying one really was John Hamilton. "I am here sketching the marbles to learn anatomy so I can improve my technique for portraits. It is my fondest hope that one of my canvases will be selected for this year's Summer Exhibition."

"I am certain Mr. Hamilton will vote for it," the shorter man assured her gravely.

"I will not." The Greek god's fists were clenched, and his Irish lilt came through gritted teeth. "I mean, he won't. Or perhaps he will, but I am *not* Hamilton."

"Pshaw." The other man waved a smooth, graceful hand. "He's—"

"Corinna!" She looked away to see her sisters hurrying near, the pram squeaking its way toward her. "I'm sorry we took so long," Alexandra said. "Are you finished yet?"

Corinna smiled in relief, certain Juliana would figure out which man was John Hamilton. The meddler in the family, Juliana had a skill for weaseling out secrets. "I'd be pleased for you to meet Mr. Hamilton," she started, turning back to the men.

They were gone.

Lifting her sweet baby boy from the pram, Alexandra frowned. "Mr. Hamilton?"

"The landscapist, John Hamilton. He was just here." Corinna scanned the crowded gallery, to no avail. "He looks like a Greek god. Or perhaps it's his friend who looks like the Greek god, or his brother-in-law—"

"Whatever are you babbling about? John Hamilton never appears in public." Looking sympathetic, Juliana touched her arm. "I think we should go. I must get home well before my mother-in-law's wedding, and in any case, you've clearly been sketching too long."

Back outdoors, Sean hauled Hamilton toward Montagu House, one hand clenched on the man's upper arm.

"It's a shame women cannot study anatomy," Hamilton remarked as though they were on a leisurely stroll, "because sketching statues is not going to help her learn anything."

"Is that so?" Sean gritted out.

"I've yet to see a portrait painted by a woman that was any good, and I never expect to, so I seriously doubt I will vote for that female's painting."

Sean had no wish to continue this conversation. In fact, he'd gladly pay a thousand pounds to avoid ever speaking with Hamilton again. But he felt sorry for the woman in question. "What if her picture *is* good? Will you still refuse to vote for it simply because it was painted by a lady?"

"Of course I wouldn't. Point of fact, I wouldn't be aware a female painted it, since I never seek signatures before I vote. Most of the Summer Exhibition judges take an artist's status into consideration, but I believe each work should stand on its own. Regardless of what the other Academicians think, I maintain that a painter's identity should never influence a judge's opinion."

It was the most reasonable statement Sean had ever heard leave Hamilton's lips. Surprisingly reasonable. Until the rotter added, "But I'm certain her paintings will not be any good, because she's never studied anatomy."

"She might surprise you," Sean shot back. "You shouldn't be so judgmental. You might vote for her painting and later on have to eat humble pie."

"I doubt it," Hamilton said blandly. "We failed to

learn her name, so in the unlikely event I ever did vote for one of her works, I'd never know it, would I?"

"Corinna."

"Pardon?"

"Her name is Corinna. Not that I learned it in the course of your shoddy introduction. Another woman called her Corinna as I was dragging you off." Her lovely face swam into his memory. "She's beautiful, isn't she?"

"You had no right to drag me off." Hamilton wrenched his arm from Sean's hand and pulled open the door to Montagu House. "Who is beautiful?"

"Corinna," Sean repeated as he followed him inside.

Wide blue eyes and gleaming dark hair. Sean had never been a fanciful sort of man, and he damn well didn't believe in love at first sight or any of the other nonsense poets regularly spouted. But something about her had seemed to crawl under his skin and clutch him low in the gut. Something had made him bunch his fists to keep from reaching to touch her. Something had made him want to kiss her.

He remembered her biting her plump lower lip, and how he'd been tempted to bite it himself.

"There's something about her . . . she's very sensual."

"Sensual? I didn't notice," Hamilton said, and while Sean was wondering how an artist could be *that* unobservant, he added, "I won the bet," in a smug tone.

"You did not. She didn't believe I was you."

"She didn't know what to believe. Which means I won. I succeeded in convincing her you may be an artist."

"Blarney."

Hamilton shrugged. "Whether you agree or not doesn't signify. You'll still pretend to be me for Lincolnshire's sake if you want to see your sister divorced."

"I believe you'll want to rethink that demand. When society discovers you deceived your uncle for your own gain, your reputation will be torn to threads. Your stellar art career will end in shame."

"Blarney," Hamilton mimicked in disdain. "No one will ever find out. Lincolnshire is incapacitated and housebound. Furthermore, he's a heartless blackguard, so who the hell would give a care whether he's hoaxed? He banished my family to the backwoods of Ireland when we should rightfully have been living the high life in London."

It was a litany Sean had heard practically since birth, not only from Hamilton himself but from both of the man's parents. They'd been none too happy to find themselves living among Irish rabble, but they'd been given no choice. Lincolnshire had ordered his younger brother to oversee his foreign interests, and the man had had no other means, short of lowering himself to common labor, to support his wife and child. He'd wanted to be a deacon or dean or archbishop, but Lincolnshire had refused to pull the necessary political strings. He'd been willing to serve in the military, but Lincolnshire had refused to buy him a commission.

Who was going to complain if such a heartless old man's nephew tricked him?

Sean stood in the museum's busy lobby, fighting his better judgment. Though he'd normally refuse to lie to a dying man—or to any decent man, for that matter—perhaps the mean old earl had it coming. But more than that, Sean loved Deirdre. He didn't want to see her forced back to Hamilton's bed or living in sin with Daniel Raleigh. And he knew that if he didn't agree to Hamilton's plan, the self-centered cur would never free his sister.

"This won't interrupt your routine," Hamilton promised. "You'll have to move to Lincolnshire's Berkeley Square town house for a couple of weeks, but you need only sleep there at night. You can tell the old man you must paint during the day and go off to do your usual work. It shan't affect Delaney and Company at all."

"What if he wants to see your paintings?"

"You mean *your* paintings," Hamilton said with a

pointed smirk. He frowned a moment, then nodded. "I'll leave you some money to lease studio space near the square—"

"I don't want your money," Sean growled. He'd come a long way in the ten years since that first fateful letter arrived. Having shrewdly invested his surprise inheritance, he thought he might now be the wealthiest twenty-eight-year-old self-made man in all of Britain. "And I don't need to lease anything. I own half of Piccadilly Street."

Not to mention a good percentage of other property in and around London.

"Do you, now? Well, that's excellent. If you've a vacant garret nearby, that would be ideal. Something very private with north-facing windows. I've a few canvases in the apartments I've been renting. I shall fetch them posthaste and put them in there for you to show him." He nodded again, more enthusiastically. "Perhaps I'll lease the space from you permanently. Once I inherit the title, I'll be forced to spend some time at Lincolnshire House, so I'll need it when I return from Wales."

An awkward silence stretched between them while people walked in and out, asking the porter directions to find the Rosetta Stone or the Egyptian mummies.

"You'll do it, won't you?" Hamilton pressed. "Otherwise—"

"I'll do it," Sean snapped. He knew what *otherwise* entailed: doom for Deirdre.

To avoid that, he'd sell himself to the devil.

Which he very probably just had.

Chapter Four

ORANGE BRANDY

Take a quart of Brandy, the peels of eight Oranges thin pared, keep them in the Brandy forty-eight hours in a closed pitcher, then take three pints of Water, put into it three-quarters of a pounde of loaf Sugar, boil it till half be consumed, and let it stand till cold, then mixe it with the Brandy.

This was served at my grandparents' wedding breakfast, and their marriage was blessed with love and health. We have had it at family weddings ever since.

—Eleanor Chase, Marchioness of Cainewood, 1730

Lady Stafford and Lord Cavanaugh's wedding was a modest affair, just family and a few friends in the gorgeous Painted Room at Stafford House. The chamber was a mite tight even for the small number of guests; the equally impressive Palm Room downstairs would have been more comfortable. But the Painted Room was perfect for the occasion, because its theme was marriage.

A famous Roman fresco was re-created on the chimneypiece, and other wedding scenes were painted directly on the plaster walls. Panels depicted music, drinking, and dancing. Cupid and Venus cavorted overhead, nymphs danced on the ceiling, lovers courted on gilt-framed canvas, and a frieze of rose wreaths and garlands of flowers went all around the cornice.

The house wasn't actually Lady Stafford's anymore. Cornelia had been the Dowager Lady Stafford for several years now, which meant Stafford House belonged to her son, James Trevor, the current Earl of Stafford. Who also happened to be Juliana's husband.

While the minister droned on, Juliana leaned close to Corinna. "Your turn will come next."

"I'm not concerned with having a turn," Corinna whispered back. "My art is more important than love."

Her gaze shifted to Aunt Frances, hugely pregnant and wearing a sentimental, romantic smile. Love had recently saved Aunt Frances from the dreary life she'd been leading as a spinster in her mid-forties. And love had transformed Corinna's sisters' lives as well. Juliana and James had wed only last August, right after Frances and Lord Malmsey. Alexandra and Tristan had been married nearly two years and took joy in their infant son.

Although Corinna sometimes feared she'd fail to find true love for herself, she also worried she'd forever remain unrecognized for her talents. Of the two, she felt the art was more under her control. The thing that defined her, the thing that mattered most. She was happy for Aunt Frances and her sisters. It was wonderful that they'd all found love, but to Corinna's mind, the three women had little else.

They *needed* love to complete them, but she had her art.

Her landscapes and her still lifes, and most of all, her portraits. Her art ought to be enough. If only she could get one of her works accepted into the Summer Exhibition, her future would be bright even without a man in the picture.

No sooner had the minister announced that the Dowager Lady Stafford was now Lady Cavanaugh than Juliana began distributing glasses of orange brandy, a concoction some ancient ancestor had claimed was guaranteed to assure a lifetime of marital bliss. How her sisters believed such nonsense was something Corinna would never fathom. But she had to admit that Lord and Lady Cavanaugh looked very happy for now. Perched together on an amazing green silk sofa with gilt arms carved to look like winged lions, they both beamed as they accepted congratulations. Clearly Cornelia had found *her* Greek god, even if he was somewhat aged and silver-haired.

Her husband, James, in tow, Juliana returned. She handed Corinna the last glass with a satisfied sigh. "Oh, don't the two of them look perfect together? I knew they'd end up married."

Juliana always knew what was best for everyone, and she never hesitated to announce it. Last Season she'd suggested her husband's mother and Lord Cavanaugh share a dance, and now here they were, man and wife.

"Her new title even begins with C," Juliana added proudly.

Corinna sipped the sweet drink. "Why should that signify?"

James laughed, slipping an arm around Juliana's waist. "My aunts," he reminded Corinna, "are Aurelia, Lady Avonleigh, and Bedelia, Lady Balmforth. But until today my mother—their sister—was Cornelia, Lady Stafford."

"Now she's Cornelia, Lady Cavanaugh, and the three sisters are Ladies A, B, and C," Juliana pointed out.

"Holy Hannah," Corinna said as James laughed again and walked off.

She'd never understand how Juliana's mind worked.

As though the conversation had summoned her, Lady A made her way over. "Wasn't the ceremony beautiful? My baby sister, married again." With a teary but happy little sniff, she tore her gaze from the new Lady C and focused on Corinna. "How are you doing these days, my dear?"

"Very well, thank you."

"And your art?"

"I've been painting madly. I hope to see one of my pictures accepted for the Summer Exhibition this year."

"Don't forget, I promised to help."

"Thank you," Corinna said, although she had no idea how the kind, plump lady *could* help. But one of the woman's daughters, who'd been artistic as well, had tragically ended her own life before the age of twenty when she'd jumped off the London Bridge, taking her unborn baby with her. And since Lady Avonleigh's daughter had hoped to be elected to the Royal Academy herself, the woman had announced last year that she wished to see Corinna succeed in her daughter's stead.

Unfortunately, wishing didn't accomplish much, and Lady A had no connections to the art world. But Corinna knew the sweet lady's heart was in the right place. "I appreciate your good intentions," she told her sincerely.

"I have a plan," Lady Avonleigh announced.

Corinna couldn't have been more surprised if the new Lady Cavanaugh had asked for an annulment. "Do you?"

"Yes, indeed. I've made a rather large donation to the Royal Academy, earmarked to provide yearly grants for deserving students to study abroad. A noble cause, do you not agree?"

"Very much so," Corinna said. The Royal Academy had sponsored student travel years ago, but such grants had been in abeyance since the wars had begun, making journeys to the Continent impossible. Following Napoleon's recent defeat at Waterloo, travel had once again resumed, and artists were now clamoring to go.

But Lady A's grants would all go to men, of course, since women were barred from the Royal Academy schools.

Corinna sighed. "I would love to go study in Italy."

"I'm sure you would, dear. My daughter always wanted to go, too." Lady A rested a sympathetic hand on her arm. "I've made a stipulation that the yearly awards be titled the Lady Georgiana Cartwright Scholarships, in her honor. I do hope that seeing a lady's name on the grant will encourage the Academy to consider admitting women in future. And in the meantime"—she smiled, her soft blue eyes going a little hazy as she gazed off into space—"it gives me pleasure to think of helping any art student achieve his dreams, no matter the recipient's gender."

"Tell her the rest," Juliana prompted.

"Ah, yes." Lady A nodded, coming back from wherever she'd drifted off. "Next month I shall hold an afternoon reception in my home, to which I shall invite the members of the Summer Exhibition Selection Committee. Thanks to my generous patronage, I am certain they will all feel obligated to attend. And, of course, I shall invite you too, Lady Corinna, giving you the opportunity to show them some of your work and, more important, charm them and influence their decision."

Corinna doubted her ability to charm. Her sisters accused her of being sarcastic much more often than they lauded her more feminine virtues. But as she was unknown in the art world—and that would be a mark against her in the judging—she was thrilled to have the opportunity to meet the committee. And flabbergasted that Lady A would go to such lengths to help her. "Thank you so much. I shall make the most of this chance, I assure you."

"I must give credit where credit is due," Lady A said. "The whole scheme was your sister's idea."

"It was *your* money," Juliana hastened to point out. "And your decision where it should be allocated."

"I was pleased to do it. My dear daughter would have approved. I shall be even more pleased when your sister becomes the first female elected to the Royal Academy in the last forty-nine years, and honored to have had a hand in it." She took a sip of her orange brandy and looked back to Corinna. "Of course, your talent will be the determining factor, my dear. I've no doubt you'll eventually find yourself elected with or without my help."

Corinna wished she could be so sure.

"Have you need of assistance with the planning?" Juliana asked Lady A.

"I could use a hand with the invitations," the older woman admitted. "My penmanship is not what it used to be."

"I'd be pleased to assist," Juliana assured her—no surprise, since Juliana loved to have her hand in everything. "Perhaps we can have a little invitation party here next week. Friday afternoon would work well. I'll invite Alexandra and our cousins. You remember Rachael, Claire, and Elizabeth?"

"Of course," Lady A said. "It was a pleasure chatting with them during your many sewing parties." Last year, Juliana had offered to make baby clothes for the Foundling Hospital, and she'd needed a *lot* of assistance. "I would be grateful for your cousins' help. And now . . ." Lady A gestured to the new Lady Cavanaugh. "I must congratulate my sister before the wedding supper."

After she left, Juliana drew Corinna toward three of their dark-haired cousins. At twenty and twenty-one, Elizabeth and Claire Chase were both pretty as pictures. Their tall brother, Noah, the Earl of Greystone, was a year older and would have been pretty too—but Corinna thought a small scar that slashed through his left eyebrow made him look a little dangerous instead.

He had an equally dangerous smile, which he flashed as she and Juliana approached. "I'm going to find Rachael," he said, referring to his elder sister. "If you'll excuse me."

As he ambled away, Juliana turned to Elizabeth and Claire. "We're helping Lady Avonleigh with the reception she's planning to launch Corinna's art career. I'm hoping you'll both come to a little invitation-making party here next Friday. And I hope Rachael will come as well, of course. Where has she gone off to?"

"The terrace. She's just staring out over Green Park." Claire looked worried. "She hasn't been herself for a long while."

"I've noticed," Juliana said. All the time Corinna's brother, Griffin, had been busy trying to marry off his three sisters, Juliana had been trying to match him with Rachael. But Rachael had neglected to attend many events this Season and last. "Rachael has always been so enthusiastic. What do you suppose has dampened her spirits?"

"She's not yet got over finding that letter," Elizabeth said.

Claire elbowed her younger sister in the ribs.

"What?" Juliana looked between them. "What letter?"

"Now you've done it," Claire accused, her unusual amethyst eyes glaring into her sister's green ones. "Rachael's kept mum on the subject deliberately, you know."

Elizabeth's hands flew up to slap her own cheeks. "Oh, fiddlesticks!"

"What letter?" Juliana repeated.

Although the Painted Room was filled with the babel of conversation, Claire and Elizabeth's silence was noticeable. "Whatever it is," Corinna said for them, "Rachael wants it kept a secret."

"Surely she didn't mean from us," Juliana said. "We're her cousins."

"No, you aren't," Elizabeth said, then clapped a hand over her mouth.

"What?" Juliana and Corinna burst out together.

Claire glared at her sister again, then sighed. "When Rachael cleared out our parents' suite at Greystone for Noah, she found a letter that revealed she had a different father than ours. It seems our mother was married before and carrying Rachael when she was widowed. Then she married our father before giving birth."

Juliana looked astonished. "Who was her real father, then?"

"She doesn't know." Claire shook her head sadly. "The letter didn't say, and there's no one to ask. We have no living grandparents, and Mama's only sister died when we were young. Rachael went through all of our mother's belongings, searching for clues to who her first husband might have been, but she found nothing."

"Is she still looking?" Corinna asked, concerned.

"She cannot think of anywhere else to look," Elizabeth said. "Griffin even helped her go through everything again last year, in case she missed something."

Now Juliana looked intrigued. "Griffin knows about this?"

"He's the only one besides us," Claire said. "Please don't tell Rachael you know now, too. She'd be mortified."

"Why?" Corinna asked. "Her parentage is certainly no fault of hers. Does she think so little of us that she believes it would change our feelings toward her?"

"I fear she's not thinking at all these days." Claire crossed her arms over her violet satin bodice and leveled another stare at her sister. "Much like Elizabeth."

"I'm sorry," Elizabeth squeaked.

Claire sighed. "I don't think Rachael even realizes you're not her cousins. She's so upset at not knowing who her father is that she hasn't thought past that. Or maybe she's blocked the truth from her mind, because she can't stand the thought of losing all the family she knows."

"She still has you two," Corinna said. "And Noah."

"But that's all. Please just let her work it out for herself in her own good time. I don't think she could take hearing anything more now."

"We promise not to tell a soul." Corinna turned to Juliana. "Don't we?"

"Of course we do." Juliana reached to touch both her cousins' arms reassuringly. "I'm sorry to hear Rachael is so upset over this discovery, but I assure you that no one—including her—will hear about it from either of us. We love Rachael, and we don't find it upsetting at all."

To the contrary, Corinna suspected Juliana was personally thrilled to hear this news. Rachael's main objection to marrying Griffin had always been that he was a cousin. That obstacle was now gone. Rachael had confided in Griffin, and Griffin had tried to help her and kept her secret. Add all of that together, and it seemed another of Juliana's constant projects was well on its way to success.

And if she actually managed to pull it off, she was going to be smug beyond belief.

Chapter Five

Few people were strolling in Green Park this Thursday evening. The undulating landscape was shadowed by the setting sun, and the gardens were very tranquil.

But Rachael wasn't.

Gripping the terrace's rail, she stared out over grassland and trees, telling herself it was time to let go of these feelings. She was never going to learn who had fathered her, and she had to come to grips with that. She'd allowed Griffin to help her as he'd wanted, and they'd found nothing—just as she'd expected. That had been months ago, months spent in a melancholy haze.

The man who had raised her had cared for her, so it shouldn't matter that they hadn't shared a blood bond, should it? And how long could she remain angry with her mother for withholding the facts? The woman was dead, for God's sake. The anger was pointless, and she had to get on with her life.

"Rachael."

Turning to see her brother step out on the terrace, she forced a smile. "Noah. You arrived so late I had no chance to talk to you before the wedding." His priorities never had been with family or the earldom. "Did you get the new racehorse settled in at Greystone?"

"Horses," he corrected. "I bought two. And they're both doing well, yes. I'm hoping for a good showing at

Ascot. While I was home I asked for an inventory to be taken—"

"An inventory of what?" Since when did Noah care about anything at Greystone Castle?

"Of everything. While dining there alone, I noticed that old portrait of the first earl over the fireplace and got to thinking about what might have accumulated in the hundred and fifty years since he was granted the title and lands. The servants aren't yet finished—I expect it will take them weeks to catalog all they find. But one thing they discovered was an old trunk in the attic with Mama's wedding dress and a few other items. Nothing important—"

"I want to see it."

"I knew you would," he said with a wry smile. "That's why I'm telling you they found it. I had it brought down and put in my room so you can go through it after the Season."

"I want to see it now. Can we go to Greystone tomorrow?"

"I just got back from Greystone, and the Jockey Club meets tomorrow. Besides, I told you nothing in it is important. You can wait a few weeks."

"No, I can't, Noah." He didn't know what was important. The trunk might have something in it that would reveal her father's identity. "I'm going tomorrow."

"I'm not going with you, and you cannot travel that far alone or with Claire or Elizabeth. It wouldn't be safe."

"I know that." But she knew another man who might be willing to accompany her in his place. "When you go back inside, will you ask Griffin to step out here a moment?"

"Can you come for me at seven?" Rachael asked, a few loose tendrils of her hair blowing in the breeze that crossed the terrace.

"That anxious, are you?" Griffin's sisters were never ready to leave the house so early in the morning, but none of them were nearly as focused as Rachael. "That will be fine. Will one or both of your sisters come along, too?"

"I think not."

"Hmm. Aunt Frances is too far gone with child, so I guess I'll ask one of my sisters to join us."

"Why?"

"As a chaperone, of course."

"We don't need a chaperone, Griffin."

He sipped orange brandy, watching her warily over the rim of the glass. "It's a long journey."

"Only half a day each direction. We won't be gone overnight. Other than you and my siblings, no one knows about my true parentage, and I want to keep it that way, at least for now. Besides," she added, "you're my cousin. Would I require a chaperone to go visiting with Noah?"

"I'm not Noah," Griffin pointed out. "A cousin is not the same as a brother." But he didn't point out that he wasn't, in the strictest sense, her cousin. Not by blood anyway, not since it had been established that John Chase hadn't been her father. He didn't want to upset her, and more to the point, he'd just as soon have her think of him as a cousin.

"You're *practically* my brother," she insisted.

Maybe having her think of him as a brother was even better. "Very well," he said. "I'll come for you at seven."

"Thank you!" she exclaimed, looking happier than he'd seen her since that disappointing day when they'd gone through her mother's belongings and found nothing. As he watched her glide back into Stafford House, her luscious derriere swaying as she went, he gritted his teeth.

Griffin remembered Rachael as an awkward adolescent, a tomboyish playmate, all skinny arms and gangly legs. At fourteen, she'd had a silly dent in her chin, wild, curly dark hair, and sky blue eyes that seemed much too big for her face. But then he'd left home for Oxford and later joined the cavalry. And during the years he'd spent away, the tomboy had transformed into a woman.

A very sultry one.

Those cerulean eyes were now alluring, those limbs long and graceful, that body anything but awkward. The dent in her chin no longer looked silly—it looked provocative instead. Her hair was sleek and tamed, excepting those few chestnut tendrils that always seemed to come loose. Or maybe she left them loose deliberately. Either way, they caressed the sides of her face in a way that made him wish his hands were there in their place.

In short, he found Rachael Chase entirely too attractive. Which was why he was happy she thought of him as nothing more than a cousin.

Although cousins often wed, Rachael's aunt had married a cousin, then sadly given birth to a crippled, feebleminded child. A doctor had said the family relationship might be to blame, and as a result, Rachael was deadset against marrying any cousin, no matter how distant. And that suited Griffin just fine, since he had no intention of marrying her.

He had no intention of marrying anyone, for that matter.

At least, not in the foreseeable future.

His sisters and Cainewood kept him occupied quite enough, thank you very much. The last thing he needed was an additional distraction, or yet another responsibility. For God's sake, he was only thirty, he thought as he downed the rest of the orange brandy and went back inside.

There were years and years left before he had to worry about taking on a wife.

Chapter Six

The homes on the east and west sides of Berkeley Square were close to the street and built cheek by jowl against one another, but Lincolnshire House stood alone on the north end, behind a high, imposing wall. Friday morning, the guard at the massive wooden gate scowled at the portmanteau Sean carried.

"Peddlers are not welcome."

Sean's hand clenched on the handle of the simple leather bag. "I'm the earl's nephew," he said, all but choking on the words.

A little gasp burst from the man's mouth. "Pardon me, Mr. Hamilton. I'm sorry; truly I am." Babbling, he swung open the gate. "Do come in, and please accept my sincerest apologies."

Sean was more than willing to do so, but he was struck dumb at sight of the house.

His own house in Hampstead was sizable and impressive. Originally built in the seventeenth century, it had been extended and remodeled some fifty years ago by the notable architect Robert Adam, for a chief justice who worked in the City but wanted to live in the suburbs. It sat in acres of gardens and ancient woodland, with a stunning view out over London. Deirdre had gasped the first time she saw it.

But it seemed a hovel in comparison to the Earl of Lincolnshire's enormous mansion in Berkeley Square.

A rather plain Palladian-style brick building, it was quite simply the largest house Sean had ever seen. Five gardeners labored industriously in the lavishly landscaped courtyard. After banging the knocker, he shifted uncomfortably on the front steps beneath the portico, wishing he'd never consented to what he was about to do.

Deirdre certainly hadn't agreed that it was worthwhile to secure her divorce. Last night's disbelieving cry—"You promised to do *what*?"—still rang in his head. "That's ridiculous!" she'd railed—and Irishwomen were nothing if not expert railers. "You fool! You knothead! I don't need you to play the martyr for me. I'll be happy together with Daniel whether we're married or not."

Well, maybe *she* would be happy, but Sean wouldn't. Not if the two hadn't exchanged vows. But although he'd been tempted to tell her Hamilton was threatening to make her move back in with him, he'd resisted that temptation. He didn't want to be the martyr; he didn't want her to feel indebted or burdened with guilt. Better she think her brother a knotheaded fool.

That was nothing new, anyway.

A butler opened the door. His dark suit was starched and pressed. His features looked as rigid as his clothing, his round face seemingly frozen.

"May I help you, sir?"

"I've come to see my uncle, the Earl of Lincolnshire."

"Your uncle? You must be Mr. Hamilton, then." As though he'd suddenly melted, the man's entire demeanor changed. "Come in, come in," he said, ushering Sean through the door. "I'm Quincy, and the earl is going to be so pleased to hear you've arrived. I shall inform Mr. Higginbotham, his house steward, that you are here so he can make certain your room is ready." He eyed the portmanteau. "That cannot be all you brought along."

"My manservant will bring in my trunks after he sees to my curricle."

"Good, good. I shall send an underfootman to assist

him. The earl has been asking after you since he opened his eyes this morning. In truth, since last night when he received your note. He's abed, so I shall fetch a maid to show you upstairs posthaste."

The butler closed the door and promptly disappeared down a corridor. Sean waited pensively. In contrast to the house's plain facade, its interior was absolutely sumptuous. The grand, pillared entrance led to a wide, sweeping curved staircase with broad steps made of the purest white marble. Grecian-style couches lined the perimeter, plushly upholstered in light-colored velvet with darker trim. Gold and crystal glittered everywhere, and there was lots of Oriental pottery scattered about. Paintings hung everywhere, too—enormous gilt-framed paintings that Sean imagined were probably famous, though knowing nothing of art, he couldn't identify a single one.

"Fancy, ain't it?"

Wondering if his mouth had been hanging open, he turned to see a little bird of a middle-aged woman wearing a dark dress with a starched white apron. "It's impressive."

"The most impressive house in London," she declared, leading him across the stone floor toward the steps. "Which is only fair, considering Lord Lincolnshire is the most wonderful man in all of England."

Wonderful? The earl was wonderful?

Hamilton's family had always described him as a heartless blackguard.

The staircase's newel post looked to be fashioned of solid crystal. Atop balusters of gilded ironwork, the handrail was crystal, too. As Sean climbed, he nodded at two more servants on their way down. "What exactly is wrong with his lordship?"

"Such a tragedy." The maid sighed. "He complained of chest pain that lasted a few hours. Before the doctor could arrive, he fell into a dead faint, and when he woke, his legs started swelling 'orribly. A dreadful sight, I tell you. And he's short of breath, the poor man. Dropsy, the doctor said."

"Dropsy." Sean knew little about the disease, but it sounded bad. "He can talk, though, yes?"

"Aye, that he can." At the top of the stairs, she turned down a corridor that had more paintings on the walls and more Oriental pottery on marble hall tables. She skirted around another woman polishing the already spotless inlaid floor. "He cannot wait to see you."

Sean was waved through a door to find Lincolnshire in a huge state bed hung with dark damask trimmed with pale silk. His face hidden from Sean's sight by a sturdy nurse dressed in white, the earl sat propped against four or five pillows. The nurse finished plumping them and stepped away.

"John!" the man exclaimed as Sean came into view. He had light-colored eyes, thinning gray hair combed forward, and an altogether dignified, pleasant appearance.

And he did not look as ill as Hamilton had indicated.

"I'm so pleased you agreed to keep me company in my final days," he added enthusiastically. "Come here, nephew. Let me have a look at you."

Feeling like the fraud he was, Sean walked closer. "Your letter implied you were quite ill, my lord."

"My lord? Please call me Uncle. And yes, I do fear I am quite ill. Began with massive pain—a great, squeezing pressure in the vicinity of my heart. As though a man were sitting on my chest." He paused. And then, "No," he corrected himself, "as though the *Prince Regent* were sitting on my chest."

Lincolnshire smiled at his own joke; the Prince Regent was grossly overweight. Although Sean had never run in court circles, even he knew that. Scurrilous cartoons were often printed in the papers, and a recent one had featured the fat prince picking his teeth following an enormous meal.

"Doctors say I won't last two weeks," Lincolnshire added, sounding a bit out of breath. "I need all these pillows because I cannot breathe lying down. I have to stay upright even to sleep, so I can breathe. Sit down, sit down." Looking much more chipper than a man with a death sentence rightly should, he indicated a tufted velvet chair close by the bed. " 'Tis dropsy, they tell me."

"What causes it?"

"That they *haven't* told me. Or perhaps they don't know. Sit, John, sit."

"You seem so cheerful," Sean commented as he lowered himself.

"I'm happy to see you. After all these years, John—"

"Sean," he interrupted.

"Eh?"

"Call me Sean, please." He couldn't stand being called by Hamilton's name, not to mention he was likely to forget to answer to it. "Sean is the same name as John in Ireland, you see, so I've been called Sean since I was a lad. By all my friends and family."

"You haven't any family left other than me, have you? Or only on your mother's side?" The old man cocked his head. "You've an Irish accent, too. How is that?"

Sean had forgotten Hamilton's parents were dead and he'd had no siblings. Sweet Jesus, whatever had made him think he could pull this off? Warning himself to tread more carefully, he ignored the first questions and answered the last. "Surely you know I was raised in Ireland."

"But you're an Englishman, after all. I made certain you always had English tutors. Paid the enormous bills myself."

Sean shrugged—casually, he hoped. "Everyone else around me was Irish. I expect I picked up a bit of an accent anyway."

"A bit?"

In all honesty, Sean had thought he'd lost most of it.

Or at least he'd tried to. He was very careful to always say *yes* rather than *aye*, and *my* rather than *me. Yes, that's my best suit*, instead of *Aye, that's me best suit.*

He knew the Irish had a less than sterling reputation in London.

"Ah, well, I suppose it doesn't signify," Lincolnshire added kindly. "I'll call you Sean if that pleases you. I'm just glad to have you here. Been lonely since your aunt passed on."

Hamilton's aunt, Lincolnshire's wife. Guilt was a fist around Sean's heart. "You must miss her."

"I surely do. After all our children died, at least we still had each other. Rather disconcerting to find oneself alone."

"You seem to be surrounded by staff, sir. Uncle." An understatement of great proportions. The nurse still puttered in the shadows, and two more maids had come and gone in the past few minutes, delivering a glass of water, fussing with the curtains, seeing to the man's comfort.

"Ah, yes, that I am." The earl smiled a bit sheepishly, revealing straight but tea-stained teeth. "Mrs. Skeffington takes excellent care of me," he said, indicating the nurse, "but she does have some help. More than a hundred servants altogether, and I cannot bring myself to dismiss a single one. My family has employed them all for years."

"*All* of them?"

"And their folk before them, generations back. My forebears housed many relations, you see. As did I, in the past." A sigh escaped his lips, a wheezy sort of sound. "While my family shrank, the families of the servants continued to grow. After so many years of loyal service, I cannot find it in myself to turn them out. It's no simple matter to find good positions these days, even with a letter of good character."

While keeping such a large staff bordered on absurd, Sean found the sentiment touching, which ratcheted his guilt up a level. No wonder the maid had described Lincolnshire as the most wonderful employer in all of England.

Sean's breakfast felt as if it were congealing in his gut. An iron collar seemed to be squeezing around his throat. How could he do this to such a nice man? Clearly Lincolnshire wasn't the blackguard Hamilton had described. And neither was he "incapacitated." Perhaps he was knocking on death's door, but for now, at least, the man was fully alert.

Lincolnshire leaned to pat Sean's hand. "I'm so glad you're here, John," he repeated gratefully.

"Sean," Sean choked out.

"Sean, yes. I shall have to grow accustomed to that." He smiled again, a fond smile that spiked Sean's guilt to new heights. "Lady Partridge is holding a ball tomorrow night. I've already sent my regrets, but I've a sudden hankering to see all my friends one last time. To show off my famous nephew. I'll have my secretary send her a note, if it wouldn't be too much trouble for you to accompany me."

Trouble?

Guilt transformed to a panic that *trouble* didn't even begin to describe.

Should Sean appear in society as Lincolnshire's nephew, the truth would be revealed when Hamilton later appeared as himself. And then where would they all be? Hamilton would lose his art career if not his inheritance. He'd kill Sean, or, at the very least, refuse Deirdre her divorce. Sean's sister would go on to live in sin, and he'd be proved worse than a knotheaded fool—a complete failure as a brother and a man.

"I'd prefer not to be 'shown off,' " he explained carefully. "I'm rather a mystery to the public, if you've heard. That secrecy adds to my cachet, and—"

"Your mysterious ways are legend. Very well, then." Lincolnshire looked resigned, and Sean was relieved—for approximately two seconds. "I'll not tell anyone you're John Hamilton. I'll simply introduce you as my nephew Sean."

"Surely people know who your heir is. . . ."

"I'll tell them you're my long-lost *other* nephew. For now. They'll learn the truth, of course, when you inherit. It will be our little secret." For a moment the earl's eyes danced with merry amusement, but he quickly sobered. "I'd . . . well . . ." The old man cleared his throat, looking embarrassed. "I'd given up living, Sean. I didn't want to see anyone. But now . . . having you here . . . it makes me want to live again. I've a short time left. With you by my side, I wish to say my good-byes." A sheen of tears glazed his eyes. "Please, nephew, do me this favor."

How could Sean deny such a fine, upstanding fellow? How could he possibly refuse? How could he disappoint the most wonderful man in all of England?

He gazed up at the exquisite painted ceiling, where the Goddess of Dawn chased away the Goddess of Night. Hamilton had been so wrong about his uncle, in so very many ways. And being introduced as Lincolnshire's *other* nephew should carry no risk. Their ruse would never come to light. Sean had no connections with high society. Before Lincolnshire, he'd never met any member of the *ton*. No one should suspect he was anything but what Lincolnshire said, and after all this was over, he would never see any of them ever again.

"Very well," he finally said, lowering his gaze to meet the earl's eyes. "I'll accompany you. Just remember to call me Sean."

Chapter Seven

Griffin spent all of Friday morning seated across from Rachael in his blasted carriage, breathing her come-hither scent and watching her lick her lips so many times his jaw ached from clenching his teeth.

It was that or leap across the space between them to kiss off that beckoning sheen. A temptation he'd managed to resist in all the months since he'd left the cavalry and returned to England. A temptation he was determined to resist forever.

Instead, he talked of politics, books and plays, family and property, and plans for the future . . . anything to keep his mind off that generous, glistening mouth. It was difficult to speak with his teeth clenched, so he was thankful Rachael kept up her end of the conversation. She always had been easy to talk to, especially for a female.

At long last, in the early afternoon, the carriage rattled over the drawbridge and into the modest courtyard before the small castle that was Rachael's home at Greystone. Spring rain pelted his head when he shoved open the door and leapt to the circular drive. He breathed a sigh of relief and reached to help Rachael out.

She hadn't worn gloves, damn it. Her hand felt entirely too warm in his, especially when she left it there while they made their way down a short, covered passageway and entered through the unassuming oak door. Her fingers trembled, either from the cold or from nervousness at what they might find; he wasn't sure which.

He was thankful she dropped his hand when the butler, Smithson, approached. "Lady Rachael. Lord Cainewood." Tall and lean with gray hair and piercing gray eyes that seemed to match the old castle, Smithson was too mannerly to show dismay at their unexpected arrival. "What a pleasant surprise."

"We'll be here but a short while," Rachael assured him. "No need for any preparations."

He glanced at the tall-case clock that stood in the square, stone-floored entry. "I'll ask Cook to prepare a luncheon. Will you be wanting anything more?"

"No, thank you. I wish only to fetch something of my mother's, and Lord Cainewood was kind enough to accompany me." She headed toward the oak staircase that marched up the wall opposite the entrance. "Please don't trouble yourself or anyone else."

Griffin followed her up the steps, past two of her mother's watercolor paintings, and along the corridor that led to what used to be her parents' bedroom. The chamber's walls were covered in pale green paper with gold tracery, the bedding green velvet of a deeper hue, the furniture light and slender, of the style popularized by Sheraton.

"Did this room not used to be decorated in red?" he asked. "And the furnishings of dark oak?"

"I changed it all for Noah." Having come of age last year, her brother had finally taken responsibility for the earldom—a responsibility Rachael had borne herself since their parents died when she was just fifteen. "To make it his, not Papa's and Mama's."

How thoughtful. How Rachael. "But some of your mother's things are in here now?"

"In that chest." She gestured toward the one heavy,

dark piece of furniture, a large carved trunk set in a corner. "Noah had it brought down from the attic." Her voice sounded thin. "He said nothing in it is important."

"He could be wrong," he said, hoping that was the case. "Let's have a look."

"Yes, let's." She crossed to the trunk and removed an embroidered covering and a lamp someone had set on top. Then she knelt and took a deep breath before reverently opening the lid. A musty scent wafted out, starch and aged leather mixed with hints of her mother's gardenia perfume. "Oh, God, Griffin."

Griffin knelt beside her. "Pretty," he murmured, lifting a straw hat from atop the contents.

"It's years out of style. I remember her wearing it when I was a child." Rachael removed a few more dated items of clothing, then shook out a white gown. "This must be the wedding dress Noah mentioned. I remember seeing it in their wedding portrait."

Though clearly out of fashion, it was lacy and beautiful. Georgiana, Rachael's mother, had been slender like her daughter, all willowy, graceful curves, and she obviously hadn't been pregnant long when she married John Chase. The dress looked like it would fit Rachael perfectly. "Will you wear it for your own wedding someday, too, now that you've found it?"

"I'd love to, but . . ." Her eyes grew misty as she stared into the trunk. "Damn. I am not going to cry."

Rachael could cuss as colorfully as a cavalryman, but that didn't bother Griffin. He considered it part of her charm. It reminded him she'd spent years as the Earl of Greystone in all but name, and he admired her for that. "But what?" he prompted.

"She wore it for her wedding to him. Lord Greystone. Not my father."

He reached out to take her chin and turn her to face him. "Lord Greystone was your father in every way that counted. I'm sure he would have wanted you to wear it. He would have been honored, as a matter of fact."

She nodded and swallowed hard. "I'm not sure I'll ever marry, anyway."

"Of course you will. Any man would be lucky to have you. I'm surprised Noah hasn't found you a match."

"Noah?" Her eyes cleared, and she laughed, turning back to the trunk. "Who would run his household should I wed? He won't be matching me anytime soon."

Though but eighteen months her junior, Noah had always seemed far less mature. But Griffin couldn't imagine any man wanting the responsibility of three sisters. Much better to find them good husbands and enjoy their company from time to time without worrying over the lot of them.

A few old books lay beneath the clothes, but they were all signed, *To Georgiana with love from Mama,* and dated with her early birthdays, giving no clues to her first husband. There were no diaries or anything else of a personal nature. A stack of letters tied with a ribbon held no pertinent information, either. They were all written in the years following Rachael's birth.

When the trunk was otherwise empty, Rachael found a tiny box in the bottom and pulled it out. It held a narrow, plain gold band.

"Her wedding ring?" Griffin guessed.

"She was buried wearing her wedding ring. Unless . . ." She glanced up at him, wonder in her eyes. "This must be from her marriage to my father." She looked inside, turning the band to catch the light. "No inscription. No clues." Sighing, she slipped it onto the fourth finger of her right hand. "It fits."

"I'm not surprised." Griffin's knees creaked when he stood and stretched. "That's it, then, is it?"

"Everything in here was old, things she didn't use anymore, things it made sense to have put away." Leaving the ring on her finger, she started putting everything else back. "I guess she didn't have a lot to keep. Mama led a quiet life."

He nodded. "My parents often left us with our governesses, but I remember your mother was always home with you."

"She never went up to London. She said the air there was bad for her lungs." Another dismal sigh escaped her lips as she replaced the last few items and shut the trunk. "Noah was right. There was nothing important here. I'm sorry I wasted your time."

"It wasn't a waste, Rachael." He watched her spread the embroidered cloth, the narrow gold ring glinting as she moved. "Did your mother have no other jewels?"

The lamp in her hand, she froze. "Yes, of course she did. I've had them all along. She may have been quiet, but she liked pretty things. She willed all her jewels to me. Claire and Elizabeth each chose a few pieces, but the rest are in my room."

He took the lamp from her and set it down decisively, then reached a hand to help her up. "We should have looked at them last time. Maybe something will be engraved—"

"Nothing is. I would have noticed."

Yes, she probably would have. Rachael was nothing if not observant. "Let's have a look, though, shall we?"

Rachael's chamber was deep rose and rich green and dark blue, a combination as classic and sophisticated as Rachael herself. Another of her mother's watercolors hung over her washstand. Fetching a mahogany box off her dressing table, she brought it with her to sit on the bed and patted the spot beside her in invitation, apparently comfortable having an unmarried man in her room.

Griffin wished he could say the same. It felt highly improper to be in here.

He sat, though, when she opened the box. Filled to the brim, it sparkled with gold and lustrous pearls, diamonds and colorful gems. Griffin didn't know much about jewelry, but he recognized a fortune when he saw it.

His eyes must have widened, because Rachael laughed at the look on his face. "This family is descended from jewelers," she reminded him. "My great-great-grandmother, or some such."

"I think you need a few more 'greats,'" he said, remembering now. "Her father's shop burned in the Great Fire, did it not? Way back in the 1660s?"

"Something like that. Some cousins own another shop in London. It was started by one of her sons, I think. In any case, there are many more jewels, including some very old ones, in the safe in Claire's workshop." Her sister Claire had taken up the old family hobby. "These were Mama's personal items. Some family heirlooms given to her by my father—Lord Greystone, I mean—and some newer things. But nothing I could identify as coming from her first husband."

Griffin sifted through the treasure trove, rings and bracelets glittering as they slipped through his fingers. He recognized a diamond necklace as one Rachael had worn to a ball at Cainewood two summers earlier. A pair of ruby earrings that looked like the ones in her mother's formal portrait. A brooch he had often seen pinned on Georgiana's dress.

A locket made him momentarily hopeful, but it held a swatch of hair, not a miniature or a note. No dates or names were engraved on anything.

Then another brooch caught his eye. "The Prince of Wales's Feathers," he murmured, pulling it from the pile.

Three silver plumes rose from a gold coronet of alternate crosses and fleurs-de-lis, studded with rubies and emeralds. Along the bottom, a gold ribbon bore a motto.

"What does it say?" Rachael asked.

"'*Ich Dien.*' I serve." He looked at her, his heart pounding. "Your father . . . I mean, John Chase, Lord Greystone . . . was he ever in the cavalry?"

"Of course not. His younger brother served in the army, but Grandfather would never have allowed his heir to risk his life."

"I thought not. This may be our clue."

She blinked. "It's a national symbol of Wales, is it not? I assumed it was a souvenir from a visit."

"It's a military badge. From the Tenth Hussars. My regiment."

Hope leapt into her sky blue eyes. "Do you think it was given to my mother by a member?"

"An officer, from the looks of this piece. An enlisted man would wear a much less expensive version." The metal felt cool in his fingers as he turned it over. Nothing was engraved on the back.

"No more clues," she said with a sigh.

"This alone may be enough. Would you mind if I keep it a while?"

"Of course not. But how can it help you find my father?"

He slipped it into his pocket. "He died in 1792, sometime in the months after you were conceived but before you were born—that much we know. We weren't at war then. Louis the Sixteenth had yet to be tried and executed, and Napoleon didn't come to power until 'ninety-nine. There shouldn't have been many deaths that year; the Tenth would have been at home; in peacetime, there are few casualties. I'll go to regimental headquarters and ask to see the records."

It would take two days to get there, a day to search the records, and another two days to ride home. Five days during which Corinna wouldn't meet any suitable men. But much as he wanted his sister married and off his hands, he didn't mind.

Rachael's happiness was important, too.

Although another woman might have made a token protest, Rachael wasn't that sort. "Thank you," she said instead, two simple, grateful words. "Do you expect you can find something that could tell us who he was?"

He shrugged, not wanting to get her hopes up. "I can try. I'll bring you back to London now, and I'd like to take Corinna to Lady Partridge's ball tomorrow night. I'll leave for regimental headquarters first thing Sunday morning and hopefully have an answer for you by Thursday."

"An officer," she breathed. "Someone important."

A bark of a laugh burst out of him. "It doesn't take importance to buy a commission. Only money."

Her eyes shone. "You were important. You led campaigns in the Peninsular War. Your patrol brought news of the Prussian retreat at Wavre, thus influencing the Duke of Wellington to fight at Waterloo."

"How do you know all that?"

"Your sisters. They're proud of you. You'd have been at Waterloo had your brother not died."

"Well, he did," he said flatly, keeping the bitterness out of his voice.

He'd never wanted to be a marquess. And he'd felt damned ineffective since becoming one. But here, now, was a chance to use his military connections to advantage. To help someone.

To help Rachael.

And that thought made him entirely too pleased.

Chapter Eight

"You're not going to stay up 'til all hours, are you?"

In a creative haze, Corinna turned from her easel and blinked at her brother in the drawing room's doorway. It was close to midnight, and she hadn't realized he'd returned home. "I'm starting a new painting."

"You didn't answer my question. I've had a long day, and I'm off to bed. Will you also be retiring soon?"

"I don't know." Irritated, she set down her palette. "It depends upon how this goes."

Griffin walked closer. "Doesn't look like much."

"Yet." All she'd done was layer the pale gray ground that she used as the undertint for her paintings, with a rough white oval in the upper middle.

"What is it going to be?"

"I'm not sure," she hedged.

But she knew what she wanted it to be: a portrait. That was why she'd laid the white oval where she planned to paint the face. Flesh tones would appear brighter over white than gray, and she wanted the face to be luminous.

And she wanted it to be a *good* portrait. That was why she'd sketched the Elgin Marbles.

"I want you to get a good night's sleep," Griffin pressed. "I've several men I want you to meet at Lady Partridge's ball tomorrow evening."

Not that again. *Your turn will come next,* she remembered Juliana saying. All she wanted was to concentrate on her art, but everyone wanted to marry her off.

Her creative haze had dissipated, like paint swiped with turpentine. "Well, then, I will certainly go to bed," she said sarcastically, thinking she hadn't decided whom she wanted to paint, anyway.

"I'm glad to hear it," Griffin said, evidently missing her sarcasm. "By the way, I need to leave Sunday morning, and I probably won't be back until Thursday. I won't be able to take you to Almack's on Wednesday night."

"What a pity." Day after day of painting without interruptions, while he was busy dealing with some problem at Cainewood or whatever. Though she vaguely wondered what he was going to do, she didn't want to prolong this discussion. "That's too bad, Griffin," she said, hiding a smile. "Good night."

Looking forward to the week ahead, she hummed as she cleaned up and put everything away. Then she went upstairs to her room, lit a candle from the fireplace, and ducked into her dressing room to grab a nightgown.

And there she stopped short.

The paintings taunted her. Hidden paintings, dozens of them stacked leaning against the walls. Portrait after portrait, none of them quite right.

She'd spent a decade and more learning to paint still lifes and landscapes. Practicing, persevering, perfecting. Eventually she'd begun putting people into her scenes, figures strolling or laboring or simply lounging in the background. But that hadn't proved enough, hadn't satisfied her dreams.

She'd always wanted to paint real portraits, detailed studies of people. She all but *burned* to paint portraits, and last year she'd put all other sorts of painting behind her.

She walked closer and flipped canvases, bringing the candle near to scrutinize the year's many efforts. Her maid. Alexandra and Juliana. Alexandra and baby

Harry. Juliana alone, her shoulders bare, her skirts hiked up to expose one scandalous, naked knee.

Juliana, the dear, had obligingly posed for Corinna in the buff. Rigidly, self-consciously nude. Unfortunately, Corinna had been unable to *paint* her sister nude, as the sight of such a work of art would have driven Griffin out of his mind.

And none of the paintings were good enough.

Sighing, she leaned them back against the wall. She knew she had it in her to produce a fine portrait. She'd long since mastered all the things she could easily study—the face, the hair, the clothing, the hands—and she portrayed her subjects' expressions with unfailing insight.

But when it came to the body, she found herself frustrated every time. The people looked stiff and unnatural, not altogether surprising, given they'd looked stiff and unnatural when they'd posed. Corinna's maid and sisters could never seem to sit still for long, and sketching them had never proved as helpful as she'd wished.

Not to mention her maid and sisters were all female. Men were formed differently, and since half the world's population was male, Corinna intended to paint them, too. But barring her brother—who so far had been uncooperative—where on earth was a gently bred lady supposed to find a male model?

Well, perhaps sketching the Elgin Marbles had done the trick, she reminded herself, lifting her chin. At least *they* had held still for hours.

Squaring her shoulders, she returned to her room and summoned her maid to help ready her for bed. But then she found she couldn't relax. She rarely rose before noon, because she retired late as a habit. Although painting by candlelight rather than sunlight could sometimes prove challenging, the night hours were quiet, almost mystical, the very best time for creativity.

It was too early to fall asleep.

She pulled out a small book tucked under her bed,

the second volume of *Celia in Search of a Husband* by Medora Gordon Byron. Smiling, she cradled it in her hands. A Minerva Press novel, a torrid romance, bound as usual in cheap marble-patterned paper.

Other than painting, reading Minerva Press novels was Corinna's favorite, most secret escape.

She bought them in secret, too. Most fortunately, a bookseller's shop sat next door to the colorman's shop where she purchased her art supplies. Her maid or a footman generally accompanied her on these excursions, since no one in the family had the patience to wait for hours while she chose the perfect oils and tints. Which was a good thing, since that meant they never saw her go into the bookshop afterward, either.

The last thing she wanted was her family discovering she reveled in such unrefined literature. Her sisters would be properly scandalized—or else they would tease her mercilessly. And Griffin would doubtless be pleased; he'd say it proved she pined for love and a husband.

She could do without any of those reactions.

To make doubly sure there was no risk of discovery, after reading a Minerva Press novel she always donated it to the circulating library. That way other women could enjoy them. She had no need to ever reread them herself, since she was afflicted—yes, *afflicted*—with the capability of remembering everything she'd ever read.

Word for word.

The printed pages simply appeared in her mind, and random sentences popped into her head at the oddest, most inconvenient moments. It was annoying beyond end. Almost annoying enough to make her stop reading.

But only almost. She set the candle on her bedside table and opened the book with a happy sigh.

Celia was rather amusing. Though the woman proclaimed loudly and often that she wanted a husband, she discarded men left and right, as though they were so many used handkerchiefs. On page 183, Celia sighed "mentally," according to the author.

Corinna often sighed silently, too.

Am I rigid? Celia wondered. *What woman of real feeling would trust her peace to the keeping of a libertine? It may prove the vanity of love to believe that we could fix the heart hitherto unprincipled, but a trusting woman must meet, in the creature of her choice, either the idol of her hopes or certain disappointment in her connubial happiness—for here is no medium.*

Exactly, Corinna thought with a sigh. A mental sigh, of course. One could not fix an unprincipled man, no matter how much she loved him, and what were the chances of her meeting her idol? Certain disappointment was much more likely, which was why she, a woman of real feeling, was *much* better off putting her faith in her art.

Chapter Nine

Lady Partridge lived in a small mansion at the edge of Mayfair. On Saturday night, the line of carriages stretched for blocks. Sean figured he could have inspected two properties and negotiated three deals by the time he and his "uncle" made their way to the front.

Two footmen reached in for Lincolnshire, who had spent most of the wait dozing. He glanced at Sean as they helped him hobble out. "You look a bit sober, eh?"

"I beg your pardon, sir? I should think so." Sean watched the footmen settle the earl in an amazing contraption. A typical dining room chair with a caned back and an upholstered seat, it had two huge wheels attached to its sides and a smaller wheel centered behind. "I am not an inveterate drinker, I can assure you."

Indeed, to the contrary—and to Deirdre's unending amusement—Sean seemed the only Irishman alive who couldn't hold his liquor.

"Downed a toddy myself before leaving," the earl said as one of the servants lifted his feet while the other unfolded a small, upholstered shelf for them to rest upon. "A swallow of spirits never hurt a fellow, should you ask me. But I plan to stick around long enough to get to know you, yet you look to be dressed for a funeral. Not mine, I hope."

"Certainly not yours, sir." Sean shook out a blanket and settled it on the earl's lap to hide his swollen legs.

Lincolnshire was a rather slight fellow in general, but his lower extremities would fit a man thrice his size. When Sean had seen them uncovered earlier this evening, he'd winced. "I'm afraid, however, that I've not spent much time at balls." He'd never been to a ball, as a matter of fact, so he'd had to guess at the proper garb. "Is something wrong with what I'm wearing?"

"Not wrong, no. Just drab for such a festive occasion." Lincolnshire himself was decked out in peacock blue and gold. "A little color wouldn't be amiss."

"Ah, I see," Sean said as he moved around to push the chair. "But I've a decided preference for black and white."

In truth, he *always* wore black and white. He'd learned early that to do otherwise meant risking mismatches often found humorous. Since he had nothing but black and white in his wardrobe, he was relieved to find his choice suitable if not stylish.

As he wheeled the man toward the door, a tall proper butler opened it. Sounds of music drifted out. "Your name, sir?"

"Lincolnshire," Lincolnshire barked. "And my nephew, Mr. Hamilton."

"My lord Lincolnshire, do please come in." Judging from the butler's tone, if Lincolnshire had been a dog, the man would have petted him. "Lady Partridge left instructions to be notified the very moment you arrived. This way, if you will," he added, motioning Sean along.

But Sean couldn't push the chair in the direction indicated. In fact, he couldn't push it anywhere at all. It seemed Lord Lincolnshire had barked his name a little too loudly, because people began streaming into the Partridge foyer, all but trapping the two of them in place.

"Lord Lincolnshire!" An aging matron took the old man's hands. "It's positively delightful to see you!"

"I'm delighted as well, Lady Fotherington. May I introduce my long-lost nephew, Mr. Sean Hamilton? He's like a son to me."

Sean tensed, waiting to be called a fraud, but the woman focused on him only briefly. "I'm pleased to make your acquaintance," she said politely, displaying no interest in him at all.

Apparently his secret was safe. He didn't know any members of the *ton*, he reminded himself, glancing around at the growing gathering. And none of these people knew him.

There was no cause for worry.

"Lord Lincolnshire, how are you feeling?" the woman asked.

"As well as can be expected. And how is your son?" Lincolnshire squeezed her hands. "Well as well, I hope?"

"Oh, he's very well indeed, thanks in no small part to your assistance."

" 'Twas but a trifle, my lady, I assure you."

A young gentleman laid a hand on Lincolnshire's shoulder. "Is there aught I can do for you, my lord? After all, there's so much you've done for me."

An older, taller man sighed. "Who will bring toys this Christmas for the children at the Foundling Hospital?"

"Who indeed?" Tears tracked down a middle-aged lady's cheeks. "We're going to miss you, Lord Lincolnshire. Mightily."

One after another people arrived, crowding the foyer to pay their respects to the dying Earl of Lincolnshire. Men sighed and women cried, young and old alike sharing their memories, expressing their affection, declaring their sorrow.

And over and over, most touching of all, proclaiming their utter desire to see him leave the world a man content.

"We would do anything for you, my lord."

"Anything."

"Anything to make your last days easier."

"Anything to please you."

"Anything at all . . ."

* * *

Corinna was dancing with a thoroughly boring man—the latest in a string that proved Griffin hadn't the slightest idea what she was hoping for in a husband—when she noticed her old neighbor Lord Lincolnshire enter the ballroom.

Well, try to enter, she mentally amended. He was making excruciatingly slow progress, surrounded as he was by adoring people, all of whom seemed to be clamoring to capture his attention at once. Propped up in a cane-backed wheelchair, he looked happier than she'd imagined a dying man could possibly be.

The sight warmed her inside. If anyone in the world deserved happiness, it was Lord Lincolnshire. Watching him glance up and back, she smiled when she saw him aim an elated grin at whoever was pushing the chair. Her gaze followed his, focusing on the man behind him.

And her heart stuttered.

That crisp, overlong black hair. Those emerald eyes. That angular, sculpted face.

Her Greek god.

She'd never finished the drawing of him she'd begun in the Elgin Gallery. He'd left too soon. She'd actually tried painting him today—she'd decided she wanted him in her portrait—but she'd found herself unable to recall enough detail. Eventually she'd concluded she'd have to choose another subject and glumly painted over her efforts before dressing for tonight's ball.

Her canvas once more had a plain white oval where there should be a face. And now her fingers itched for a pencil.

She hadn't expected to see him ever again. He'd certainly never appeared at a society event before this. What was he doing here? How had he come to be with Lord Lincolnshire, pushing the dear old earl in a wheelchair?

"Whom are you staring at?" her partner asked.

She'd forgotten the dratted man. Indeed, she was suddenly thankful her mother had forced her to dance lessons those countless times when she'd protested she'd prefer to paint. All of that practice had allowed her to continue dancing by rote when she hadn't been paying attention. "I was watching Lord Lincolnshire. I'm so glad he managed to attend tonight. Might you know that gentleman with him? I'm wondering if he could be the artist John Hamilton."

"I've not seen him before, but I seriously doubt he's John Hamilton. John Hamilton never appears in public." The music came to an end, and the man bowed. "Thank you for the dance, Lady Corinna."

"My pleasure," she assured him, smiling distractedly.

Thinking Juliana knew everyone, after curtsying Corinna looked around and found her sister conversing with her mother-in-law, the new Lady Cavanaugh.

"Might either of you know that man accompanying Lord Lincolnshire?" she asked, barging right in.

Juliana glanced over and shook her head. "A handsome devil, though, is he not?"

A vast understatement. Corinna wanted to rip his clothes off and see the godlike body underneath. "I met him the other day at the British Museum. When you and Alexandra went off, remember? Another man introduced him as John Hamilton."

"John Hamilton, the artist? You said you'd met him, but—"

"Yes, the artist. But then everything became very confusing, because this man claimed he *wasn't* John Hamilton, but the other man was instead. And why would John Hamilton be with Lord Lincolnshire?"

"Lord Lincolnshire collects art," Juliana reminded her. "Ming vases and paintings."

"More to the point," Lady Cavanaugh said, "John Hamilton is Lord Lincolnshire's nephew. And his heir. Everyone knows that."

Corinna hadn't. But if John Hamilton was Lord Lincolnshire's nephew, that explained why the two men were together. Suddenly everything made perfect sense. His protests in the museum notwithstanding, her Greek god *had* to be the elusive John Hamilton. Being a recluse, he'd obviously claimed otherwise in order to retain his anonymity.

But Corinna knew the truth now.

Rising excitement fluttered in her chest. Her pulse pounded in her ears. She'd actually met John Hamilton.

The John Hamilton, a member of the Summer Exhibition Selection Committee.

A man who could help her dreams come true.

She had only to renew their acquaintance in order to set her future plans in motion. "Come along," she told her sister, grabbing her hand. She motioned to Lady Cavanaugh. "I'll introduce you both."

Chapter Ten

Lord Lincolnshire held up a hand, interrupting an effusive outpouring of affection from yet another of Lady Partridge's guests. "Nephew."

"Yes? Do you need something, Uncle?" Concerned, Sean moved around the front of the wheelchair, wedging himself between two hovering matrons. "Some laudanum? Are your limbs paining you?" He reached into his pocket for the vial the nurse had pressed into his hands.

"No laudanum. I'd as soon not dull my senses." The earl smoothed the lap robe that covered his legs, looking amused. "That pretty young lady is calling you."

"What pretty young lady?"

"That one." Lincolnshire motioned with his head. "The lovely Lady Corinna."

Corinna. Though London was surely home to more than one woman with the name, when Sean looked to where Lincolnshire had indicated, he already knew what he would see.

Shining dark hair, beckoning blue eyes. That air of sensuality that made his fists bunch at his sides to keep from reaching out to touch.

Bloody hell, he *had* met another member of the *ton*.

"Mr. Hamilton!" she gushed as she approached, making him realize she'd already called out, "Mr. Hamilton," several times. Sweet Jesus, he'd known he would forget to answer to his brother-in-law's name. "What a pleasure it is to see you again!"

"Again?" Lincolnshire asked.

"I met your nephew in the British Museum," she explained enthusiastically. "But when I went to introduce him to my sisters, he was gone." She turned to two other women who had followed her. "Here he is at last, the talented and reclusive John Hamilton. Mr. Hamilton, this is my sister, Lady Stafford, and her mother-in-law, Lady Cavanaugh."

Both women curtsied. Lady Cavanaugh looked kind and motherly. Lady Stafford was pretty like her sister, but not nearly as voluptuous. The petite and sprightly type.

"I'm sorry, but I'm not Mr. Hamilton." Sean turned to Lord Lincolnshire. "Tell them, Uncle."

The earl's eyes danced; clearly he was enjoying this bit of subterfuge. "Of course you're Mr. Hamilton." His papery lips curved into a smile as he focused on the three women, making Sean imagine he must have been a bit of a flirt back in the day. "But he's *Sean* Hamilton," he told the ladies. "Sean, not John. My *other* nephew."

Never in his life had Sean heard anyone sound less convincing.

Lady Cavanaugh leaned down to give Lincolnshire's shoulder a sympathetic pat. "I know you're not feeling yourself these days, my lord, but you've only one nephew."

"I may have lost the use of my legs, but I assure you, dear lady, I have not lost my mind along with them." An unapologetic grin spreading on his face, he turned to Sean. "I'm afraid our ruse didn't work."

"I knew it!" Corinna exclaimed loudly enough to wake the dead. Heads snapped around as other guests looked to see what was up. "You *are* John Hamilton!"

Sean didn't know whether he wanted to kiss her or strangle her. Both, he decided as whispers ricocheted around the room.

"John Hamilton?"

"*The* John Hamilton?"

The whispers became a buzz. "John Hamilton!"

"It's John Hamilton!"

Sean moved behind Lincolnshire to prevent the earl from seeing him, and shook his head wildly in an attempt to wordlessly inform Corinna she was wrong. But she only frowned in confusion, and he was too late in any case. A matron was already waddling near, pulling an obviously shy, marriage-aged daughter by the hand.

"Lord Lincolnshire, may I beg an introduction to your illustrious nephew?"

Another lady seemed to appear from nowhere. "Is this your heir, Lord Lincolnshire?"

A third lady shoved in front of her. "Mr. Hamilton, my Matilda is a diamond of the first water."

Lincolnshire puffed up like a peacock, albeit a seated one. "Our secret is out." Pride was evident in his tone. "I am pleased to have you all meet the next Lord Lincolnshire. My nephew, Mr. John Hamilton."

Sean cringed as matchmaking mamas came out of the woodwork, their eligible daughters in tow. Corinna disappeared, or maybe she was pushed away by the expanding crowd. He spent the next few minutes at Lincolnshire's side, pondering how to escape this coil while he made small talk with an unceasing parade of all-but-identical insipid misses.

"Sean."

Feeling a tug on his tailcoat, he breathed a sigh of relief. "Uncle, you must be exhausted. Shall we leave? I'll take you home."

"Balderdash. I've not felt so energetic in weeks. I wish to see you dance with one of these lovelies."

The not-so-lovely mamas started shoving their charges Sean's way.

"I couldn't choose," he protested amiably. But he wasn't feeling amiable at all. What he felt instead was a rising pressure in his chest. The last thing he wanted to do was dance.

His mother had dragged him to many a village *ceili. A vicar's family should be social,* he heard her sweet voice in his memory. But he'd never been a man who enjoyed dancing. Even more to the point, Irish dance parties featured jigs and reels. No ceili band ever played a waltz.

And Lady Partridge seemed partial to waltzes. Or perhaps the musicians she'd hired preferred playing them. Either way, the last dance had been a waltz, and a waltz was playing now, and he'd lay odds a waltz would also come next.

He aimed a smile at Hamilton's uncle. "I think I should stay with you."

"I think not." One of the earl's grizzled brows went up. "I've a mind to see you settled before I die."

Settled? Posing as the man's nephew was bad enough—Sean would go only so far in an effort to placate the old fellow. And a wedding went rather beyond that boundary.

Miles beyond that boundary.

And then he remembered.

"I'm quite settled already. I'm married, if you've forgotten." The real Hamilton was married, after all. Had he *not* been married—to Deirdre—Sean wouldn't have been in this mess in the first place. "I've been married for ten long years."

Audible sighs could be heard from all the females.

"Ah, yes," Lincolnshire mused. "I'd forgotten about that. And I've never seen your wife in all that time."

The old man hadn't seen Hamilton in all that time, either, but Sean wouldn't be the one to remind him. "Deirdre is a wonderful lady."

The earl's forehead furrowed. "I seem to recall rumor has it you two don't rub along."

"To the contrary," Sean assured him. "The two of us rub along grandly."

Someone snorted, and a few other bystanders murmured, evidently recalling the same rumors. Or, more likely, rumors of the artist bedding countless women.

Well, Sean supposed, it wasn't all that surprising to find Hamilton's reputation preceded him. Some of the man's bastards probably resided right here in London.

"Where *is* your wife?" Lincolnshire asked.

"In the countryside," Sean told him, not actually stretching the truth. Though Hampstead lay but four miles northwest of Charing Cross, many Londoners did consider it "way out in the countryside." Which was precisely why he'd bought his house there. While he needed to be close to the City, he had no wish to live in it. Having been brought up amid wide-open spaces, he preferred not to be hemmed in.

"In the countryside," Lincolnshire repeated, and sighed, a protracted sound positively flush with disappointment. His gaze turned wistful, the soft, yearning gaze of a puppy dog. "I do understand. But since I can no longer dance myself, I was so hoping to see you in my stead."

The current waltz ended, and sudden silence pervaded the ballroom.

"Dance for him," a woman coaxed.

Her daughter smiled. "Make him happy."

The music—another waltz, naturally—restarted. "It's just a dance," someone else said.

The crowd seemed to press closer. "Lord Lincolnshire wants to see you dance."

"Humor him, will you?"

Although attempting a waltz was sure to prove humorous indeed, Sean felt his resolve disintegrating under the assault. The damn earl was making puppy-dog eyes. What the devil was a man supposed to do?

One of the identical insipid misses gazed up at him beseechingly. "Don't you *want* to make Lord Lincolnshire happy?"

"Oh, very well," he gritted out. "One dance."

Then he turned on a heel and headed straight for Corinna.

As he elbowed his way through the crowd, Corinna's startled gaze met his, and it seemed as though a fist grabbed him in the gut. Half of him wanted to wring her neck for interfering; the other half wanted to drag her into his arms.

He settled for snatching her hand and pulling her toward the dance floor.

He threaded them between other couples to the center, enduring bumps from various dancers along the way. It seemed a whirling obstacle course. But at least here he wouldn't be on display.

He turned her to face him. "I hope you can lead."

She looked a little dazed, standing still with everyone moving around her. "I beg your pardon?"

"Thanks to you, I've been commanded to dance. And I've never waltzed in my life."

"Oh." She smiled, a rather sheepish smile that made the fist inside him twist. "I confess I've been accused of leading before. I fear it's one of my bad habits."

" 'Tis glad I am to hear it."

Mimicking the other dancers, he wrapped an arm about her waist and grasped her gloved right hand. She began to move, keeping her body tense so that he moved with her.

Not very gracefully, but they moved.

"May I sketch you sometime?" she asked.

"Sketch me?" he echoed, amazed to find them actually swirling among the other couples. He stumbled, but managed to keep upright. "I think not."

"Never?"

"Ever," he reiterated, treading on her toes.

A wee "Eek!" escaped her tempting lips, but then she gave him another smile. An understanding one this time. Not that it had any less of an effect on him. It was a wonder she didn't react to the naked desire he suspected was evident on his face, but it was probably best that she was oblivious to it.

"Very well," she said on a sigh. "I suppose you're too busy with your own art to sit for someone else."

She was exasperating. "You're ruining my life."

"How so?" she asked. "I've done you a favor, Mr. Hamilton. Society is all aflutter to finally meet Lord Lincolnshire's famous, mysterious nephew. They'll pay even more for your paintings."

He leaned improperly close, catching a whiff of a light, floral scent with something odd layered underneath it. Paint, maybe. "I'm not an artist," he hissed in her ear. "I'm Sean Delaney, not John Hamilton."

She drew back, making them lurch, and the look she gave him was uncomfortably close to a smirk. "I haven't heard you say that in front of Lord Lincolnshire."

"For his sake." Revealing the truth would doubtless destroy the kind old earl, not to mention infuriate Hamilton and jeopardize Deirdre's divorce. "I wish not to embarrass the poor man by disagreeing with him in the company of his friends."

"I understand that you prefer the privacy that anonymity affords you, Mr. Hamilton. But as the real Mr. Delaney said in the museum, you are much too self-effacing. You'll grow accustomed to being famous, and it is long past time you met your adoring admirers."

He considered stepping on her feet on purpose. "They wouldn't adore me if they knew the truth."

"Of course they would. You're a fortunate man, Mr. Hamilton. They all love Lord Lincolnshire and will transfer that affection to you. In fact, they already have. I was squeezed right out of the earl's circle by all the ladies who want to marry you."

So she hadn't heard he was married. Or rather, that Hamilton was married. Well, he wasn't going to inform her. That would only serve to reinforce her conviction that he was Hamilton.

"Lincolnshire *is* well loved," he muttered instead in disgust. Had the earl been the blackguard Hamilton had described, he'd not have been welcome at this ball. And Corinna would never have introduced Sean as his *famous nephew*. "Everyone seems absolutely devastated that he is dying."

"Of course we are," she said, pulling his hand back to keep him from ramming into someone. "Throughout his life, Lord Lincolnshire has given generously to charity and done countless good deeds for various members of the *ton* and their children."

"Everyone says they'll do anything for him."

"Anything but the one thing we cannot, which is to save his life," she said mournfully.

"Then why didn't you believe him?" He stumbled again, and her hand gripped his shoulder harder. "When he told you I was Sean, not John, you disagreed with him. Loudly."

The look she gave him said he was a complete idiot. "The dear man does enjoy his games. And Sean is the same name as John in Ireland anyway, is it not? You sound like you come from Ireland."

That he couldn't deny. Not without appearing to be the idiot she already considered him. Luckily for him, the musicians stopped playing. The dance had come to an end. Corinna curtsied, thanked him politely, and walked off.

He'd survived his first waltz. But as her sweet, paint-tinged scent wafted away, he found himself wishing it had lasted longer.

And wasn't that absurd? He was lucky he had come out alive.

Chapter Eleven

Shortly after noon on Monday, Sean paced outside the gate in front of Lincolnshire House, planning his day as he waited for his curricle to be brought around. Thanks to a long breakfast with Lincolnshire, he was getting a very late start. He needed to stop by his main offices and make sure everything had gone well in his absence. Two contracts should be waiting for him to sign, he had three pending transactions to review, and he hoped to open negotiations for a factory he wished to sell. In addition, he expected barrels of wine he'd imported to arrive, he had a hotel to inspect in the center of London, and he wanted to talk to Deirdre—which meant a drive out to Hampstead and back.

Across the street, Berkeley Square hummed with activity. From his vantage point at the north end, he watched people traipse in and out of the fenced, grassy park in the middle. In the row of houses along the west side, a blue door opened, catching his eye. Two footmen emerged, burdened with boxes and an easel. As they headed across the street toward the park, a young woman came out and followed, her lithe figure clad in a pale blue gown with a white apron tied over it. Her dark hair, worn unfashionably loose, shone in the midday sun.

As his curricle pulled up, he blinked, suddenly recognizing Corinna.

"Wait here," he told the stableman before dashing out into the square.

By the time he reached her, the servants had positioned her easel beneath a giant plane tree and were setting a canvas upon it—one covered with blotches of gray and white. She riffled through a box filled with little pots of paint, her gaze focused, her plump bottom lip caught between her teeth.

"Good day to you, Lady Corinna."

Startled, she looked up, narrowing her eyes. Impossibly gorgeous blue eyes.

To Sean, most everyone's eyes—including his own—appeared brown. Green, hazel, brown . . . they all looked brown. Only shades of blue looked truly colorful, and Corinna's eyes seemed the most brilliant blue he'd had the pleasure to see.

A man could lose himself in those eyes.

"Have you decided to let me sketch you?" she asked.

"No," he said, not lost after all. "I was waiting there for my carriage"—he gestured toward Lincolnshire House—"when I noticed you entering the square. I came over to tell you I'm not Hamilton. I'm not Lincolnshire's nephew."

She lifted a dull knife. "So you keep saying." Using it to scoop brown—or maybe red or green—paint onto a palette, she slanted him a glance. "Yet you're living in Lincolnshire House."

"I am. I can explain. Hamilton is my brother-in-law, and—"

"You said that in the museum."

"Because it's true."

She seemed to stare at his mouth for a moment before she wiped the knife on her splotched apron and used it to add a smidge of a lighter color. "I don't believe you," she said, apparently as blunt as she was beautiful. "I understand that you've enjoyed your anonymity in the past, but your secret is out now. You're going to have to get used to the fact that everyone knows you're John Hamilton."

She was staring at his mouth again, almost as though she wanted to kiss him. He certainly wanted to kiss her. Or throttle her. "But I'm *not* John Hamilton."

"And I'm not here in Berkeley Square." With a saucy smile, she picked up a brush and turned to her canvas. "I expect you should get to your own painting, Mr. Hamilton. I wish you a successful day."

Clearly he was dismissed. He strode back to his curricle, bunching his fists—as much to keep from throttling her as to keep from touching her this time. If he didn't manage to convince her of the truth soon, his hands were going to be permanently clenched.

With Griffin gone, Corinna had been looking forward to a few peaceful days to work on her portrait, but she wandered the drawing room Tuesday, still pondering whom to paint.

She'd decided her picture would be set outdoors. She was an accomplished landscape artist, after all, and it was important that her backdrop be as impressive as her central subject. She wanted the play of light and shadow, the varied greens of grass and trees, the bright hues of blooming flowers. She'd started painting all of that yesterday in the square, and she was happy enough with how it was coming along. But she couldn't make up her mind whom she wanted in the foreground and what, exactly, he or she should be doing.

She didn't care for formal portraits where the sitter just stared at the viewer. She preferred to see subjects in context. Conversation portraits, they were called. Quite popular in the previous century, they often featured whole families or groups of friends posed casually, as though caught in some everyday action. Although it wasn't common to do the same with a single subject, she wanted to give it a try. She hoped it would make her painting a little different—and therefore more noteworthy.

If the painting turned out well, it would not only be the first work she submitted to the Summer Exhibition, but also the first portrait she put on public view. She wanted to choose someone who would be memorable. Someone whose personality would shine from the canvas. Someone she knew well enough to portray in such a manner that the viewer would feel he or she was a close, personal friend.

That was why she'd painted family members over and over.

She stopped and scanned all the many old Chase family portraits on the wall, settling on one dated 1670. The gentleman wore a long surcoat and a lace-trimmed cravat, the lady a full, heavy brocade gown with an old-fashioned stomacher fronting the bodice. A small engraved metal plate on the frame read:

JASON AND CAITHREN
8TH MARQUESS AND MARCHIONESS OF CAINEWOOD

She'd never known this couple, of course. They'd both died long before she was born. But unlike the ancient, more sober portraits, which invariably featured stern, unsmiling subjects, this husband and wife looked happy. They looked like they had been in love.

And they looked very much like Corinna's present family.

Juliana resembled Caithren, sharing her ancestor's warm hazel eyes and straight, streaky blond tresses. Griffin had inherited Jason's dark hair and square jaw, and both men had deep green eyes.

Not as startling a green as the eyes belonging to the man Corinna really wanted to paint. She couldn't keep her mind off him. The way he kept lying to her was infuriating, but now whenever she picked up a Minerva Press novel she pictured him as the hero. No matter if the author described the hero as having fair hair and blue eyes; in her head his hair was dark, his eyes that startling green. When the dark-haired, green-eyed hero touched the heroine, a pleasurable shiver ran through her. And whenever the hero and heroine kissed, she imagined Mr. Hamilton kissing her, and her lips tingled.

But he'd refused even to let her sketch him, so painting him was out of the question. She was as likely to paint him as she was to kiss him.

Neither was going to happen.

And no, she decided, she didn't want to update the family portrait collection by continuing to paint new pictures of people who looked eerily similar to the ones already on the walls. She'd been doing that for nearly a year, and none of her efforts had turned out well enough to hang on the walls, anyway.

Sighing, she collected her art supplies and summoned two footmen to accompany her into the square. Until she decided on a subject, she would continue working on her setting. Carrying her box of paints, she followed the servants out the door and across the street.

Or at least she tried to cross the street. Rounding the curve from Lincolnshire House, a curricle drew to a halt in her path. The driver looked down from his high perch.

"I'm not Hamilton," he said coldly.

She shrugged, thoroughly vexed. Apparently he hated her. And since he wasn't going to let her sketch him—let alone paint him—she wished he'd just leave her alone. If he'd cease popping into her life, perhaps she'd be able to concentrate on finding someone else to kiss.

To *paint*, she mentally amended. She didn't want to kiss him; she only wanted to paint him.

Holy Hannah, she was a liar.

And was there anything worse than lying to oneself?

"Fine," she snapped. "You're not Hamilton. Now will you please drive on so that I can paint?"

A hoot of laughter burst from his throat. Or maybe it was a snort of frustration. Whichever, he flicked his reins and drove off, leaving her to think about painting him and kissing him . . . and very little else.

At the rate she was making progress, she'd be lucky to finish a new portrait before *next* year's Summer Exhibition.

Chapter Twelve

"Nephew?"

"Hmm?"

"I wish to see your studio today."

Sean looked up from reading the *Morning Chronicle* at the breakfast table, thinking it was way too late for breakfast. By this hour on a normal morning, he'd generally have risen, eaten, and driven all the way into town to his offices. On a normal morning, he'd have already gone through the day's mail, sat in on several meetings, dispatched employees to see to his interests. On a normal morning, he'd be elbow-deep in business by now, expanding his empire, increasing his fortune. On a normal morning . . .

This wasn't a normal morning.

No morning had been normal since he'd agreed to this damned scheme. Lincolnshire had trouble falling asleep and, in consequence, stayed abed late. And then he wanted his "dear nephew Sean" to keep him company at breakfast. He ate very little and very slowly, and in consequence it all took very long.

Sean folded and set aside the newspaper. "My studio is private," he said carefully.

"From me?" The earl looked hurt. "I'm your uncle. You're my heir."

"I have work to do—"

"I know. Work that makes me mighty proud, work

that rivals the very best." He gestured to all the old masters on his dining room walls. "I want to see where you work. I shall sit and watch quietly; I promise. It's not as though I could move around much even if I wanted to," he added with his usual good humor.

But Sean's smile was regretful, not amused. "I'm sorry, but I wouldn't be able to concentrate—"

"You won't even know I'm there."

He *did* want to make the old man happy. But he couldn't—he just couldn't—allow Lincolnshire to see Hamilton's studio.

At least, not in its current state.

No more than an hour after leaving the British Museum, Hamilton had fetched a few paintings and stuck them in an empty garret in one of Sean's buildings. He'd even included a half-finished canvas and propped it on an easel, so it would appear as though Sean were in the middle of a project.

But after that, he'd run off to Wales. Immediately and without a backward glance, with only a promise that he'd return in two weeks. Other than the pictures and a few well-used sketchbooks, he'd provided nothing.

No paint. No brushes. The earl would expect to see more than art, wouldn't he? He'd expect to see art *supplies*.

Still and all, Sean had no wish to disappoint Hamilton's uncle. Lincolnshire's condition was worsening by the day, and he was a nice fellow who deserved a happy ending. There was nothing for it; Sean had no choice.

He was forced to twist the truth once again.

"Unfortunately," he explained, "I find it impossible to paint with anyone watching over my shoulder. And I'm in the middle of something I fear I'm quite anxious to finish today. Will tomorrow be soon enough? I should be done then, and I'll be happy to bring you to the studio. Not to watch me paint, mind you, but to see the space. And to view the latest Hamilton canvases."

He hated lying. This whole exercise was mentally exhausting. For the umpteenth time, he silently cursed himself for allowing Hamilton to talk him into it.

"Very well," Lincolnshire finally conceded. "I shall look forward to visiting tomorrow."

Sean thanked him and finished breakfast, then went off to work. Or rather, to purchase art supplies.

Normally he wouldn't have a clue where to buy anything related to art. But he'd noticed Hamilton's sketchbooks all had REEVES & SONS stamped on them. Recalling a tenant by that name in one of his buildings in the center of the City, he was able to drive straight there.

It took him a good while to choose the supplies, particularly the colors. Completely at a loss, he finally consulted one of the Reeveses—father or son, he knew not—who selected the proper pigments for him. After hearing the man rattle on about tone harmony, warmer and cooler variants, transparent as opposed to opaque, and the benefits versus the drawbacks of a broad palette compared to a more limited one—this particular "palette" apparently referring to a list of colors rather than a thing one put the colors on—Sean felt as though his head might explode.

When at long last he came out of the shop—a "colorman's shop," he'd learned it was called—he also feared more than half his day had slipped away.

He was in a hurry. So much so that, on his way back to his curricle, he glanced twice at a woman in the bookshop next door before realizing she was Corinna.

A footman in Chase livery stood outside the shop, looking bored. Corinna stood on the other side of the window, her nose buried in a book. A bell on the door jangled when Sean opened it, but the noise failed to rouse her. Ignoring the bookseller's muted "Good afternoon," Sean walked past the front desk and right up to her. Still reading, she didn't acknowledge his arrival.

"I'm not Hamilton," he said.

She jumped. Then slammed the book shut as her gaze flew to his face. "I don't believe you."

"So you keep saying. But I don't paint."

Her blue, blue eyes focused on the bulky package in his hands. Wrapped in brown paper and tied with string, it had REEVES & SONS stamped on it in smudged black ink.

A tiny smile tugged at her lips. "Then what did you buy at the colorman's shop?"

The sarcasm in her tone was unmistakable. Answering truthfully would only dig him in deeper. But he was tired of lying. He'd been trying to *correct* a lie. He didn't want to claim he'd purchased anything other than oil, pigments, and brushes.

So instead he said, "What are you reading?"

Her reaction was astonishing. She blushed and stuttered and quickly shoved the book onto the nearest shelf. When he looked to see the title, she grabbed his upper arm and maneuvered him down a row of bookcases. And around a corner and down a second row. She didn't stop until she'd backed him into a dead end.

He smiled down at her. She looked very becoming with flushed cheeks. And though she'd finally released him, he'd rather liked having her touching him.

He'd liked that to an alarming degree.

A small part of him wondered what she'd been reading. A very small part of him. The rest of him was busy contemplating the fact that the two of them were quite alone here, tucked amongst the quiet bookshop's tall shelves. There didn't seem to be any other customers, the bookseller was well out of view, and the footman who'd accompanied Corinna was apparently still outside daydreaming.

Sean set the package on a high, empty shelf.

The shop smelled like paper and dust, but Corinna smelled of flowers and paint. Her breathing seemed loud in the pervasive silence. Loud and a wee bit ragged. Watching him, she sank her teeth into her bottom lip—that plump, tempting lip—and swayed toward him, perhaps involuntarily.

Without thought, he leaned in to kiss her.

She tasted as sweet as she smelled, her mouth yielding against his. He brushed it once, twice, then settled into place, taking possession. She gasped, parting her lips just enough to let him in.

He knew he shouldn't, but he couldn't help himself—didn't *want* to help himself. He'd been imagining this kiss since that first day in the British Museum. He wrapped his arms around her and slipped his tongue into her mouth, half expecting her to bite it in protest.

But she didn't.

She kissed him back.

First she angled her head to make their lips match more closely. Next she sighed into his mouth. Tentatively, she touched the tip of her tongue to his. Then, seeming to go boneless in his arms, she simply sank into the experience.

She felt . . . wonderful. Soft and warm and curving in all the right places. Sean wasn't a man to think in poetic terms, but the word that sprang to mind was *divine*. She molded her body to his and wound her arms around his neck, threading her fingers into the hair at his nape. By degrees she grew bolder, the kiss deepening, an exciting, arousing dance of lips and tongues. He sensed she was learning as she went along, but she seemed a very apt pupil. And an extremely talented one as well.

When she finally pulled away, he was left rather witless.

Her cheeks were even more flushed than before; her breath was now ragged enough to make her breasts heave beneath her thin dress; her eyes looked as hazy as he felt. "Why?" she asked in a voice so throaty it kicked his lust up a notch. "Why did you do that?"

He wasn't sure why. "I suppose because I wanted to."

"But you hate me!"

"Obviously, I don't. Although I will admit to finding you somewhat exasperating." He measured her in return. "Why did you *let* me do that?"

Her hazy eyes widened. "Are you jesting? What woman—most especially what woman *artist*—wouldn't let John Hamilton kiss her?"

For once he didn't protest that he wasn't John Hamilton. He was too stunned. "So it was a trophy kiss?"

"I beg your pardon?"

"You kiss artists? You thought to add me to your collection? A particularly shiny prize?"

She splayed a hand on her heaving cleavage. "I have never kissed another artist."

She had not, he noted, claimed she'd never kissed another *man*. Evidently she'd been kissed before. But while she'd been an enthusiastic participant, she'd not been precisely schooled, making him suspect that she'd never been kissed before in the French manner.

He found himself pleased by that notion. A man liked to be first. However, he was very much aware that he had no business kissing her at all, in the French manner or otherwise.

He wasn't John Hamilton. He wasn't Lincolnshire's nephew. He wasn't an English peer, or a soon-to-be English peer, or remotely related to any English peer at all.

He wasn't even English.

He was an upstart Irish commoner with lots of money but apparently no sense. Aristocratic young misses like Corinna were off-limits to men like him.

"I'm sorry," he said.

"I'm not."

She was very blunt, he thought, not for the first time. And very beautiful.

He'd thought that before, too.

"I won't kiss you again," he vowed.

"I hope you will." Her lips curved, making him want to kiss them again, vow be damned. "I enjoyed kissing you very much," she added artlessly.

In the sense of being free of guile, of course. Of stating something simply and sincerely. She was certainly not *artless* in the literal definition.

"You shouldn't have enjoyed kissing me," he informed her, "because I am not John Hamilton."

"Not that again." Reaching up to the shelf, she shoved his package toward him. "Don't forget your art supplies," she called over her shoulder as she walked away. "You're going to need them the next time you paint."

He was still standing there when the bell jangled and the door shut behind her.

Chapter Thirteen

Corinna stood before her easel in Berkeley Square the next day, painting.

Oh, very well, daydreaming.

Or—since she was determined to stop lying to herself—reliving yesterday's kiss.

For at least the hundredth time.

She'd been kissed before, of course, but never like *that*. She'd never tangled tongues with a man. She could have sworn her legs had turned to water. Not only her lips, but her entire body had seemed to tingle. She was surprised her pounding heart hadn't cracked a rib.

She couldn't say she hadn't been aware that such kisses were possible—she'd certainly read of them in Minerva Press novels. In fact, standing right there in the bookshop, she'd read in *Children of the Abbey* how Lord Mortimer had clutched Amanda close and *straining her to his beating heart, he imprinted a kiss on her tremulous lips*.

And the sort of kiss she'd shared with Mr. Hamilton was exactly what she had imagined.

It had seemed an excellent novel, and she'd had every intention of buying it. Until he'd kissed her—until he'd *imprinted a kiss on her lips*—leaving her head spinning and her mind blanker than a fresh canvas. And she'd forgotten all about buying the book.

Truthfully, though she relished reading of such kisses,

she hadn't expected to experience one until after she married. After all, the most proper ladies considered even a chaste kiss to be scandalous before a man proposed. But she'd never been proper, and she couldn't be sorry she hadn't waited.

Kissing Mr. Hamilton had been glorious. Magnificent. Awe-inspiring.

The most memorable, most erotic moment of her entire life.

And in all the hours since, when she wasn't daydreaming about the kiss, when she wasn't reliving it over and over in all its shocking, knee-weakening glory, she'd been engrossed in trying to figure out if that sort of kiss would have proved so incredible with any man, or only with Mr. Hamilton.

She suspected only with Mr. Hamilton. And despite what she'd said in the heat of the moment, that wasn't just because he *was* John Hamilton, either. Mostly because something about him called to her; something about him just—

"Lady Corinna." A familiar voice interrupted her musings.

It sounded weaker and more breathless than she'd like. Lord Lincolnshire wasn't doing well. Her heart sinking, Corinna looked over to see him sitting in his wheelchair outside the fence that enclosed the park.

Setting her palette down on a bench, she walked over to greet him, feeling a bit better as she got closer. He looked flushed and swollen . . . but happy. Happier than she'd seen him in ages.

Mr. Hamilton stood behind him, his hands on the back of the chair drawing her gaze. Only yesterday those hands had held her, had pressed her tight to his hard body. They looked tanned and large and square, appealingly masculine.

"My nephew is taking me to his studio," Lord Lincolnshire informed her brightly, snapping her attention back to him. "I'm going to see his newest paintings."

"We really must be on our way," Mr. Hamilton said without meeting Corinna's eyes. "I have much to do today after this."

Lord Lincolnshire smiled up at her. "Would you like to come along?"

"No," Mr. Hamilton shot out at the same time Corinna exclaimed, "Oh, yes!"

"Thank you for the invitation," she added. "I'd be delighted to come along."

"No," Mr. Hamilton repeated more forcefully, finally looking at her. "My workspace is private. There's a reason I am known as a recluse."

"Come now, nephew," Lord Lincolnshire chided. "You're about to be an earl. Your days as a recluse have come to an end."

"Uncle—"

"Mr. Hamilton," Corinna interrupted, having never been one to hold her tongue. "Your uncle would like me to accompany you. Will you disappoint such a kindly man?"

Mr. Hamilton opened his mouth, most likely to argue, but then apparently had second thoughts, because he closed it. Into a very straight line. And he glared at her.

Obviously, she'd won.

Remembering that stern mouth *imprinting a kiss on her lips*, she smiled. "I'll be but a moment. I'll meet you gentlemen at the gate." After quickly returning to her easel and instructing the footman to take it home, she removed her apron, smoothed her pink dress, and joined the Hamilton men outside the fence.

It was a short walk to Piccadilly Street, where the studio apparently was located. Mr. Hamilton remained grim and silent the entire way. Lord Lincolnshire chattered breathlessly. Though Corinna maintained her half of the conversation, her mind was on other things.

She was impatient to see the studio, to see new Hamilton paintings before anyone else. To see exactly where Mr. Hamilton worked, and what sorts of supplies he used, and maybe, if she was lucky, a canvas or two that wasn't finished yet, so she could study his technique.

But mostly she was excited that after she'd visited his private space—his secret, reclusive hideaway—he'd no longer be able to keep claiming he wasn't John Hamilton. Because honestly, enough was enough.

She was growing rather weary of this act of his. It was becoming more than childish. She was going to let him kiss her again—she could hardly *wait* for him to kiss her again—but she wanted him to own up to the truth first.

The studio was in a very nice building. Shops filled the ground floor, and the two floors above were divided into large flats. Unfortunately, the studio was in a windowed garret above those, and it was no small feat helping Lord Lincolnshire up the stairs.

Even though Mr. Hamilton took most of his uncle's weight, they went very slowly, and Corinna found the man much heavier than she expected. He was also shorter than she'd thought, quite a bit shorter than his nephew. Having known Lord Lincolnshire her entire life, she supposed she still thought of him as tall compared to the child she'd once been, but she wasn't a child anymore.

Especially after that tongue-tangling, spine-tingling kiss.

The minute they got inside, Lord Lincolnshire shuffled to a threadbare sofa and plopped down, out of breath. Corinna would have sat, too, but he was sprawled right in its center. And the studio had no other sofa or any chairs.

In fact, it hadn't much of anything.

Six pictures rested on the floor, leaning against the bare walls. An easel held one more work of art in progress. Clearly it would be a lovely scene once it was finished, a beautiful meadow bordered by trees more realistic than any others she'd ever seen rendered in paint. Tiny, individual leaves seemed to be rustling in the wind, casting shadows on the grass below. She looked forward to studying it, to figuring out how Mr. Hamilton had managed such incredible detail.

A small table sat beside it, with a few sketchbooks piled on top. But no pencils.

Odd, that.

Mr. Hamilton's supplies were on the table, too. All of them. There was no cupboard, no shelf in the room, no place for anything to be hiding. She walked over to have a look and found a selection of various pigments, a big bottle of linseed oil, a pristine palette, and two—only two!—seemingly brand-new brushes. Neither of them was nearly fine enough to paint the tiny leaves she'd seen on the trees.

And that was it. There was nothing else. No extra jars to hold leftover mixed paint. No turpentine, no varnish.

No rags, no blank canvases, no knives.

No little spots of paint on the wooden floor.

Since Corinna painted in her family's drawing room, she always spread a large tarpaulin to prevent spotting, but the floor here was bare and clean. And no folded tarp was in sight.

"Where do you make your paints?" she asked.

Mr. Hamilton shifted uneasily. "Right here. Where else?"

"What do you use, then? What surface do you grind them against?"

"I make them directly on the palette," he said, slanting a glance to his uncle.

She frowned. "Isn't that too porous? I've always used glass. And a glass muller."

"A muller?" Lord Lincolnshire asked.

"It's sort of like a flat pestle," she explained. "One has to grind the pigment into the oil in order to completely combine them."

He looked to his nephew. Mr. Hamilton lifted a shoulder. "With enough elbow grease, one has no need of a muller."

There were, she acknowledged, different methods. "I

suppose a palette knife would do if one worked the mediums well," she conceded.

Lord Lincolnshire nodded approvingly. "He's very talented, you know."

"*Extremely* talented," she agreed. But there were no palette knives. And she still wondered how he could grind against a surface as permeable as wood. She wandered to the painting on the easel, admiring its incredibly detailed trees. "Which pigment do you use as the base for your greens?" she asked.

"The green one."

"Hmm?" He had no green pigment. She turned and glanced back to the table to verify. Black, white, yellows, blues, reds, and earth tones. Other pigments were available for purchase, of course, but these were the basics, the same ones she used herself. With these colors, one could mix any other color one might want. Greens were generally created from blues and yellows.

When she'd asked which pigment was his base, she'd meant which blue. Ultramarine, Prussian, cerulean? "I'm partial to cobalt," she said, "even though it's the most expensive."

"I can afford it," he said haughtily. "I'm partial to cobalt green, too."

Cobalt was *blue*. Transparent, neutral blue. The truest of all the blues, which was why she preferred it.

She thought a moment. And then she smoothed her pink skirts, moving closer to Mr. Hamilton so Lord Lincolnshire wouldn't overhear. Walking right up to him, she rose to her toes, placing her mouth close by his ear and giving him an eyeful of her scooped neckline.

"Do you like my new green dress?" she whispered.

Chapter Fourteen

"You look grand indeed in that dress," Sean murmured, trying not to stare at the enticing pale mounds peeking from beneath it. He'd noticed Corinna's dresses weren't generally as low-cut as most of those worn by other ladies of her class. Evidently she was too practical to paint while wearing fashionable, tiny-bodiced dresses. But the way she was leaning toward him afforded him a view that made him swallow hard, anyway. "The, um, green color is very flattering."

"Thank you," she said, and stepped back.

And, miraculously, she stopped asking questions.

"May I see your paintings, Sean?" Lincolnshire asked.

"Of course, Uncle," Sean said, and brought them over, one by one.

The earl examined each picture minutely, making thoughtful and considered comments. John Hamilton might have argued or agreed, but Sean was only confused. He was an entrepreneur, not an actor. Devising responses proved mentally exhausting. But he was thankful that at least Corinna had ceased making everything more difficult, had stopped asking question after question that he couldn't answer.

In fact, he suddenly realized while Lincolnshire was rhapsodizing over yet another painting, she wasn't saying anything at all. She was just standing by the table with his supplies, watching him. She seemed dumbstruck.

And all Sean had done was tell her he liked her dress. Whoever would have guessed a simple compliment could have such an effect? Contrary to the wise old saying, apparently flattery could get a man anywhere. He'd have to remember that going forward.

After Lincolnshire finished perusing all the pictures, Corinna still remained quiet while they assisted him back down the steps, a slow and painful process even with her help. She didn't say much as they wheeled the chair home, and her farewell at Lincolnshire's door was uncharacteristically reserved and polite.

Mystified by the change in her, Sean saw the poor, exhausted earl upstairs and into bed. With that finally done, he stepped out into the corridor, shut the door, and slumped against it, shutting his eyes, willing the tension to drain out of his body.

Mother Mary, that had possibly been the longest afternoon of his life.

This won't interrupt your routine, Hamilton had promised. *It shan't affect Delaney and Company at all.*

The rotter had obviously been lying through his teeth.

Sean was seriously considering ending the whole thing now. Not only because he was constantly neglecting his interests—which was no small consideration—but also because deceiving the nice old man was increasing his guilt by the moment.

Well, he was free for the time being, he told himself, opening his eyes and straightening his shoulders. Maybe he could finally attend to some business. He traipsed downstairs, asked a footman to see that his curricle was brought round, and headed out of the house.

Then stopped dead on the doorstep.

"You're not Hamilton," Corinna said.

"Sweet Jesus." Sean blinked. "What are you doing here?"

"Waiting to talk to you. You're color-blind. Which means you cannot be Hamilton—or any oil painter at all. At least not a good one."

Once the shock subsided, he cracked a smile. "I take exception to that. I expect I could paint a tolerably good brown scene. Assuming I had an artistic bone in my body, that is." A stableman arrived with his curricle, but he ignored it. "What was the telltale sign, then?"

"My dress is pink, not green."

"Ah." It looked pale brown. And so much for flattery getting him everywhere. "After you figured that out, you didn't say anything. What made you keep the truth from Lincolnshire?"

"Are you jesting? The last thing I'd want to do is disappoint that man. He's wonderful."

"That he is."

"And he'd be crushed to learn you're not his nephew." She pursed her lips. Those plump, tempting lips he'd vowed not to kiss again. "Who are you?"

"Sean Delaney. Hamilton's brother-in-law. I've been telling you that all along."

"If you're not an artist, what do you do?"

"I own property. I buy and sell buildings. Among other things." He shifted uneasily. "I'd like to explain. Not about that, but about how I ended up here. Will you walk with me in the square?"

She seemed to consider that for a moment. "Will you buy me an ice from Gunter's?"

"You're hungry?"

"Not particularly. But Gunter's Tea Shop is probably the only establishment in London where a lady can be seen alone with a man without ruining her reputation."

"Agreed, then," he said when he stopped laughing.

She was a clever one.

Leaving the curricle in front of Lincolnshire House, they made their way across the square to Gunter's, where he ordered a lemon ice for himself and a strawberry ice for Corinna. They took them back into the square.

"This is such a relief," he said as they walked.

"The other man in the museum was really Hamilton,

then. Given how he acted at the time, I'm guessing this was his plan. Why did you go along with it?"

"I didn't want to—"

"But you did it anyway."

"For my sister." Sean sighed. "Hamilton's wife."

By the time he explained, both their dishes were empty. They sat on a bench beneath a large London plane tree. Corinna slowly licked her spoon.

It was an amazingly erotic sight.

"I don't blame you," she declared. "I'd have done the same to save my sister from being unhappy all her days."

"I feel like a bastard tricking Lincolnshire, though. I'm going to tell him the truth."

"You cannot!" She turned to him, her lips slick with melted ice. "You'll ruin your sister's chance to get her divorce. And you'll ruin Lord Lincolnshire's final few days. The earl is the most wonderful man in the world, and he's tragically lost everyone he loves, and he's so thrilled to have his nephew in his life. . . . How can you even think of depriving such a kind old man of his last chance at happiness?"

" 'Tis sorry I am for that. But I cannot continue perpetrating this hoax." Sean thought of telling her what it was costing him personally, but that wasn't really the point. "It isn't right to deceive him—"

"It's kind, and what is so wrong about that? How is it hurting him? He'd be much more hurt to learn his real nephew is so very selfish, and there'd be nothing he could do about it, anyway. The law is the law. John Hamilton is his nearest blood relative, his legal heir. He will inherit no matter what Lord Lincolnshire would prefer."

"He'd inherit the title and any entailed property. But Lincolnshire could will everything else to anyone he wanted."

"Yes, he could, Mr. Delaney. But—"

"Sean."

"I beg your pardon?"

"My name is Sean. And I'm thinking we should have leave to call each other by our given names."

He already called her Corinna in his head. He'd thought of her as Corinna ever since he'd heard her name called out in the British Museum. And not being accustomed to the company of the peerage, he was likely to forget to add the *Lady*.

"I don't know," she said slowly. "That seems rather . . . intimate."

"You're the only one who knows my secret," he pointed out. "That's a rather intimate thing, don't you think? And we've kissed."

A dreamy look crossed her face. A look that doubled the speed of his pulse.

"Not that that's happening again," he quickly added, thinking maybe they'd be better off not using first names after all.

"All right," she said. "Now where were we . . . Sean?" She paused, looking dreamy again. "Oh, yes. You'd said that should Lord Lincolnshire learn the truth, he would be able to will everything but his title to anyone he wanted. But at what cost? He'd be unhappy and disillusioned the rest of his days, and once he's gone, will it really matter whether Mr. Hamilton does or doesn't inherit? Lord Lincolnshire deserves happiness," she concluded with conviction. "That is the deciding factor."

She had a point. A lot of points, actually. But Lincolnshire's happiness wasn't the only consideration. "He's going to find out regardless. I'm not an artist, and I seem to keep proving that, over and over. The earl may be physically deteriorating, but his mind is sharp as a knife. It's only a matter of time before he realizes I cannot possibly be an accomplished landscapist, which means I cannot possibly be his nephew. How will he feel then? Wouldn't it be better for me to admit the truth than for him to discover it himself?"

"*I'm* an artist. I can cover for you. I can help you keep up the masquerade."

"You're not around enough to do that."

"I can *be* around enough. I'll visit Lord Lincolnshire every day. I'll keep close. You won't mind that, will you?"

Sure, he wouldn't mind. He *liked* torturing himself, *lived* to spend hours in her presence, bunching his fists to keep from touching her.

She licked her spoon again, an act so innocently sensuous, it took everything he had not to kiss her on the spot.

He grabbed the spoon instead. "I won't mind," he muttered, only adding to his legion of lies.

Chapter Fifteen

TEA BUNS

Mix a lot of Flower with some Sugar and a little Salt in a bowl, then put in Egges, Butter, halfe a cup of Milk and a measure of Yeast to make a thick dough. Allow to rise, then flatten and make rounde buns and allow to rise again before you bake.

A most genteel addition to afternoon tea, these buns encourage serenity.
—Georgiana Chase, Countess of Greystone, 1806

Yesterday's discovery that John Hamilton was really Sean Delaney—well, that and constantly reliving the kiss—had kept Corinna too distracted to take notice of the calendar. But today she'd realized it was May. The second of May, to be precise. The reception was on the fourteenth, and her painting was due on the nineteenth.

It usually took her at least two weeks to complete a painting. And for this one, she had yet to choose a subject.

Griffin had been gone a day longer than he'd said he would, yet with all the peace and quiet, she still wasn't making progress. The thought of that had kept her mind buzzing the entire afternoon at Juliana's home, where everyone had assembled in Stafford House's beautiful

Palm Room to pen the invitations to the reception Lady A was planning to introduce Corinna to the art world.

All of Corinna's female relations had come, and people related to her relations, too. Alexandra and Juliana, and their three cousins, Rachael, Claire, and Elizabeth. A hugely pregnant Aunt Frances. Lady Avonleigh, of course, and her two sisters, Lady Balmforth and Lady Cavanaugh, who was also Juliana's mother-in-law.

It was touching. Corinna had never considered herself the sentimental type, but the thought of them all helping her made her throat feel tight.

"It was so kind of you all to come," Lady A said now as she rose to fetch her pelisse. "I was dreading writing these invitations, but with all the help, we finished in no time."

Juliana piled the leftover tea buns she'd served into a basket. "Have you need of any more assistance, Lady Avonleigh? With anything else at all?"

"Just encourage everyone to attend, please, all of you. Royal Academicians in particular, but anyone else influential as well. You all know the wording for the invitations now, so feel free to write out more should you think of anyone else who might be able to further Corinna's career. Above all, we must make certain the committee members all attend." Buttoning the pelisse, she turned to Corinna. "I am sure John Hamilton will accept, as he's your personal acquaintance—"

"I wouldn't call him that," Corinna interrupted, suddenly nervous.

"You've danced together, my dear."

"He's a very busy man." Sean couldn't attend the reception—the Academy members would surely expose him as a fraud. "And you know he doesn't like to appear in public."

"Now that he's inheriting Lord Lincolnshire's title, I am certain that will change. Do not fret, my dear; he shall attend." Lady A leaned closer and kissed Corinna's cheek, enveloping her in a cloud of gardenia and camphor scent. "Should you run into the man, you might encourage him to see that the other committee members accept as well."

Lady A certainly seemed more confident than Corinna felt. "I don't know. . . ."

Shrugging into her own light pelisse, Rachael paused. "Are you all right?"

"I'm fine," Corinna fibbed. "Perfectly fine."

She couldn't help wondering if she'd done the right thing encouraging Sean to continue deceiving Lord Lincolnshire. In fact, it seemed she could think about little else. Besides the kiss. And the reception. And her looming deadline to finish her portrait.

But she was fine. Perfectly fine.

And she was lying to herself again.

Rachael patted her shoulder. "Don't get yourself in a dither. I know this reception is important to you, but we shall all contrive to make certain it's a wild success."

Lady A's sisters reached for their reticules as Alexandra lifted baby Harry out of his pram. "Yes, we will," they all confirmed in unison.

Aunt Frances pushed slowly to her feet. "Yes, we will," she echoed, sounding a little bit breathless.

Apparently noticing that, Juliana laid a hand on her arm. "Are you feeling poorly, Aunt Frances?"

"No, just fat and ugly and short of breath. My friend Lady Mabel swears this city isn't good for the lungs once a lady reaches a certain age, but then again, she has asthma." Frances laughed. "I'm only with child."

Elizabeth grabbed her cloak, but as it was a warm day she didn't put it on. "Our mother always said that about the London air, too. But I don't remember her ever having any trouble breathing."

"That's because she refused to come to London," Claire said, and turned to Juliana. "I hope you put those extra tea buns in the basket for us. Mama used to make them, but we haven't had them in years."

"I figured as much." Juliana handed her the basket. Leaving Corinna and Alexandra behind, she started walking the rest of her guests toward the door. "Your mother copied the recipe into our family cookbook. She said the tea buns encourage serenity."

"Is that why you made them?" Rachael asked. "Do you think Corinna feels a need for serenity?"

Before Corinna could go after them and speak for herself, Juliana answered. "Of course she feels a need for serenity. Her entire future hangs in the balance!"

Corinna heard everyone laugh before they said their good-byes. Then she heard the door shut, and Juliana returned to the Palm Room.

Going to a sideboard that had gilt legs carved to look like palm trees, she poured three glasses of sherry before joining her sisters on one of the many sofas covered in palm tree–themed satin fabric. "Here," she said, handing Corinna a glass. "I expect you will find this encourages serenity much more than tea buns."

Corinna sipped gratefully. "I didn't expect to be nervous about this reception."

"That's natural," Alexandra said, shifting Harry in order to take a sip.

"And you're nervous about something else, too." Juliana crossed her legs. "I can tell. Out with it, Corinna."

They knew her too well; there was no sense pretending. She sighed. "I have a secret."

Her sisters exchanged meaningful glances. "Well?" Alexandra asked.

"Lord Lincolnshire's nephew isn't John Hamilton," Corinna confessed in a rush. "I mean, John Hamilton *is* his nephew, but the man you met at Lady Partridge's ball isn't. He's his brother-in-law. He wanted to tell Lord Lincolnshire the truth, but I convinced him not to, and now I'm not sure that was right."

"Whoa." Juliana's sip of sherry was more like a gulp. "Explain that again. Slowly, and with more detail."

Corinna did so, then held her breath before asking, "Was I wrong? Should he tell Lord Lincolnshire the truth?"

Juliana shook her head. "Absolutely not."

"I agree." Alexandra patted her son's back. "Lord Lincolnshire deserves a happy ending."

Corinna blew the breath out. "You're right. I love Lord Lincolnshire."

"So do we," Alexandra assured her.

"I'm going to visit him more often. I promised Mr. Delaney I would, to help him keep up the pretense that he's an artist."

"You'll get to see more of Mr. Delaney that way, too, hmm?" Juliana's eyes danced. "That shouldn't be a hardship."

Alexandra looked to Corinna. "She's meddling again, isn't she?"

"Doesn't she always?"

"I can tell you're attracted to the man," Juliana said defensively. "And I cannot say I blame you. He's a handsome devil—"

"You're a married woman!" Corinna interrupted.

"A very happy one," her sister agreed. "But a lady doesn't go blind when she takes her marriage vows. Or deaf, either. That accent—"

"You make him sound like a pretty box. You know nothing about the man inside." Neither did she, for that matter.

"I know he's being very nice to Lord Lincolnshire. And that his sister is married to John Hamilton, which means he's connected to the right people."

"He's not a peer, Juliana. He owns property."

"Doesn't every gentleman own property?"

"I mean he buys and sells buildings for a living. Among other things." She wondered what. "And he's Irish." With that Irish accent. She'd gone back and bought *Children of the Abbey* this morning, and she'd already read up to page 43, where Amanda thought, *the harmony of his voice imparted a charm that seldom failed of being irresistible.*

"Does his being Irish bother you?" Juliana asked.

"Of course not." Just thinking of that melodic Irish voice made her imagine hot kisses, which hardly bothered her. Well, maybe it did, but not in the way her sister meant. "But it might bother Griffin."

"Griffin would be a hypocrite if it did," Juliana scoffed. "His own name comes from an Irish ancestor."

"That's right," Alexandra put in. "Our fifth or sixth or seventh great-grandfather, wasn't he? Aidan Griffin, Baron Kilcullen from Ballygriffin, Ireland. Born 1568, died 1648 at Cainewood."

"How do you remember such things?" Corinna asked.

"Family is important to me." She smiled at little Harry, who was named after her husband's uncle. "Besides, you remember every word you've ever read."

"That's different. I can't help it. And I don't even like it. My brain is always filled with all those stupid lines." She sighed. "In any case, I'm not interested in Mr. Delaney that way." Maybe for a few kisses, but that was a far cry from what Juliana had in mind. "I've only seventeen days to finish my portrait. And spend some time with Lord Lincolnshire while I still can."

Juliana nodded so thoughtfully that Corinna could almost see the scheming going on in her head. She hadn't given up. But apparently she'd decided to back off for now. "I think that's very kind of you," she said. "You should bring Lord Lincolnshire a sweet to brighten his last days."

"Corinna doesn't bake," Alexandra reminded her.

Corinna *couldn't* bake. The women of their family were famed for their sweets, and she was the only Chase female in history with no talent in the kitchen. She couldn't measure anything properly; she couldn't mix without creating lumps. If she so much as approached the oven, biscuits burned and cakes collapsed.

"I didn't say she should make it," Juliana pointed out.

"I only said she should bring it. *I'll* make something for her to bring."

"Thank you," Corinna said. It wasn't so bad being a bungler in the kitchen, really. In truth, she'd much rather paint.

Chapter Sixteen

"I wonder why Corinna's so nervous," Rachael said to her sisters during the drive home in their carriage. "There's the reception, of course, but she seems to be worrying about more than that."

Corinna was very far from calm and collected. As a person who wasn't quite herself these days, Rachael recognized the signs. Griffin was supposed to have returned yesterday, and she was on pins and needles waiting to hear what he might have discovered.

"I don't know what's bothering Corinna." Elizabeth shrugged. "But I've been thinking."

"That's a novelty," Claire teased.

Elizabeth rolled her eyes and stuck out her tongue. "I meant I've been thinking about something else. I've been thinking about how Mama never wheezed like Lady Mabel."

"I told you, that's because she refused to come to London." Claire fiddled with a new amethyst ring she'd made, twirling it on her finger. "She knew better than to aggravate her condition."

"But Mama was very quiet," Elizabeth pointed out. "I'm wondering if she actually suffered from asthma at all. Maybe she just didn't want to socialize, so she made that up as an excuse."

Claire stopped twirling. "You think Mama *lied*?"

"I didn't say she lied. I said she might have used it as an excuse."

"She would never have—"

"Mama wasn't perfect," Rachael interrupted. An understatement, considering the woman had hidden the truth from her all of her life. "It's possible Elizabeth could be right." Thinking back, she couldn't remember her mother ever having difficulty breathing. "Mama never attended large social gatherings. She always preferred to stay home with her needlework and her watercolors and her children."

"She went to Cainewood," Claire argued. "Often."

"But only to visit with family. Never for a ball or any other major occasion."

"I don't believe it," Claire said, looking pouty.

"Well, it doesn't signify anyway, does it?" Rachael sighed. "We'll never really know."

They all rode in thoughtful silence until the carriage came to a stop before their town house in Lincoln's Inn Fields. Elizabeth climbed out first, then emitted a little yelp.

"What are you doing here?" she cried.

Rachael followed Claire out to find Griffin standing in the courtyard.

"Good afternoon, ladies," he said with the crooked smile she always found disconcertingly attractive. But when his gaze swung to meet hers, his expression grew more serious. "I've been waiting for you. I have news."

"What news?" Claire demanded.

"I'll explain later," Rachael told her sisters. She didn't want an audience when she heard what Griffin had learned. "Go inside. Griffin and I will talk in the square."

Grumbling all the way, her sisters entered the house while Rachael and Griffin crossed the street and went through the gate to the private park in the center of the square. It was a nice day, sunny but not hot, and Lincoln's Inn Fields was filled with people enjoying the fine weather. Choosing a bench beneath a large tree, where the shade would hide them from view of the houses all around, she sat and smoothed her pelisse's thin lavender skirts. "You took longer than I expected."

Angled toward her, he pulled her father's jeweled badge from his pocket and placed it in her palm, folding her fingers around it. "Rachael . . . I know who he was."

"Was," she repeated. "He's dead, then."

In a cousinly, concerned way, he took one of her hands in both of his. "You knew that, didn't you?"

"Yes. Yes, of course." But apparently part of her had hoped that wasn't true, because a pang of disappointment seemed to spear her in the vicinity of her heart.

"There's more," he said, squeezing her fingers. "Not all of it good."

She nodded and pulled her hand free, staring down at the badge on her palm. She couldn't think straight with him touching her. "Start at the beginning. Please."

He took a deep breath. "I searched all the records for the time in question and found a member of the Tenth who took leave to wed a woman the month before you were conceived. An officer, a lieutenant. His name was Thomas Grimstead."

"Grimstead," she echoed, testing the word on her tongue. She should have been Rachael Grimstead, but that sounded so very wrong. "Are you sure he was the right man?"

Griffin nodded. "He married a woman who was thereafter known as Lady Georgiana Grimstead."

Startled, she looked up at him. "He was titled, then?"

"No. She must have been a nobleman's daughter."

"But my mother was a commoner. She was born plain Georgiana Woodby, not a lady. She always said she was uncommonly lucky to have wed an earl. You found the wrong man."

"I also thought so at first. That's why I was gone the extra day. I combed the records going back years, in case your mother married long before conceiving you. But very few men from the Tenth wed in the correct time frame, and no one else married a woman named Georgiana."

"You're sure it was her, then?"

"There's no other explanation. Your mother acted the lady through and through, did she not? And would she not have thought herself, a woman ripe with another man's child, 'uncommonly lucky' to have wed at all? It cannot be a coincidence that Grimstead's wife had the same given name. He had to have been your father."

"Maybe." The name sounded wrong, but she still couldn't seem to think straight. She focused on a wooden stand in the distance, where lemonade was sold in the square. "This Grimstead . . . did the records say how he died?"

"They did."

She waited, but no more information seemed to be forthcoming. She looked back to Griffin and found his green eyes flooded with sympathy.

She didn't want sympathy; she wanted the truth.

"What?" she asked, but still he didn't answer. She clenched her hand around the badge. "Out with it, damn it! I've already learned that my mother lied to me all of my life, came from a different family than she claimed, and my name should be Rachael Grimstead." Grimstead, for heaven's sake! It wasn't a cold day, and she was wearing a pelisse in any case, but she wrapped her arms around herself as though she might ward off a chill. "What could you possibly have to tell me that would be more upsetting than all of that?"

Griffin blew out a breath. "He was executed, Rachael. For treason."

She opened her mouth to respond, but suddenly all the air seemed to have been sucked right out of her. The birds in the tree overhead sounded entirely too cheerful. The people strolling by, chatting and drinking lemonade, sounded too cheerful, too.

"Treason?" she finally managed to say, her voice thin and not cheerful at all. "What did he do?"

"That I don't know; the records of the court-martial must be elsewhere. But he joined the Tenth in 1782—transferred from a disbanded regiment—and there was a notation of his family's address at that time. In Yorkshire. I've hired a man to see whether they still live there. I'll let you know when I find out. Then take you to meet them."

Treason. She hugged herself tighter, the edges of the hard metal badge digging into her clenched fist. "I'm not sure I want to. Meet them, I mean. Not if their son committed treason."

"You don't have to, of course. It will be up to you. They're your family, but I'm willing to wager they don't know of your existence. Perhaps that's why your mother used another name. So they couldn't find you."

"That makes sense." As much sense as anything else she'd heard this afternoon. "Treason," she murmured. "My father was executed for treason."

"I'm sorry." He started to reach for her, then apparently thought better of it and crossed his arms instead. "It doesn't change who you are, Rachael, or make you any less good than you are."

"No," she said, "it doesn't."

But she must not have sounded convincing.

" 'Fathers shall not be put to death for their children,' " he quoted solemnly, " 'nor children put to death for their fathers; each is to die for his own sins.' "

That dredged up a tiny smile. "Griffin Chase, referencing a Bible passage? Now I've heard everything."

In all the years she'd known him—which was her whole life—he'd never been a man given to prayer.

"Thank you for the information," she said, rising and smoothing her pelisse. "I do appreciate your taking the time to find it. I'm sorry it proved so difficult." She started back home with a sigh, taking a little comfort when he fell into step beside her. "My sisters are going to be very interested to hear all of this."

Chapter Seventeen

GINGERBREAD CAKES

Take four pints of Flower with Ginger and Nutmeg and rub Butter into it. Add to it Brandy and Treacle and mix it altogether. Let it lay till it grows stiffe then pinch pieces and make into little balls. Flatten cakes on a tin and add a Sweetmeat if you please and bake.

These spicy little cakes are known to raise the spirits. Not ghosts, that is, but spirits of the emotional variety. Excellent to bring when paying visits to the ill.

—Anne Chase, Marchioness of Cainewood, 1775

Upon arriving at Lincolnshire House the next afternoon, Corinna was shown to a drawing room, where Sean sat holding a book that he'd apparently been reading to Lord Lincolnshire. He rose immediately. "I waited for you all yesterday. Where were you?"

He'd waited *all day*? "I was helping Lady Avonleigh make invitations for a reception. And I was painting. And earlier I went back to the colorman's shop." Well, really to the bookstore to buy *Children of the Abbey*. "What were you doing here all day? Didn't you need to . . . ah"—she slanted a glance to Lord Lincolnshire—"paint?"

"I have a lot of work to do, yes. But my uncle is my priority," he said pointedly.

"Of course." The strain in his voice sparked her guilt. And *her poor mind was all topsy-turvy* like Pamela's had been in the book *Pamela; or, Virtue Rewarded.*

She'd promised to visit more often, and she imagined Sean did have some work to do—though she didn't know what—but she couldn't spend all day with the earl in his stead, could she? If she wanted to submit a portrait for the Summer Exhibition, she had to work, too.

"Good afternoon, Lord Lincolnshire," she said, walking toward the older man. "I brought you some gingerbread cakes. They're supposed to raise one's spirits."

"Says who?" Sean asked, taking the basket.

"Says my family's heirloom cookbook. Each lady in the family adds a recipe every year, and they all have legends attached. Not that I believe such nonsense," she hastened to add. "My sister Juliana baked these. I'm hopeless in the kitchen."

"I wasn't aware any ladies in Mayfair ever entered a kitchen."

"All the Chase ladies do," Lord Lincolnshire said, pausing for a breath. "They're famous for their sweets."

"All except me," Corinna said.

Sean handed Lord Lincolnshire a sweet and took one for himself. "Please, have a seat."

Corinna looked around the room, which she'd never been in before. The butler, Quincy, had called it the "yellow drawing room" when he'd shown her in here. The walls were covered with yellow silk printed with pink roses, green leaves, and some blue flowers she couldn't name. All the sofas, chairs, and footstools were upholstered in yellow brocade. Part of Lord Lincolnshire's extensive Ming vase collection was in here, and there were several excellent paintings on the walls, including two Rembrandts.

She wanted to study them, but Sean had asked her to

sit, and he still seemed a bit peeved. Since she wanted another kiss from him, she decided to study them from a chair.

After she chose the seat with the best view, Sean reseated himself, too. "This gingerbread is delicious," he told her.

"I'll tell Juliana." She turned to Lord Lincolnshire. He was covered to the waist with a heavy blanket, making her wonder what might be concealed underneath. His hands looked a little puffy, and he'd taken only a tiny bite of the cake. "How are you feeling today, sir?"

"Better than one might expect, thanks to my nephew." He smiled at Sean, apparently waiting to catch his breath before continuing. "I've been thinking, nephew"—pause—"that I'd like to meet your wife."

Sean exchanged a panicked look with Corinna. "I left my wife in the countryside, sir, as I told you. She prefers the quiet life."

Lord Lincolnshire looked disappointed, but apparently he accepted the state of affairs, since his response was, "Very well." But then he added, "As I was saying when Lady Corinna arrived—"

"Shall I continue reading?" Sean interrupted.

"Not now, nephew. We have a lovely . . . young lady visiting. And as I . . . was saying—"

"Would you care for another sweet, Uncle?"

"I've not finished this one." Pause. "I've been—"

"Have you need of another pillow?"

"No." The poor man was already leaning against at least five of them. "I've—"

"Are you certain—"

"Will you let the man speak?" Corinna cut in. In the awkward silence that followed, she tore her gaze from one of the Rembrandts and turned to the earl. "What did you want to say, Lord Lincolnshire?"

"I wanted to say . . . that I've been thinking I'd like Sean . . . to paint a portrait of me. One last portrait . . . before I depart this fine world."

Sean glared at her. Apparently he'd known this was coming. But how was she supposed to have known?

"I don't think he can do that, Lord Lincolnshire," she said carefully. "Mr. Hamilton paints only landscapes."

"Surely he can paint . . . one portrait."

Sean shook his head. "I've never painted a portrait."

Truer words were never spoken, Corinna thought.

"You're a skilled artist, nephew. One of the very best . . . in the land." Lord Lincolnshire gasped and waited a moment—a moment during which Corinna racked her brain for a way to help Sean, as she'd promised. "Surely—"

"May *I* paint you, Lord Lincolnshire?" she interrupted. "Please? I'd be honored if you'd allow me. I've been dying to paint a portrait to submit to the Royal Academy for the Summer Exhibition. If it turns out well, perhaps it will be selected. A subject of your stature could absolutely make my career."

"Me?" Lord Lincolnshire wheezed. "In the Summer Exhibition?"

"Possibly," she reiterated. "None of my portraits have turned out stellar so far, since I've not had any anatomy lessons. But lately I've been sketching the Elgin Marbles for practice, and I shall try my best—"

"I'm certain," Lord Lincolnshire interrupted, "it will turn out brilliant." He smiled at her as though she'd brought the sun. "But my days are . . . numbered. Tomorrow being Sunday, I'm hoping . . . my dear nephew . . . will take me to church. May we begin Monday?"

"I think we should start now." Her painting was due to the Royal Academy a scant sixteen days hence, and she hoped to show it at Lady A's reception five days before that. "If you've some paper, I can begin sketching you immediately."

"Excellent." Lord Lincolnshire lifted a silver bell from a table beside him. "I shall have a footman . . . fetch paper . . . posthaste."

While he rang the bell, Corinna glanced rather triumphantly to Sean.

His expression took her aback. A page from *Children of the Abbey* flashed into her mind, where Amanda had looked at Lord Mortimer and thought *seducing sweetness dwelt in his smile.*

A matching sweetness seemed to melt in Corinna's middle, making her remember she wanted another kiss.

In fact, she'd planned to let Sean kiss her again just as soon as he stopped pretending he wasn't John Hamilton, hadn't she? But instead, he'd convinced her he'd been telling the truth. That was equivalent, wasn't it? Either way, the truth had come out Thursday, and today was Saturday, which meant they'd had two whole days of truthfulness between them . . . and still she hadn't been kissed.

Actually, she suddenly realized, he hadn't even tried. Whatever could that mean? He couldn't have *meant* it when he said he'd never kiss her again, could he?

Holy Hannah, she hoped not.

A footman handed her a pencil and some paper. She blinked and looked back to Lord Lincolnshire. "What would you like to be doing?"

"Doing?"

"In your portrait. I don't care for portraits where the subject simply stands there and stares at the viewer. I would prefer for you to be doing something."

"Well, I cannot . . . simply stand there . . . in any case." With a faint but good-natured smile, Lord Lincolnshire gestured to his covered legs. "I shall . . . have to be sitting." His expression turned contemplative. "I've always . . . enjoyed a good book. Perhaps I can be . . . reading a book."

While she'd been hoping for something a bit more active, she decided that would have to do. If the man had always loved to read, it was suitable, after all. Thinking Sean had pleased the earl by reading aloud, she glanced back to him.

He was still smiling at her with seducing sweetness.

Oh, very well, maybe it wasn't seducing sweetness; maybe it was only gratitude that she'd saved him from having to paint Lord Lincolnshire. But either way, he was smiling. He was happy with her.

She'd get him to kiss her one way or another.

She returned his smile. "Would you care to read while I sketch, Mr. Hamilton?"

He nodded and opened the book.

Letting his melodic voice wash over her, she settled back and put pencil to paper. And even though Sean wasn't reading a romantic novel, she kept smiling as she listened and sketched.

Chapter Eighteen

"Thank you," Sean said simply as he walked Corinna toward the door later. "You saved my skin by offering to paint him."

"I told you that you could count on me. May I look in here?" she asked, indicating another drawing room. Lincolnshire House seemed to have a surplus of drawing rooms. "I'd like to see if there are any more Rembrandts."

"I can't think why not." He walked in with her. "What color is this room?"

"Mostly green. The walls are lined with bright green silk damask, and the draperies are green silk trimmed with black velvet. The furniture is all covered in golden and dark red brocade. It's beautiful. I'm sorry you cannot see it."

"I can see it," he told her. "It just looks different to me. The color I can see best is blue. All the rooms in my house are blue, except for Deirdre's."

"Where is your house?"

"In Hampstead. Who painted that landscape you're staring at?"

"John Hamilton." She laughed, a joyful, unselfconscious sound. "All the paintings in this room are Hamiltons. It seems Lord Lincolnshire truly is quite proud of his nephew."

"Figures," Sean muttered in disgust. "It's good to know that, though. I imagine I'd make a holy show of myself if he took me in here and I didn't recognize my own paintings."

"A holy show?"

"A great fool of myself," he translated. "A massive embarrassment." Apparently he hadn't ridden himself of the Irish as much as he'd thought. "Thank you again. I really do appreciate all your help."

"I'm glad to hear that," she said, moving to a fine Kent fireplace. She leaned against the mantel flirtatiously.

Well, not precisely flirtatiously, because she wasn't a flirtatious woman. She was much more straightforward than that. But seductively.

And effectively.

"I think you owe me a kiss," she said softly.

He laughed. What else could he do? "I'm not John Hamilton, remember? I'm no longer a trophy. Why should you want to kiss me again?"

"Maybe I liked it the first time," she said blithely.

Except she didn't look blithe. She looked seductive again. *Bloody hell.*

It was her eyes, Sean decided. Those blue, blue eyes. They made a man grateful for being color-blind. And her voice. Something in her voice appealed to him. So low and sweet. He was amused to hear sarcastic words come out of her mouth, and when she wasn't being sarcastic and he wasn't being amused, well, then . . .

Well, then he wanted to kiss her.

"I told my sisters your secret," she said, interrupting his tangled thoughts.

"What?" He was appalled. Any thought of kissing her fled his mind.

"I had to share it with someone," she said. "I had to. I feared I'd done wrong encouraging you to keep it up, and—"

"What did they say?"

"They heartily approved. They assured me I'd done exactly the right thing. I'm not at all sorry I told them."

"Do not tell anyone else."

"But—"

"Do *not.*"

She hesitated, then nodded. "I won't."

"I want your promise."

"I promise. And a Chase promise is never given lightly," she added solemnly.

And seductively. *Bloody hell.*

It was that voice, those eyes.

Bloody hell.

"All right, then." It seemed disaster had been averted. But that didn't stop him from sighing. He just wished he could decide what he was sighing about. "You'll be back Monday to start the actual painting? Early, I hope?"

"First thing in the morning."

"Excellent." Maybe he could finally escape and get something done. "I—"

"Of course, 'morning' for me starts at noon."

"Noon?"

"At the earliest. I like to paint through the wee hours, so I sleep late." She straightened away from the fireplace and walked closer. Right up to him. So close he could see her blue irises were rimmed in a darker, midnight shade. So close he could smell her floral fragrance and the faint scent of paint underneath it.

Thoughts of kissing her flooded back.

"Do you know what else my sisters said?"

"How could I? But I'm sure you'll tell me."

"Juliana said it doesn't signify that you're not a peer, because you're connected to the right people. And she was impressed that you own property."

"She doesn't know how much I own," he pointed out. "And neither do you."

"Houses in Hampstead are very expensive," she said

dismissively. "And Alexandra reminded me that our brother, Griffin, is named for an ancestor. Aidan Griffin, Baron Kilcullen from Ballygriffin, Ireland."

"And the significance of all that is . . . ?"

"They think it's all right for you to kiss me." She stepped even closer. "Are you certain you don't want to? I might get up earlier in the morning for a kiss."

What was a man supposed to do when a woman made such an offer? A woman who looked like an angel and tasted like sin? A woman who'd just brushed off every reason he'd considered her off-limits?

Besides, he really did need to attend to his work.

"How much earlier?" he asked.

"Ten o'clock."

"Eight."

"Nine."

He yanked her against his body and fastened his lips on hers.

For a brief moment he cursed his own weakness, but then he lost himself in the immense pleasure of kissing such a warm, willing woman. She pressed closer. Sweet Jesus, he could feel every curve of her through his clothes. Her hands drifted up and fisted in his hair. He felt his heart beating against hers and the seductive heat of her mouth. He'd never wanted anyone with such a fever, with such a hunger. She wasn't for him, but she'd crawled into him, held him in her grip.

When she stepped back, she had a dazed smile on her face that he was certain reflected his own.

"I'll see you Monday at nine," she said softly, and quit the room.

He heard her footsteps cross the stone floor in the entrance hall, the door open, Quincy bid her a polite farewell. By the time the door closed, he'd gathered his wits.

Somewhat.

Another man would head straight to the bottle, down a stiff drink for fortification. He'd never taken up the habit, but if anything could drive him to it, it was this damned charade.

Well, maybe he could leave now, get a little work done.

He went back to the other drawing room, where Lincolnshire was dozing in the chair. He touched the man gently on the shoulder and smiled when his eyes fluttered open. "Would you like me to see you to bed, Uncle? I think you could use the rest. And I could use a few hours to paint."

"Very well," Lincolnshire said. "But I really do . . . wish to meet your wife."

Sean mentally winced. He'd thought they'd dispensed with this subject. " 'Tis truly sorry I am, but as I told you, she's in the countryside."

"You can summon her . . . can you not? She'll be the next countess . . . and the mother of my eventual heirs. I wish to . . . get to know her." The earl paused for a much-needed breath. And another. "Please, Sean."

The dear man's eyes shone with hope. How could Sean refuse him?

He couldn't.

Bloody hell.

"No." In her beautiful floral-painted bedroom, the only room in Sean's house that wasn't blue—in fact, he wasn't sure *what* color it was—Deirdre tossed a pile of shifts into the trunk she was filling. "I've told you twice already, no."

It felt like days since Sean had been home. Hell, it *had* been days since he'd been home. He'd neglected his work yet again to come talk to his sister, and this was not the welcome he'd hoped for. "Why are you packing your things, then?"

"I'm moving to Daniel's house tomorrow. I'm bored out of my mind here alone in Hampstead. I'm going to live in the middle of London, where a body sees another face once in a while."

Oh, no, she wasn't. "You'll live in London, all right, but with Lincolnshire." He was allowing his empire to go to hell in order to obtain her precious divorce, and she couldn't even wait and see this thing through? "I want you to arrive early Monday evening. That will make it believable that you had to come in from the countryside. You owe me, Deirdre. I'm doing a favor for you. Now you'll do this favor for me."

"I didn't ask for any favors. I don't *want* any favors." She pulled three dresses out of her clothespress. Brown, brown, and brown. "I still cannot believe you allowed John to talk you into this ridiculous scheme."

"Well, I did." And didn't he regret it even more than she? "And now Lincolnshire is insisting he meet Hamilton's wife. Which is *you*, in case you don't remember."

"Oh, I remember," Deirdre said dryly. "But I don't care." The dresses clenched in her hands, she turned to him. "What is the man going to do, after all, should you fail to bring him a wife to meet?"

"He'll be disappointed."

"I've news for you, Sean: We're all disappointed sometimes. Lincolnshire will survive."

"He won't survive, no. Either way. And he deserves happiness in his final days. He's a nice man, Deirdre."

"John never thought so."

"John is an idiot."

"You've a point there." She folded the dresses, then sighed and went back for more. "But I don't want to play your wife."

Sean echoed her own words. "I've news for you, Deirdre: We all have to do things we'd rather not sometimes."

"Sometimes, maybe. But not this time."

"If I don't produce a wife," he argued, "Lincolnshire may retaliate by withholding his fortune from your husband."

"John deserves that. Nothing would make me happier."

"Think again, little sister. If Hamilton isn't satisfied with the job I do placating his uncle—if he loses his inheritance as a result—I'd lay odds he won't grant you your divorce."

She shrugged. "I don't care. I told you not to do this in the first place. I'll be happy living with Daniel whether I'm married to him or not."

Sean stayed silent a moment, deliberating. And then, "You won't be living with Daniel Raleigh," he said quietly.

"I will. Is something wrong with your ears, Sean? I told you, I'm moving to Daniel's house tomorrow."

"No, you're not. You're moving to Lincolnshire House on Monday."

"Something *is* wrong with your ears."

He hadn't wanted to tell her the whole truth, hadn't wanted her to know the worst. Hadn't wanted her to feel guilty or indebted.

But he didn't see where he had a choice.

"Whether he inherits Lincolnshire's fortune or not, Hamilton will soon be an earl. He's going to require an heir. In lieu of divorcing you, he intends to force you to move back in with him until you bear him a male child."

That stopped her halfway from her clothespress to the bed. She swiveled to him, a blue dress and a brown one clutched tight to her middle. "He wouldn't. You're making this up to get me to do what you want."

"I'm not making anything up." He walked closer, put a hand on her shoulder, eased her toward the bed and down to sit. "He told me this, Deirdre. When I refused to do his bidding, he told me to force me to agree. And the law is clear. If he demands you back in his bed, you'll have no choice but to comply." He sighed and sat beside her. "You're already packed. Come play Mrs. Hamilton at Lincolnshire House, will you? With any luck, it will be for the last time."

Her fingers uncurled; her arms dropped to her sides. The dresses slid from her lap to the floor. "You win," she said.

But he didn't feel like a winner.

Chapter Nineteen

Early Monday evening, Corinna was cleaning her palette and gazing at her work in progress when she felt the hair stir on her neck. Felt it swept aside. Felt warm lips pressed to her nape. A little thrill rippling through her, she bowed her head to allow better access, sighing at the tender caress.

It ended too quickly, and she turned to see Sean.

"I had a good day," he said. "A productive day. Thank you."

His eyes were so green, so sincere. It was amazing how comfortable she felt meeting them, how easily she'd slid into this intimacy. He'd met her at the door at nine o'clock this morning, walked her into this salon, and greeted her with a kiss that had left her weak at the knees and light in the head.

"Was that worth getting up for?" he'd asked.

She'd nodded, robbed of words for once. And he'd laughed, then left to do whatever it was he did while she spent the whole day painting.

She felt light-headed again now, just locking eyes with him. She hoped he would kiss her again, a real kiss on the lips this time, but instead he shifted his gaze past her. "I'm impressed."

Feeling the way she did, for a moment she thought he was impressed with the salon. It was a most unlikely room to use for painting, by far the most grandiose room in London's most grandiose house.

The salon was mostly blue, so she knew Sean could see just how gorgeous it was. Designed for lavish entertainments, it was decorated in the Italian style. Splendid blue and gold furniture matched ornate blue and gold curtaining that hung from gilt rods. The coved ceiling was painted in the palazzo manner, and the walls were broken up by alternating silk panels and mirrors in highly ornamental frames, the latter reflecting the room's sparkling gold and crystal chandeliers. All day Corinna had feared she'd splatter paint and ruin something. But of all the rooms in the house, it had the largest north-facing windows, so Lord Lincolnshire had insisted it was the best place to sit for his portrait.

Then her head cleared, and she realized Sean wasn't impressed with the salon. He was looking at her painting.

"I'm glad you like it," she said, turning to see it herself. She resumed wiping her palette. "But I've just started, really."

"You started this morning, before I left. You've been working all day."

"Time flies when I'm involved in a painting. But I think I wore out poor Lord Lincolnshire. Two footmen helped him up to bed two hours ago." She set the palette on the mosaic table she'd covered for her use. "Do you think it would be all right for me to leave everything here overnight?"

"I'm sure it will be fine. The man's unlikely to hold an entertainment anytime soon." Walking closer to the painting, he peered at it. "You've laid in the basics of him already. And the background is magnificent. So detailed. How did you do that so quickly?"

"Oh, that was already done." She began cleaning her brushes. "I've been working on it for days in the square. I just hadn't decided who to put into it."

He paused for a significant beat before he turned to her. "So you *wanted* to paint Lincolnshire. You didn't offer only to save my skin."

"You've caught me out," she admitted. Swirling three brushes in turpentine, she grinned. "I think I'm finally going to complete a good portrait. One fine enough to put on display. I've always wanted to, but . . ."

"But what?"

"Women don't usually, you know? Paint portraits, I mean. It's not considered very ladylike. We're supposed to paint only scenes and still lifes." Setting the brushes aside, she sighed. "I'm tired of painting apples and bottles and trees."

"You paint very good trees," he pointed out, gesturing toward her picture.

"I've had lots of practice," she said dryly.

"You have goals," he said. "I admire that."

"Everyone has goals. Of some sort."

"But your goals go beyond those expected of your gender. You'll have to overcome great odds to achieve them, yet you're not letting that stop you. I applaud you for that."

"Thank you," Corinna said softly. She'd never had a man say he admired her, let alone claim he expected her to reach her goals. Griffin was supportive, of course, but that was his job. He was her brother. And while she had no doubt he wished the best for her—while she was sure he wanted her happy—she'd never felt he truly believed she'd see the success she hoped to achieve.

He believed her art was a hobby, something to keep her occupied until she married.

Sean, on the other hand, seemed to believe in *her*. And as Amanda had thought in *Children of the Abbey*, in return *her heart felt he was one of the most amiable, most pleasing of men*.

Oh, God, she really had to stop this.

It was just kisses. No matter what her sisters said, she

knew Sean wasn't the sort of man her brother wanted for her. And she wasn't looking for marriage now, anyway. Her painting was more important.

"Thank you," she repeated. "I'm finished here and expected home for dinner. I'll be back tomorrow morning."

"At nine?"

"For another kiss, I'll be here at nine."

He laughed. "You aren't anything like I expected a marquess's daughter to be, do you know that?"

"I'm an artist," she said, and he laughed again.

"I'll walk you to the door." They headed out of the salon. Unusually for this mansion full of servants, the entrance hall was empty. Quincy wasn't there, and there were no footmen, no maids scurrying from one side of the house to the other. "My sister will be here soon," Sean said quietly. "She's going to live here until this is all over."

"Will she?" Corinna asked, surprised.

"Lincolnshire's insisting upon seeing my wife. And she's Hamilton's actual wife, so . . ."

"So at least that one thing won't be a lie?"

"Exactly." Reaching the front door, he stopped and opened it. "But I'm afraid something will slip now that Deirdre's getting involved."

"You're not having second thoughts, are you?"

He shrugged, making it obvious he was.

She clutched his arm. "*Please* don't reveal the secret. It might be easier, but it won't be best. I don't like keeping secrets, either, you know. I feel terribly guilty keeping Griffin in the dark."

"Don't tell him," he warned under his breath. "You promised."

"I remember. That's why I haven't told him until now. But my sisters think we're doing the right thing, and I'm certain he would, too—"

"He wouldn't. He'd expose me forthwith; I'm sure of it."

"You don't know Griffin—"

"He's a marquess, is he not? That's all I need to know. I'm everything the *ton* despises." Standing there in the open doorway, he raised a hand and began ticking off all the marks against him. "I'm Irish—"

"I told you, we're part Irish, too."

"What, a quarter?"

"Probably a tenth," she admitted, thinking it was probably even less than that.

He ticked off another finger. "I'm untitled, I'm in trade, I'm richer than any three members of society combined—"

"Really?" She hadn't known he had that much money. "Where did you get your fortune?"

He looked like he was sorry he'd let that slip. And like he was scrambling to decide what to tell her. But just then the wooden gate opened outside, and a woman walked into the courtyard.

Without hesitation, looking quite sure of herself, she crossed to the portico and mounted the steps. She was blond, green-eyed, and very pretty. Or at least, she looked like she would be very pretty if she weren't scowling.

"Corinna, this is my sis—," Sean started, but stopped when the woman gestured discreetly.

He turned to see Quincy approaching the door.

"My wife has arrived," he said loudly instead.

Chapter Twenty

Five minutes later, after Corinna departed following her introduction to his "wife," Sean found himself standing in Lincolnshire's bedroom with his sister beside him.

"Uncle," he said, "this is Mrs. Hamilton. Deirdre, the Earl of Lincolnshire."

Deirdre curtsied. " 'Tis pleased I am to meet you, Lord Lincolnshire."

"I'm pleased you've come." Struggling to sit higher against all of his pillows, Lincolnshire blinked and yawned. "Please excuse me. I sat all . . . day for a portrait, and I fear that . . . left me exhausted."

To Sean's relief, Deirdre didn't seem fazed by the man's shortness of breath, or repulsed by his ever-swelling body. "I understand that you're ill, my lord."

"I'm dying," Lincolnshire said in his plainspoken way.

"That, too. And 'tis sorry I am to hear it."

"No fault of . . . yours." The old man cocked his head. "You're Irish."

She exchanged a wary glance with Sean. "Born and raised in Kilburton, sir. Your nephew married me while he was living in Ireland."

Lincolnshire nodded. "Kilburton is a pretty place."

"And how would you know that?" Deirdre raised a brow. "I don't recall your ever visiting."

Sean winced. Deirdre never had been one to think before opening her mouth. But Lincolnshire only laughed—a laugh that ended in a wheeze. "Haven't been there . . . since before you were born," he told her, and then added to Sean, "I like her."

Releasing a breath, Sean smiled and moved closer to his sister, wrapping an arm about her shoulders. "I like her, too."

"You should, considering . . . she's your wife. Whyever did you leave her in the countryside? She's . . . lovely." The old man grinned. "Give her a kiss."

The look sister and brother exchanged this time wasn't wary. It was panicked.

"Go on," Lincolnshire demanded.

Sean turned to Deirdre and pecked her on the cheek.

"That will never do," the earl declared in apparent disgust. "Word is you two . . . don't get along. Rumor has it you live apart."

Was that why the old man had insisted Deirdre be fetched? Was he intent on seeing a reconciliation? "You've said that before," Sean reminded him. "Wherever did you hear it?"

"Everywhere. I'm dying, not deaf. And I won't countenance . . . such a relationship in Lincolnshire House." He paused, all but gasping for air, but when Deirdre went to open her mouth, he waved a hand to stop her. "Everyone here has been happily . . . married, and I mean to see . . . that tradition continue."

"You shouldn't listen to rumors," Sean protested. "I love Deirdre."

Maybe not *that* way, but he did love her.

"Then . . . kiss her . . . like a man," the old earl wheezed.

There was nothing for it. Reluctantly, Sean faced Deirdre once again. Sucking in a breath, he leaned down and laid his lips on hers, lightly, for the briefest instant.

It was all he could manage.

When he pulled back, Deirdre looked rather pale.

Slowly, Lincolnshire shook his head. "Before I expire . . . I want to see better than that."

Saints preserve us, Sean thought.

"And I've a favor . . . to ask of you."

"Anything, Uncle. Anything at all." So long as it didn't involve kissing his sister.

A weak smile twitched on the man's lips. "Were I you . . . I'd wait to hear it first." He paused for a breath, and then another. "I wish you to . . . keep this house—"

"I will. You have my word." Arrogant Hamilton wouldn't be selling the most impressive house in all of London. "You won't mind living here, will you, Deirdre?"

She glanced around in patent disbelief, taking in the towering damask-hung bed, the scenes painted on the ceiling, the gold-stamped leather wallcoverings. "What sort of knothead would mind living here?"

That prompted another smile. But Lincolnshire wasn't finished. "And all of my staff . . . in perpetuity."

Tempted as he was to agree to that, too, Sean couldn't add to his mountain of lies. "He has more than a hundred servants," he informed Deirdre.

Her eyes widened. No knothead herself, she was well aware Hamilton wouldn't keep nearly that number. He was a man who valued his privacy.

"Oh, Lord Lincolnshire, my husband doesn't like spending much time in London. The scenes he paints are all in the countryside. We won't be needing so many servants when he isn't here."

"For me, my dear. I cannot stand to think . . . these loyal people . . . *my* people . . . will be forced to fend for themselves."

Exchanging a glance with his sister, Sean shook his head.

"I need to know . . . this house will remain in your hands. And my staff . . . will retain their employment."

"I'll keep the house," Sean promised, "as I've said, although it is overly large for just Mrs. Hamilton and myself." Indeed, it was overly large for anyone unrelated to royalty. "But as to the other—"

"Sean," Lincolnshire cut in gently. Beseechingly. "Did you not say . . . you would do anything for me?"

In the long silence that stretched between them, Sean's mind raced. He was more likely to go to bed with Deirdre than Hamilton was to retain the old earl's enormous staff. "What if I could find new, better employment for them all instead?"

A wee snort emerged from the man's throat. "Better than working . . . for me?"

"Very well, I misspoke. There exists no kinder, more thoughtful employer. But more prestigious positions exist, certainly. And . . ."

"And I won't . . . be here."

Sean nodded.

The earl remained unconvinced. "How can you find them all . . . employment? You're an artist, not . . . a man of business."

"I know people. Trust me."

"I do," Lincolnshire said meaningfully, making Sean writhe inside with guilt. "But I want . . . I need to know they're settled. That . . . they'll be happy."

"You will. I'll find them all employment."

"Better positions?"

"Better positions than they have now."

"Before I'm gone?"

"Before you're gone. Uncle, this I promise."

One promise he could keep. One promise he *would* keep.

The man nodded, apparently satisfied. "Now, as to you two."

Deirdre's eyes widened again. "What now?"

"I want to see you dance . . . at the Billingsgate ball . . . on Saturday."

Chapter Twenty-one

APPLE PUFFS

> Pare the fruit and bake them. When cold, mixe the pulp of the Apple with Sugar and lemon-peel shred fine, taking as little of the Apple-juice as you can. Orange marmalade is a great improvement. Put in paste with a little Sugar inside and on top. Bake in a quick oven a quarter hour until browne.
>
> *The homely apple is always dependable. Serve at family gatherings to assure harmony.*
>
> —Helena Chase, Countess of Greystone, 1776

"A lovely first vintage." Lamplight glinted off deep ruby as Alexandra held up her glass on Tuesday night, toasting her brother during their family dinner at his Berkeley Square town house. "You did it, Griffin."

Her husband smiled. "A toast to England's newest wine producer."

"I don't know that *wine producer* is an apt description." Griffin grinned at his brother-in-law. Tristan had helped him save Cainewood's fledgling vineyards. "It implies producing enough to sell a quantity. We're likely to consume this year's entire production ourselves. Within a week. Perhaps tonight."

Alexandra laughed. "You'll make more next year, and

still more the year after that. Eventually there may be enough to sell."

"Charles would be proud," Juliana said softly.

Charles, their eldest brother, had planted the vines when he was the marquess. But he hadn't lived to see them bear fruit. Two years ago, when Charles died of consumption, Griffin had been forced to leave the cavalry. To come home to take Charles's place. To accept Charles's title. He'd also found himself saddled with their three unmarried sisters, a diverse collection of mainly unprofitable properties, and a field full of dying grapevines.

Today the vines were thriving, the family holdings had been reduced to those that were manageable, and two of his sisters were happily wed. Not bad, Griffin thought, relishing a sip of the heady wine. One by one, all of his problems were being resolved. Now he had only to find a husband for Corinna and puzzle out the mystery of Rachael's parenthood.

He was making good progress on the latter. Having heard from his man today, he looked forward to giving Rachael the news when he saw her at the Billingsgate ball on Saturday. Corinna, however, was another matter altogether.

Paint, paint, paint . . . all she ever wanted to do was paint. Clearly she had little interest in finding a husband. He'd introduced her to countless fine gentlemen, and though on the surface she looked cooperative, she always danced and smiled and moved on, never giving any of them a second thought.

All he wanted was her happiness. And women were happier married, were they not? But lately it seemed Corinna paid attention to only one man. He'd be decent husband material, Griffin supposed—a little old, but wealthy, unmarried, and kind. . . .

If only he were expected to last out the week.

"Corinna has been spending a lot of time with Lord

Lincolnshire," he commented as Juliana served the apple puffs Alexandra had made and brought to the family dinner.

"I'm painting Lord Lincolnshire's portrait. I hope to submit it for the Summer Exhibition."

Juliana put a puff on a plate and moved to give it to her husband, James. "How is the old earl doing?" she asked.

"Well enough, considering the circumstances. He seems to be holding his own." Corinna paused for a sip of her wine. "He's very happy to have his nephew to keep him company."

James frowned. "His nephew? Oh, you mean Mr. Delaney."

Griffin tilted his head, confused. "Who is Mr. Delaney?"

Juliana paused with the plate in her hand, apparently torn between setting it before James or bopping him on the head with it. "That was a secret."

"Oh." He winced. "You didn't tell me."

Corinna blindly jabbed a fork in her own apple puff, glaring at Juliana. "Why on earth did you tell *him*?"

"We don't keep secrets," Juliana explained apologetically. "We promised before our wedding."

"Well, when you tell a secret, you could at least tell that it *is* a secret."

"I'm sorry," Juliana squeaked.

"What the devil is this about?" Griffin demanded. "Who is Mr. Delaney?"

Corinna sighed. "The man you met at Lady Partridge's ball—the man introduced to you as John Hamilton—is actually Mr. Hamilton's brother-in-law, Sean Delaney. Mr. Hamilton asked him—"

"Blackmailed him," Alexandra interrupted.

"Well, yes. He blackmailed him into posing as himself. As John Hamilton, I mean. Lord Lincolnshire's nephew. But now he's having second thoughts, even though it's the right thing, and—"

"I beg your pardon?" Griffin cut in.

None of this made sense. The name, Sean Delaney, seemed familiar. Yet the man introduced as John Hamilton at Lady Partridge's ball hadn't seemed familiar at all. In fact, Griffin was certain he'd never set eyes on that man before in his life.

He swung toward his old friend Tristan, more confused than ever. "Did you know about this, too?"

"Not all of it." Looking down, Tristan speared a bite. "And only for a short while."

"A short while," Griffin growled.

Alexandra released a melancholy sigh. "The apple puffs don't seem to be working."

"Come again?" Tristan asked.

"They're supposed to assure harmonious family gatherings."

Her husband and Juliana's both looked amused. Griffin wasn't. "Would someone *please* explain—"

"Excuse me a moment," Juliana interrupted. "And don't you dare discuss anything in my absence. I'll be right back."

While she was visiting the water closet, or wherever else she might have rushed off to—Juliana was female, which meant it was much too dangerous to inquire—Griffin shoveled apple puff into his mouth and tried to puzzle out what was going on.

He failed. Miserably.

"Explain," he demanded when she returned. "And don't leave anything out."

Between them, with much mind-boggling back-and-forthness, his three sisters explained.

And explained.

And explained.

A quarter hour later, when they finally finished, Corinna paused for a breath. "You won't give away Mr. Delaney's secret, will you? Not only would it imperil his sister's divorce, but it would also make Lord Lincolnshire's final days unhappy ones."

"I don't know," Griffin grated out. While his sisters' reasoning was not unsound—assuming one took into consideration their female brand of logic—none of it really sat quite right with him. "I don't like tricking that kindly old man."

"You're not tricking him," Juliana said with that same typical—illogical—logic. "You're only allowing it to happen."

"Which isn't very honorable."

Alexandra shook her head. "Seeing to Lord Lincolnshire's happiness is the *epitome* of honor."

"It's lying," Griffin disagreed.

Now Corinna shook her head. "It's only failing to reveal the truth."

Semantics. It was all semantics. And it was *wrong*.

Griffin was opening his mouth to say so when a footman stepped into the dining room. "A caller, my lord. A Mr. Sean Delaney."

"What a coincidence," Griffin said. "Show him in."

No sooner had the servant left than Corinna snorted. "It's not a coincidence."

"I sent a message to Lincolnshire House," Juliana explained. "I told Mr. Delaney that you're aware of his true identity and there is something we need to discuss."

"So that's what you were doing when you went off." Tristan nodded contemplatively. "I wondered."

James spread his hands. "I thought she was visiting the water closet."

"We should have guessed," Griffin muttered. "She always *has* been the family meddler."

When Mr. Delaney walked in, Corinna motioned to a footman to fetch him a chair, then scooted over so the servant could fit it in beside her own.

A tall man, Delaney looked like he spent all his free hours in Gentleman Jackson's boxing salon. Griffin wouldn't care to challenge him to a match. And he was even more certain they weren't acquainted. "Had we already met?" he asked him. "Before Lady Partridge's ball?"

Delaney gave a little bow before he sat. "Not that I recall, sir."

The man had a distinct Irish accent, and Griffin hadn't ever met very many Irishmen. "Yet your name seems familiar."

"Is it?" Although he took the glass of wine Corinna handed him, Delaney didn't drink from it as he seemed to consider. "I think I may have bought a piece of property from you. Last year, through your solicitor, which explains why we never met."

"Ah, yes." Now Griffin remembered seeing the name on the contract. "A tumbledown boardinghouse near Lincoln's Inn Fields, if I recall aright. Cannot imagine why my father and brother held on to it for so long. I was pleased to get rid of it."

"I take it you haven't been by there of late." A corner of Delaney's mouth twitched as though he wanted to grin. "That 'tumbledown boardinghouse' is now a sound four-story building with sixteen tenants. Shops and offices on the ground floor, residential above." He looked to Corinna. "I received your note. What is it you feel we need to discuss?"

"It was *my* note," Juliana said. "And you've been summoned in order to convince both you and my brother that your posing as John Hamilton is the very best thing."

Which she proceeded to do, of course, with the help of her sisters.

Though Griffin didn't know Delaney, he judged him a man with a quick mind and sound business sense. Together they put up a good fight. In the end, however, they both reluctantly agreed to preserve Lincolnshire's happiness for his final few days.

It was inevitable, Griffin supposed.

Three Chase females against two hapless men was nowhere near a fair match.

Chapter Twenty-two

"Very handsome gentleman," Juliana commented as Corinna came off the Billingsgates' dance floor Saturday night. "Who is he? Did you kiss him?"

"I cannot remember his name. Lord Stonehurst, or maybe Lord Brickhaven. Something to do with building materials." Corinna watched the man walk away, expecting Griffin to bring another one by at any moment. "And no, I didn't kiss him," she added under her breath. "I just met him, for heaven's sake."

"Tonight?" Juliana's smile was a tad too innocent. "Then I expect you'll make him wait a week?"

"At least," Corinna confirmed, tilting her chin up into the air. She'd once told her sister she never let gentlemen kiss her right after meeting them; she made them wait at least a week. But the truth was that since her first kiss with Sean, she'd had no interest whatsoever in kissing anyone else.

Unfortunately, she'd received no kisses in the last three days. Lord Lincolnshire was so anxious to see his portrait finished before he passed on that he'd been ready and waiting when she arrived each morning at nine, making it impossible to sneak a kiss. And although the earl tired easily and went up to bed every afternoon, Sean never returned before it was time for Corinna to go home.

Lord Lincolnshire had taken his rest extra early today, because he was bringing Sean and Deirdre here tonight. He'd told Corinna he wanted to see his nephew "dance with his lovely wife." Corinna was very much looking forward to their arrival, not least because she hoped to get Sean alone for a kiss or two.

The lack of kisses certainly hadn't made her want to kiss another man instead. It seemed she belonged to Sean in a sense, or he to her. Or both. It was a very mild relationship, and a very innocent one, but it was also wonderful, thrilling, and just illicit enough to make her feel like a true, free-spirited artist. Yet it was disconcerting, too. She felt like Pamela had when she'd bemoaned, *I shall never be able to think of anybody in the world but him!*

And she couldn't marry him. Or could she? She was no longer sure. She still knew very little about him, really. But yesterday she'd casually asked Griffin what he thought of Sean—well, she'd called him Mr. Delaney, of course—and he'd said he was impressed with the man's business sense and was hoping to buttonhole him sometime soon to ask him for advice regarding property management.

In other words, he hadn't sounded at all disapproving.

Thinking of her brother made her realize he seemed to have abandoned the Billingsgate ballroom. For now, at least, he wasn't shoving another man at her. She relaxed a little bit. "Do you know where Griffin went off to?"

"I don't. Who is that woman?" Juliana indicated the direction with a flick of her dark blond head. "The one who just came in with Lord Lincolnshire and Mr. Del—um . . . Mr. Hamilton."

They were here! And fortunately no one was nearby to hear Juliana's slip of the tongue. Discretion was important. "That's Deirdre," Corinna whispered. "His sister. We were introduced earlier this week, but I didn't have a chance to actually talk to her. She never seems to be around in the daytimes when I'm at Lincolnshire House painting."

"Let's talk to her now," Juliana said.

Corinna wasn't sure how wise that would be, considering Sean feared his sister might give them away. But she had no choice. In her usual decisive manner, Juliana was already heading Lord Lincolnshire's way.

"Lady Corinna!" he wheezed when they arrived, grinning up at her from his wheelchair. He looked to Juliana. "And Lady Stafford. Please . . . allow me to introduce Mrs. Hamilton, the next . . . Countess of Lincolnshire."

Behind him, Sean shifted uncomfortably. But Deirdre *was* Mrs. Hamilton, after all. And she *would* be the next Countess of Lincolnshire—at least until she managed to secure the divorce she was seeking.

"It's a pleasure to meet you," Juliana told Deirdre.

" 'Tis my pleasure to meet you. I've been hearing so much about your family, especially your sister."

Corinna flushed, wondering what Sean might have told Deirdre. But then she realized it was probably Lord Lincolnshire who'd done the talking. She was painting him, after all, and he was rather pleased by that.

"Mr. Hamilton!" Lady Ainsworth, a tall woman who looked even taller wearing a golden turban, bustled over. "What a delight to see you again! What are you painting these days, if I might ask?"

"A landscape," Sean said.

"A landscape!" Lady Ainsworth's loud laugh had more people coming to join them. Evidently Sean's celebrity had yet to wear off. "Have you ever painted anything that *wasn't* a landscape, Mr. Hamilton?"

"I suppose I haven't."

"You suppose?" Lady Ainsworth's laugh was really quite annoying. "What is it a landscape *of*?" she asked.

"It's a meadow scene," Corinna said.

Lady Hartshorn turned to her. She was a short, round

woman who had very wide eyes at the moment. "You've *seen* it?"

"I have." Corinna smiled, thinking Lady Hartshorn looked rather envious. "The trees are exquisite, their shadows most intriguing."

"Speaking of intriguing shadows," a gentleman said, looking to Sean, "I've been wondering about *Allegory of Shadow.*"

"I beg your pardon?"

"*Allegory of Shadow.* Your most famous painting?"

"Oh, yes." Sean's own laugh sounded rather forced. "Of course. I was still thinking about my new painting, I fear. Once I finish a piece, I quite put it out of my mind."

"May I ask what inspired you? What made you decide to focus so on the shadows?"

"The, ah . . . the trees. I've always found trees very inspiring. Lush trees of the English countryside that grow from wee acorns to cast large shadows—"

"But Mr. Hamilton," Lady Ainsworth interrupted, her turban bobbing as though it were as indignant as she. "I don't recall seeing any trees in *Allegory of Shadow.* It portrays a stone circle, does it not? And not in England, but in Ireland, I do believe?"

"Well, I was raised in Ireland—"

"Exactly," Corinna cut in. "Allegories are symbolic representations, as you know. If one looks closely, one will see that the shadows cast by the standing stones resemble trees. English trees."

"Oh," the woman said.

"I cannot believe you didn't know that," Lady Hartshorn scoffed. "It's brilliant, Mr. Hamilton. Simply brilliant. How long did you take to paint it?"

"Three days, my lady."

"Three *days*? The thing is the size of a drawing room wall! The largest painting in the history of the Summer Exhibition, was it not?"

"When one is inspired," Corinna said, "the image simply flows from the hand through the brush. I myself have completed a painting in a single day." Once. One tiny painting, no more than eight inches square. *Allegory of Shadow* was eight feet by sixteen, at the very least. "Have you ever painted, Lady Hartshorn?"

"No. No, I haven't."

"I thought not," Corinna said in a superior tone of voice.

Just then Lord Lincolnshire coughed. And coughed again.

"Do you need something to drink, Uncle?" Sean took the back of his chair, looking not at all unpleased to have a plausible excuse to escape the conversation. "Let me bring you to the refreshment room."

Without the celebrated Mr. Hamilton as a point of focus, the gathering quickly dispersed. Shifting uneasily, Deirdre watched her brother wheel the earl off.

"Would you like to go outside?" Juliana asked her kindly. "Lord Billingsgate has a lovely garden."

"Oh, yes," Deirdre said, sounding grateful. "I would like that very much."

"Why don't you take her?" Juliana suggested to Corinna, her gaze straying to where James stood in a circle of men engaged in a heated argument. All members of Parliament, no doubt. "I've a mind to rescue my husband by asking him for a dance."

Corinna nodded, taking Deirdre's arm to steer her around the perimeter of the dance floor, toward French doors that opened to the terrace. "Thank you," Sean's sister breathed when they finally made it outside. "I'm thinking I don't really belong in there, do I?"

Corinna led her down a path where twinkling lanterns hung overhead. "Whyever would you say that?"

"I'm a simple country girl, a vicar's daughter from a village in Ireland. I've no place in London society."

"You're married to John Hamilton."

"In name only," Deirdre said darkly. "He's not paid me any mind since . . . well, for a long time."

In all the time since Deirdre lost their baby, Corinna knew. Although Sean had told her little about himself, he'd spent much time explaining Deirdre's situation and how it had led to the mess they were in now. She imagined it was hard for Deirdre to speak of it. "You've every right to be here. And at least you know more about art than your brother."

"I know less about my husband's art than you might think. You did a grand job deflecting those questions. I can see why my brother admires you."

Sean had told her that? Corinna's heart skipped a beat at the thought. "I'm surprised to hear he said so."

"Not in so many words, mind you. But he told me all about you, and I could hear it in his tone of voice."

"He likes my paintings."

"Sean doesn't care a fig about art. But he likes the way you're not afraid to face great odds to get what you want. He did the same himself, you know. He started with nothing, and now he's richer than a pot of gold at the end of a rainbow."

Corinna hadn't brought Sean's sister out here to glean information about him, but she couldn't resist taking advantage of that opening. "How did he manage that?"

Deirdre shrugged. "He says he has a knack."

"A knack?"

"I don't know what he means, exactly. All I can tell you is that shortly after I wed John, Sean moved to London, using a small inheritance he received from our uncle. A *small* inheritance," she emphasized.

"And?"

"The next time I saw him, he owned several pieces of property, including his own house. Twenty years old, and he had his own house." Wonder suffused her voice, and she shook her head disbelievingly. "I never saw my brother often, since John doesn't care to live in London. Once a year, maybe, if that. But the next time I saw Sean, he owned more property, and some manufactories, and any number of other businesses. Ships, too. And a bigger house. And, a couple years later, a bigger one still. Now he lives in a house so big all of Kilburton could move in. The whole village would fit in a corner of the acreage."

"Kilburton?"

"Perhaps that's a bit of an exaggeration." Deirdre shrugged rather sheepishly. "Kilburton is where we grew up in Ireland."

"Tell me more," Corinna said, thinking she knew even less of Sean than she'd thought. "Tell me how he came to own all he does."

"I don't know that much," Deirdre said with a quiet smile. "I think you should ask him yourself."

Chapter Twenty-three

"Griffin," Rachael said. "What are you doing here?"

In his cousins' Lincoln's Inn Fields town house, Griffin stopped pacing the drawing room and turned to find her leaning against the doorjamb. Even in a simple day dress, she looked entirely too sultry for his comfort. Her lips appeared freshly licked. Her dark hair fell in soft waves around her face. Her eyes looked large and luminous.

And sad.

"I'm waiting for you, as I suspect your butler told you. Why aren't you at the Billingsgate ball?"

"I didn't feel like going," she said.

Her wan expression broke his heart, but he embraced the emotion. Pity was much safer than lust. "You cannot withdraw from life, Rachael."

"I'm not." She scanned his evening clothes. "Why did you *leave* the Billingsgate ball?"

"To fetch you."

"What if I don't want to be fetched?"

He shrugged and said nonchalantly, "Then I won't tell you my news."

"What news?" she demanded, straightening and coming toward him. "Tell me."

"I'll tell you on the way to the ball," he promised her with a smile—the charming smile that worked on everyone.

But it didn't work on Rachael. Not tonight. "I don't want to go to the ball."

"Then I don't want to tell you my news. I'll stop by again tomorrow."

"Griffin!" Moving closer, she laughingly punched him on the shoulder. "You cannot do this to me!"

He was happy to see her more animated, but that wasn't enough. He wanted her joyful. He wanted her socializing. He wanted to see her dancing with eligible gentlemen and getting on with her life.

"Would you care to bet?" he asked, starting from the room.

She grabbed his arm. "All right, I'll go to the ball."

"Excellent." With any luck, she'd find a love interest tonight. Then it wouldn't matter that she wasn't his cousin, because she'd be taken anyway. "I'll wait here while you change."

"Oh, no, you won't." Still holding his arm, she pulled him toward a sofa. "Tell me what you learned." With both hands, she pushed him to sit. "Now, damn it."

"Has anyone ever told you you're demanding?"

"Most everyone." She sat beside him and licked her lips, kicking his pulse up a notch even though that was the last thing he wanted. "Did the man you hired find my father's parents?"

"His mother is dead, but the man found his father. His name is Thomas Grimstead, same as his son. Colonel Thomas Grimstead—he was a military man, too."

She nodded, looking vulnerable in a way that made him want to hug her. "Is he still living in Yorkshire?"

"Not anymore. He's living at the Royal Hospital in Chelsea."

"So close," she murmured. The Royal Hospital wasn't a hospital for the ill, but rather a government-funded home for pensioned soldiers. "I have a grandfather so close, and I never knew it." She licked her lips again, proving Griffin a pathetic weakling of a man. "I want to see him. I want to meet him and find out if my father really committed treason."

"I'm glad," he said. It was better to know than to stay

in denial. "I'll take you Monday. No, Tuesday. I've got a meeting with my solicitor scheduled for Monday. I'm sorry."

"You're entitled to live your own life. I can wait. I've waited twenty-four years already."

"I guess you have. Now *I'll* wait while you change for the ball."

She sighed. "You're not really going to hold me to that, are you? I don't want to dance, so what is the point in going? I don't feel up to having men paw me."

"They wouldn't dare. I'd issue a challenge on the spot."

"To a duel? Just what I need . . . your death on my head."

"You think I would lose? You wound me." He playfully clutched his heart. "Get changed. You can dance with me," he offered, vaguely wondering what the devil he was doing suggesting something that would result in his clenching his teeth all night. "Nothing but innocent, cousinly dances."

The Billingsgates had a rather impressive art collection, one Corinna had spent much time studying during the ball the Billingsgates held last Season. This year, although she once again found herself hovering in their picture gallery, she wasn't enjoying herself nearly as much.

And she wasn't studying the paintings this time, either. Mostly, she was trying to help Sean escape both the room and the guests who insisted on surrounding him. If she could manage that, maybe she could also manage to get him off alone.

She wanted to talk to him without everyone's eyes on the two of them. She wanted him to look at her without it being a look of distress. She wanted to touch him and feel his touch in return. She wanted to be close enough to breathe in his scent.

And she was dying for a kiss.

Unfortunately, Lady Billingsgate's guests weren't co-operating. And neither was Lord Lincolnshire.

"Wouldn't you care for some air, Uncle?" Sean asked for the third time.

"Oh, no. I'm . . . enjoying this conversation."

No doubt he basked in seeing his heir command so much attention. But Corinna had already had to save Sean from mistaking a watercolor for an oil and justify his description of a piece of William Hogarth's as a "groundbreaking new work."

Not an easy task, considering Hogarth had died in 1764.

"It was groundbreaking when it *was* a new work," she'd said. Fortunately, the hangers-on bunched around Sean had nodded as though they'd interpreted his comment that way all along.

"Oh, I do adore mythology as the subject for a painting," Lady Trevelyan said now, moving on to the next piece of art. "What do you think of this one by Kauffmann, Mr. Hamilton?"

"Very detailed," Sean said—a safe enough comment. But then he added, "I admire his—"

"His?"

"Joshua Reynolds, he means," Corinna rushed to say. "Am I right, Mr. Hamilton? You were referring to Sir Joshua Reynolds, since *Angelica* Kauffmann was one of his protégées?"

"Joshua Reynolds, yes." The smile he sent her was a grateful one. "As I was saying, I admire Reynolds for being open-minded enough to recognize a female artist."

"That's what I thought." Corinna breathed a silent sigh of relief. "Although, of course, Kauffmann was widely recognized as one of the founders of the Royal Academy. One of only two female Academicians in its history, as a matter of fact."

Sean's smile now was warm rather than grateful. "I look forward to your being the third."

Their gazes caught and held. He really *did* want to see her succeed. "I appreciate your support," she said softly.

A gentleman cleared his throat. "Speaking of Reynolds," he said, moving along to stand before two large portraits. "What do you think, Mr. Hamilton, of Reynolds's work as compared to Gainsborough's?"

"Hmm." Corinna saw Sean glance to the artists' signatures. "This Gainsborough is rather sentimental, is it not, while the Reynolds here is, ah, more grand. Establishing the importance of the man portrayed rather than sympathy with the subject."

Though Sean looked quite proud of his analysis, the questioner frowned. "I meant in *general*, Mr. Hamilton, not these particular portraits. One man's body of work juxtaposed against the other."

"I do not judge entire bodies of work, sir. I never seek signatures prior to evaluating a painting. Each work should stand on its own—the artist's identity shouldn't influence my opinion of any specific picture."

The gentleman was clearly taken aback. "I thought all artists studied the masters' techniques."

Corinna didn't quite know what to say to that, so she was relieved when Juliana stepped forward and laughed. "Ah, there is your mistake, Lord Prescott," her sister said. "One cannot make suppositions regarding 'all artists.' Artists are known to be eccentric, individualistic. They pride themselves on not conforming to convention. Therefore you should never expect a particular artist, such as Mr. Hamilton here, to approach other artists' work in any singular, conforming manner."

Thank God for sisters, Corinna thought. Lord Lincolnshire also looked impressed with Juliana's speech. He blinked madly. And then he coughed. And coughed again. A bit of froth appeared on his lips.

Looking alarmed, Sean dug out a handkerchief and dabbed it off. "I really think you need some air, Uncle. I insist."

"Take me to the . . . doors, then. And . . . let me see . . . you dance"—gasping, he looked to Deirdre—"with your wife."

Corinna was alarmed, too. "He cannot even get three

syllables out before needing a breath," she said to her sister as they followed Sean, Deirdre, and Lord Lincolnshire into the ballroom. "Maybe you should ask James to have a look at him." Besides being an earl, Juliana's husband was also a physician.

"I'm sure Lord Lincolnshire has his own doctors."

"But he's getting worse."

"He's dying," her sister reminded her gently.

"But he might die before I finish his portrait, and he really wants to see it completed."

Juliana measured her for a moment. "All right. I'll ask him."

"Thank you," Corinna said.

They watched Sean wheel Lord Lincolnshire over to the French doors, then turn to Deirdre and reluctantly escort her to the dance floor. The musicians struck up a country tune.

Corinna breathed a sigh of relief. "Thank goodness it isn't a waltz."

"Why is that?" Juliana asked.

"Sean cannot waltz to save his life."

"Sean?"

"Mr. Delaney," Corinna corrected quickly. "And thank you for stepping in to save him. With any luck, that was the last in our long series of close calls."

A slow smile curved her sister's lips. "*Our*, hmm?"

"Yes, our. You, me, Mr. Delaney, Alexandra, Griffin. We're all in this together. All of us who know the secret."

Juliana's smile remained. "*Our* could also mean just you and Sean—I mean, Mr. Delaney." Now her smile widened at her own deliberate mistake. "The two of you belong together. Anyone can see it."

"We do not." The last thing Corinna wanted was her meddlesome sister interfering. "He's not from our world, Juliana. Griffin would never agree."

"Griffin has nothing against the man. In fact, he said he admires him. I asked him what he thought of Mr.

Delaney earlier this evening, before he left and came back with Rachael."

Rachael and Griffin were dancing together even now. Unsurprisingly, Corinna's sister was looking rather smug about how *that* relationship was progressing. And Corinna wasn't at all surprised to hear Juliana had questioned Griffin about Sean, either. "Mr. Delaney is color-blind. He cannot even appreciate my paintings."

"There's something between the two of you," Juliana insisted.

"A mutual desire to see Lord Lincolnshire happily through his last days, that's all."

Her sister shrugged. "If you say so," she said agreeably, not sounding like she really agreed at all.

"Holy Hannah," Corinna muttered. "Go dance with your husband, will you? And don't forget to ask him to have a look at Lord Lincolnshire."

Chapter Twenty-four

Sean had decided that the day he'd brought Lincolnshire to Hamilton's studio hadn't been the longest one of his life, after all.

This damn ball felt at least a week longer.

Escorting Deirdre off the dance floor, he noticed Corinna standing by the open French doors. She caught his eye, motioning her head toward the Billingsgates' garden before slipping outside.

Sean brought Deirdre in the same direction, walking her back to Lincolnshire. "Are you enjoying the fresh air, Uncle?"

"Very much. And . . . I enjoyed . . . seeing you dance."

"We enjoyed the dance, too." For the dear gent's benefit, Sean smiled at his sister and kissed her on the cheek. "I'm feeling a wee bit overheated after that, though, I'm afraid. Would you mind keeping my wife company while I step outdoors for a moment?"

"Not at all," Lincolnshire said, reaching for Deirdre's hand.

Leaving the two of them, Sean entered the garden, knowing he probably shouldn't, and immediately spotted Corinna on a path lit with twinkling lanterns. Beckoning for him to follow, she disappeared.

He briefly thought of turning back, but having come this far, he didn't feel it fair to leave her waiting. Following the sound of her light, running footsteps, he found her quite a distance down the path and off to the side, in the darkness of a small stand of trees. Though the area was shadowed, he could see the outline of her lovely form, not at all hidden by her slim, high-waisted dress. He walked closer, telling himself he shouldn't touch her, knowing he would.

Her scent wafted to him through the starlit night, flowery and sweet, underlaid with that astringent hint that reminded him she was an artist, a talented woman who went her own way. But she was aristocratic, too. Beneath her facade of originality and forwardness, she was sheltered and unspoiled, a woman who had never wanted for anything. Like a bright, newly minted coin, nothing had tarnished her. She was shiny and pretty, and that perfection drew him. Tempted him toward a world where he didn't belong.

He knew that, and he'd tried to stay away the past few days because of it. He'd kissed her three times already—four if he counted the occasion he hadn't resisted pressing his lips to the nape of her neck—and he knew that was three or four times too many.

He knew also that she hadn't the same reservations. She was impulsive and eager and ardent. He drew close, and when she raised her fingers to brush along his jaw he wasn't the least bit surprised. A moment later they were in each other's arms, their lips locked together.

It was frightening, this mad passion. He felt swamped. But the fear didn't stop him from taking what he wanted, from feasting on her mouth and running his hands down her back. From tasting her and finding that taste intoxicating. From pressing her against his body and reveling in the feel of her and enjoying her small sounds of delight.

When he drew back, they were both breathless. She moved closer again, close enough to lay her head against his chest. "I missed you the past three days," she said softly.

" 'Tis sorry I am for that," he said, because he *was*

sorry, for disappointing her but also that he'd let things get to the point where she would be disappointed. And that he wasn't doing anything to stop that progression. "I've had things I've had to do."

"What things?" She pulled away a little and gazed up at him, her blue eyes looking black in the darkness. "What do you do, Sean, exactly?"

"Unfortunately, very little for myself since this all began. Now Lincolnshire has asked me to find new positions for all of his servants. Well, actually he asked me to *keep* all his servants after he passed, but I told him I'd find positions for them instead. So that's what I've been doing. Finding placements for them." He smiled down at her, and because he couldn't help himself, he gave her another kiss. A short, gentle one this time. "Thank you for making that possible."

"It sounds like a horrible imposition. You'll be glad when this is all over, won't you?"

"Very glad." Although he wondered if he would ever see her again. How he possibly could. And whether he'd find himself content again if he couldn't. "I'll miss seeing you, though, when it's over."

"I think we'll see each other again. My brother wants to talk to you. He wants to ask your advice about property management."

"Does he now?"

"He likes you. He's impressed with your business sense."

"I didn't think marquesses were interested in business."

"They're not, mostly, but Griffin's a little different. He never wanted to be the marquess. He likes being in the center of things. He was in the cavalry, you know, before our older brother died. An officer. He led campaigns in the Peninsular War. Although he complains of too many responsibilities, I think in his heart he feels a little useless now. He'd like to find something of his own, something more challenging, more involving."

"Managing property can be very involving." Her brother sounded like a man he might admire. And if the man admired him as well, then . . .

There was no sense thinking in that direction. But he held Corinna a wee bit closer and pressed another kiss to the top of her head, inhaling the warm, floral scent of her hair. "We'd best get back," he said regretfully, taking her hand and easing them both out of the trees. "Or people will come looking for us."

"That wouldn't be good," she agreed, moving with him. "Juliana would come looking for us first, and then who knows what would happen." While he was wondering what *could* happen, they turned onto the path. "I liked what you said in there," she said. "In the picture gallery."

"In the picture gallery. Saints preserve us. I don't think I said anything that wasn't a disaster."

"But you did. You said that an artist's work should stand on its own, that his identity—or hers, I'm hoping everyone who was listening would agree—should not influence the viewer's opinion of any specific picture." Her hand warm in his larger one, she looked over and up at him and smiled. "Wherever did you come up with that?"

"Hamilton," he admitted with no small measure of disgust. "Hamilton said something very like that, and I remembered it. In my desperation to sound artistic, it just came flying out of my mouth."

"I know you despise him, and for good reason, but I'm so glad to hear he thinks that way. It makes it so much more likely that he'll vote for my painting."

Sean didn't think so. She didn't know the rest of what Hamilton had said—the part about females never painting anything good. But he wasn't going to tell her that, not now. He wasn't going to ruin the last of these few stolen moments together.

"He should be back by now," he told her instead, pulling his hand from hers as the house came into sight. Faint snatches of music floated to them from the open

French doors. "He said he'd be gone two weeks, and it was two weeks on Thursday. But instead of coming home to deal with everything, he sent a letter."

She clasped her hands before her, like maybe she was missing holding his. He hoped so. But he knew he shouldn't. "That's just as well," she said. "If he came home now, he might ruin his uncle's last days. What did the letter say?"

"He's painting the Lady of the Waterfall, and he doesn't want to leave. But I'm suspecting the lady he doesn't want to leave is the one in his bed." The rotter. "He told me not to worry; he'll be home well before the Summer Exhibition vote."

"I don't expect you were worrying," Corinna said. "You obviously cannot do that for him. Just like you cannot come to Lady Avonleigh's reception next week in his place. Ten days," she added with a sigh as they approached the open French doors, instinctively moving farther apart so it wouldn't appear they'd done anything but talk. "In ten days my painting will be turned in and Hamilton will come home."

"He should return before that. He said he'd be here well before the vote."

"Then in less than ten days, you'll be free."

Sean wouldn't be free until Lincolnshire passed on, unless Hamilton stirred everything up.

But he didn't want to say that.

Much as he wanted his life back, much as he knew he and Corinna were growing too close, ten days in her company didn't seem nearly long enough.

Chapter Twenty-five

"How does Lord Lincolnshire fare today?" Sean asked as he stepped into the man's house late Monday afternoon.

Quincy sighed, a maudlin sound that spoke volumes. "Perhaps you should ask his new physician."

"New physician?"

"He's with him now. Second doctor to visit today."

Alarmed, Sean headed for the crystal staircase. Glimpsing Corinna inside the salon as he passed, he was tempted to stop. But her back was to him, and she looked absorbed, humming tunelessly while dabbing vigorously at her painting.

And Lincolnshire took precedence now, regardless.

Sean took the steps two at a time, wincing at the sound of Lincolnshire's cough. Apparently hearing her brother's footsteps, Deirdre hurried out into the corridor. "You're back early today," she whispered.

"He wasn't doing well this morning."

"That's why I decided to stay home with him. He was sitting for Lady Corinna when he started coughing blood. Just a wee bit, but . . ."

"A wee bit is too much."

She nodded. "Lady Corinna sent him upstairs. Nurse Skeffington summoned his doctor, and then Lord Stafford arrived, too. Dr. Dalton was livid." Her eyes were wide. "He packed up his leeches and left."

"His leeches?" Sean pulled a face before registering the rest of Deirdre's words. "Lord Stafford? Corinna's brother-in-law?"

She nodded again. "Lady Corinna sent him a note. He's in with Lord Lincolnshire now." She motioned to the door, and they headed toward it.

"My recommendation is that the leeches and bleeding and blistering be stopped," Lord Stafford was telling the earl as they walked in. "Your choice, of course, but I don't believe those treatments will accomplish anything, unless you're aiming to hasten the end."

Lincolnshire shook his head wildly and coughed again.

"There now." Lifting a cup off the earl's bedside table, Lord Stafford leaned closer and held it to his lips. "Have a little sip for me, will you? It will soothe your throat, and the warmth will ease your lungs." He straightened and looked to Sean. "Good evening, Mr. Hamilton."

Considering the man knew he wasn't Hamilton, he'd said that smoothly, Sean thought. "Thank you for attending him. I thought you ran a smallpox facility."

"I spend most days vaccinating, yes. But I also see a few very special patients." He aimed a gentle smile at Lord Lincolnshire. "Another sip for me, as a favor?"

The earl took a very tiny one.

"He doesn't have but a wee appetite," Deirdre said.

"He's doubtless nauseous," Stafford explained. "Although we cannot see it, of course, his internal organs will be swelling along with those parts we can see. He'll not be wanting to eat much, but you should encourage him to take what he can. Especially the tea."

"We will," Sean said. "And we shouldn't allow Dr. Dalton to apply more leeches, then, yes?"

"It's my belief such treatments will only make Lord Lincolnshire more uncomfortable. Better to let things progress naturally, as I see it. But I don't expect Dr. Dalton will be returning in any case." Stafford set an affectionate hand on the earl's shoulder. "I'll be attending Lord Lincolnshire now."

Lincolnshire gave him a weak smile. "Thank you," he whispered, closing his eyes.

"Think nothing of it. I'd do anything for you—just like everyone else who's had the good fortune to be part of your life."

Not Hamilton, Sean thought darkly, watching the earl's breathing even out. His head lolled against the pillows. No matter his cheerful front, Lincolnshire was weakening. He wouldn't last much longer. Though Sean regretted spending the day out of the house, he'd needed to talk to his people, figure out where more of Lincolnshire's servants could be placed. He wanted to assure the earl's peace of mind before he passed.

Stafford dropped his stethoscope into his black leather bag and fastened it with a *snap*. "I'll return in the morning. I trust Nurse Skeffington to take good care of him in the meantime."

Deirdre glanced gratefully at the sturdy woman hovering nearby. "Sure, and she will. And Sean and I will be caring for him, too."

Lord Lincolnshire's actual niece by marriage, Deirdre was proving more devoted than Sean had expected. More grown-up than he'd imagined. He gave her a sad smile of approval before following Stafford downstairs.

The two men paused at the salon door. Corinna still had her back turned, but she wasn't painting anymore. She wasn't humming, either. She just stood there, gazing at her canvas.

Her hair was swept up, and the nape of her neck looked vulnerable. Something inside Sean stirred, a long, liquid pull.

As though she could sense it, she turned. "Sean. And James." Joining them in the entry hall, she looked to her brother-in-law in concern.

"Lord Lincolnshire has fallen asleep. I put a drop of laudanum in his tea. He's resting easily for now."

"Might he get better, then, do you think?"

"I fear not," Lord Stafford said gently. "It is, of course,

difficult to predict the path of an illness. He could have an hour or a day when he seems better, but overall he will continue to decline." He leaned close and kissed her cheek. "You were right to send for me. Juliana suggested I see him, but I didn't realize the situation was so urgent."

"Thank you for coming." She walked him to the front door, which the competent Quincy was already holding open. "I know Lord Lincolnshire is in the best of hands," she added softly.

She watched him go down the steps, then waited for Quincy to close the door before turning to Sean. "When did you get home?"

This wasn't home, but he shrugged wearily. "A while ago. You looked very busy."

"I'm finished."

"Leaving for the evening, then?"

"I'm *finished*. With the painting."

"Oh." He blinked. "May I have a look?"

"Yes, I was hoping you would." She hesitated a moment before heading back to the salon, motioning him to follow. She seemed to hold her breath as they drew near the canvas. "What do you think?"

"It looks just like Lincolnshire. A healthier, more vital Lincolnshire." The man who'd sat for her, blended together with the younger Lincolnshire of her memories, Sean guessed.

It was a full-body portrait, a natural pose in lieu of the typical head-and-torso formality. The painting showed the earl seated on a bench beneath a plane tree in Berkeley Square—perhaps the same bench where Sean had explained the truth to Corinna. Lincolnshire wasn't eating a Gunter's ice, though; instead he held a weighty, leather-bound book. Rather than reading it, he looked like he'd just glanced up, distracted by the viewer walking by. He seemed relaxed, contemplative. And very much alive.

"It's good," Sean said simply.

Corinna exhaled in a rush. "You know nothing about art."

"I know what I like, and it looks very well done to me. You'll submit it for the Summer Exhibition, won't you?"

"I hope to. But first I'm going to show it at Lady Avonleigh's reception on Wednesday." She'd have it delivered, along with a selection of her other paintings, to Lady A's house tomorrow. "I want to see what the artists say of it."

"The judges."

"Yes." She met his gaze, nerves suddenly jumping in her stomach. "I hope they'll like it."

Her voice quavered, and she wondered if he had heard it. He didn't say anything, so she couldn't tell. He only looked at her for a moment. Just looked at her, while she stood there wishing she hadn't eaten any luncheon, because she felt like what she had eaten was about to come back up.

Abruptly he turned and walked back to the salon's huge carved and gilded door. Shut it with a heavy *thump*. Then turned again to face her. "You're nervous," he stated in that low, melodic tone that made everything shift inside her. "Come here, Corinna."

She rushed into his arms, raising her face for his kiss. But he didn't kiss her. He only held her. He only held her tight, murmuring wordless sounds of comfort, or maybe they were Irish words—she didn't know. But just at that moment, she fell in love.

The realization robbed her of breath, made her heart stutter once before it raced faster. She slid her hands beneath his tailcoat and around him. Squeezed him as he was squeezing her, as hard as she could.

"There's nothing to be nervous about," he said soothingly, running his hands up and down her back. "It's a lovely painting."

She turned her head, laid her cheek against his warm, comforting chest, wishing there weren't a shirt and waistcoat between them. "I know."

"And you've many more paintings at home, do you not? So if the judges don't agree, they could choose another one."

He smelled like starch and soap and man. "I know." Impossibly masculine man.

"And if they don't choose another one, there's always next year. You won't give up. I know you."

She knew him, too. And she loved him. She didn't think she could tell him—there was so much happening around them, so much else complicating his life. But she raised her face again, hoping this time he'd kiss her so she could tell him without words.

He did.

It was a gentle kiss, not at all like the ones they'd shared before. Their kisses tended to be stormy. But this was calm and slow and soothing—and exactly what she needed.

Tender and caring, his lips slid over hers, taking their time. His tongue swept her mouth, languid and unhurried, luxurious and deliberate, as though tasting her and discovering her and making her feel better were the only things he cared about in the whole world.

She quivered. But not with nervousness now, because he was right: There was always next year, and at the moment this give and take, this lingering caress, seemed so much more important. She lost herself in him, lost herself in the magic of love and all of its promise.

A knock came at the door, and they jerked apart. Sean whirled and opened it. "Deirdre."

His sister blinked, looking between them. "I'm sorry. I wasn't meaning to interrupt."

"No, no." He drew her inside. "Lady Corinna was just showing me her finished picture."

Corinna feared the other woman could see the truth on her face—or rather her lips, which were tingling and felt thoroughly kissed. But if Deirdre could tell, she didn't let on. Her own lips curved in a faint smile as she walked toward the painting.

"Oh, Lady Corinna, this is absolutely lovely. Tell me about it, will you?"

Behind Deirdre's back, Corinna shared one last, lingering glance with Sean, feeling so much better about everything. She was in love, and she knew that mattered more than any painting.

Hugging her new secret to herself, she went to join his sister.

Chapter Twenty-six

ALMOND CAKES

Grinde halfe a pound of Almonds and mixe with halfe a pound of Sugar and Orange or Lemon Water. To this add ten Yolks of Egges beaten and the boiled skins of two Oranges or Lemons grounde fine. Mixe together with stiff Egge Whites and melted Butter gone cold and bake it all in a good Crust.

Good for nibbling during nervous occasions, such as when my daughter brought my first grandchild into the world earlier this year. Oh, my, what a day and night. I think I'd much rather give birth myself!

—Elizabeth Chase, Countess of Greystone, 1736

As was customary, the furniture in Aunt Frances's Hanover Square home had been rearranged to prepare for the birth of her child. On the ground floor of Malmsey House, a room had been designated as the lying-in chamber, and a portable folding bed had been brought in for the occasion. A larger connecting room provided a gathering place for relations during the labor, and more rooms across the corridor had been outfitted to house the accoucheur—the obstetrical doctor—and the monthly nurse, called such because she not only assisted the accoucheur and attended the mother during the birth, but stayed for a month afterward to care for the baby.

The accoucheur and monthly nurse had arrived yesterday in anticipation of Aunt Frances's due date a week hence. But Dr. Holmes had apparently reckoned incorrectly, because today, while Corinna and her family nibbled at the almond cakes Juliana had baked and brought, Frances was laboring in the inner chamber.

As she had been for half a day already.

Corinna had been forced to rush this morning to get her paintings sent to Lady A's house before coming here to be with Aunt Frances. Along with the portrait, she'd chosen all her best landscapes and a few of her favorite still lifes. At least waiting for the birth was keeping her from fretting over whether she'd made the right selections.

Well, a little bit, anyway.

Hearing more moans and murmurs through the door, she winced. "How long is this going to take?"

"It hasn't been that long." Alexandra smiled down at her infant son. "If you'd attended Harry's birth, you'd know that."

Alexandra had delivered in the wintertime, at Hawkridge House in the countryside. Two weeks early, a full week before her sisters had planned to arrive. Her accoucheur had miscalculated, too, and at the moment, Corinna was grateful for that. The thought of Alexandra groaning like Aunt Frances made her want to groan herself.

"Oh, damn," Griffin suddenly said.

"What is it?" Corinna asked. Had he heard something through the door that she hadn't? Something bad? Something dire?

"It's nothing," he said. "I just forgot something." He rose and went over to a little desk in a corner of the room, where he started pulling drawers open. "I need to send a message."

Juliana rose, too, and found paper and quill for him.

"It seems this is taking forever," she said, looking rather pale as she returned to her seat. "James, maybe you should help."

"I don't deliver babies," her physician husband said for the fifth time. "But there's no need to fret. Dr. Holmes is the best."

"He could take some measures," Griffin muttered as he scribbled.

"It's usually better not to intervene as long as the labor is making progress. What would you have him do?"

"Bloodletting, perhaps."

"James does not believe in bleeding," Juliana said quickly. Juliana hated the sight of blood. She said it made her sick to her stomach.

Griffin folded his letter and started scribbling again, adding the direction to the outside. "Then maybe forceps."

"The use of forceps," James said, "can result in tearing the mother."

"I don't want to hear this," Corinna said. The sight of blood didn't bother her, but her stomach was turning anyway with all of this talk. She didn't want to see Aunt Frances bled, and the thought of forceps was equally upsetting. But something needed to be done, because she didn't think she could listen to what was coming from behind the closed door a moment longer.

"Are you all right?" Juliana asked her.

"I'm fine. I just never want to give birth."

Everyone laughed. But this was no laughing matter. She was never going to tell Sean she loved him, because what if he wanted to get married? And though Griffin probably wouldn't assent, what if he did? She could end up wedded and bedded and moaning and groaning behind a birthing room door herself.

A particularly piercing scream came from the room beyond, and she felt the blood drain from her face.

"It's worth it," Alexandra said softly, still smiling down at her child.

"I think I'll stick to producing pictures," Corinna muttered.

"Your husband may not agree with that," Griffin said, rising from the desk. He strode toward the room's door. "I'll be right back. I need to give this to a footman to have it delivered."

I believe all men are deceitful, Corinna remembered Amanda saying in *Children of the Abbey*. Well, her brother was not deceitful. Oh, no, he was perfectly straightforward. He was determined to marry her off, and there was nothing the least bit deceitful about the way he was going about it. To the contrary, he regularly announced it to the world.

Your husband may not agree with that.

Corinna was yelling at him in her head, deciding just what words to use to make it clear to him, once and for all, that she wasn't looking for a husband in the first place and wouldn't accept one who didn't support her art career in any case—when the moaning and screaming suddenly stopped.

Corinna's breathing stopped, too. "Do you think Aunt Frances is . . . ?"

She couldn't bring herself to utter the word *dead*. And evidently no one else could, either, because a tense silence flooded the room.

And then a thin cry came through the closed door.

"Of course not, you goose." Juliana grinned. "She's had her baby."

"Thank God." Corinna bit off a hunk of almond cake. Her aunt's ordeal was over. Marriage and childbirth hadn't killed her, after all. "When can we see it?"

"Not for a while," Alexandra told her. "The baby will be covered in mucus and blood, so it will need to be cleaned up first, and Aunt Frances will need to deliver the afterbirth—"

"Stop." Griffin walked back in, looking rather green. "I don't think Corinna needs to hear this."

Corinna laughed softly. She was feeling better already. Her stomach fluttered with excitement as they all waited to be invited inside. The baby stopped crying, and the murmurs that came through the door sounded contented rather than distressed. She heard Frances's familiar soft chuckle and knew everything had gone well.

At last the connecting door opened. From the bed Frances smiled, propped comfortably against her pillows. Lord Malmsey came out of the room, a short man with a receding hairline, a wide smile, and a pink bundle cradled in his arms.

"It's a girl," he said, sounding bemused.

Everyone seemed to sigh in unison.

Slowly he unwrapped the blanket, revealing a little heart-shaped face, a shock of straight dark hair, and large, unfocused blue eyes.

Corinna rose and walked toward him.

"What are you calling her?" she asked.

"Belinda," he said quietly.

"Oh, God." Frances's sister's name. Corinna's mother's. "May I hold her?"

Griffin laughed. "I thought you didn't want a baby."

"There's a big difference between having one and holding one," she retorted, opening her arms.

Lord Malmsey reluctantly handed his daughter over. Belinda felt warm and smelled divine. And holding her close, Corinna fell in love for the second time in two days.

Chapter Twenty-seven

Hanover Square, Tuesday 13 May

My dear Cousin,
I regret that I shall be unable to accompany you to Chelsea today, as my Aunt Frances is most inconveniently delivering a child. I shall take you tomorrow if that agrees with you.

Fondly,
Cainewood

"A useful skill indeed, miss." Sean made a notation in his notebook. "Perhaps I can find a position for you cleaning Delaney and Company's main offices."

"Offices?" the scullery maid squealed, her cracked and work-reddened hands flying up to her cheeks. Clearly she considered cleaning offices a huge step up in the world. "A place of business? Not a kitchen?"

"I cannot make any promises, since decisions have not yet been made. But you won't be working in a kitchen." One business he *wasn't* involved in was food service. He stood, and when she stood, too, he stuck out his hand. "Whatever your final assignment, you should expect to begin the Monday following Lord Lincolnshire's loss."

"Will I still live here?"

"I'm afraid not." Sean was certain Hamilton would never allow it. "But have no fear, miss. I shall arrange lodging in a boardinghouse for you until you can find a situation of your own."

She clutched his hand in both of hers, her eyes wide with disbelief. "Thank you, my lord. You cannot imagine—"

"I'm not a lord," he interrupted. "Merely a mister."

"You'll be a lord soon—"

"And you're very welcome. Before you return to the kitchens, please ask Mr. Higginbotham to step in."

He sat and made a few more notes while she all but danced out of the room. When the house steward entered, he rose again. "Was she the last one then, Mr. Higginbotham?"

A tall, thin man with a gaze that didn't miss anything, Higginbotham ran Lincolnshire's household like clockwork. "Other than Eugene Scott, one of the gardeners, yes. I allowed him the day off to sit with his ailing mother."

"A gardener." Sean nodded and made another note. Perhaps Mr. Scott could be assigned to work with the crews that landscaped new buildings following construction. "Please sit down, Mr. Higginbotham."

The steward did so, smoothing his palms on his striped trousers. "I must tell you, sir, that everyone, from the basement of this house to the attics, is extremely grateful for your seeing to their continued employment."

"Think nothing of it. They are uncommonly loyal employees, and as such, will prove to be assets in their future positions."

Now that Sean had interviewed them all—mostly in the evening hours over more than a week—he would assess their relative strengths so he could appropriately distribute them among the varied businesses he owned. Some would be involved in property management, others in import or export, manufacturing, construction, and many other of his endeavors.

"I hope everyone will be pleased with their final assignments," he said.

"I'm certain they will be pleased to have any employment at all. Although they wish to remain with Lord Lincolnshire until he's gone, of course."

"Of course. I'd not have it any other way."

Higginbotham hesitated. "If you don't mind my asking, Mr. Hamilton . . ." He cleared his throat. "How is it you've come to know of enough available positions? And come by the authority to hire—"

"I know a lot of people," Sean interrupted dismissively.

"I expect as a well-known artist you've commissions from all the best—"

"Something like that." He tapped his quill on the notebook. "As for *your* future, Mr. Higginbotham . . ."

The man sat forward, apprehension crossing his long face. "I assumed I'd remain here. If I may say so, Mr. Hamilton, you're going to require a minimum of staff at the least."

Sean wouldn't think of leaving such a fine man at the mercy of Deirdre's husband. "Your efficiency has impressed me. I know of a factory in Surrey in need of a foreman. If you're amenable, I'd like to see you in that position."

Higginbotham's eyes widened. "A factory?"

"They manufacture lamps, the new gaslights. As it's a growing industry, it's a very large factory indeed, with upward of three hundred employees."

The steward squared his shoulders. "I have managed a sizable staff here."

"More than a hundred, by my estimate." Sean felt like he'd interviewed a thousand. "You'll have to relocate outside London, of course, but compensation will include a foreman's house and the staff to manage it, leaving you free to focus on the factory's needs."

"I'm to have my own servants?"

"You'll need them. The factory is a major responsibility."

The man's eyes filled with determination, perhaps

tempered by a touch of excitement. A house steward was a respectable position, but managing a factory was something else altogether. Rather than a glorified servant, he'd be a man of industry, a man of business. "I'm up to it, sir, I assure you."

"I've no doubt." Sean snapped the notebook closed. "We're agreed, then, and I'm finished here. Let Lord Lincolnshire know, if you please. I'm off to . . . paint."

Lincoln's Inn Fields, Tuesday 13 May

My dear Cousin,

It should have been better had you notified me of your delay sooner than four hours after I expected you. You seem to have forgotten that Lady A is holding her reception tomorrow, possibly the most important day of your sister's life. As I plan to attend, Thursday afternoon will be more agreeable for Chelsea.

Yours very sincerely,
Rachael

P.S. I wish Lady Malmsey the best.

Chapter Twenty-eight

ROUT CAKES

Take Flour and mix with Butter and Sugar and Currants clean and dry. Make into a paste with Eggs and Orange Flower Water, Rose-water, sweet Wine, and Brandy. Drop on a floured tin-plate and bake them for a very short time.

My mother said these cakes bring luck, and indeed, I fed them to my husband the day he proposed! Serve to ensure the success of your rout or any other event you'd like to see turn out well.
—Katherine Chase, Countess of Greystone, 1765

Finally, the day of the reception dawned. Corinna arrived at Lady Avonleigh's town house, where an ancient butler ushered her inside. Her knees were shaking. Lady Balmforth, who shared the house with her sister, came over to greet her and bring her to the drawing room.

"Welcome, my dear. Where is Mr. Hamilton?"

"He . . . ah . . . he couldn't come," she said, which was the truth. Mr. Hamilton couldn't come, as he was in Wales, and Sean couldn't come in his place, either. "I haven't actually seen him the past few days, Lady B. Apparently he's very busy."

That was true, too. She hadn't seen Sean since she'd finished the portrait.

"Well." The older woman huffed, sucking in her already thin cheeks. Lady B was as skinny as Lady A was plump. "My sister is not going to be happy about this."

Some of the ladies' friends were already there, exclaiming over Corinna's paintings. Lady A and Lady B had taken all the other pictures off their peach-painted walls and hung Corinna's art there instead.

Everything in their house seemed to be peach. The color unfortunately clashed with some of Corinna's work, but there was nothing she could do about that. Nothing but cross her fingers and hope that the artists would like what they saw when they arrived.

Alexandra showed up next, a platter in her hands. "Rout cakes," she explained. "They're supposed to ensure the success of your rout."

"It isn't *my* rout. In fact, it isn't a rout at all. It's a reception."

"It's a fashionable gathering, and as Lady A's home isn't overly large, it's bound to be a crush. That's a rout in my book." Alexandra leaned to kiss her sister's cheek. "You look nervous."

A sarcastic retort hung on the tip of Corinna's tongue, but she felt too frazzled to make jests. "I am," she admitted instead. She abruptly realized that, other than the rout cakes, Alexandra held . . . nothing. And there was a decided lack of squeaky wheels. "You left Harry at home."

"Babies don't belong at routs." Alexandra set the platter on a side table of mahogany inlaid with lighter, peach-colored wood. "Show me your newest painting."

But before Corinna could do so, Juliana walked in. Then Rachael and Claire and Elizabeth. Then more of Lady A's and B's friends, and their other sister, Lady Cavanaugh, and the first of the artist judges.

Suddenly, it was a rout.

Corinna could barely move among all the people. Lady A pushed through the crowd to give her a hug, enveloping her in camphor and gardenias. "Our honored guest! Where is Mr. Hamilton, my dear?"

"He couldn't come."

"Well. I . . . Well. I never—" More guests were arriving, cramming the drawing room. Her plump cheeks quivering with indignation, she turned to the nearest new arrival. "Have you heard, Mr. West, that Mr. Hamilton isn't coming?"

Benjamin West! The president of the Royal Academy! Corinna found herself speechless with terror, which was not a good thing, considering the man looked mightily confused.

"I'm sorry to hear that, madam, but it's hardly a surprise, considering he's currently in Wales."

"When did he leave for Wales?"

"Last month, I do believe."

"Last month? I think not." Lady A looked even more confused than he did. "Lady Rachael," she called, motioning her over. "Did we not see Mr. Hamilton last Saturday at the Billingsgate ball?"

"Why—"

"No," Corinna cut in, sending her cousin a pitiful, pleading look. Although Rachael didn't know the truth, surely she'd respond to such obvious silent begging. "That was *Sean* Hamilton, remember? Sean, not John." Before Rachael could disagree or Lady A could protest further, Corinna clutched Mr. West's arm and began pulling him toward her painting of Lord Lincolnshire.

Though she was no shrinking violet, she surprised herself with that kind of boldness. But she didn't see where she had much of a choice. She had to get Mr. West out of there before—as irreverent Rachael would put it—all hell broke loose.

"Will you have a look at my newest painting, Mr. West?" she asked, coming to a stop before it. "As I'm considering submitting it to the Summer Exhibition, I'd surely appreciate your thoughts."

Before commenting, he studied the picture quite a while. Corinna studied him. He was balding, what was left of his hair was gray, and he looked rather dour overall. But not really unfriendly, she decided with some relief.

Mr. West was famous for his paintings of recent battles that depicted their heroes wearing modern dress rather than traditional, classical garb. Since Corinna thought it rather silly to paint contemporary men sporting flowing Roman robes, she heartily approved—and she hoped his willingness to take the less traveled road meant he was more open-minded than most.

"It's very nice, Lady . . . Corinna, is it?" he finally said in his disarming American accent. "Your basic techniques demonstrate fine skills. But I'm not certain your model's form looks quite realistic."

"His form?"

"His body, under his clothing. Not quite natural, I'm afraid."

Her heart turned to lead in her chest. She'd done her best, considering the Academy refused women access to anatomy lessons. Maybe she should point that out to him. As the Academy's president, maybe he would see how unfair that was, how detrimental to a lady's chances, and decide to change the Academy's rules.

No, that would never happen. And he might consider such a request to be very bad form. She'd never get elected to the Academy if its president thought she was vulgar.

On the other hand, maybe he was wrong. Maybe Lord Lincolnshire's form looked perfectly fine. West was known for painting all of his subjects with large almond-shaped eyes, so maybe he wasn't one to judge. Although his portrait clients thought those eyes most dashing—and doubtless commissioned him for that reason—it wasn't accurate, after all. Some of them had narrow, squinty eyes, or small round ones.

"Thank you very much for your opinion," she told him as sweetly as she could. "I surely appreciate it, and I shall take your thoughts under consideration."

Suppressing a sigh, she returned to Rachael after he took leave. "Well, *that* didn't go well."

Rachael's sisters came to join them. "Who was he?" Claire asked.

"Benjamin West, the president of the Royal Academy. He said Lord Lincolnshire's body doesn't look natural beneath his clothing."

Elizabeth glanced over toward the painting and shrugged. "Looks fine to me. Rather impressive, in fact."

"He did say my techniques demonstrate fine skills. And maybe he's wrong about the other, but that doesn't really matter, does it? Either way he won't vote for my painting unless I change it."

"His is just one opinion." Rachael touched her arm. "There are other committee members, are there not? How many in total?"

"Nine. The president plus eight elected Academicians."

"So you have eight more men to influence. Seven if you count Mr. Hamilton as being on your side. And he should be, considering you've become friends with him."

"I'm not sure *friends* is an accurate description of our relationship." But although Rachael didn't know the truth, in a sense she was right. The real Mr. Hamilton *should* be on Corinna's side, considering how hard she'd been working to keep his uncle happy. And he believed each work should stand on its own and not be judged by the gender of its creator. "However, I think he probably will vote for me," she decided.

"So you've already balanced Mr. West's negative opinion with a positive." Rachael smiled; then her brows drew together in a frown. "Why did you claim you didn't see Mr. Hamilton at the Billingsgate ball on Saturday? That he was Sean Hamilton, not John? I've heard you *call* him Sean, and Lord Lincolnshire calls him that as well, but it's just a nickname, after all."

"Mr. West seems to think Mr. Hamilton is in Wales

for some reason. I didn't want to argue with the president of the Royal Academy. Better to go along with what he said, I was thinking."

Rachael exchanged puzzled glances with her sisters. "I don't know about that."

Corinna gave what she hoped was a casual shrug, then smiled at Lady A, who was approaching with another man in tow.

"I cannot understand why everyone thinks Mr. Hamilton is in Wales," the older woman muttered darkly. And then more graciously as she drew near, "Mr. Mulready, I'd be pleased for you to meet Lady Corinna Chase. Corinna, William Mulready."

Mr. Mulready looked *much* younger than Mr. West, probably not a decade older than Corinna herself. "A pleasure to meet you, my dear," he said in an accent that reminded her of Sean.

That thought made her smile. "Oh, Mr. Mulready, your painting in last year's Summer Exhibition was my absolute favorite!"

She wasn't making that up; the enthusiasm in her voice was genuine. And judging from the man's expression, he rather liked hearing it. "Which one, my dear?" he asked.

Academicians were allowed to display six paintings each—works that were hung without question, without being judged by the committee. "*The Fight Interrupted.* I adore the seventeenth-century Dutch masters, and it reminded me of their work. An updated version, if you will."

"I too admire the Dutch masters," he said, sounding like he also admired her for admiring them. "Their work inspired *The Fight Interrupted.*"

Encouraged by how much better this was going than her last conversation, Corinna started inching Mr. Mulready toward her painting of Lord Lincolnshire. "I also much admire your wife's landscapes, Mr. Mulready."

"Elizabeth does lovely work."

"Since you married a female artist, may I assume you don't disapprove of us?"

He laughed, apparently enjoying the saucy question. "A valid assumption. I've had a look at your paintings, my dear. Your own landscapes are quite remarkable."

Oh, this was going *astoundingly* better. "Here is my latest portrait. What do you think?"

"Lord Lincolnshire, is it not?" Cocking his head, he perused the picture. "I think, Lady Corinna, that you've truly captured the essence of the man."

Corinna couldn't help but grin. She couldn't think of a more wonderful compliment than hearing she'd *captured the essence*. That was exactly what she tried to accomplish, not only with this portrait but with all of her paintings.

And the score was now two to one. Mulready and Hamilton on her side, and only Benjamin West on the other. Clearly her chances were good.

She *loved* William Mulready.

Until she heard the next words out of his mouth. "But he seems a wee bit . . . stiff."

"Stiff?"

"Yes, stiff. I've had the pleasure of meeting Lord Lincolnshire—quite the art collector, isn't he?—and he struck me as a relaxed sort of fellow. It's something about this fellow's frame beneath his clothing that looks stiff, I think. . . ." Smiling, he patted her on the shoulder. "Not to fret, Lady Corinna. Your landscapes are brilliant. I'm sure the committee will be more than pleased to choose one of them."

She didn't want them to choose a landscape. She was no longer sure she even wanted to submit any. She was going to have to fix Lord Lincolnshire's portrait.

"How is it going?" Alexandra came and asked when Mr. Mulready had walked away.

"He likes my landscapes."

"Well, that's good, isn't it?"

"He's not nearly as impressed with my portrait. He

thinks Lord Lincolnshire looks unnatural beneath his clothes. And Benjamin West said the same thing."

"Oh, my. I think you need a rout cake."

Alexandra fetched one from the platter and handed it over. Corinna bit into it morosely, thinking she could use their luck.

No matter that she disbelieved such nonsense.

"How many works will be chosen?" Alexandra asked.

"There were almost a thousand in last summer's Exhibition."

"Well, then, I should think your chances will be good."

"But there were more than *eight* thousand submitted. And there are eighty Academicians who get to show six pieces each, which leaves only five hundred twenty for the rest of us."

"*Only* five hundred twenty," Juliana said with a laugh as she joined them. "I should think there'd be room for one of yours in all of that. And I cannot believe you did that calculation that fast."

Juliana never had been very quick with numbers, but that was beside the point. "I've done that calculation a hundred times," Corinna admitted. "At the very least."

"How are the pieces chosen?" Juliana asked.

Corinna was about to confess ignorance when a man stepped up and gave a little bow. "I'd be pleased to explain to such fine ladies." Although he wasn't as handsome as Sean, he, too, had a similar lilting accent. She'd had no idea so many Academicians were Irish. "Martin Archer Shee, at your service," he added.

Martin Archer Shee had studied with the late, great Sir Joshua Reynolds. Corinna was awed that such a man would bother to introduce himself, let alone take time to explain a mysterious procedure. "I'd adore hearing all about it."

" 'Tis a simple process, if a wee bit tedious. The works are marched past the Committee by a chain of human art handlers. The first round cuts the mass of submissions to about two thousand, and the next round is much more rigorous. From the Academy's earliest days, two metal wands have been used to stamp labels attached to each painting. One wand is surmounted by a letter D, the other by a more ominous X. A work that receives the vote of three or more Academicians is awarded a D for 'Doubtful' and passes to the next round of selection. Works that get an X are eliminated. The rounds are repeated until the paintings that remain are reduced to a reasonable number. Beef tea is served to keep the Academicians' spirits up during the ordeal." His eyes twinkled. "Which isn't really very much of one, in reality. Hanging the exhibition is a much more arduous affair."

"That takes days," Corinna told her sisters. "More than a week."

"With much politics involved regarding whose picture goes where. All done in a veil of secrecy, to protect the Hanging Committee from being hanged ourselves."

Mr. Shee smiled at his own joke; a quite engaging grin, Corinna thought. "Thank you kindly for the explanation."

"I'm much impressed by your work, Lady Corinna. Your textures are quite admirable. I wish you the best of luck in the selection process," he added before taking his leave.

Corinna turned to her sisters. "He likes my work," she breathed. Maybe her chances weren't so dire, after all. "Martin Archer Shee likes my work. And he studied with none other than Reynolds."

"Ah, but *I* wrote *Life of Reynolds*," another man said, rivalry evident in his tone.

He stepped up to take Shee's place. Though she'd never seen him before in her life, Corinna knew who he was immediately. "James Northcote, I'm honored to meet you. I read your book four years ago, when it first came out, and I found your recollections of your old master to be quite enlightening."

"He was an enlightening man," Northcote said. "And a discerning one. He'd have been impressed, as I am, with your portrait of Lord Lincolnshire. The man's suit looks like real velvet, his lace truly handmade, the trees in the background wet and glistening. An admirable endeavor, Lady Corinna. Not perfect, of course. The underlying anatomy seems a mite off, and—"

"I'm so pleased you think well of it," Corinna interrupted before she was forced to hear that complaint again. "I realize it's not usual for a female to paint portraits."

"Half the things that people do not succeed in are through fear of making an attempt," he told her solemnly. "You've an excellent start. I wish you well in proceeding with your portrait career."

"I think you have a good chance," Juliana said as he walked away. "He sounded very impressed with your realism."

Corinna smiled at her sister's use of one of the newest terms in art. But then she sighed. "He didn't think the underlying anatomy looked very real."

"He said you have an excellent start."

"Exactly. One doesn't submit a painting that looks like a *start*, does one? Clearly he was implying I need more practice."

She mentally counted her votes. Against: Benjamin West and James Northcote. For: John Hamilton and Martin Archer Shee. William Mulready would vote for a landscape but not for a portrait.

She wanted to submit a portrait.

Well, maybe Mr. Mulready or Mr. Northcote would vote for her portrait if she fixed it. And there were still four other committee members. With either Mulready or Northcote on her side, she needed only two of them to swing the vote.

"How are things going?" Lady A asked, joining their little circle.

"All right," Corinna said. "Mr. West was lukewarm,

but Mr. Shee said he was impressed by my work, and so did James Northcote." She wouldn't mention that Mr. Northcote had also said she needed improvement in portraying anatomy.

"Mr. Hamilton will certainly vote for you, although I'm still miffed with him for not attending. He could have influenced the others positively. What did William Mulready have to say, my dear?"

"He loves my landscapes, but he's not as enthusiastic about the portrait."

"Well, that doesn't signify, now, does it? My daughter painted wonderful landscapes. You should be happy enough to get a landscape into the Summer Exhibition."

Corinna wasn't certain that would make her quite happy, but she didn't say so. She didn't want to sound ungrateful. She was thankful to Lady A for giving her the opportunity to meet all the committee members, even if things weren't working out the best.

Besides, things weren't looking all that dire, either. She needed only two more artists to love her work, and she had four more chances to find them.

"I spoke with William Beechey," Lady A added. "I'm sorry to tell you, my dear, that it doesn't seem he approves of females painting portraits."

Corinna couldn't say she was surprised. Disappointed, but not surprised. A portrait painter himself, Mr. Beechey had painted the royal family and nearly all the most famous and fashionable people. A steady stream of very sober portraits. Obviously he took life seriously and wouldn't be wanting competition from anyone, let alone from female artists. "Well, then, I don't need to meet him. There are still three committee members I've yet to speak with."

Lady Balmforth threaded her way to them. "I talked to William Owen," she reported. He was principal portrait painter to the Prince Regent.

"And?" her sister asked.

Lady B just shook her head. Mournfully.

Another artist to cross off Corinna's list. Now there were just two left . . . and her stomach felt as though rocks were collecting inside it.

"How about Henry Fuseli?" she asked. "Or John James Chalon? Have either of you talked to either of them?"

"Our sister has one of Mr. Fuseli's pictures in her bedroom," Lady B said. "Let's ask her if she'll introduce you."

Lady A nodded. "That would be good. I'll find Mr. Chalon in the meanwhile."

As Lady B took her to find Lady C, Corinna wondered what sort of picture the woman had in her bedroom. That she had one at all was rather intriguing. Mr. Fuseli painted weird, often sensual scenes, fantasies that were daringly inventive. His most acclaimed painting, *The Nightmare*, was an unforgettable image of a woman in the throes of a violently erotic dream.

She was a bit nervous to meet Mr. Fuseli. He seemed attracted to the supernatural, and he was bound to hold strong opinions. She almost hoped Lady Cavanaugh would be too hard to find.

But she wasn't, of course. The house simply wasn't large enough to get lost in it. Lady B found her sister very easily, and Lady C was positively pleased to provide the introduction.

Mr. Fuseli had masses of curly white hair and a face that looked oddly like a lion's. He'd already examined Corinna's artwork on the walls.

"Your paintings are very well-done," he told her in a booming voice. "Very accurate, Lady Corinna."

"Thank you, Mr. Fuseli. I admire your paintings, too. I'm inspired by your inventiveness. I find your work fascinating. Very visionary."

"I do believe that a certain amount of exaggeration improves a picture."

Was that a criticism? He'd described her work as *well-done* and *very accurate*. She always did her best to portray the truth or, as William Mulready had put it, to *capture the essence*. There was nothing exaggerated in her pictures at all.

"Our ideas are the offspring of our senses," he continued.

What was *that* supposed to mean?

"It was lovely speaking with you, Lady Corinna," he concluded. "I wish you the best of luck."

That was it? He was done? She hadn't the barest idea what he'd been talking about, or whether he'd liked her pictures.

Her sisters appeared as if by magic—or perhaps as if they'd sprung from one of his strange paintings. "What did he say?" Juliana asked.

"I don't know, exactly. He didn't quite make sense. But he did wish me the best of luck."

"Then he goes in the 'for' column," Juliana said firmly, being the type to always look on the bright side.

Corinna wished she were half so certain. But maybe Mr. Fuseli did like her paintings. And there was still John James Chalon.

The crowd seemed to be thinning out. Spotting Lady A, who was looking rather flustered, Corinna made her way over to see her.

Her sisters followed in her wake.

"Did you talk to Mr. Chalon? Did he say he was willing to meet me?"

"I couldn't find him," Lady A said. "It seems he's left."

"Oh, no. He was the last committee member." Her final opportunity to convince herself she still had a chance. "Now I won't know if he liked my portrait."

"It's all right, dear." The sweet lady smiled. "Everyone loved your landscapes. This all went brilliantly, don't you think?"

Corinna nodded. It was all she could manage. Her only other options were to scream or to cry.

"Have another rout cake," Alexandra said.

Chapter Twenty-nine

The earl's health was failing fast.

Lord Lincolnshire hadn't left his bedroom in two days . . . two days during which he wanted his nephew nearby. Stuck in the house for hour upon hour, Sean was at his wit's end. He had so much to accomplish, so much that wasn't getting done.

And he missed Corinna.

For a solid week she'd spent long days painting in the salon. Morning to evening, she'd been there. Though he hadn't been there much himself, he'd liked seeing her portrait every night, checking her progress. He'd liked thinking that if he wanted to see her, he knew exactly where to find her.

She'd been a fixture. A comfort. A temptation.

But since she'd finished the portrait, all her time had been spent with her aunt or Lady Avonleigh. Now that he was here, she was gone. He didn't know when he might see her next, and the house felt empty.

Fearing the situation would drag on, yesterday Sean had asked Higginbotham to have his art supplies fetched from the studio on Piccadilly Street. Thinking it was what Hamilton would do himself, he'd set everything up in the drawing room that had Hamilton's pictures all over the walls. Then he'd summoned his secretary, Mr. Sykes.

Sykes had been in Sean's employ for almost eight

years. He was a short, dark man with round gold spectacles, a quick, precise mind, and an encyclopedic knowledge of Sean's many and varied enterprises. During the hours the earl slept—which, fortunately, were many—the two of them worked quietly behind closed doors in the drawing room. The staff had been told that Sykes was Sean's "assistant," there to mix paint for him and such. In reality, they were allocating positions for all of Lincolnshire's many servants.

Sean was thankful that was now done. He'd begun notifying each member of the staff of his final decisions. Were it not for the sadness of Lincolnshire's impending demise, he suspected some of them might be singing as they worked. They were obviously looking forward to what lay ahead. And very relieved overall.

But Sean was not.

In deference to Lincolnshire's wishes, he was neglecting his own concerns. In defiance of Hamilton's plans, he'd been introduced as the man in public. And other than the last few days—and despite knowing what was best—he was kissing Corinna too often and growing much more attached to her than was prudent.

Nothing was working out the way it was supposed to. And lately he'd found himself wondering if maybe he could stay with her. Marry her. He kept thinking about how her brother reportedly thought him a fine man, and attaching way too much significance to that.

This had to stop.

When she showed up unexpectedly Thursday morning, he was entirely too happy to see her.

"How is he?" she asked quietly, poking her head into the earl's room.

"The same." Sean waved her to the chair next to him beside the towering bed, where the earl slumbered almost upright against a dozen pillows. "Sleeping as comfortably as I expect we can hope." It seemed the only way the man could sleep these days, the only way he could breathe.

"You look upset."

"It's not pleasant," he said with a shrug, "but it cannot last much longer." He looked closer at her, noticing her tense jaw, a certain wildness in her eyes. Or maybe panic. "You look upset, too."

She lowered herself to the chair and sighed. "Lady Avonleigh's reception did not go well."

"Didn't it?"

"She kept asking why you weren't there," she said, keeping her voice low. "Or rather, why Mr. Hamilton wasn't there." She winced and flicked a wary glance at Lincolnshire, apparently worried he might have overheard. "Sorry."

"He's asleep. Though we should be careful."

She nodded. "The committee members were mystified, since they believe Mr. Hamilton to be in Wales. Lady A and her sisters and my cousins and others all kept saying he'd been seen at various social events, and the artists kept saying that was impossible. . . . It was a mess, Sean."

" 'Tis sorry I am about that." Not that there was anything he could have done. "How about the rest? Did the committee members like your new painting?"

She sighed again. "For the most part, they didn't seem enthralled with my portrait of Lord Lincolnshire."

"Why not?" He was outraged. These artists were obviously idiots. Temperamental idiots, one and all—with the exception of Corinna, of course. "It's brilliant."

"It isn't." When he might have protested further, she laid a hand on his arm. "They liked Lord Lincolnshire's expression well enough. One said I captured the essence of the man." A hint of a smile transformed her face; she'd obviously liked hearing that. "And they admired the textures overall. They thought his suit looked like real velvet, his lace truly handmade, the trees wet and glistening."

"But . . . ?" All of that sounded grand. There had to be a *but.*

"But they claimed Lord Lincolnshire's form doesn't seem real beneath his clothes. He looks stiff and unnatural."

"Did they?" Sean hadn't looked for such a thing. Hadn't known to look for such a thing. He'd been impressed with the way she'd rendered Lincolnshire's face, and aye, his clothes and the background. Even colorblind, he could see that. But he'd paid no attention whatsoever to the man's body.

Well, another man wouldn't, would he? Unless he were an artist.

Hurting for her, he tried to point out the positive. "It doesn't sound all that bad. They had lots of good things to say."

"One of them really loved my work—"

"One?"

"Yes, one. Or rather, only one had no reservations about it. Martin Archer Shee, that was."

"How about the rest?"

"Benjamin West liked my basic technique but didn't have anything else good to say. William Mulready and James Northcote both think I paint excellent landscapes, but they weren't so enthusiastic about my portrait."

He didn't know any of those names, but this was not the time to tell her. "That's four out of how many?"

"Eight, not counting Mr. Hamilton. Two were hopeless. William Owen and William Beechey. They simply don't approve of women painting portraits. I have no idea what the last two thought. I found Henry Fuseli's comments completely indecipherable, and John James Chalon left before I could hear his opinion."

"They might approve, then, the both of them."

"They might. But they might not. Or they might, like some of the others, like my landscapes but not my portrait."

"You can submit landscapes, then, can you not? Or landscapes along with your portrait? How many paintings are you allowed to turn in?"

"Three. Non-Academicians are allowed to submit three. . . ." She trailed off with yet another sigh.

She looked tortured, which made his heart seem to squeeze in his chest. He wanted to gather her into his arms, but he couldn't do that in Lincolnshire's bedroom. He fisted his hands to keep from reaching for her. "What is it, *cuisle mo chroí*?"

For a moment, she looked puzzled instead of distressed. "Cooshla-macree? Whatever does that mean?"

"Nothing," he said quickly. "It just slipped out. The language of my childhood . . . sometimes it just slides off my tongue."

He shouldn't be calling her that. Not as a slip of the tongue or anything else.

The tortured look was in her eyes again. "What is it?" he repeated, without the Gaelic this time. "What has you so troubled?"

"I don't know how to explain it," she said slowly, her gaze focused on the canopy above the earl's bed. "I don't quite understand it myself. As the reception wore on, it became more and more obvious that one of my landscapes would surely be accepted. Which has been my goal all these years, hasn't it? Yet it seemed the more they said they liked my landscapes, the more I wanted to submit a portrait. Only a portrait." She lowered her gaze, finally meeting his eyes. "I want to be known as a portrait painter, Sean. I think I'm going to try to fix Lord Lincolnshire's portrait."

"Can you do that?"

"I hope so. I think so. I have four days before the submission is due. I painted him into the scene in a week, so I should be able to fix him in a shorter time."

"That sounds hopeful." It made sense. But she still didn't look very sure of herself. "Well then, is there another problem?"

"There is." The two wee words sounded so despondent. "Even should I fix it, two of the committee members will refuse to vote for it just on the grounds that I'm a woman. And I cannot count on all six of the other members, either. If it's better—if it's brilliant—I imagine some of them may come around. But others may not. I'm counting on Mr. Hamilton to be the deciding vote, but that will work only if three others besides Mr. Shee vote for me, too. So I was wondering . . ."

"Wondering what?"

"When he gets here, before the vote, do you think you could ask him to talk to the committee?" she whispered in a rush. "I don't want my painting selected if it doesn't merit the honor, but if he could just ask them to seriously reconsider it even though they've seen it before, to give the revised version a fair look even though I haven't yet made a name for myself. Do you expect he might be willing to talk to them, as a favor? After all, you and I have done *him* a big favor by appeasing his uncle."

Sean couldn't believe she'd said that aloud in the earl's bedroom, even in a whisper. He slanted a nervous glance toward Lord Lincolnshire, but the man was snoring peacefully. Or at least as peacefully as a dying man could.

Their secret was still safe.

That knowledge did not, however, allow him to rest easy.

He was not at all sure Hamilton would vote for Corinna's portrait, let alone encourage others to do so. *I seriously doubt I will vote for that female's painting,* he remembered Hamilton saying. *I'm certain her paintings will not be good, because she's never studied anatomy. Sketching statues is not going to help her learn anything.*

"I'm not sure," he said apologetically. "Hamilton is not known for being cooperative."

"But we saved his inheritance."

Darting another glance toward Lord Lincolnshire, he rose. "Let's have our chat somewhere else, shall we?"

"We cannot leave him alone."

"I told Mrs. Skeffington to rest her bones a spell, but I'm sure she wouldn't mind returning."

Indeed, Mrs. Skeffington was coming down the corridor when Sean peeked out. He thanked his lucky stars she'd not returned a minute earlier and overheard Corinna. After seeing the nurse settled by Lincolnshire's side, he guided Corinna downstairs and into the salon.

He closed the door behind them both. Took a seat on a blue and gold sofa. Smoothed his palms against his thighs.

Cleared his throat.

Corinna settled beside him, closer than he would have liked. Well, he liked it, but he needed to keep a clear head for this conversation.

"I'm sorry I said that out loud," she apologized. "I wasn't thinking."

"No harm done." He drew and released a breath. "I have an idea."

"For what?"

"For helping you fix the portrait of Lincolnshire."

"Helping me? How can you possibly help with that? I only want you to have a talk with Mr. Hamilton."

"You've a need to learn anatomy, haven't you? Since you're wanting to make him look more natural?"

She looked perplexed. "That's why I sketched all those Elgin Marbles."

"But that wasn't good enough, was it?"

He couldn't believe what he was about to say. He'd spent the last two days thinking about how they were getting too close, and this would make it even harder to keep any sort of distance. But he saw no other way to make certain Hamilton would admire her portrait. No other way to repay her for all the assistance she'd so generously given him.

There was nothing for it. He drew one more deep

breath and took the plunge. "I'm thinking I can pose for you."

"What?"

"I can pose for you. If you practice painting me, that might help you fix the portrait in time."

Chapter Thirty

Holy Hannah. Corinna had to forcibly close her mouth.

"You want to pose for me?" she asked when she'd more or less gathered her wits. "So I can learn anatomy?"

His gaze caught hers and held it, looking rather apprehensive. "I said so, aye."

Aye. Sean never said *aye*. "You do realize . . ."

He looked no less wary, but a corner of his mouth turned up in a half smile. "That I shall have to take off my clothes?"

She glanced away, scandalized. But she recognized a good opportunity when she was offered one. She needed to fix Lord Lincolnshire's portrait, make his body look more realistic, and sketching marble gods had quite clearly left her unprepared for the task.

She would never have asked Sean to pose for her. Never. The idea would never have occurred to her, even after a hundred more kisses.

But now that he'd brought it up . . . well, how could she possibly refuse?

It was scandalous, but it could be her one and only chance to truly study male anatomy. And it was certainly her only chance before this year's Summer Exhibition. While it would be no more than a session or two, perhaps a live model would make the difference. She might be able to master figure drawing once and for all.

Though she was staring through the large windows that overlooked the garden, she wasn't seeing trees and flowers and blue sky. Instead she was picturing the sofa where Lincolnshire had sat for her . . . with Sean on it instead.

Naked as the day he was born.

She swallowed hard. Her heart thumped unevenly. Warmth flooded her cheeks.

Biting her lip, she met his gaze again. "You won't have to take off *all* of your clothes."

"Will I not?" He raised a brow. "Lord Lincolnshire's portrait isn't just head and shoulders, as I recall. His body wouldn't look 'stiff and unnatural' had it not been shown, would it?"

"But there's no need to sketch all of you at once. I can do parts."

"Parts?" The corners of his eyes crinkled with amusement.

"A part at a time. You can undress just a little bit."

"If you say so." He looked unconvinced. But perhaps he also looked relieved. "Where shall we do it?"

"Not here. And not in my brother's drawing room." *God forbid.*

"In the square, then? Where the painting is set?" Reacting to her shock, he released a laugh. But it sounded a little bit shaky. "I was jesting, *mo chroí.* We can use Hamilton's studio."

Macree again . . . what did that mean? "That sounds good. When shall we meet?"

"Time is of the essence, is it not?"

"I've four days to fix the painting. I'd best not sketch more than two."

"We shan't delay, then. I shall meet you there in an hour."

"So soon?" Time might be of the essence, but she wasn't at all sure she was ready for this. "Can you leave Lord Lincolnshire? I thought he wanted you to stay here."

"Saints preserve us. Lincolnshire *does* want me here. But we surely cannot wait for the poor man to die."

Oh, that was so irreverent.

And so true. "Sean . . ."

"Let's make it in the evening, then. Lincolnshire's been falling asleep early these days, and if he doesn't, I'll come up with some excuse."

"What excuse can I give Griffin to leave the house alone in the evening?" She preferred, of course, to be honest with her brother, but she could hardly tell him she was going to sketch a nude man.

Her cheeks burned at the mere thought.

"Tell him Lincolnshire's invited you for dinner. I'll come for you, and we'll walk to the studio together." Sean grabbed her by the shoulders and pressed a kiss to her lips. Quick and hot. Her senses were spinning when he pulled back. "It'll be fine, Corinna. Don't worry yourself. This plan is going to work."

Chapter Thirty-one

Her grandfather was here somewhere.

Nervously smoothing the lavender dress she'd chosen to wear—after trying and rejecting six others—Rachael stared down the length of the Royal Hospital's great hall. The black-and-white marble floor seemed to stretch forever. "Which one is Colonel Thomas Grimstead?" she asked the guard at the door.

It was early evening—dinnertime, to be precise. Sixteen long tables crowded the hall, each seating twenty-six pensioners. Every man wore the same outfit: a scarlet coat and tricorn hat based on the service uniform of the Duke of Marlborough's time. They were all sixty-five or older, and they all, to Rachael's eye, looked alike.

Maybe none of them was her grandfather. Maybe Griffin had been wrong.

"I'll show you to Grimstead, milady," the guard said. Griffin offered his arm, and she clutched it tightly as they followed him. Cutlery clinked, and the hall rang with the deep voices of so many men. Chandeliers overhead seemed too few to light the towering chamber, but the last of the day's sunshine streamed through many tall, arched windows.

The guard stopped at one end of a table covered with white cloth. "Colonel Grimstead?" A gray-haired man glanced up—a man who looked eerily familiar.

Griffin hadn't been wrong.

"This fine lady and gentleman are here to see you," the guard told him, and walked off.

The man blinked and rose, standing at attention, his narrow chest puffed out in the smart red coat. He was medium height, with a long nose on a long, pleasant face. He had Rachael's dented chin and, beneath the black tricorn, Rachael's sky blue eyes.

But they were blank.

"Who are you?" he asked, not rudely but not in a welcoming tone, either.

Griffin took Rachael's hand. "I'm the Marquess of Cainewood, and this is my cousin, Lady Rachael Chase. Your son's daughter."

"Hmmph." He reclaimed his seat and picked up his fork, silently dismissing them. "My son has no daughter."

Would he send her away without even listening? Rachael looked to Griffin and back to the man. Her grandfather. "Sir." She swallowed hard. "I know this must come as a shock, since your son—my father—is dead, but—"

"Thomas is not dead." He lifted a tankard and took a swallow of beer.

"Sir." Rachael felt tears sting her eyes and cursed herself. It would have been nice to be welcomed with open arms, but if that wasn't to be, she at least wanted some answers. "I know your son did something shameful, but I just want to ask you—"

"My son has done nothing wrong." The words weren't said angrily but rather matter-of-factly, his blue gaze unfocused on his dinner. "Thomas will be an important man someday; just you wait and see. He'll be marrying John Cartwright's daughter, he will. *Lord* John Cartwright's daughter. Course, the gel ain't yet born, so I cannot be telling you her name." He glanced back up, cocking his head in apparent confusion. "Who are you?"

Flustered, Rachael freed her hand from Griffin's so she could dig in the beaded reticule that matched her lavender dress. "I'm your granddaughter." She pulled out her father's badge and held it out toward the man. "See, this is your son's badge."

"My son has no badge," he said flatly. "Where would he get such a thing? The lad is not even a year old."

The man across from him, an aging fellow with big ears and a hooked nose, reached to take the badge and examined it with a low whistle. "Tenth Hussars. Old Grimstead's son must have done well for himself." He handed it back. "He don't mean to be uncivil, milady," he said sympathetically. "Colonel Grimstead, he's not quite here, if ye catch my drift. Thinks it's 1760. If you stay long enough, he'll start nattering on about how he just saved some fellow's life and the bloke promised his firstborn daughter to his infant son."

"John Cartwright," Grimstead confirmed with a nod. "A bloomin' a-ris-to-crat." He drew the word out into four distinct syllables and ended it with a chortle. "My name will be connected to nobility."

Rachael dropped the badge back into her reticule. "Dear heavens." She stared down the hall toward an old, faded mural of King Charles II on a horse with the Royal Hospital in the background. He'd commissioned these buildings, she suddenly remembered—a disjointed thought that came out of nowhere—but never lived to see them finished.

Like her father hadn't lived to see her.

Disappointment was a physical ache, a knot in her middle. She looked back to her grandfather and tried again. "Sir—"

"Yes?" He looked up, appearing startled to find her there, blinking at her through eyes just like her own. "Who are you?" he asked.

"Our thanks for your time, sir." Griffin curved an arm around her shoulders. "Let's go," he murmured under his breath. "Staying here will accomplish nothing."

She nodded and allowed him to draw her back toward the door. The huge room felt suddenly close and stifling, making her grateful to step out into the cool evening air. In the center of the deserted courtyard, a grand, bronze statue of King Charles thrust toward the sky, and she sat on its marble base, smoothing her dress over her knees and hugging them.

"He's gone," she said. "He's there, but he's *gone.*"

"I'm sorry." Griffin stood gazing down at her, looking as solid as the old brick building behind him. "I should have come to see him myself before bringing you."

"No. I'd have wanted to see him, anyway. Just to convince myself he was my grandfather."

"He has your eyes."

"And my chin. We're related; I've no doubt of that at all." She hugged her knees tighter. "But he'll never be able to tell me what happened to my father."

"No, he won't." Griffin lowered his rangy frame to sit beside her. "He thinks your father is still a child."

A lone hawk circled overhead, looking as solitary as Rachael felt. "I'll never really know who I am."

"Ah, Rachael." He shifted closer, wrapping an arm about her to pull her against him. "What your father did, however heinous, has nothing to do with who you are."

She dropped her head to his shoulder, taking comfort from his nearness, breathing in his warm male scent. "I know. I just wanted to *know*. I assure you, I wouldn't have fallen apart had I learned the truth."

"I never thought you would. You're strong, Rachael."

"You think so?"

"I know so."

There was conviction in his voice, and admiration, and something else she couldn't identify, but it helped the knot in her middle loosen a little. It helped to have Griffin here. She'd always considered him an unreliable scapegrace, yet he'd been by her side all through this. Which seemed to lend her the strength she'd been missing. The strength he believed she had.

It was amazing what a difference it made to have someone believe in her.

Chapter Thirty-two

"How shall we work this?" Setting his large case full of art supplies on the table, Sean glanced around the sparsely furnished garret studio. "Will you sit on the sofa?"

"Lord Lincolnshire sat on a sofa for the portrait," Corinna pointed out, "so I think you should pose there. Did he fall asleep?"

"He didn't. I think he might be getting better." Sean wasn't sure whether he was happy about that or not. Much as he liked the man, this couldn't continue forever, could it?

"Then how did you manage to leave him? What excuse did you give him?"

"I told him my painting wasn't going well at Lincolnshire House, that I needed to work here instead. That's why I brought along these supplies. I'd have looked a liar otherwise."

He'd brought candles, too, knowing it would grow dark as the evening wore on. He pulled them out of the case and set them up around the room and began lighting them.

"Lord Lincolnshire didn't mind, then?"

"I sent for Deirdre to keep him company."

Though his sister was nominally living at Lincolnshire House, she spent most of her waking hours at Daniel Raleigh's place of business—or his home, where she planned to live with or without a divorce. Sean was less than thrilled with that, but he didn't want to fight with his sister. He'd told the earl his wife was very fond of shopping.

Yet another lie, he thought with a sigh. "She wasn't happy, but she agreed."

"She should. You're putting yourself out to secure her future."

If only Deirdre saw it that way. "Lincolnshire likes her," he said dryly. "Thinks I chose a fine wife."

"That's good," she said distractedly. "I like to paint standing, but I usually sit when I sketch." She moved his case to the floor. "This table will do fine."

He lit the last candle. "I'll get you a chair."

"From where?"

"From one of my tenants." At her blank look, he smiled. "I own this building, Corinna. And half the others on this street."

"Oh." Now she looked stunned. "I thought you said the studio was Mr. Hamilton's. I guess you didn't mean literally."

"Hamilton said he plans to lease it when he returns. I intend to charge him a small fortune. I'll be right back."

It took but a few minutes to run downstairs and borrow a chair from one of the shopkeepers on the ground floor. He returned to find Corinna with her sketchbook open, chewing on her bottom lip. She'd worried it pink and plump with her teeth.

At least, he assumed it was pink. It definitely looked darker than usual. And very enticing. He wanted to kiss away the marks, wanted that so badly he could already taste her. But if he kissed her now, he knew, this session would get way out of hand.

"Sit," he said instead, "while I undress." He set down the chair so it faced the sofa.

"Just a little bit," she reminded him as she lowered herself to it.

He sat across from her and pulled off his shoes and stockings. "Will this do?"

She stared at his bare feet, seeming rather riveted by them, to his amusement. "Lord Lincolnshire's feet aren't in the picture," she finally said. "Just a little more."

He rose and shrugged out of his tailcoat. "Will this do, then?"

She cracked a smile. "A little more."

He unbuttoned and took off his waistcoat.

"More."

He untied and drew off his cravat.

"A little more."

He saw her swallow as he removed his braces. He unfastened the top button on his shirt.

"Wait."

"Wait?" His fingers paused on the second button as he raised a brow. "You're going to draw this wee bit of my throat?"

A nervous laugh escaped. "Your hands. Lord Lincolnshire's hands are in the picture. I've decided to start with your hands."

"I'm thinking you've sketched hands before. Your sisters', perhaps?"

"Yes, of course. But I need a man's hands."

"Lincolnshire had two, I believe. Quite naked at the time he sat for you."

"Old hands. I painted him younger."

"Your brother's hands, then. Surely he's sat for you."

"Not without grumbling. And never long enough."

"I don't remember you mentioning that any of the artists criticized Lincolnshire's hands. I'm thinking you've probably mastered the painting of hands."

"It is notoriously difficult to paint hands," she said in clipped tones. "Will you just sit down and show me your hands?"

Evidently she was anxious, which was hardly surprising. This was rather unnerving for him as well. "All right," he said, sitting and placing his hands on his spread knees. "Will this do?"

"That will do fine." She blew out a breath. "Just relax."

"I might suggest you do the same."

"Yes. Of course. Right." She scooted her chair closer, put pencil to paper. "However did you come to own half this neighborhood?"

He didn't usually talk to people about his property, his businesses, his company. He'd learned over the years that it made others envious. They couldn't understand how a single man could have so much, and they certainly didn't believe he'd worked hard and earned it honestly. They figured he'd come by it through luck or fraud or chicanery—or all three.

He'd grown up tithing, and these days he gave quite a bit of money to charity—more money every year than most people ever saw in a whole lifetime. But people didn't seem to care about that. They wanted what he had for themselves, and they resented him for having it when they didn't. They thought he should simply agree to give them some of it. Or they plotted ways to steal some of it, or destroy some of it.

Mother Mary, he'd never been able to decide which was worst.

Quite a few people did know, of course. People in high places, people he often dealt with. People those people had told. It was inevitable, he supposed, and he accepted that, even though it sometimes made life difficult. But he operated on the general principle that anyone who didn't already know—and had no reason to know—would be better kept in the dark.

But Corinna . . . How could he justify keeping Corinna in the dark any longer? He'd been kissing her. She stirred his blood, and he'd become equally attracted to her intellect. He admired her. She seemed to fill a void in his life he hadn't known was there, and he'd been thinking of marrying her.

Though he remained far from convinced he actually could, the thought had surely crossed his mind. And she'd been asking for details for quite a while now. Not forcefully, but sweetly. Under the circumstances, it didn't feel right to keep dodging her questions.

"I have a knack," he finally said.

Her eyes were on her sketch, but a faint smile curved her lips. "Deirdre said you'd say that."

"When was that?"

"At the Billingsgate ball." She focused on his left hand, drew a few lines. "She told me you departed Ireland with nothing, and the next time she saw you, you owned several pieces of property."

"I didn't start with nothing," he corrected. "My uncle left me an inheritance."

"How much?"

"Ten thousand pounds."

She nodded, clearly unimpressed. Sean hadn't expected any different. Ten thousand might be a fortune to a vicar's son in Ireland, but to a marquess's daughter in Mayfair?

It was a pittance.

Such different people they were, from such different backgrounds. He might have money now and dress like a gentleman, but he'd never have met her were it not for Hamilton. He'd never have spoken to her. Never have danced with her or shared ices in Berkeley Square.

And they'd certainly never have kissed.

He shifted uneasily, thinking he shouldn't be doing this. *Knowing* he shouldn't be doing this. It was too tempting for them both, and he didn't know how he was going to take off any more of his clothes without her attacking him and him allowing it. Or, more likely, encouraging it.

She was only sketching his hands so far, he reminded himself. There was no need to panic yet.

"What happened after you received the inheritance?" she asked.

"I left my family, came to London, bought a small, run-down building. By myself I fixed it up, and then I sold it for a profit. That's when I discovered I have a knack."

"For buying and selling property?"

"For making money," he said with a grin.

He couldn't help himself. He rarely talked about this with anyone, and he was rather proud of himself, after all. The seventh deadly sin, his father would have reminded him had he been alive to see how far his son had come. But Sean would have laughed, because he believed a man was entitled to find satisfaction in a job well done.

As was a lady, he thought, watching her sketch. "I bought a larger building and did it again," he explained. "And again. Eventually I had enough funds to hire other people to fix up the buildings, so I could concentrate on finding and buying them faster, and after that, I realized it might be more profitable to keep some of the buildings—select ones, based on criteria—and make money leasing them out."

"Deirdre said you own more than buildings. Businesses. Manufactories. And ships, too, she told me."

His sister had a big mouth. No wonder Corinna had been so curious. "Well, now, one of the tenants I leased to had a business that was about to fail, and I realized I could fix that, too. So I bought it and made it profitable. And then I bought other businesses. And started some. Some of the businesses required supplies that came from outside the country, and I realized I could make more profit by importing such supplies myself. And importing supplies for other people. And exporting some of the things I was manufacturing, and some other things other people were manufacturing—" He cut himself off and shrugged. "I seem to have a knack for making money all sorts of ways."

She froze midsketch, stunned. And admiring. All the

men she knew were wealthy, of course, but their wealth came from owning land. Mostly from owning land for generations—the same land, for hundreds of years. None of them had started with nothing, or even ten thousand pounds, and built their wealth all by themselves.

No other men she knew had a knack for making money. Or a knack for much of anything else, come to think of it. Except maybe sitting a horse or tying a perfect cravat.

"How is it coming?" he asked.

"I beg your pardon?"

"The hands."

"Oh. They're . . . they're fine."

"You need to see more than hands, Corinna, if you're going to fix Lincolnshire's portrait."

She nodded, knowing he was right.

Apparently taking that as agreement, he rose and finished unbuttoning his shirt. In one single, fluid movement, he pulled it off over his head. Then he draped it over the arm of the sofa and . . . just stood there.

He was absolutely magnificent.

Better than the Elgin gods. Human, not marble, and very, *very* male. His chest rippled with muscles and ridges, and he looked warm and smooth and altogether enticing. It was all she could do to keep from reaching out to touch him.

She'd never seen another man without his shirt. Did they all look like this? Somehow, she thought not. All the gentlemen of her acquaintance led lives of leisure. It seemed fixing buildings had toned Sean's body in a way that made him different.

And much, much better.

His hands moved to the buttons on his trousers.

"No." She swallowed hard. "That's enough for now." She wouldn't be able to concentrate if presented with anything beyond that splendid torso. "You need a book."

"A book?"

"In the painting, Lord Lincolnshire is holding a book."

He reached for one of the sketchbooks Mr. Hamilton had left behind. Another fluid movement that made something flip-flop in her stomach.

"Will this do?"

"What? Oh, yes. Have a seat. Like Lord Lincolnshire did, if you'll remember."

He sat and held the book, looking nothing like Lord Lincolnshire, even though the pose was similar. She sketched a few lines. Shaky lines, since she couldn't seem to take her eyes off him. "I fear you don't really look like Lord Lincolnshire."

"Close enough, I imagine. You're painting him younger, are you not?"

"I thought the portrait would be more compelling that way. And please Lord Lincolnshire more as well. But I seriously doubt he ever looked like you. That he looked so . . ."

Hard and hot. Strong and overwhelming. Just looking at Sean robbed her of words. She was growing more confident, though. Her fingers flew across the page, capturing every detail while she had the chance.

She'd remember this evening always.

"So . . . what?" he asked.

"Hmm?"

He smiled and settled back. "How many sessions do you expect you'll need?"

A thousand. Maybe more. "I've time for only two," she said regretfully. "After that I'll really need to paint. I hope Mr. Hamilton won't return and expect to use this studio before then."

"Don't worry yourself about that." Disgust filled his voice. "I got another letter from him yesterday. He's staying longer. Claims he's seeing fairies in the falls or some such blarney," he added with a snort. "I know he's really lingering with his lover."

His lover. Corinna felt her skin heat just hearing those two words. Her eyes traced Sean's form, her pencil traced the lines on the paper, and she imagined him kissing her.

Her lips tingled.

She blew out a tense breath.

"Is something wrong?"

"I'm just concentrating."

Sean shifted, reclining a little to one side, raising an arm to lay it along the back edge of the sofa. He was looking more relaxed—and not at all like Lord Lincolnshire had posed. She considered asking him to move back, but she didn't want him to.

In the flickering candlelight, he looked absolutely delicious. So delicious she wanted a bite. It was a shocking thought, but she wanted to do it. She wanted to sink her teeth into all that smooth, warm skin—

Oh, this would never do.

She had to concentrate on sketching him, not biting him. Or kissing him.

She sketched a while more in pensive silence.

"I know you're worried." She heard compassion in his voice. He shifted again, raising a bare foot to the sofa's surface. He rested the hand with the sketchbook on his bent knee. "But Hamilton is aware I cannot pretend to be him at the Royal Academy. He'll be home in time to vote on the Selection Committee."

"I know that," she said.

"Is something else wrong, then, *a rún*?"

Oh, yes, something was wrong. He kept saying words she didn't understand, for one thing. Words that sounded so lovely and melodic they made her melt inside, even not knowing what they meant. And the way he was looking at her, the way she was looking at him. She wanted to touch him and bite him and kiss him, and she needed to sketch.

It was all just unbearable.

Her sketchbook and pencil both fell from her hands.

"Oh, Sean, I don't think I can do this anymore. Not tonight."

His foot slid back down to the floor. The hand with the book dropped to his side. "Why not?"

She didn't answer. She didn't think she could tell him. Looking concerned, he took his arm off the edge of the sofa back and sat straighter, ruining the delicious pose.

But she found him delicious, anyway.

"Because I cannot concentrate," she said, feeling her temper rise, although she couldn't figure out why. "All I can think of is bi . . . kissing you."

"Oh. Well, then. I think we can fix that." She thought he might smile, but he didn't. In fact, he looked a little apprehensive. "Why don't you come over here and give me a kiss, get it out of your system?"

Well, she wasn't going to resist *that* invitation. She simply couldn't. She all but flew out of the chair and into his arms, sprawling over him on the sofa.

He'd intended it to be a little kiss. A get-it-out-of-your-system kiss. She knew that. She could tell by the way he looked startled, by the way his mouth felt a little stiff when she planted her lips on his.

But that didn't last long, of course. Most of their kisses had been rather wild, and this one was no exception. A moment later he was kissing her back, slanting his mouth over hers, sweeping his tongue inside to claim her.

And, oh, she wanted to be claimed. She remembered reading *Ethelinde* last summer, and how Ethelinde had cried, *I am yours whenever you come to claim me.* That was exactly how she felt.

But Minerva Press novels hadn't prepared her for everything else Sean made her feel. When he kissed her, the world disappeared . . . she knew only the exciting heat of his mouth and her own blood rushing through her veins, the fierce pounding of her heart and that wonderful melting feeling inside her.

He undid her.

Feeling like that now, she touched him like she'd been

wanting to. She ran her hands over his bare skin, and it was hot and silky and made an ache form low in her middle. And she wanted more.

"I want you, Sean," she murmured.

He stopped kissing her. "What?"

"I want you." She hadn't realized that until she'd said it, but it was true. That was why her temper had flared; she wasn't getting what she wanted. "I want all of you."

He didn't pretend that he didn't understand her. "I want you, too," he said wryly, but she also heard frustration in his voice. "This is difficult, isn't it?"

"No, it's wonderful. You feel wonderful." She ran her hands over him again, feeling his muscles jump beneath his warm skin, beneath her fingers. A soft groan sounded in his throat, and he shut his eyes, making a little thrill run through her. "Touch me, Sean," she breathed. "Touch me like this."

Instead, he opened his eyes and took her hands. Took them off himself.

"I cannot." He sat up, moving her to sit beside him, shifting so he could meet her eyes. "Not now, not before . . . It wouldn't be right, Corinna. I cannot do that." A strand of her hair had come loose, probably when she'd leapt on him, and he reached to gently tuck it back. "What you're offering me isn't mine to take. Not now."

"But I want you to take it." More than she'd wanted anything before in her life. "That *makes* it yours to take."

"It doesn't." He shook his head. "I shouldn't even be kissing you, though God knows I enjoy it. You're an innocent. A sheltered, aristocratic miss."

"I'm an artist," she argued. "Artists are eccentric, individualistic. Free-spirited." Maybe she wasn't all of those things, exactly, but she'd always wanted to be. "We don't conform to convention."

"Well, I do. Sweet Jesus, I'm the son of a vicar. I don't go around ruining women. I won't do to you what that bastard Hamilton did to my sister. I like to think I'm better than that."

Corinna was startled silent. How could she argue with that? How could she say she wanted him to act like the man he despised most in the world? He was only being honorable. And she'd known all along he was honorable, hadn't she?

He'd proved his honor so many times, in so many ways. The way he'd wanted her to know the truth from the very beginning, and kept at her until she believed him. The way he still felt guilty deceiving Lord Lincolnshire, even though he knew it was best.

And then there was the way he didn't want Deirdre to live with the man she loved unless she could marry him. She should hardly be surprised he held himself to the same standards. Sean was the most honorable man she knew.

That was one of the many reasons she loved him.

It wasn't that he didn't want her. She wasn't stupid enough to believe that. She could see the wanting in his face, feel it in his kiss, in the way he touched her. He'd said *not now*, hadn't he? He was planning a future with her. He hadn't told her yet, just like she hadn't told him she loved him. All of that had to wait until this was all over. She was going to have to content herself with his kisses until then.

He wanted her. He just didn't want her *now*. And he seemed so distressed, so troubled. The way he was looking at her broke her heart.

"You are *much* better than that," she said quietly. "That's why I want you so much, but I understand." And then, because she couldn't help herself: "But I wish you wanted me now."

"Of course I want you now," he burst out, sounding exasperated, sounding like he couldn't believe he had to explain it. "You obviously *don't* understand. I want you now, and a minute ago, and a minute from now. All I ever *think* about is wanting you. I want you more than

I want to breathe, but I want what's best for you even more than that."

And when those words came out of his mouth, that was when Sean knew.

He loved her.

Yes, she made his blood sing; yes, she'd crawled under his skin; yes, he admired her drive and ambition. But it was more than that, much more. When a man put a woman's interests before his own, when he denied what he wanted most because it wouldn't be best for her . . . well, if that wasn't the definition of love, he didn't know what was.

He loved her.

He was going to ask her to marry him.

Not now, not until all of this was over. Not until he'd seen everything through, eased Lincolnshire to his rest, settled things between Hamilton and Deirdre. Not until he'd reclaimed his life and had something to offer Corinna besides subterfuge and lies. Not until he could approach her brother with his head held high.

Even then, the marquess was likely to refuse him. But he was going to ask.

And though he was a busy man who rarely stopped to pray anymore, right now he was praying harder than he ever had that the answer would be *yes*.

He kissed her, because he'd already done that and there was no going back. It was a gentle kiss, slow and heartfelt, a kiss he hoped told her without words what he wasn't ready to say.

Then he rose and reached for his shirt. "I'm thinking it's a good idea for us to stop now, as you said. We'll do this again tomorrow afternoon."

Chapter Thirty-three

The next day, Lincolnshire perked up.

When Lord Stafford made his usual early morning call, he was pleased to see his patient more comfortable. "He's more awake than he's been for days," he reported when he came out of the earl's bedroom following his examination. "And he can speak whole sentences—entire paragraphs—without pausing for breaths between words."

Sean had suspected the man might be getting better. "Do you expect all the sleep has revived him?"

"Perhaps, but only temporarily," the doctor reminded him. A gentle warning. "This sort of disease tends to progress and regress in uneven waves, but he's not recovering by any means." His brown eyes met Sean's with sympathy. "You'd best enjoy your uncle's alertness while you can."

Lincolnshire wasn't his uncle, but Sean nodded and thanked Stafford and saw him out. Only to find another man coming in.

This man carried a leather valise. A quite official-looking one. "I'm Mr. Lawrence Lawless," he said by way of introduction. "Lord Lincolnshire's solicitor. Here to consult with him at his request."

Lawless was a tall and very sober sort of gent—not a man Sean normally would greet with a grin. But he couldn't squelch a smile at meeting a lawyer named

Lawless. He turned away to hide it, allowing Quincy to escort the man upstairs.

It was the last time Sean smiled that day.

The solicitor spent a full hour closeted in Lincolnshire's bedroom, and no sooner had he left than the earl summoned his nephew. On her way out to go to Raleigh, Deirdre turned back and went upstairs with Sean.

"Good day to you, Lord Lincolnshire," she said softly as they entered his room.

"Good day to *you*, my dear," the earl wheezed. Sean was amused to hear Deirdre's Irish phrasing echoed rather than *good morning* in the English way. And very happy that, wheezing or not, Lincolnshire had indeed rattled off that whole sentence without pausing for breath.

But when the earl added, "I'm getting my affairs in order," any smile that might have sprung to Sean's lips died before it could emerge.

That sounded so dire. So final. Despite the doctor's warning, despite his need to get on with his own life, Sean must have been harboring some small hope that Lincolnshire might recover after all, because his heart squeezed painfully in his chest.

"I'm sorry," he mumbled.

"For what?" The older man coughed. "Sit . . . both of you."

Sean and his sister exchanged a glance. Playacting, or perhaps sensing Sean's distress, Deirdre took his hand as they slowly lowered themselves in unison.

The earl swiped the back of a swollen hand across his face, clearing his mouth of a bit of froth he'd coughed up. When his hand dropped, his lips were curved in a half smile of his own. "I'm pleased to see the two of you holding hands. I cannot imagine why rumors of infidelity persist, when I've seen for myself you've a wonderful marriage. Devoted, close . . . understanding."

Sean's guilt spiked to record levels. He'd have dropped

Deirdre's hand like a hot coal, except she sensed that and gripped his tightly.

"Give her a kiss," Lincolnshire coaxed.

There was nothing for it. Suppressing a sigh, Sean turned to his sister and gave her a wee peck on the cheek.

Lincolnshire nodded, still smiling. "Discreet in public, as usual. But I'd wager that behind closed doors—"

"Uncle," Sean cut in. He couldn't take hearing more about his *wonderful marriage* to Deirdre. Not without losing his breakfast. "Was there something else you wished to tell me?"

"Indeed. I wanted you to know that I'm pleased—or shall I say overjoyed—at the success you've had finding new positions for all my staff."

"It was nothing," Sean muttered.

"It was everything," Lincolnshire disagreed. "My heart sings to know all my holdings will be going to such a worthy man. My nephew—my blood." Tears sprang to the older man's eyes: not tears of pain, but tears of regret for devotion discovered much too late. "I'm so sorry I never came to know you before this. That your undeserved reputation and my unresolved feelings about my brother kept me from seeking you out earlier—"

"There is nothing to be sorry for," Sean interrupted, having had enough of this guilt-inducing affection. "My life has also been enriched by our time together. But your brother . . . this is the first you've mentioned these 'unresolved feelings' concerning him."

Lincolnshire shrugged. "I loved him, of course. He was my twin—"

"Your twin?" This was the first Sean had heard *that*.

"Surely you've noticed your father and I look identical?"

"I hadn't . . . thought about it." Now *he* was the one pausing between words. "My, uh . . . father . . . died years ago. He never mentioned you were twins. What happened between you? What made you banish your brother to the wilds of Ireland?"

"Banish him?" Lincolnshire snorted. "He should have been down on his knees kissing my feet. I saved the ungrateful bastard." He cocked his head, measuring Sean for a long, silent moment. "He never told you what happened?"

"Never." And if Sean could judge by Hamilton's attitude, Lincolnshire's brother hadn't given his real son the facts, either. "What happened?"

"You honestly don't know?"

Sean shook his head.

"When we were young men," Lincolnshire said, settling back against his pillows, "our father died, leaving me the earl. Your father was less than happy I inherited everything and he nothing. He was furious, as a matter of fact. A mere five minutes' difference in our births made me the heir and him the second son."

" 'Tis understandable he might feel that way," Deirdre said, no doubt remembering her father-in-law's underlying anger.

"I agree. But that's the way the world works. I assured him I'd take care of him, support him and his new child and his young wife—a wife he'd been forced to wed after getting her in the family way, I might add."

"Like father, like son," Sean whispered beneath his breath.

"Why do you say that?" the earl asked, proving his hearing wasn't affected by the dropsy. "My father's marriage was a love match. No one forced him to wed our mother."

"No, of course not," Sean assured him, thinking back. Hamilton's parents' marriage hadn't been a happy one. He'd always figured that was a result of their displeasure at being stuck in Ireland, but maybe it had been more than that. "Just a slip of the tongue, a commonplace expression. Pray, go on."

"Well, promising to support my brother and his family was not enough. He wanted more than just a generous allowance. Shortly after I inherited, I went off to Ireland, to Kilburton, to see my steward, meet my villagers and tenants. I returned to a scandal of unimaginable proportions."

"What?" Deirdre breathed.

"In my absence, William had decided to take some of what he considered his due. He'd pretended to be me, and we looked so much alike that people had believed him. He'd lived in this house, worn my clothes, gone to my club. He'd attended dinners and card parties and breakfasts and balls and soirees. He'd even paid my respects to King George at court, and while doing all of this, he'd run up debts that amounted to thousands. The biggest gaming debt in all of London, in my name. He couldn't pay it, of course. And a man's vowels, a debt of honor, is expected to be paid before any other."

"They must have been livid," Deirdre said. "All those men to whom he owed money."

"Oh, they were livid, all right. All the gentlemen and the ladies, too. But not because of the debt. I paid that immediately upon my return."

"Why then?" Sean asked. "Why should they remain livid after having been paid?"

"Because he'd tricked them," the earl said. "Made fools of them, one and all. He'd made them believe he was me, and for that they would never forgive him. Society has a long memory, and they hold a grudge even longer." Lincolnshire's sigh was one of heartache, of sorrow and deepest regret. "Only the gravest misdeeds will ever warrant the cut direct, but my brother had crossed that line."

"He had to leave," Deirdre concluded. "He couldn't live any longer in London."

"Indeed, he couldn't. Many wanted him banished to the countryside, to live in poverty and anonymity, or even better, they'd have preferred to have seen him shipped off to America. He hadn't the option of entering the clergy, and I couldn't buy him a commission in the military—the peerage is too well connected to both for him to have held posts in either. So I did what I could. I sent him to Ireland, where no one knew him. Where he could hold up his head and play the lord in Kilburton. Live in the drafty old castle—"

"He built an enormous new manor house."

"I know that, my dear." Lincolnshire smiled sadly at Deirdre. "He wanted a fancy new house, and I wanted him to be happy. Or at least as happy as possible. He was my brother, you see, my twin. If I never fully forgave him, it wasn't because of what he did, but because I lost him as a result."

"He never forgave you, either," Deirdre said.

"I know that, too. But I also know I did my best." He looked to Sean, who hadn't said anything for quite a while. "I hope you don't blame me for your father's disgrace. Under the circumstances—"

"No," Sean said in a dead tone. It was the only tone he could manage, because he felt dead inside. "I don't blame you."

"You understand, then?" Lincolnshire pressed.

Sean nodded. He understood perfectly.

He understood that the aristocracy wouldn't countenance being duped. He understood they held grudges forever. He understood that, having impersonated Hamilton, Lincolnshire's nephew and heir, he'd earned the cut direct from society himself.

Once the people of Mayfair learned the truth, none of them would speak to him ever again. They'd look right through him as though he weren't there. And should he marry Corinna, she and all of her family would be rejected along with him.

How had he not realized this? How had he convinced himself that he, an Irish vicar's son, could ever dream of wedding the daughter of a marquess? They'd been doomed from the first. If not by his background, then by Hamilton's games. *Damn the rotter.*

Damn him to hell and beyond.

The fact that Sean would never have met Corinna if not for Hamilton was entirely inconsequential. He'd been happy before he met her, or if not happy, at least content.

Now he'd never be either again.

And how was he going to explain all of this to her? Although they'd never discussed marriage, he wasn't a knothead. He knew she was thinking in that direction. Sweet Jesus, she'd offered herself to him. And she had but three days to fix Lincolnshire's portrait before she had to submit it.

After Sean posed for her this afternoon, she'd have only two days left to paint. The truth would devastate her, break her concentration, destroy any chance she had of achieving her lifelong dream. How could he tell her now?

He couldn't.

He couldn't tell her for three long days, until after the painting was finished. He was going to have to lie again, for her sake. He hated lying. And lying to the woman he loved seemed the worst lie ever.

It felt like a knife had sliced his heart, and his gut felt heavy. Like an anvil were lodged in it.

"Nephew . . . Sean." The earl was tiring, but clearly struggling to make amends. His eyes were pleading. "I wish I'd . . . known you all these years. I'm so . . . sorry—"

"Please, Uncle," Sean ordered himself to respond. "It's all water under the bridge, isn't it? We've come to know each other now, have we not? And nothing makes me happier than seeing how very gratified we both are at the outcome."

"Gratified? I am . . . euphoric. You came running when I asked . . . you've cared for me like a son. You've found positions . . . for my servants . . . seen all my concerns . . . are alleviated." Lincolnshire wheezed, then coughed, then placed a hand on his chest. His lids fluttered, then slowly shut.

But before he drifted off to sleep, he uttered one more sentence in a ragged whisper. "You're the best man . . . I've ever met."

And Sean felt like the worst man who'd ever lived.

Chapter Thirty-four

ICED CAKES

Mix sugar together with butter and rose-water. Mix this together with six eggs leaving out two whites and beat for a quarter of an hour. Put in your flour and mix them together well. Put them in your patty pans in an oven as hot as for manchet. Then make your icing. Put fine sugar in a mortar with rose-water and the white of an egg. When the cakes are cold put them on a tin then dip a feather in the icing and cover them well. Set the cakes back in the oven to harden.

These are sweet as a newborn baby. Eat them for the baby's health.

—Belinda Chase, Marchioness of Cainewood, 1799

"Oh, Aunt Frances, she's beautiful." Balancing her own son on her hip, Alexandra leaned close to run a finger down Frances's daughter's downy cheek. "Is she a good baby?"

"When she isn't crying." Frances cuddled Belinda closer. Reclining on a chaise longue that had been moved to her drawing room, she looked around at all the seated ladies who were visiting her and smiled a weary smile. "Which seems to be most of the time."

"For her first three months, my youngest daughter

cried all the time, too," Lady A said. "She almost drove me to Bedlam. Luckily she soon outgrew that and turned into a lovely child."

"I'm certain Belinda will outgrow it, too," Claire said.

Elizabeth nodded. "And besides, you do have the monthly nurse."

Rachael took an iced cake from the plate Juliana offered. "I expect the nurse sees to the baby's needs?"

"True," Frances said wryly. "The monthly nurse sees to her needs, and she's instructing the permanent day nurse and the night nurse. I'm only surprised Theodore hasn't hired a governess to start teaching Belinda her letters and numbers already. Nothing is too much for his daughter."

"As it should be," Lady A said approvingly. "It was the same with mine."

"But *three* nurses? When I'd as soon care for Belinda myself?"

"Alexandra feels the same way." Juliana set down the platter. "I expect I may be that way, too. May I hold her?"

"Of course." Frances held out the baby. "Support her head."

"I know," Juliana said, taking Belinda like an expert. "I learned that with Harry."

Watching her sister, Alexandra smiled and cuddled her son. "Does she make you want one of your own?"

"I'm going to have one of my own," Juliana said quietly. "In the winter."

A hush fell over the room while all of the ladies absorbed that information. Someone let loose an excited squeal. Then it seemed everyone was talking at once, exclaiming and congratulating and jumping from their seats to rush over and give Juliana a hug.

Except for Corinna, who seemed riveted in place.

She was happy for her sister, but suddenly she wanted a baby of her own more than she'd thought possible.

Regardless of her protests the day Belinda was born,

she'd never considered that she might not ever have a child. She'd always planned on marrying someday, after she made her mark on the art world. And while she'd never shared her brother's urgency regarding the matter, because her art came first, now she was thinking there might have been another reason, too. It had been difficult to feel urgency when she'd never had any mental picture of the man who would father her children.

But now she did.

The man in the mental picture had dark hair and fathomless, deep green eyes. Square, masculine hands. A firm, defined chest. Rippling muscles, a disarming grin, a charming Irish accent. And Sean Delaney's face.

She wanted Sean's baby. He was so honorable. He would make such a wonderful father.

Of course, she'd have to marry him first, but she'd already been thinking about that, hadn't she? And she couldn't imagine having a child with anyone else. No one else had ever made her feel like Sean did, and she was certain no one else ever would.

Marriage to him would be unbelievably exciting. He was going to pose for her again this afternoon, and now, as she imagined him disrobing, a shimmering heat seemed to shudder through her—

"Are you all right?" Juliana asked, interrupting her reverie. She stood in front of Corinna, looking concerned. Sometime in all the commotion, she must have handed the baby back to Frances. "You don't look very excited."

Odd, considering she'd certainly felt excited at the thought of seeing Sean later. But Corinna wasn't about to confide that to her sister. And in the back of her mind, she felt disturbed somehow, as though something bad might happen.

"Of course I'm excited. And I'm thrilled for you and James and, oh, all of us." Corinna forced a smile, deciding she must be more worried about fixing Lord Lincolnshire's portrait than she'd thought. She rose and gave her sister a heartfelt hug, then sat down again. "I'm just being selfish as usual. Worrying about my upcoming submissions. I need to bring my paintings to Somerset House on Monday."

"Who is going with you?" Lady A asked.

Corinna hadn't thought that far ahead, but of course she couldn't go alone. It wouldn't be proper.

Being female proved terribly inconvenient at times.

"I suppose I'll ask Griffin."

"I'd be honored to accompany you, my dear." Lady A's smile looked wistful. "It would be my pleasure. I'm supposed to assist my nephew at the Institute until four o'clock on Monday, but I can tell him I need to leave at noon." The New Hope Institute was James's facility, where he provided smallpox vaccinations for the poor. Lady B was his assistant today—she and Lady A took turns. "Will that be early enough?"

"That will be fine." Considering all the kind woman had done for her, she wouldn't think of denying her this pleasure. "I'll come for you in my brother's carriage at one o'clock. The submission deadline isn't until five."

"Oh, then two o'clock would be better, if you wouldn't mind. That way I'll have time for luncheon first. And there is nothing to worry about." She leaned to give Corinna's hand a pat. "The committee members said lovely things about your paintings. My daughter would have been overjoyed to have such important men give her such recognition," she added with a sigh.

Corinna didn't know whether Lady A's sigh indicated happiness for her prospects or sadness for her own daughter's failed dream. But regardless, she sighed along with her. "Most of them did say nice things, but they also said my portrait wasn't quite right. I need to fix it before Monday."

"You're not going skip the Teddington ball tomorrow night, are you?" Juliana asked. "Or Lady Hartley's breakfast on Sunday? It's the event of the Season."

"I probably should skip both." Which meant her

brother would be hovering over her all weekend, badgering her to leave the house and meet more men. "I wish I could find somewhere peaceful to paint."

"Chelsea Physic Garden is very peaceful." Juliana rubbed her belly, even though it was still flat as a canvas. "Only physicians and apothecaries can generally gain entrance, but James could obtain a ticket for you."

"I was just in Chelsea yesterday," Rachael commented rather absently. "At the Royal Hospital."

Corinna still felt disturbed. Maybe it would be better to change the subject. "Why is that?" she asked.

When Rachael looked flustered and hesitated, Claire slanted her sister a glance and then answered for her. "It was a charitable visit. Rachael brought books for the pensioners."

"That was very kind," Lady C said.

A footman came in and set a tray of tea things on a table by the door.

"Would anyone like tea?" Since Aunt Frances wasn't up to acting as hostess, Lady A rose and started toward the teapot to pour. "My younger daughter's father-in-law is a Chelsea Pensioner. But I haven't seen him in years."

While Lady A was across the room, Rachael nudged Corinna. "Lady A seems to take any excuse to mention her younger daughter," she whispered. "I think the poor woman really misses her."

"Brilliant observation," Corinna whispered dryly.

"James told me Lady A's younger daughter took her own life," Juliana said quietly. "Lady A doesn't have any grandchildren. Her oldest daughter eloped against her father's wishes, and he banished her from their lives. Her middle child, a son, drank too much and accidently drowned. And her younger daughter was in the family way when she jumped off the London Bridge, taking Lady A's last chance at having a grandchild with her."

"Oh, poor, poor woman!" Rachael sighed. "I really

like Lady A. She reminds me of my mother. I think it's the gardenia scent she's wearing. Mama always loved gardenia perfume." She smiled, but the expression was sad. "I think I'll go help her pour tea."

As their cousin went off, Corinna nudged Juliana. "I think Lady A smells as much of camphor as gardenias."

"I agree." They shared a smile. "But as Rachael has been suffering from dampened spirits of late," Juliana added, "I don't think we should say anything to ruin her comforting illusion."

Corinna wished *she* had a comforting illusion. All the way through the rest of the visit, and all the way home, she continued feeling disturbed. As she went up to her bedroom to ready herself before meeting Sean, she told herself things weren't that bad.

Sean was still willing to kiss her. She still had time to fix Lord Lincolnshire's picture. And her life certainly wasn't as tragic as Lady A's. She'd lost her parents and a brother, yes, but only to illness, which was sad but not completely unexpected. She hadn't lost anyone to drink, or to suicide, or because they'd eloped without permission and been banished from the family.

She plopped onto her bed, suddenly realizing why she felt disturbed.

She wanted Sean's baby more than anything. She wanted to marry him. But what if she had to elope with him in order to accomplish that?

She hoped Griffin would agree to their marriage, but what if he didn't? Sean wasn't anything like the men her brother pushed on her, and not only because he was Irish. He could certainly support her—after what she'd learned yesterday, she suspected he could support half of London. But he wasn't aristocratic. Griffin's saying he admired Sean and wanted his advice did not equate to an endorsement of marriage.

She was willing to defy her brother's wishes to marry Sean, should it come to that. She was willing to run off to Gretna Green to elope. Her family wasn't the type to banish her. And she was an artist, after all, wasn't she? Freethinking, a rebel, unconventional.

But none of that mattered . . . because Sean *was* conventional.

He wouldn't elope with her against her brother's wishes. She was certain of that. He was too honorable.

Now that she'd figured out why she felt disturbed, the disturbance grew. The iced cakes she'd eaten felt like they were congealing in her stomach. The tea she'd sipped was threatening to come back up.

How could she persuade Griffin to allow them to marry if he disapproved? She didn't know. All she knew was that unless she came up with a plan, her future with Sean was very uncertain. And should Griffin discover she was meeting Sean, this might be the last time they were alone together, ever.

She'd best make the most of it.

She'd work on a plan, she decided as she rose to change and gather her things. In the interim, she wanted more of Sean's kisses. And she couldn't afford to be nervous about sketching him this time. If she were to have a prayer of fixing Lord Lincolnshire's portrait, she needed to study Sean. *All* of him.

Her stomach churning with a mixture of anxiety and anticipation and who knew what else, she felt more disturbed than ever. Thinking she needed what she'd sometimes heard referred to as "Dutch courage," she grabbed a bottle of her brother's first vintage on her way out.

Chapter Thirty-five

They met in the afternoon this time, so Sean didn't bother lighting any candles. "I'm thinking we don't need them with all of this light," he told Corinna. "Hamilton chose this place because of the north-facing windows."

"I'll be able to see you fine without candles," she said softly. "*All* of you, I'm hoping."

Sweet Jesus, he was in trouble.

How on God's green earth was he going to take off all his clothes without the two of them ending up tangled together on the sofa? It had been a close thing yesterday. Never had he come so near to going against everything he believed. And he'd removed only his shirt last time.

Now she wanted to see *all* of him.

"I'm thinking you won't see all of me at once, though," he said, noticing she'd brought two glasses and a bottle of wine with her. He would have to make sure he didn't drink much. "I'm remembering you said you wanted to sketch part of me at a time."

"I really need to see all of you if I'm to fix Lord Lincolnshire's portrait." Turning away, Corinna made herself busy pouring the wine. "Male artists sketch live models day in and day out. I have only these two sittings to get it right." With an apologetic smile, she turned back and held out a glass filled to the brim. "I brought some of my brother's wine to help us both relax."

Sean accepted the wine reluctantly, telling himself he needed to keep a clear head. He took a tiny sip, just to be polite.

She drank down nearly half of her own large glass. "Don't you like the wine?"

"I like it fine. But I don't drink very much, so I've never built up a tolerance."

"Now I'm remembering you drank only a little that night you were summoned to our family dinner. Just a couple of sips."

"I watched my maternal grandfather drink himself into the grave. An effective advertisement for moderation."

She touched his hand, a brief contact that left him wanting more. "I'm sorry."

He'd felt the warmth of her skin, and now he smelled her sweet floral fragrance and the slight hint of paint underneath it. He had come to love that hint of paint, because it was uniquely Corinna and he loved *her*. To keep himself from reaching for her, he abruptly sat and sipped again. "He was a happy drunk, but he never made anything of himself."

"You've made a lot of yourself," she said, moving to sit across from him. After draining the rest of her glass and setting it on the floor, she reached for her sketchbook. "You're the best man I know, Sean."

She was the second person to tell him that today, which served to remind him of the first and what he'd learned before Lincolnshire had said that. The reminder cut him to the core.

He took a full swallow of wine.

Her blue, blue eyes locked on his, she opened the sketchbook. "You can disrobe now. I'm ready."

He wasn't ready—he didn't think he'd ever be ready—but there was nothing for it. He'd offered to pose for her, and he wanted her painting to be a success. He took another swallow of wine and put his glass down carefully, then stood and tugged off his shoes and stockings, his cravat, his coat, his waistcoat. Feeling her gaze on him, he swiftly removed his braces, then unbuttoned his shirt and stripped it off over his head.

Like last night, his hands moved to the buttons on his trousers. But this time she didn't stop him.

He stopped himself instead.

Taking a gulp of air, he reached for his glass and swallowed more wine.

"Sean?" she whispered, then bit her lip. She looked as tense as he felt. And as aroused. Her cheeks were flushed, her eyes wide and yearning.

The sight devastated him.

Her sketchbook lay open on her lap, ignored. He felt sweat break out on his brow, a sheen slick his bare chest. Her gaze was fastened on the front of the trousers he'd yet to open, on the obvious bulge straining against them. He knew it was only a matter of time before that sketchbook was on the floor and they were in each other's arms. A short time.

Maybe he should just tell her the facts, tell her they had no future together, cut this off before it got out of hand.

No, he couldn't tell her, not until she'd finished the portrait. The knowledge wouldn't just cut this off; it would devastate her. He was devastated already, so he knew exactly how she would feel. Completely, utterly devastated.

And she wouldn't be able to paint.

Corinna couldn't sketch. She could only stare. She felt a heat beginning to build in her, and she wanted nothing more than to leap across the space between them. And Sean wanted her, too, didn't he? More than he wanted to breathe, he'd said last night, and hadn't hearing *that* melted her to the consistency of fresh paint?

Just like she felt melted now.

The glass of wine had gone to her head, and she licked her lips, feeling a bit woozy. The sketchbook slid to the floor as she leaned over to pull off her slippers.

"What are you doing?" Sean murmured.

She didn't quite know what she was doing, so she didn't answer. Instead she reached beneath her skirts and untied one garter and then the other, dropping the lace-trimmed ribbons atop her discarded shoes.

She could scarcely believe she was acting so wanton. It had to be the Dutch courage, because she'd never been the beguiling sister. That was Juliana's role. But suddenly she remembered Juliana demonstrating something she called *the look*, a practiced flirtation so contrived Corinna had never been able to imagine herself doing it. Now she glanced down and then swept her gaze up, looking at Sean full on as she curved her lips very slowly in a deliberately seductive smile.

His pupils dilated, and she saw his respiration quicken.

Seduction was so much easier than she'd ever thought it would be.

Maybe it was the wine, but she thought it was also Sean. He was so seductive himself that any woman would feel seductive around him. Every word he said in that lyrical Irish voice seeped right into her, dissolving her bones. She hadn't even touched him yet, nor had he touched her, but her blood was already sluicing through her in a seductive rhythm.

Soft afternoon light slanted through the north-facing windows, illuminating his sculpted face, glinting off the slight dark stubble that had grown since he'd shaved this morning. Her fingers itched to stroke that roughness, that glorious maleness, just as her body yearned to press against him, to mold her curves to his muscled form.

She drew the hem of her dress up to rest on her knees and began rolling down a stocking, watching Sean's face. What she saw there made the heat build more. He was *watching her with the most impassioned look*, like in *Children of the Abbey*, a look more intoxicating than any wine. She pulled the stocking off of her foot and dropped it to the floor and started on the other.

Transfixed, Sean stared at the pile of satin and lace

and silk that was building up. He knew he should stop her, but he couldn't seem to make himself move. She drew the second stocking off her foot, baring her toes. Small toes they were, pale and tender-looking. Imagining sucking on them, he thought he might die. He looked up to her bare, curvy calves and died a little more. He raised his gaze to her naked knees, and saw the hem of her dress rucked up there, and imagined her wearing a gauzy bit of a shift under it. Or a chemise, as the high-born called it. A gauzy, enticing chemise.

He tried to take another swallow of wine, but his glass was empty.

What was he doing? He couldn't tell her he couldn't marry her, so he had to keep his wits about him. He had to fight this. He shouldn't be imagining what was under her dress; he shouldn't be imagining anything. Feeling light-headed, he carefully set down the glass. He wouldn't allow her to refill it.

"Sean," she said in a tone so husky it made his breath catch. She rose and walked close, so close he felt heat shimmering between them. Lifting a hand to his cheek, she turned his head to face her.

All over again, her blue eyes devastated him.

"Are you all right, Sean?"

He wasn't all right, no. He was growing so hard he was in pain. He was dying.

"Sean," she breathed, moving her fingers on his face so gently he wondered that he could feel it. But he did feel it, so strongly the feeling seemed to permeate his body. She shifted and leaned closer. "Oh, God, Sean, I want you to kiss me."

Oh, God, Sean thought. He could see down her dress. *Sacred heart of Jesus.*

There *was* a gauzy chemise under it, just as he'd imagined. Beneath that, her breasts looked high and round and firm, making him want to touch them. Hell, he didn't just want to touch them—he wanted to rip off her dress and fasten his mouth on them. She leaned closer, and he could see their rosy tips strain against the chemise like he was straining against his trousers. Her scent swamped him, and she raised her other hand to cradle his face, and then . . .

He kissed her. It was a defensive move, because he couldn't stare down her dress a moment longer without exploding. But he was lost the moment his lips touched hers.

Lost in the kiss, lost in her, lost in his own longing. She consumed him.

He was devastated.

Somehow they made it down to the sofa, and she was pushing him back and crawling over him. She was running her hands over his chest and around to his back. Her fingers left fire in their wake, a hot trail of burning sweetness that seemed to devastate him yet more.

"Touch me, Sean," she murmured. "Touch me like I'm touching you."

She devastated him. He was going to die if he didn't touch her. So, God help him, he touched her.

His hands went everywhere, everywhere they shouldn't, everywhere he wanted. Under her bodice to tease a nipple, to cup a breast when she moaned and asked for more. He was going to die if he didn't taste her, so his mouth followed. He nibbled on her neck, her shoulders, unbuttoned her dress in back and dragged it down and suckled her, feasted on her.

Corinna wanted more. She'd never imagined she could feel like this. What she'd felt last night when she'd thought she wanted him was nothing compared to this. Nothing. The little ache that she'd felt then was nothing compared to how she ached now. Sean's mouth on her breast felt hot and made her ache everywhere, but especially between her legs, where the ache was exquisite, almost painful, just unbearable. She wanted more.

"Sean," she whispered, "I want you to take me."

"I want to take you," he echoed in a tone so ragged it tore at her heart. "I want all of you." He reversed their positions, climbing over her. He slipped a hand under her skirt and skimmed it up her calves to her thighs. Still he suckled her breasts, one and then the other, a sensation so astounding she was grateful she'd found the courage to act wanton. His fingers felt wonderfully warm on her legs, stroking, inspiring her to do the same. She ran her own hands over his skin, feeling his muscles underneath, and sinewy tendons, crisp hair where he had it and the smooth, soft places where he didn't.

His breath became as rough as hers, making her heart thunder just to hear it. He moved his hand higher, brushing her curls, cupping her where no one had touched her before. He nibbled up her neck and took her mouth with his again, thrusting his tongue inside while his fingers slowly parted her below and began to stroke. He caught her gasp in his mouth and continued moving his hand, slowly, patiently, stroking her while excitement built until she couldn't keep still, until she couldn't stop a little sound of frustration that came from her throat.

And then he slipped a finger inside her.

"Oh, God, Sean," she breathed. "Oh, yes."

"Sweet, so sweet," he murmured into her mouth. He buried his face in her neck, moving his finger in and out of her. "So hot, so wet, so tight," he whispered against her skin. He did something with his thumb, touched a spot so sensitive her hips bucked off the sofa, and when he lingered there, circling, circling, she felt she might tumble off a ledge.

And then she did. She tumbled and tumbled, over and over, gasping and crying out his name. Sensation rocked her, sprinting along all her nerves, spreading everywhere. "Sweet, so sweet," he choked out.

She felt dizzy; she felt lethargic. She felt drained, but she wanted more.

She wanted *him*.

"I want more," she whispered. "I want you."

He lifted his head then, kissed her, and lifted his head

again. "Open your eyes, *críona*." She did, and he met her gaze, his own hazy with desire. He kissed her again and again, little nipping kisses and slow, deep ones. "This is wrong," he whispered, "but it feels so right."

"It *is* right. Oh, Sean, I still want you."

He held her gaze for so long, so steadily, she felt they might be locked together forever. Then he nodded and began tugging up on her dress, gathering it around her waist.

This is it, she thought. *Finally he's going to join his body with mine and make me his.* Her heart soared with the rightness of it, her pulse pounded, and every inch of her strained to feel him. She reached to help unbutton his trousers, but he moved down instead. Nibbled his way across her jaw and down her throat and past her breasts, nipping and licking her abdomen and her belly and lower, kissing her thighs, little feathery kisses that coaxed her to open them, baring her to his gaze.

And then he was there between her legs, his breath washing over her, hot and heavy. He kissed her there, touched her lightly with his tongue.

What was he doing? She'd never imagined such a thing. But the pleasure was even more unimaginable. She'd thought she was finished, drained past sensation; she'd wanted only to feel him inside her. But suddenly every fiber of her being was sparking alive again, driving her up once more, crowding every lucid thought from her head. She couldn't think; she could only feel: the incredible heat of his mouth; his tongue, licking slick and unbelievably exciting; the tension building; her body straining toward a peak of passion she feared might tear her apart.

And it did. She splintered into a million shards of sensation, waves rushing, shimmering, and making her soar.

Sean felt her tremble, felt her shudder, heard her gasp and cry out his name, and thought it the sweetest moment he'd ever known. He held his mouth to her, savoring the taste of her, a honeyed flavor he would never taste again.

He loved her, and he'd wanted to give her this. He knew there could be only this once, and he'd wanted to give her what he could before it was too late.

He crawled up her body and laid his head against her soft breasts, listening to her heart thunder like his. He wanted her, wanted her more than he'd ever thought possible. She whispered, "Take me, Sean; I still want you," in a tone so desperate, so filled with yearning it made him want to weep with despair. He wanted to take her; he wanted to bury himself inside her and stay there forever.

But he couldn't. Somewhere in the madness, somewhere in the midst of giving her what he could, he'd discovered he still had a shred of clarity.

The wispiest shred, the barest fog, but just enough.

He wasn't going to take her. Not forever, not for a moment, not at all. He couldn't do that; he couldn't ruin her. Lust and drink had brought him closer to that than he'd intended, so close a hot rush of shame and regret overwhelmed him, but it wouldn't take him any farther.

"Take me now," Corinna whispered desperately, pressing herself up against him.

She felt divine, but he couldn't take her now. Not even if he'd wanted to. The shame and regret had stolen his desire.

"I'm sorry," he murmured. "*Cuisle mo chroí,* I'm so sorry."

"I feel like I've been waiting forever."

"I'm sorry." She was going to be waiting forever. He was never going to take her. He wasn't going to be able to do that, ever, because they had no future together.

But he couldn't tell her, not now, not until her painting was finished.

More shame and regret overwhelmed him, tightening his throat, making it difficult to breathe as he watched her eyes slowly clear, watched her come to her senses.

"Oh, God," she whispered. "Oh, Sean. I cannot believe what happened. It was more wonderful than I can possibly describe. It wasn't exactly what I wanted, but it was heaven."

"It was, yes," he said, meaning it. He'd been in a terrible state physically, but feeling her tremble in his arms had been the sweetest moment he'd ever known. He would never feel such sweetness again, but to feel it even once was a gift beyond measure.

"Next time—"

"Hush," he said, and kissed her, a short kiss, because his throat was so tight he feared he couldn't breathe. There wouldn't be a next time, but he couldn't tell her that until her painting was finished.

He feared he might never be able to breathe again.

And he still had to help her fix the painting. She hadn't sketched yet, and she needed to sketch. He couldn't marry her, he would never have her, but he could still do what he'd come here to do. Three days from now, when he gave her the facts, when he devastated her, at least she would have her art. She'd have fixed her painting, and when it was accepted for the Summer Exhibition, she would still have her dreams, and they would help console her.

That thought in mind, he rose from the sofa and pulled her up, too. Ignoring her startled face, he tugged her bodice back up. Fortunately, the rest of her dress fell into place all by itself.

"Go sit in the chair, Corinna."

"What?"

"It's time to sketch now." He started unbuttoning the left side of the falls on his trousers.

"You've got to be jesting. I couldn't possibly sit and sketch now."

"We came here so you can sketch," he said, unbuttoning the right side. "Go sit down."

She did, watching him shuck off his trousers. Her eyes

widened. Thank God he'd lost his desire, he thought, sweeping a used sketchbook off the table.

"Sketch, Corinna." He sat, holding the book as the earl had in her picture, arranging himself in a similar pose. "I want you to sketch."

Her gaze wandered over him. Wandered everywhere. A melting softness came into her eyes.

She devastated him.

But he hadn't the luxury of being devastated, not anymore. "Start sketching."

"I cannot possibly concentrate after what just happened. We'll have to do this again tomorrow."

"We're not doing this again, Corinna. I'm not leaving here until you've sketched enough anatomy to fix Lincolnshire's portrait. And I'm not touching you again; that I promise. I'm not kissing you or touching you . . . so sketch."

Chapter Thirty-six

Corinna had never painted so fast in her life.

As she swept her brush along the canvas, she remembered all the hours she'd spent sketching earlier tonight. Intense hours. She hadn't thought she'd be able to concentrate, but she'd found herself focusing, fascinated, simply sinking into the experience. After sketching a full hour and realizing that wasn't nearly enough, she'd sent home a note with a contrived excuse, and Sean had lit candles, and she'd kept sketching.

Still caught in the lush aftermath of Sean's lovemaking, she'd captured him, all of him, head to bare toe. Captured his essence, she was sure of it. Her painting instructors had spoken of this, but studying a real, live man had made the difference. Finally, after months and years of trying, it had all clicked into place. She'd come home with page after page of sketches that would help her fix Lincolnshire's body beneath his clothes.

She wouldn't see Sean again until the portrait was finished. He'd made it clear, very clear, that he expected her to spend the entire weekend painting. Knowing she needed that time, she hadn't argued. As much as she would miss seeing him, she had but two days left to paint.

Three hours ago, in the darkness, Sean had walked her to her doorstep, graced her with a single, heart-stopping kiss, and sent her inside to fix the portrait. Instead, without conscious thought, she'd grabbed a blank canvas. In the quiet house, while Griffin and his staff slumbered upstairs, she'd surrounded it with lanterns.

And started another portrait, more vivid than any she'd ever imagined.

Now, in the middle of the night, the picture was simply pouring out of her, the brush an extension of her body, its movements seemingly undirected. Hour by hour, stroke by stroke, the portrait was taking form, coming to life.

Unlike the vast majority of the portraits she'd ever seen, this portrait wasn't posed, it wasn't contrived, it wasn't meant to convey the importance of the man it portrayed. The gentleman's clothes were not carefully chosen to imply his level of status or wealth. He wasn't meticulously groomed, nor did he hold objects imbued with significance. His gaze did not issue a challenge. It didn't say, *Look at me; I'm superior and distinguished.*

Rather the man reclined half-clothed, sprawled with casual abandon on a sofa upholstered with sumptuous fabric. He held nothing, one strong arm relaxed along the back edge of the furniture, the other on a bent knee. His shirt had been removed and draped negligently on the sofa, revealing a splendid toned chest that gleamed in the candlelight. His feet were bare, his lower body concealed by only trousers tight as a hug. His gaze was focused off-canvas, lost in contemplation. It didn't say anything direct at all, allowing the viewer to draw his own conclusions.

It was Sean, of course. Sean in a richer version of the garret studio, Sean in Corinna's mind's eye. Warm, golden skin and firm, rippling muscles. Raven hair curling at the neck. Eyes of deepest emerald edging toward black, a shadowed hint of shaven stubble on cheeks and chin. All she'd touched, all she'd experienced, all her emotions, all she still yearned for . . .

Exposed for all to see.

As she created, snatches of lines tumbled through her mind.

. . . a passion, which virtue cannot sanction or reason justify . . .

. . . the soul-soothing certainty of being beloved by him . . .

. . . life, without him, would lose far more than half of its charms . . .

She painted without thinking, only feeling. Flesh tones, candlelight and shade, crisp white linen, velvet-dark fabric. The sofa, ruby red and decadent. Richly paneled walls behind, an exotic carpet underfoot.

Her brush followed the ridge of a ropy thigh, the slope of a brawny shoulder. The angle of jaw, the curve of cheek, the line of flexed and bended knee. She was melting inside. Hot and melting and deliciously languid, melting right onto the canvas.

She wanted him. She wanted him again, wanted more of him next time. Twice he'd shown her heaven—she couldn't believe the things he had done—but she wanted more.

She wanted all of him.

The wanting was a ball of heat gathering in her middle, a sweet, yearning ache growing down lower. He was going to be hers. The words remained unspoken between them, but she was going to marry him. She had a plan now, a solution, something to guarantee Griffin's cooperation.

This painting.

An hour ago, well into painting it, she'd suddenly realized that proof Sean had posed nude for her was all she needed to make sure Griffin would allow them to wed. In fact, if Griffin saw this portrait, he'd *insist* she and Sean wed.

He'd insisted Tristan marry Alexandra after they were caught together in a bed, even though they'd both sworn nothing had happened that night. The mere sight of this portrait would make Griffin suspect she and Sean had shared a bed, too.

She *wished* they had shared a bed. She wanted Sean, and remembering how it had felt almost having him, remembering how he had made her feel with his hands and his mouth and his tongue, sent a stunning thrill rippling through her.

Her knees threatening to buckle, she stepped back and examined her work.

It was marvelous. The portrait looked breathtaking in the lanternlight. Though it was still quite unfinished, she had no doubt it would be her most inspired painting ever. Sensual and scandalous and altogether brilliant.

And all at once she knew: She wanted to submit it for the Summer Exhibition.

No.

Blinking, she took another step back.

She couldn't.

Should it be selected, it would be hung for all to see. Sean would be mortified when people saw him half-naked. And her heart was laid bare on the canvas—anyone looking at the portrait would be convinced, unequivocally, that the artist was in love with her subject. It would be like announcing to the world that she and Sean were lovers.

But wait . . .

Maybe she could change Sean's hair color, his eyes. Then no one would recognize him. There might be whispered speculation about the artist's lover, but she could laugh it off, because no one would find a man who looked like him anywhere.

That was a plan.

And she was a rebel, wasn't she?

She was going to forget Lincolnshire's portrait. Forget her landscapes and still lifes. *This* would be the painting she submitted for the Summer Exhibition.

The one she wanted to be known for, the one that would launch her career.

* * *

Sean was in a beastly mood when he joined Deirdre for breakfast the next morning. A cup of coffee was waiting on the table, strong and black the way he liked it, and she pushed it toward him after he slammed into his chair.

"You look upset," she observed, sipping her own tea.

Upset didn't begin to describe the depths of his self-loathing. It didn't so much as scratch the surface. He'd allowed drink and lust to overcome him last night, all but ruining the woman he loved. And keeping the truth from Corinna was tearing him up inside, like coarse gravel tumbling around in his gut.

He'd been fooling himself all along. There'd never been a chance he'd end up with Corinna. And Deirdre wasn't going to get her divorce, either. Hamilton was going to be furious Sean had appeared in public pretending to be the earl's heir; the moment Sean had agreed to that, he'd sealed his sister's fate. All that was left was seeing Lincolnshire through his last days—nothing else was going to work out.

But he wasn't going to tell Deirdre any of that.

"Lincolnshire's sliding downhill," he said, taking a gulp of the hot, bracing brew. "He's too weak to come down and join us."

"Someone to see you, Mr. Hamilton." A footman appeared in the doorway. "Your assistant, Mr. Sykes."

"Mr. Sykes? Send him in. At once. Please," he added as an afterthought.

"By all means," the man said, and left.

"Just what I need," Sean muttered.

Deirdre frowned. "What could he want?"

"I haven't a clue." But it couldn't be good. "It's Saturday. Sykes doesn't work on Saturday."

"Maybe it's nothing bad."

"Maybe it isn't."

And maybe the sun would fail to rise tomorrow. Maybe it wouldn't rain for the whole of the summer.

Maybe London's poor would stop drowning their sorrows in gin.

"Shut the door," he instructed when Sykes walked in, then waited until the man had. "I don't remember summoning you today to play my art assistant."

"I apologize for the interruption."

"Sit down. I'm certain you've a fine reason."

After pulling out a chair, Sykes wasted no time coming to the point. "All of your concerns are being investigated. Inquiries are being made." He pushed up on his round spectacles. "Not only at your main offices, but at your factories, your shipyards, your—"

"I get the picture," Sean interrupted.

It was horrendous timing, but he wasn't altogether surprised.

It was those *people who knew*, probably someone he'd dealt with. Perhaps someone whose failed endeavor he'd acquired for pennies on the pound and turned into a high-producing concern. Or someone whose property he'd bought and improved and made profitable. Or someone whose employees he'd hired and paid better, or . . .

The possibilities were endless.

He liked to think he was a pleasant fellow, if perhaps a bit driven. He'd never forced anyone to do anything. He believed every man had the right to his own property and the right to make his own choices regarding it, so long as he respected others' rights in the process.

All of his business dealings were honest and straightforward, within the law, and—most important—within his own moral code. He took responsibility for himself, had no sense of entitlement, didn't ask anyone for anything. All he wanted was the opportunity to pursue his goals, the chance to realize his potential. There were few bywords he swore by, and they all reflected a similar theme: mutual consent, live and let live, the Golden Rule.

But this wasn't the first time someone had tried to ruin him, and he knew it wouldn't be the last.

"I'll look into it." Downing the rest of his coffee, he pushed back from the table. "If Lincolnshire needs me," he told Deirdre, "send for me. You know where I'll be."

He was out the door, on his way to Delaney and Company's main offices, before the cup stopped rattling in its saucer.

Chapter Thirty-seven

Berkeley Square, Saturday 17 May

My dear Cousin,
I have an idea I wish to discuss with you. As I'll be bringing Corinna to the Teddington ball tonight, I hope you will also be attending.

Fondly,
Cainewood

Arriving at the Teddington ball on Saturday night, Rachael waved to Lady A and looked around to locate Griffin. She found him in the refreshment room, talking to Juliana.

Or rather, complaining to Juliana.

"I cannot believe she refused to come tonight. How the devil am I supposed to find her a husband?"

"Corinna's submissions are due on Monday, Griffin. This is important to her."

"Well, she said she doesn't want to go to Lady Hartley's breakfast tomorrow, either, but I won't hear of it. It's the event of the Season, and I've already lined up three men for her to meet."

Juliana looked as though she might argue with that, but then she noticed Rachael standing there. "Good evening, Rachael."

Griffin turned and looked at Rachael, too. Or rather,

he skimmed her from her toes on up, his gaze lingering on her sky blue silk bodice before it reached her face. "What are you doing here?"

"You sent me a note," she said, confused. "You asked me to come." What kind of a fool would ask her to come and then ask her why she was here?

"Well, I didn't ask you to wear a dress like that."

"It's a ball gown. This is a ball." What else was she supposed to wear? "Your note sounded important." She glanced around, seeing entirely too many people. "Is it something we should talk about privately?"

"Let's go to Lord Teddington's library."

"All right." They'd gone to the library during the Teddingtons' ball last year, too—in fact, it was where she'd first asked Griffin if he might help her find her father—so she knew exactly where to head: down a long corridor past several other doors. Slipping inside, she walked over to a leather sofa and sat, irritated that she'd responded to his note. "What did you want to discuss with me?"

Leaving the door open, Griffin joined her on the sofa, sitting sideways to face her. "I thought of something," he said quietly. "Maybe your grandfather wasn't the last chance to learn what became of your father. If we can find your mother's family, perhaps they will know the truth."

The irritation rapidly dissipated, shifting to disbelief. She stared at him. "We cannot find her family."

"We have a name now. John Cartwright. If we can believe the old man's ramblings, he saved John Cartwright's life and Cartwright promised his daughter in return. I know your mother called herself Georgiana Woodby, but she must have been Georgiana Cartwright."

Having seen her grandfather, Rachael could no longer doubt that Griffin's reasoning made sense. "But even if she was Georgiana Cartwright, she had no family left. There is no family to find."

"Maybe that's not the case. If she gave a false name,

she might have told other untruths. She might have had living family, after all."

"Maybe." Though the implications made her reel, she was willing to concede the possibility. "But how would you find them with just a name, and such a common one at that?" The man who'd raised her had also been called John, as were many other men of her acquaintance. John Hamilton, for instance. "There must be a hundred John Cartwrights." Maybe more.

"But how many of them are titled? At the time of her marriage, your mother was Lady Georgiana, which means her father was an earl at the very least. We can look him up in *Debrett's Peerage*. Even if he did die young, the succession will be listed in the pedigree. If you have any living relations, I can find them."

Of course he could. "I'm a bloody idiot." She rarely considered herself a fool, but it was so simple. "Why didn't I think of that?"

He shrugged. "I expect your mind was on other things. Your life has been rather traumatic lately. Besides," he added artlessly, "I'm here to think for you."

She preferred to think for herself, but she had to admit—if only to herself—that it was comforting to have Griffin's support. And surprising. Never in a million years had she thought she'd lean on Griffin.

A man dumb enough to ask her to a ball and then ask her why she'd come wearing a ball gown.

"I'm going to go home right now and consult *Debrett's*," she said. "Do you want to come with me?"

"There's no need to go anywhere," he said, rising from the sofa. "Why do you think I suggested we discuss this in Lord Teddington's library?"

She *was* a bloody idiot. Everyone had a copy of *Debrett's*. It didn't take long for Griffin to find the Teddingtons'. He drew it off a shelf and came back with it in his hands, a small but very fat volume bound in deep green leather.

"Here," he said, handing it to her as he reclaimed his seat by her side. "You look it up."

With shaking fingers she opened the cover and turned to the table of contents. All they had to go on was a last name.

"There," Griffin said. " 'Surnames and the Superior Titles of the Peers and Peeresses of the United Kingdom of Great Britain and Ireland.' That's the section you want."

"I know," she said dryly. "I've looked in *Debrett's* before." She turned to that section and flipped to the second page, where the Cs were listed. "Cartwright—Avonleigh."

There was a little e by the listing, indicating Cartwright was an earl. "Your mother's father was the Earl of Avonleigh," Griffin said.

"Maybe." She wouldn't believe it until she saw her mother's name in the Earl of Avonleigh's pedigree. She simply couldn't make herself believe it. Although the earls were all listed in one section, they were in no particular order that she'd ever been able to discern, so she went back to the front, where all the titles were indexed.

"Avonleigh," Griffin said. "There it is. Page two thirty-three."

"I can read, Griffin." He may have done all the research up until now, but she could do *this*. She turned to page 233. "Robert Cartwright, Earl of Avonleigh . . ." She scanned down past the current earl's birth and marriage dates. ". . . succeeded his uncle, John, the late earl, born 1739, married 1765 to Aurelia Egerton, daughter of William, Earl of Wilton, by whom he has issue Alice, born 1767, married 1785 to George Egerton, youngest son of John, Earl of Wilton, died 1799; Harold, born 1770, died 1791; Georgiana—" She broke off.

"There she is," Griffin said softly.

"Yes." There it was, in black and white, her mother's name.

"What does it say about her?" he prompted.

She swallowed hard and refocused on the tiny print. "Georgiana, born 1774, married 1792 to Thomas Grimstead, died 1793."

"The year you were born," he said.

"Yes. She didn't die. She married my father—Lord Greystone—and had me." She glanced up, looked at Griffin, confused again. But something seemed to be tugging at her mind. Something significant.

Griffin's green gaze was unfocused, as though he were deep in thought. "Everyone thought she died, obviously. She was officially dead. Then she married Greystone and hid herself in the countryside."

"She pretended she had asthma and couldn't go to London because the air here was bad for her. She never liked to socialize."

"Are you sure?" Griffin asked. "I'm thinking she never came to London because someone here might have recognized her. Someone here would have realized she wasn't actually dead."

"Maybe," she said. "That does make sense. Maybe her family was here in London. John Cartwright, the Earl of Avonleigh, my grandfather. And his wife"—she glanced back to the pedigree to find the name—"Aurelia . . ."

When she trailed off, Griffin laid a gentle hand on her arm. "What?"

"Aurelia, Lady Avonleigh. I don't believe it." That was what had been tugging at her mind. "We know her, Griffin! She's Juliana's aunt by marriage, one of the ABC sisters. She hosted the art reception for Corinna. She smells of gardenias, like my mother. Lady Avonleigh is my grandmother!"

At ten o'clock, Sean arrived back at Lincolnshire House, exhausted. Deirdre met him at the door and hurried him into what he thought of as the Hamilton drawing room. "What did you learn?" she asked, closing the door.

"Nothing. " He shut his eyes, not wanting to see all of Hamilton's damned pictures.

"Nothing?"

"I spoke with dozens of my people around London and learned nothing concrete," he told her, opening his eyes. "Whoever is making inquiries is going about it very discreetly. Asking who owns each place and what sort of man I am—but nothing else. Nothing to help me figure out what he's actually looking for. Or so my people told me."

"They haven't any reason to lie to you, have they?"

"I wouldn't think so, but even good people manage to justify all sorts of misdeeds." Another lesson he'd learned over the years. "They could have been bribed, or . . . oh, I don't know. Nothing surprises me anymore." He wandered to an armchair and dropped onto it.

"What happens now?"

"I've asked for reports from the concerns farther out, but I won't be hearing anything back until tomorrow, at the earliest. More likely Monday and later in the week. I'd go interview them myself, but I cannot leave Lincolnshire."

"You cannot, no." Stepping behind him, she rubbed his shoulders. "I'm sorry, Sean."

The massage didn't help, but he didn't want to tell her that. It was a chilly night, and someone had laid a fire on the hearth. He stared at the dancing flames for a while, wondering how Corinna was doing with the painting. Wishing he could talk to her, explain their impossible situation.

Wishing he didn't have to explain anything, that there were no impossible situation to explain.

"You didn't send for me," he said finally. "How is Lincolnshire? I suppose I should go up and talk to him."

"He's with Mr. Lawless. His solicitor."

"Again? This late at night?"

"The man's been here for hours. I cannot imagine what the two of them are doing in there."

"Getting Lincolnshire's affairs in order." Wishing he could get *his* affairs in order, Sean sighed and rose. "Thank you. That felt good." He turned and pressed a kiss to his sister's forehead. "I'm after going up to bed."

"Good night to you, Sean. I hope tomorrow will be a better day."

"I hope so, too," he said.

But hoping, he knew, never accomplished anything. He was a doer, not a hoper . . . but there seemed nothing he could do these days to make things right.

Chapter Thirty-eight

"I saw her here earlier," Rachael said, wandering the Teddington ballroom for the second time.

Griffin walked with her, keeping his eyes off her damned clingy dress. Or at least trying to. "I saw her here as well, I think." He wasn't exactly sure which woman was the Dowager Countess of Avonleigh. He realized she was one of the ABC sisters, but Lady C, Juliana's mother-in-law, was the only one of them he knew at all well. He'd always thought of Lady A and Lady B sort of lumped together. One was plump and one was skinny, but he wasn't sure which was which. "Has she got some meat on her bones, or is she a stick?"

"Really, Griffin. She's a perfectly lovely, kind, healthy-looking woman."

The plump one, then. The other one looked like she hadn't eaten in a week, which couldn't possibly be healthy. "Let's check the refreshment room again. And then you can check the ladies' retiring room again."

"And we should check the garden again, too." Rachael turned toward the refreshment room, then turned back. "There's Lady C. I bet she'll know where her sister went. Lady Cavanaugh!" She waved, and Lady C started walking toward them.

They met her halfway. "You look lovely tonight, dear," Lady C told her. "That's a beautiful ball gown, and it matches your eyes, which are sparkling like diamonds."

"Thank you," Rachael said, her eyes sparkling even more. "I'm looking for your sister, Lady Avonleigh. Do you know where she might have gone off to?"

"I'm afraid she went home, dear."

"Oh, no. Is she unwell?"

"Not at all. But my sisters are older and don't stay out as late as they used to, especially since they began helping my son run his New Hope Institute. I expect she's sound asleep by now." Lady C put a hand on Rachael's arm. "What did you want with her? Is it something I can help you with?"

"No. I . . . well, I just need to talk to her. Do you think she'd mind my paying a call on her tomorrow?"

"I'm sure she wouldn't mind at all," Lady C said, looking curious but obviously much too polite to press. She pulled her reticule off her wrist and opened it, fishing out a scrap of paper and a pencil. "She lives just off Oxford Street. I'll write down her direction for you."

"I know where she lives. I was at her house for my cousin Corinna's art reception."

"How could I have forgotten that?" With a little laugh, Lady C dropped the items back into her fancy little purse. "I'm sure she'll be happy to see you again."

"Thank you so much," Rachael said, and waited patiently while Lady C walked off. Or at least, she *looked* patient. No sooner had the older woman got out of earshot than she whirled to Griffin. "Lady Cavanaugh is my aunt—can you believe it? She's such a nice lady. The wait is going to kill me. Can we visit Lady Avonleigh first thing tomorrow? You'll come with me, won't you?"

"I need to take Corinna to Lady Hartley's breakfast."

"That doesn't start until half past one. The best people won't get there until three o'clock. It isn't fashionable to arrive at parties on time."

He'd never understand why a garden party that

started after one o'clock was called a breakfast. He ate breakfast every morning at eight. And why the devil was it "fashionable" to arrive late? But maybe Corinna would be more cooperative if he allowed her to paint until three. "Very well, then. We'll go see Lady Avonleigh right after church."

"How about before church?"

"You can't wake up an old lady to give her this news, Rachael. Or interrupt her toilette. And then no doubt *she'll* be in church, and then she'll want luncheon." Lady A was the one who liked to eat, after all, and Lady Hartley wouldn't be serving "breakfast" until the fashionable people arrived. "I'll pick you up at one o'clock."

"Then we won't get to Lady A's until half past one. What if she's left for Lady Hartley's house already?"

"You just told me people won't arrive until three. Half past noon, then. That ought to be safe."

"I cannot wait that long."

"You've already waited twenty-four years, remember? I expect you'll survive."

"All right," Rachael muttered, sounding more than disgruntled. But her eyes were still sparkling. She looked better than she had in months, as though she were blossoming, as though a weight had lifted off her shoulders. Not that she'd looked bad before . . .

She licked her lips.

Good God, he would really be in trouble now.

"How is it going?" Griffin asked.

Startled, Corinna jumped, then quickly stepped from behind her easel, struggling out of the fog she'd worked in all day.

"All right," she said, although the painting was going brilliantly. It was faced away from him, but she raised her palette before it like a shield.

She couldn't risk Griffin's seeing it before she'd changed Sean's hair and eyes—she didn't want him to know Sean was her model unless he had to know. Unless she decided she had no choice but to tell him. With any luck, Griffin might decide she could marry Sean without ever learning he had posed nude.

"I don't want you to see it until it's finished."

He only shrugged, in any case. He'd never cared overmuch about her art. "I'm glad to hear it's going well. I want you to attend Lady Hartley's breakfast tomorrow."

"I'm not going, Griffin. I already told you that. How was the Teddington ball?"

"It went well. I lined up three men there for you to meet tomorrow. You should go up to bed now, so you'll be fresh."

She glanced toward the clock on the drawing room's mantel. "It's but one in the morning, and you know I rarely stop painting before three. And I don't need to be fresh tomorrow, because I'm not going to the breakfast."

"How about if we compromise and you paint until three o'clock tomorrow afternoon? That sounds fair, doesn't it? It's the event of the Season."

"The Summer Exhibition is the event of my *life*." He was such a brother. She decided to change the subject. "Have you asked Mr. Delaney's advice yet regarding property management?"

"I've been too busy. And why do you care?" His eyes narrowed speculatively. "Juliana asked me about that, too. You're not interested in Mr. Delaney, are you?"

She wondered whether he would consider that a good thing or a bad one. "Interested in what way?"

"As a suitor. A potential husband."

She still couldn't tell what he was thinking. Better to play it safe, she decided; better he should get to know Sean before she admitted anything. "Of course not. I just remembered you'd said you wanted to talk to him, and I wondered if you had yet, that's all." She hoped that when he *did* talk to Sean he'd be impressed, which would save her from having to tell him who had posed for her portrait. "Now leave me alone, Griffin. I need to paint. And I'm not going to Lady Hartley's breakfast."

"I'll send our regrets," he gritted out, and then, as he walked off, Corinna heard him mutter, "Why do women always seem to get the best of me?"

Fog-free for the first time all day, she turned back to appraise her picture. It really was coming along brilliantly, she thought, smiling. Just brilliantly.

But, oh, my.

This was one extremely sensual painting.

Maybe no one besides the committee should see it before it was hung in the Summer Exhibition. It was her best work ever, but someone might express shock and talk her out of submitting it. Griffin especially—even though he wouldn't be able to tell it was Sean, he might not be entirely thrilled that his sister had painted such a portrait. After all was said and done, after she'd been honored by its selection, it would be a different story. He'd be proud of her then, surely. But before then . . .

Thank heavens Lady A had offered to go with her to deliver it. She'd have to cover it up so the dear woman wouldn't be able to examine it in the carriage. Then somehow get through the submission process without her ever seeing it.

How she'd manage that, she couldn't imagine, but she'd worry about that later. After the painting was finished, after she'd changed Sean's hair and eyes.

Until then, she wanted him just as he looked now, she thought, raising her brush to the canvas and letting the fog close in again.

Chapter Thirty-nine

"Did you not sleep well?" Deirdre asked solicitously when Sean slammed into the breakfast room again Sunday morning.

"I didn't sleep at all." He'd spent the entire night alternating between worrying about his company and arguing with himself over whether to devastate Corinna now or allow her to paint in peace.

There was nothing he could do about the former that he wasn't already doing. He knew that. As for the latter, he also knew what was best for Corinna. But it didn't feel best for him.

The gravel had torn his insides to a pulp.

Still deliberating and ignoring Deirdre, he gulped down coffee and little else, then stomped upstairs to play nephew to Lincolnshire.

Coming to a halt in the earl's doorway, he listened to the man's ragged snores for a long minute, calming down somewhat. "How is he doing?" he finally asked Mrs. Skeffington quietly.

Sadness etched on her kind, plain face, the nurse shook her head.

The ragged snores ceased, making them both turn. "Cainewood?" Lincolnshire croaked.

"I'm here, Uncle." Sean walked closer and touched the man's hand, wincing when his fingers left indentations in the swollen flesh. "It's Sean."

Lincolnshire slitted his eyes, but just for a bare moment. "Cainewood?"

"He's not here, Uncle. But I am."

"Wake me . . . when . . . Cainewood . . . arrives," he wheezed again, and drifted off.

Sean looked to Mrs. Skeffington. "He thought I was Cainewood. Is he delirious, then?"

"Not delirious, but very tired. He was up quite late last night, closeted with his solicitor. And I fear . . ." She sighed and shook her head again. "I cannot say it."

Sean also feared the earl's end was near. "I cannot say it, either," he muttered, wondering why that should be so depressing. Life would be much easier when this was over. Maybe not happier, but surely easier. "Why would he want to see Cainewood?"

She shrugged. "Lord Lincolnshire asked for the marquess last night. Instructed Mr. Lawless to summon him first thing in the morning. I expect he wants to say goodbye. They've been neighbors for thirty years, after all, since the marquess was born." She forced a smile and patted Sean's hand with her own sturdy one. "I'll watch your uncle, Mr. Hamilton. You go paint. There's nothing you can do for him now."

"I cannot . . . Well, perhaps I will." The earl didn't seem to want or need him right at the moment. He wouldn't paint, of course, but perhaps he would leave for a while. Go talk to Corinna or return to his offices. See if any reports had come in yet from outside London. "Please ask my wife to send for me if my uncle has need of me. She'll know where to find me."

He went downstairs and asked a footman to see that his curricle was brought around. As he headed for the door, the knocker banged, and Quincy opened it to reveal Corinna's brother.

Cainewood stood stiffly, his arms folded behind him. He looked impatient, or maybe furious. Sean didn't know him well enough to be sure which, but he was exhausted out of his mind—and he knew he'd taken liberties with the man's sister.

For one delusional moment, he imagined Cainewood was hiding a pistol behind his back.

"It won't happen again," he promised quickly. Stupidly. Once had been more than enough.

Cainewood frowned and raised both his hands. Empty hands. "I beg your pardon?"

Sean blew out a breath, remembering Lincolnshire. "The earl has been asking for you."

"Yes, his solicitor summoned me. I know not why. But I've another appointment this morning, so I'm hoping this won't take long."

"I think he just wants to say good-bye," Sean assured him, moving past him.

On the street, waiting for his curricle, he found his gaze drifting to the town house with the blue door on the west side of the square. As though drawn by unseen cords, he walked toward it, stopping on the pavement in front of the large window that fronted the drawing room.

Corinna wasn't in the drawing room, of course. It wasn't even ten o'clock, and she slept until noon unless someone offered her a kiss for getting up early. Her easel was visible, though, so he walked closer to have a look at how Lincolnshire's portrait was coming along. But it sat sideways, and the painting was covered by a crisp white sheet.

And it wasn't finished. He knew that. She'd use every minute she had left before it was due. It wouldn't be finished before tomorrow, which meant he couldn't devastate her until then. He couldn't wake her—that wouldn't be fair.

He needed to see this thing through the right way, he lectured himself, heading back to where his curricle waited. He'd known that all along. There had been no use losing sleep over a decision so obvious.

* * *

Lady Avonleigh's town house was near all of Oxford Street's many shops. As Griffin banged the knocker, Rachael couldn't help hoping that Lady A might invite her to visit often. They could go shopping and get to know each other. It would be such fun. She'd never had any living grandparents to spend time with—at least not any she'd known of.

The butler who answered the door looked as old as Lady A and Lady B put together. "Yes?" he croaked.

"I've come to call on Lady Avonleigh," Rachael said.

He cleared his throat. "She's not here. She's left for Lady Hartley's breakfast."

"But it's not even one o'clock."

He shrugged his bony shoulders. "She doesn't like to be late for anything, my lady."

Her heart sinking, she swiveled to Griffin. "I told you we should have come first thing in the morning."

He shrugged, too, but his shoulders were much wider. "I don't mind waiting."

"Lady Hartley's breakfast will probably last until midnight! It's the event of the Season."

"We'll change our clothes, then, and go to the breakfast."

"I've already sent my regrets. And it's in a garden, under a tent. There will be no place to talk privately."

"We could walk with Lady Avonleigh in the garden."

"Any number of people might be walking as well and overhear us."

"Then we could take her into Lady Hartley's house."

"You cannot go into someone's house during a garden party, Griffin. It's not polite to go where you're not invited."

"Juliana went into Lady Hartley's house during last year's breakfast," he pointed out.

"And look what happened! It was the scandal of the Season!" When it came to the social niceties, men didn't know anything. She sighed. "We'll come back tomorrow. In the *morning*."

Chapter Forty

As the clock on the mantel struck ten on Sunday night, Corinna dipped her smallest brush in coffee-colored paint and carefully covered the green irises on her canvas. Over the next quarter hour, she added black pupils, curvature, depth and highlights, glints where the flame of a candle reflected.

Blowing out a breath, she stepped back.

Sean's eyes were brown now, and the portrait was done.

She'd already changed his dark hair to a streaky blond, made it a little straighter and a little longer, made it positively glow in the candlelight. The rest of the picture remained the same—the shockingly sensual pose; the sculpted, faintly stubbled face; the ridged, toned torso; the heart-stopping, contemplative gaze—but she was sure no one would recognize Sean now.

The painting was going to be a sensation.

Blond or black-haired, brown-eyed or green, his image looked compelling. Captivating. Spellbinding. Seductive. Like the man himself.

She'd never completed such a large painting in only two days before, and she could hardly believe she was finished. The hours had sped by in such a frenzy since late Friday night. But done was done, and there was no sense in fiddling with it any longer. She'd be as likely to ruin it as she was to improve it.

Although she couldn't show it to Sean, of course—she wasn't yet ready for anyone, including him, to learn he was her portrait's inspiration—she couldn't wait to tell him it was complete. He'd be so surprised to hear she'd finished half a day early. Bursting with happiness and excitement and energy, she hefted the canvas off her easel and started upstairs, holding it at arm's length, where she could smile at it as she went.

She was hauling it down the corridor toward her bedroom when the door to Griffin's study opened. She whirled to face him, watched him raise his hands to grip the jamb on either side of his head. Such a casual pose, when she was feeling her heart pound in her throat.

"What are you doing, Corinna?"

"Bringing this to my room. I'm finished."

"Are you?" He looked pleased. Probably because he could get back to shoving men at her now. "Let's see it," he said, moving into the corridor.

"No!" In reaction, she pulled the canvas closer to her body, nearly smearing paint against her apron. She'd have killed him if that had happened, just *killed* him. "Not yet. It isn't varnished yet." Artists rarely varnished their paintings before submitting them to the Summer Exhibition. There was a tradition called Varnishing Day, after the selected pictures were hung but before the Exhibition opened, when all the artists came to make last-minute changes and coat their works in varnish. "I don't want anyone to see it until after it's varnished. If it's accepted, you can see it in the Exhibition."

"Well, that's just silly."

She shrugged. "I'm an artist, temperamental and all that." She started backing down the corridor. "I'm going to put this in my room now, and you'd better not go looking at it."

It was his turn to shrug, as though he couldn't be bothered to walk that far, anyway. He backed into his study, and she backed into her room and closed the door behind her. After leaning the painting against a wall, facing in, she covered it with a sheet. Then she balanced a hairpin precariously on the top edge, where it would be knocked off if anyone disturbed it.

There, she thought with a grin.

Impatient to see Sean, she ripped off her apron, smoothed her dress, left her room, and poked her head into Griffin's study. "I'm going to tell Lord Lincolnshire his portrait is finished," she said, although, of course, it wasn't.

Scribbling on some paperwork, Griffin didn't look up. "Lincolnshire will be sleeping now, Corinna."

"Maybe, but maybe not. I won't wake him. If he's sleeping, I'll go back in the morning."

"Take a footman with you. I'll not have you walking alone in Berkeley Square in the middle of the night."

Did he really think she'd walk alone in London at night? *That* much of a rebel she wasn't. A lady could get herself raped or worse, even in Mayfair.

"I'm not the ninnyhammer you seem to think I am," she informed him. "I won't be long." Then she all but ran down the stairs and all the way to Lincolnshire House, pausing just long enough to request a footman. Leaving the footman panting at Lincolnshire's gate, she lifted her skirts, raced up the portico steps, and banged the knocker.

Quincy answered. "Good evening."

"I wish a word with Mr. Hamilton."

"I'm sorry, but he's not at home, milady."

"He isn't? Oh." Disappointment was a sudden ache in her middle. *How many hours must intervene ere she could press him to her throbbing heart, as the sweet partner of her future days?* she recalled reading in *Children of the Abbey*. "I'll return tomorrow then, I guess."

She had just started to turn away when Deirdre came to the door. "Lady Corinna?"

Turning back, she dredged up a smile. "I was hoping to see your . . . your husband, Mrs. Hamilton. I have something exciting to tell him."

"He's been gone all day. A wee bit of trouble with his, ah . . . his latest painting." Deirdre slanted a glance to Quincy. "Would you care to come in?"

"Is Lord Lincolnshire awake?"

"I fear not." Sean's sister sighed. "He spent the morning closeted with his solicitor yet again. Then he complained of some pain—claimed the Regent was sitting on his chest again or some such thing. He passed out for a moment, then woke and fell asleep. He's been sleeping ever since."

"That doesn't sound good," Corinna observed, the ache of disappointment growing sharper. "I'll return tomorrow, when I hope he'll be better."

Deirdre nodded and took a step back to allow Quincy to shut the door.

"Wait," Corinna said, remembering something. "I've a question, if you wouldn't mind. About a word or a phrase I'm thinking might be Irish."

"Is that so?" Coming forward again, Deirdre looked curious. "What is it, then?"

"Cooshla-macree. Does that mean something? Or is it only a few syllables of nonsense?"

Sean's sister frowned a moment before her expression cleared. "*Cuisle mo chroí*," she repeated, the words sounding a bit different as they rolled off her tongue. "It means 'pulse of my heart.' Or 'sweetheart,' I suppose you might say."

"Sweetheart," Corinna breathed. "How about creena?"

"*Críona*, 'my heart.' "

"Ahroon?"

"*A rún*, 'my love.' " Sean's sister cocked her pretty blond head. "I find myself wondering where you heard these words, I do confess."

"I expect you know." Bursting with happiness once more, Corinna gave a startled Deirdre an impulsive hug before she ran back home.

Chapter Forty-one

Sean didn't slam into the breakfast room Monday morning. He was much too drained, much too discouraged for so much emotion. At half past seven, he simply walked in and slowly sat down, feeling brittle, as though his bones might crack in the process.

Deirdre slid his cup of coffee toward him just as slowly. "No good news?"

"No news at all." He reached for the cup but didn't drink from it, just cradled its warmth between his palms. "No helpful news, at any rate. Maybe today."

She sipped her tea, watching him. "Lady Corinna came by to see you last night before you returned. Late, but I hadn't yet gone up to bed. She seemed rather . . . excited. Out of breath. I'm thinking she must have run all the way here from her house. She said she had something to tell you."

"Her painting must be finished," he said glumly. She'd completed it half a day early, which meant it must have gone well. But it also meant it was time to explain the facts.

"You don't sound happy for her. It's a good thing, isn't it?"

"Sure, and it's excellent." Now he could devastate the love of his life.

They both glanced over as the door opened. "Mr. Hamilton?"

A maid entered. The one who'd shown Sean upstairs the first day he arrived, the little bird of a middle-aged woman who'd informed him Lincolnshire was the most wonderful man in all of England.

Today she looked like an old woman, her face drawn in tight lines. "Nurse Skeffington asked me to fetch you," she said. "Your uncle is dying."

In her family's Lincoln's Inn Fields town house, Rachael was going downstairs to have breakfast when her brother started up. "Oh, there you are," he said. "I was coming to look for you."

"You're up and about early." Pausing on the steps, she noted he was wearing shoes rather than boots, a double-breasted tailcoat rather than a riding coat. "And isn't it Monday morning, Noah?"

"Of course it is, yes."

"I thought all you horse-mad young bucks met at Tattersall's on Mondays to settle your accounts. Or is Monday an auction day? Either way, you always seem to head for Tattersall's every Monday, but you're not dressed for that."

"Maybe I'm not horse-mad anymore," he suggested, a challenge in his blue eyes.

Hearing a challenge in his voice, too, she wondered if he could possibly be serious. "You're off to your club, then, I expect?"

"No, I'm not." Noah lifted his square chin. "I was hoping you'd come with me to Oxford Street. To Robert Gillow and Company, to be more precise, to pick out a desk."

"Did you say a desk?" She must have heard him wrong. "What kind of a desk?"

"An oak one, I'm thinking. Something sturdy, in any case, with many drawers. The one in the study seems to be growing rather rickety."

"I imagine it's a hundred years old, at the very least. But however did you come to notice it's rickety?"

He raised his scarred brow. "I *used* it, Rachael. Is that such a surprise?"

"Frankly, yes." *Surprise* seemed too mild a word—she was positively shocked. First he'd asked for an inventory at Greystone, and now this. Could it be her younger brother was growing up? At twenty-two, he was looking like a man, but was he actually becoming one?

"Well?" he asked, still looking like a man, but one who was rather annoyed. "Will you come with me or not?"

"Oh, I wish I could." The sight of Noah inspecting desks rather than horseflesh was bound to be a spectacle. But she expected Griffin to arrive in half an hour. "I've other plans for today, I'm afraid, but let me talk to Claire and Elizabeth about going with you to Gillow's instead."

"Lord Lincolnshire! Mr. and Mrs. Hamilton!"

Corinna hurried toward Lord Lincolnshire's bedroom, having been told at the front door that Sean and Deirdre were with him. She'd risen at the crack of dawn this morning and come before even eating breakfast, because she couldn't wait a moment longer to share her news.

"I finished my portrait!" she announced, stopping in the doorway. "I'm going to submit it this . . ."

The sentence trailed off when she saw James by the bed, leaning over the earl with his stethoscope. All her excitement dissipated along with the words.

". . . afternoon," she finished in a small voice. "How is he?"

Sean rose from where he sat by Deirdre. "I think Lord Stafford is just about finished and ready to tell us."

"I am, yes." James drew the covers up to the earl's chin and straightened, looking grim. "I fear the end is imminent. He may last the night, but not any longer. I don't believe he'll wake, either. He'll likely just continue like this until his breathing and his heart simply stop. I'm sorry," he concluded with a sigh. "We'll all miss him."

Corinna looked back to the huge crimson-draped bed where Lord Lincolnshire slumbered, propped upright against a dozen pillows. When the covers were down, she'd noticed his belly appeared swollen now, along with the rest of him. His skin looked tight and wet, as though it were weeping fluid. Gurgling noises came from his throat.

Her heart sank even lower. "He must be suffering so. That sounds dreadful."

"He sounds like that because his lungs are filling," James explained gently. "But he's sleeping. I don't think he's really suffering in the sense you imagine." He dropped the stethoscope in his leather bag and snapped it closed, looking to Sean. "I can stay if you wish, but there isn't anything I can do. It's only a matter of time now."

"I understand," Sean said. "We'll not be needing you to stay, though I appreciate the offer. I'll be with him."

"I'll stay with him, too," Deirdre added softly. "And Nurse Skeffington will be back within the hour."

"All right, then." James moved to Corinna and lightly kissed her cheek. "I'm sorry," he said again, and left.

For a moment, Corinna just stared at Lord Lincolnshire. Hot tears pricked her eyes. Deirdre rose and came to place a hand on her shoulder. "I'm sure he knows you finished his portrait."

Guilt flooded her. She *hadn't* finished it. But she would. She'd promised to paint his final portrait, and she'd follow through with that. She had only to fix the underlying anatomy, and she knew how to do that now. His portrait wouldn't be exhibited at the Royal Academy, but it would hang here at Lincolnshire House.

Which would be John Hamilton's house, unfortunately. At that thought, a rush of anger tempered her guilt. But it would be Deirdre's house, too, at least until she got her divorce, and that thought was a little mollifying.

She raised a hand to touch Deirdre's on her shoulder. "Thank you for saying that."

"Which other pictures will you submit along with the portrait today?" Sean asked.

"I'm not submitting any other pictures," she told him, turning to him. "I've decided to submit the portrait alone." She neglected to mention it wasn't the one he expected. "It's my best work, the painting I wish to exhibit as my debut. Should it not be chosen, I'll try again next year."

" 'Tis pleased I am to hear you're that happy with the way it turned out," he said.

But he didn't look pleased. Or sound pleased. At all.

"I'm sorry you're losing Lord Lincolnshire," she said, her heart breaking for him. "I know you've grown close."

He nodded. "I need to talk to you about something. Something important. Not here, though," he said, slanting a glance to his sister. "Later."

"Take her out of the room," Deirdre said. "I'll stay with Lord Lincolnshire." When he hesitated, she added, "Go," and waved a hand. "Lord Stafford said he might last the whole night. Nothing will be happening in a few minutes."

After hesitating a moment more, Sean took Corinna's arm and drew her out and down the corridor. But when he turned to her, he didn't say anything. He just looked at her, his heart in his deep green eyes.

"What is it?" she asked. Remembering he'd called her *sweetheart* and *my heart* and *my love*, she raised a hand to his cheek. "You look so sad."

"I am sad." Turning his face, he raised his own hand to hold hers to his mouth and pressed a warm kiss to her palm before releasing it. "I'm very sad, Corinna. I cannot do this standing outside Lincolnshire's bedroom. Will you meet me at Hamilton's studio one last time?"

"Of course." She'd soothe his sadness then, show him how much she loved him. She'd kiss him and more, and . . . He was right: None of that could happen here. But sad as she was herself at losing Lord Lincolnshire, her heart started galloping at the thought of meeting him. "What time?"

"In an hour," he said, and then: "No. I need to stay with Lincolnshire right now. I'd never forgive myself if he—"

"I understand." He looked tortured. "James said Lord Lincolnshire wouldn't last the night, and you need to be with him until then. And I need to submit my portrait later this afternoon. How about tomorrow?"

"That's too long . . . but all right."

"I don't want to wait that long, either." It seemed so very long since they'd last been together. Only two and a half days since he'd last held her in his arms, but it felt like forever.

"Shall we say ten o'clock?" he asked.

"All the ladies are visiting Aunt Frances tomorrow at eleven, but I can—"

"Let's make it in the afternoon, then." He shut his eyes briefly, then opened them with a sigh. "This will probably be best," he said as though trying to convince himself. "I'll spend the morning making arrangements for Lincolnshire's funeral."

"But you won't need to play his nephew once he's gone," she said, then clapped a hand over her mouth.

He glanced quickly around, but fortunately no servants had overheard. Looking relieved, he ran his hands slowly down her arms, then linked his fingers with hers, lacing them together. "I owe him that, Corinna," he said softly. "And who else is going to do it?"

He was such a good man. And he looked even more tortured. The rush of happiness she'd felt at the thought of spending time with him seemed suddenly overshadowed by his distress.

She couldn't kiss him here outside Lincolnshire's bedroom, but she threw her arms around him, holding him tight. "This will all be over soon," she murmured against his chest, thinking much better times lay ahead.

"Yes," he said in a flat tone. "It will."

Chapter Forty-two

Half an hour later, Griffin found himself on Lady Avonleigh's doorstep again. In the *morning*.

The ancient butler opened the door. "Yes?" he croaked.

"I've come to call on Lady Avonleigh," Rachael said.

He cleared his throat. "She's left the house, milady."

"I don't believe this!" She turned to Griffin. "We should have come earlier."

He'd picked her up at nine o'clock, and now it was half past. "How much earlier could we have come?" He'd been sure they'd be dragging poor Lady A from her bed. In his experience, ladies slept until at least ten. Except Corinna, who slept until at least noon. "What time does Lady Avonleigh rise?" he asked the old geezer at the door.

"Six o'clock," Lady Balmforth said, apparently having overheard them and come to see what was up. She looked curious. "When you get to a certain age, dearie, you won't sleep late in the morning, either."

"Good morning, Lady Balmforth," Rachael said before swinging to him again. "I told you we should have come earlier."

"We'll come earlier tomorrow." With any luck, he wouldn't receive another surprise summons from Lincolnshire.

"I'm not waiting until tomorrow. We'll wait here today."

Yesterday he'd been willing to wait, and she hadn't wanted to. Today he'd assumed she wanted to leave, but she wanted to wait. He would never understand women. "Fine," he said, "we'll wait."

"Well, maybe we shouldn't wait." She turned to Lady B. "When will Lady Avonleigh be back?"

"It was Aurelia's turn to assist our James today at his Institute," Lady B said. "Then she's accompanying Lady Corinna to the Royal Academy this afternoon."

"Oh, damn," Rachael said softly, making the older woman's eyes widen at her language. "I'd forgotten about that. The two of them planned that right in front of me, too, when we were visiting Lady Malmsey and the new baby."

Lady B briefly touched Rachael's hand. "My sister will be at home for a short while in between. She told our nephew she had to leave before luncheon." The skinny lady leaned closer. "Aurelia never likes to miss her luncheon."

Griffin had guessed as much.

"What did you want to talk to my sister about?" Lady B asked, looking very curious. "Is it important?"

Rachael nodded. "Very. But I . . . well . . . you're welcome to listen, but I'd rather wait until Lady Avonleigh is here to talk about it."

Lady Balmforth looked even more curious. "If it's that important, perhaps you ought to send Lady Corinna a note, saying she should find someone else to accompany her to Somerset House."

"That's an excellent idea," Rachael said, "but I think *you* need to write the note. That way Corinna won't be suspicious about what I'm doing with Lady Avonleigh."

"She's not going to be suspicious," Griffin said.

"Yes, she is. Your sisters aren't stupid, Griffin."

"Why don't you just tell them the truth?"

"I'm still not ready," Rachael said.

And Lady Balmforth looked very, very curious. "I think we'd better send for Cornelia, too," she said.

At one o'clock, Corinna came downstairs with a footman trailing behind carrying her painting, which she'd framed—by borrowing one off a family portrait—and wrapped in brown paper. "I need a hackney coach," she told Adamson, their butler. "My brother took the carriage, and I must pick up Lady Avonleigh."

Adamson was a very short man, but he prided himself on being quite dignified and proper. "I don't know if that is wise, Lady Corinna."

"It is necessary. Please hail a hackney."

"Lord Cainewood has been gone since the morning. It is likely he will be home soon."

She was early, true. It wouldn't take an hour to reach Lady A's house, and the woman had said two o'clock. But she was too anxious to wait. "Hail a hackney," she repeated, and paused before adding, "now."

He hemmed and hawed and clucked his tongue, clearly reluctant to put Lord Cainewood's sister in a hackney coach. Corinna crossed her arms, knowing he would eventually comply. But before that happened, the knocker banged, and Adamson opened the door to reveal a messenger with a letter.

"Ah," the butler said, looking not at all displeased to have an excuse to put off hailing a cab. "It's directed to you, Lady Corinna."

She grabbed it and broke the seal, swiftly scanning the missive.

My Dear Lady Corinna,

I am sorry to inform you that circumstances prevent my sister, Lady Avonleigh, from accompanying you to the Royal Academy this afternoon. Unfortunately, I can-

not do so in her place. Please accept my sincerest apologies.

Yours sincerely,
Lady Balmforth

"Circumstances? What is that supposed to mean?" Corinna sighed. "It seems I need paper instead of a hackney. I must send a note to Alexandra."

Chapter Forty-three

"I don't really know where to begin, Lady Avonleigh." Rachael hadn't expected to be nervous. But now that Lady A was finally home and they were all seated in her peach drawing room, she didn't know what to say.

Sitting across from her in a peach wing chair, Lady A gave her a kind smile. "Through the years I've learned what's important. Both my sisters are here, and I just came from seeing James, which means all the people I love most are healthy. I cannot imagine anything you could tell me that could be so terribly bad."

"Oh, it isn't bad." Rachael clenched her hands in her lap. "At least, I'm hoping you won't think it's bad. I'm hoping you'll think—"

"Say it already," Griffin interjected, sitting on the sofa beside her. He'd seemed a bit annoyed that they'd had to wait so long, but that was his fault; if they'd come early, as she'd wanted to, they wouldn't have had to wait at all. "Good God, I've never seen you so flustered. You're always so levelheaded and composed."

Was that what he thought? She'd never felt that way inside. But she rather liked him having that opinion of her. And he was right: She needed to just say it.

"You're my grandmother," she told Lady Avonleigh in a rush. "I'm Georgiana's daughter."

Lady A looked at her. Her face went rather white,

and from across the room she just looked at Rachael, making her feel very uneasy. It was rather awkward, really. She'd been picturing Lady Avonleigh welcoming her with open arms. She'd been picturing them shopping together.

Griffin leaned closer. "Maybe she's a bit peeved because she hasn't had her luncheon yet," he whispered.

Rachael was about to elbow him when Lady Balmforth finally broke the silence. "You cannot be Georgiana's daughter," she said, not unkindly. "Our Georgiana jumped off the London Bridge."

"She must have just pretended to jump off the London Bridge and then run away and married my father. I mean, not my real father, but the man who raised me."

The awkward silence resumed. Rachael looked back to Lady A, but her grandmother was still just looking at her. No matter how much she wanted to be welcomed with open arms, it was clear that wasn't going to happen. Griffin wrapped one of his own arms around her shoulders, and she leaned into him, taking the comfort he offered, forgiving him for being annoyed and saying the stupid things men often said.

"Who is that, dear?" Lady Cavanaugh asked. "Who was the father who raised you?"

"John Chase," Rachael replied. "The Earl of Greystone."

And Lady Avonleigh suddenly came to life. "What did you say?"

"John Chase, the Earl—"

"Oh, my goodness!" she squealed, and then she rose from her chair and rushed over to the sofa and welcomed Rachael with open arms. Probably the most welcoming arms Rachael had ever felt. They clung together, and Rachael inhaled her grandmother's gardenia perfume, remembering her mother smelling the same.

Griffin moved to Lady A's chair so she could share the sofa with her granddaughter. Tears ran down both their faces, and they just held on to each other for a good long while. Until Lady B leaned over and tapped her older sister on the shoulder.

"What convinced you?" she demanded.

"My daughter was in love with John Chase," Lady A said tearily. She released Rachael, but still held her hand tightly. "My husband and I wouldn't let her marry him."

"That's right!" Lady C exclaimed. "I'd forgotten."

The whole story came out.

John Cartwright had been a second son. While a young man in the army before his marriage, a man named Thomas Grimstead had saved his life on a battlefield in Germany during the Seven Years' War. Cartwright had granted the man a boon, and Grimstead wanted his newborn son married to the aristocrat's firstborn daughter. After Cartwright's older brother died, he'd sold out of the military and become the Earl of Avonleigh and married Aurelia. They'd had a daughter, Alice, who was promised to Grimstead's son. And a son, who'd sadly drowned at twenty-one, and another daughter, Georgiana.

"How did Georgiana end up married to Grimstead," Griffin asked, "if Alice was promised to him?"

"Alice fell in love with her cousin," Lady A explained. "Her father forbade her to marry him, but they eloped to Gretna Green. Then my husband cut her out of our lives. I've heard she eventually died, but I've never really known what happened to her—"

"I know!" Rachael said. "I knew Aunt Alice. We saw her all the time. I know what happened to her. She had a child before she died, a little boy named Edmund." She wouldn't tell Lady A that the child had been crippled and unable to talk. Not now, at least. "After that, Mama raised Edmund, but he, too, died a few years later."

Her grandmother's eyes glazed with tears. "Was she happy in her marriage, my Alice?"

"I think so. I was young when she passed away, but

she never seemed unhappy to me." Even though having Edmund must have been heartbreaking. "She and Mama visited often. They loved each other very much. And I loved Aunt Alice, too." She squeezed her grandmother's hand. "Go on, please."

But it seemed Lady A couldn't. "I'm so happy to know Alice and Georgiana were together," she whispered, and waved her free hand toward her sisters.

With a teary smile, Lady C took over the story. "After Alice failed to follow through with the betrothal, Georgiana was next in line. When she turned eighteen, she begged for one London Season before marrying Grimstead—"

"I never had been able to deny her anything," Lady A interrupted. "Georgiana was the sweetest child."

"I'm sure she was," Rachael said. Maybe Georgiana had lied to her—a lie by omission—but she'd loved Rachael and her siblings dearly. Georgiana had been a wonderful mother. In the past months, it seemed she'd forgotten that. "She loved you, too, Lady Avon—"

"Grandmama. Please call me Grandmama."

Rachael's heart swelled. "She loved you, too, Grandmama. She always wore gardenia perfume. I think that must have been because she missed you. Did she meet my father that Season?"

Her grandmother waved a hand again, overtaken by emotion.

"That's when she met John Chase, yes," Lady B said. "She begged to marry him, but my sister's husband wouldn't hear of it. He'd made a promise and had no other daughters left to satisfy his debt to the man who had saved his life. Georgiana hadn't seen her sister in seven years, and she didn't want to disobey her parents and end up estranged like Alice. So she reluctantly agreed to go through with the ceremony."

"That sounds like Mama," Rachael said. "What happened then?"

Her grandmother was recovered enough to continue.

"Grimstead took a leave of absence to wed her, and got her with child right away. Then he went back to his regiment, and Georgiana came home to London to live with us." Her voice dropped. "She didn't love him, so she didn't mind, really, and she was so looking forward to having her baby."

"Me," Rachael whispered.

"Yes. And then she received a letter saying her husband had been executed for treason. No details. She was furious with us, I'm afraid, for making her abandon her love and wed a traitor. She wrote a suicide note and jumped off the London Bridge, taking her baby with her. Her body was never found."

"Because she didn't jump off the London Bridge," Griffin said, "no matter that the note said she would. She ran to the countryside and married John Chase instead."

They could only guess what had happened after that. She hadn't wanted her child to grow up as the son or daughter of a traitor. She'd claimed she was Georgiana Woodby, a commoner, and stayed far away from London in order to avoid ever seeing her parents. Far away from any social situation, to avoid running into anyone she might have known in her previous life.

"Did she have asthma?" Rachael asked.

"Not at all," Lady Avonleigh said. "She was the healthiest of all my children."

"I thought so," Rachael said with a sigh. "So no one ever learned what had become of my real father. How he came to be labeled a traitor." She sighed again, but supposed it wasn't all that important. She'd been making much too much of the whole thing. Her mother had only wanted to protect her from being tainted by her father's shame, and she had new family now, and—

"Oh, I know what happened," her grandmother said. "After my younger daughter's death, I paid a visit to Grimstead's father."

"My grandfather? I met him at the Royal Hospital. But—"

"He's lost his mind, poor man, yes. But I talked to him a long time before that." Lady Avonleigh—Grandmama—shifted on the sofa to face Rachael and took her other hand. "It wasn't all that bad, my dear. If Georgiana had known, she might have forgiven him. Although I suspect she would never have loved him. She was in love with John Chase."

Rachael's parents—the two she'd grown up with—had been very much in love. No matter how angry she'd been with her mother, she'd never forgotten that. "What did Grimstead do?" she asked. "What did he do that wasn't so bad?"

"It was during the war against the colonies in North America, just six years after Georgiana was born. He was much older than she was, you see—probably another reason she preferred Chase. In any event, he and a fellow soldier, one William Smith, killed a British officer to keep him from murdering a number of American civilians. They managed to convince the authorities that the man was shot by a revolutionary. And all was well for twelve years, until Smith fell ill in 1792 and revealed in a deathbed confession that the two of them had killed the officer."

"But if they killed him to save innocent people," Rachael said, looking to Griffin, "the officer might have been a bad man. They might have done a good thing."

"That officer probably was a bad man," Griffin said sympathetically. "But that wouldn't matter. If Grimstead killed a superior, he'd have been arrested, court-martialed, and convicted—regardless of how bad the man had been."

"It doesn't signify," Lady A said. "Not now. Instead of being sorry for everything that happened, let's just be glad we've found each other." She squeezed Rachael's hands, and her smile reminded Rachael of her mother. "I have a granddaughter."

"You have three granddaughters," Rachael said. "Don't forget Claire and Elizabeth. They're Georgiana's daughters, too." Watching her grandmother's soft blue eyes widen, she added, "And you've a grandson as well. Our brother, Noah." Lady A was holding her hands so tightly, her own were beginning to hurt. But she didn't care. Her mother had only wanted to protect her, and her father most likely hadn't really done wrong, and Grandmama had welcomed her with open arms.

"I cannot wait to see your sisters and brother again." Lady B's smile resembled Georgiana's, too. Rachael wondered how she'd never noticed. "I'm their aunt, you know," Lady B added. "And yours. And so is Cornelia."

Lady C, being the youngest, looked closest to her mother of all. "I never had a daughter," she said. "I'm so happy that now I'll have nieces again. And a nephew, too. Oh, my."

"My sisters are out with Noah at present," Rachael told her new family. "They're helping him choose a new desk. But they should be at home later, so we can all go tell them our good news."

There were numerous murmurs of agreement to that plan.

"Maybe we'll all go shopping," Grandmama suggested. "I want to spoil my grandchildren. But first, let's have luncheon."

Chapter Forty-four

Corinna paced the foyer, watching the clock tick toward the hour when it would be too late to submit her painting. Two hours earlier, the messenger she'd dispatched to Alexandra's house had returned with the news that her eldest sister wasn't at home. Corinna had then sent a desperate note to Juliana and another to Rachael, Claire, and Elizabeth.

Since then she'd heard nothing. Nothing. Nothing at all.

"What is taking them all so long?"

"Pardon, my lady?"

"Nothing, Adamson." She paused midpace. "No, not nothing," she revised, glancing at the tall-case clock once again. It was four o'clock, and she had to get to Somerset House by five, or she'd have to wait a whole year for another chance to submit to the Summer Exhibition. "Hail a hackney, now, please. I shall have to take a footman. I cannot wait any longer."

Adamson opened his mouth to protest, but the knocker banged once again. He opened the door to reveal another messenger with a note—and Juliana out in the street, just alighting from the Stafford carriage.

"Thank God," Corinna breathed. "I won't need a hackney after all. Adamson, do please see my painting put in the Stafford carriage immediately. And carefully.

The paper shouldn't be allowed to touch the paint, because it's still not dry."

The butler handed her the note. "It's for you, Lady Corinna. Do you not want to read it?"

"Oh, very well." She broke the seal and scanned it as Juliana joined her on the doorstep. "None of the cousins are at home, either," she said with little surprise.

"Either?" Juliana echoed.

"Alexandra wasn't home, and neither is Griffin. And Lady A and Lady B are both busy this afternoon. And apparently Rachael, Claire, and Elizabeth are all busy, too. I'm grateful you could accompany me. Let's go."

"Everyone else was busy? Everyone? Dear heavens, what are the odds of such a coincidence?"

"I don't know, but I can't think about that now. We'll find out tomorrow when we all visit Aunt Frances and the baby." She ushered her sister toward the carriage, where the painting was already tucked inside. "I must get to the Royal Academy before five o'clock."

They settled against the squabs, side by side facing forward, with the painting leaning against the other seat. As the carriage lurched into traffic, Juliana patted her sister's knee. "You aren't nervous, are you?"

"No," Corinna lied. "Just rushed. I feared no one would get here in time to accompany me. You weren't arriving, and the cousins live all the way in Lincoln's Inn—"

"Mr. Delaney is right nearby. Did you think to ask him?"

"I couldn't."

"Why is that?"

"Lord Lincolnshire is dying, and he has to stay with him. And besides, I couldn't let him see the painting."

"Why is that?"

Holy Hannah, why had she said *that*? The frustrating afternoon had evidently robbed her ability to think straight.

"Why?" Juliana demanded. "You're hiding something, Corinna; I can tell."

There was nothing for it. Her sister would never give up badgering her, and if her painting was accepted, everyone was going to see it in the Summer Exhibition, anyway.

Corinna drew and held a breath. "Have a look," she finally said, reaching across to tear off the brown paper. Or rather, to tear a corner. She seemed to have trouble doing any more. "It's not varnished," she said.

Juliana shrugged. "Is it not?"

"If it's accepted, if it is hung, I'll get a chance to make last minute changes and then varnish it right there on the wall."

"All right." Juliana nodded. "So . . . ?"

"Very well," Corinna said, and ripped the rest of the paper off.

Juliana's eyes widened. "Oh, my goodness."

"Is that all you have to say?"

"It's . . . well, it's different." She stared at the painting. "Nudes of women are fairly common, of course, but not of men."

"He's not nude," Corinna pointed out, feeling a bit queasy. "He's wearing trousers."

"Very tight ones," her sister agreed. "He's absolutely . . ." She blinked. "Dear heavens, don't you just want to take a bite out of him?"

Well, yes, as a matter of fact . . . but Corinna wasn't sure she liked her sister speaking of biting the man she loved. And Juliana was still staring.

"He's compelling," her sister murmured now. "I cannot seem to take my eyes off of him." But she did, finally meeting Corinna's. "It's magnificent, Corinna. You've always done good work, but this is spectacular."

Corinna's breath went out in a rush. "Do you really think so?"

"I know so. It's groundbreaking." She shifted her gaze back to the painting. "Why did you not want Mr. Delaney to see it?"

"Does it not . . . remind you of anyone you know?"

Juliana tilted her head. "Blond hair and brown eyes. That's an unusual combination, isn't it? I don't think so."

Corinna had counted on no one looking past the coloring, but she must not have been completely convinced, because relief sang through her veins now. "I feared Mr. Delaney would find it shocking, that's all. His father was a vicar, you know."

"Really? I know very little about him."

"I don't know much about him, either," Corinna said, averting her gaze.

Chapter Forty-five

In the wee hours, the earl died.

He slipped off peacefully, leaving the world in his sleep as Lord Stafford had said he would. One instant his breath rattled noisily; the next he went eerily silent. Sean and Deirdre both held their own breath for a tense moment, then turned to each other, embracing and holding tight. Deirdre's tears wet her brother's shirtfront, but they were quiet tears. Tears born of grief mixed with relief.

Sean felt exactly the same.

He sat by the earl's side the balance of the night, because it seemed like the right thing to do. And because he wasn't ready to begin what he needed to do next. Because eventually he would finish with that.

And then . . .

Dawn was a faint glow through the bedroom window when the household stirred to life. Mrs. Skeffington appeared on the threshold, holding a ewer of fresh water. "Is he . . . ?"

"Gone," Sean said quietly. "With the angels."

A sound of sorrow escaped her throat, and she turned and fled, returning a few minutes later with Higginbotham.

"My lord," the steward said, "what shall we do?"

For a moment Sean was nonplussed. He wasn't a lord; he didn't belong here. But Higginbotham didn't know that, of course, and no one else at Lincolnshire House did, either. The lot of them wandered at loose ends, passing by the earl's chamber as though they were all ghosts themselves.

When Sean failed to respond, Higginbotham released a shuddering breath. "There must needs be funeral arrangements, and—"

"I'll see to everything," Sean assured him. It would be a busy morning.

And then . . .

"Thank you, my lord earl." Higginbotham forced a wan half smile of gratitude. "I fear I am . . . numb."

Sean wished he could say the same. He wasn't numb. Pain suffused every fiber of his being. He had to force himself to move, to do what needed to be done.

And then . . .

Then his empty life stretched ahead.

Seemingly forever.

Chapter Forty-six

ORANGE CUSTARD

Boil a pint of Cream with a little sack. When it be cold, take four Yolks and two whites of Eggs, a little juice of Orange and peel of Orange and Sugar to your palate. Mix them well together, and bake them in cups. Before serving, put your cups on ice.

This tastes lovely, and brings love as well. My sisters and I each made this when we were looking for love, and we found it.
—Anne Chase, Marchioness of Cainewood, 1772

Excitement still simmered in Corinna on Tuesday when she arrived to visit Frances and the new baby. Her submission had gone even better than she'd hoped. Though she'd half expected to be asked what made her think she, Corinna Chase, was worthy of submitting to the Summer Exhibition, nothing of the like had occurred. No one had looked askance. Not only had her painting been accepted for consideration, but Henry Fuseli, who'd taken possession of it, had exclaimed loudly over its brilliance.

She supposed she shouldn't be surprised that a man who painted weird, erotic pictures might approve of a portrait like hers.

She wasn't sure whether Lord Lincolnshire had died

yet or not, but she knew he probably had, and that was the only thing that marred her happiness. And she was very much looking forward to this afternoon, when she would meet Sean at Hamilton's studio.

When she entered Aunt Frances's drawing room, Ladies A, B, and C were the only ones there, and they were chattering enthusiastically. Corinna wondered what could possibly have happened to make them babble like that, but when she appeared in the doorway they all fell silent. She saw the three of them exchange significant glances before Lady Avonleigh met her gaze.

"Oh, my dear," she cried. "I'm so sorry I couldn't accompany you to Somerset House yesterday. Did you manage to submit your artwork?"

"Yes, I did," Corinna assured her. She was about to excitedly explain what had happened, but then Aunt Frances came slowly downstairs, supported by her maid and a footman, followed by a nurse with the baby. It took quite some time for her to get settled on her chaise longue with Belinda in her arms. Then Alexandra arrived with *her* baby, and Juliana showed up with a huge, flat basket filled with cups of orange custard, which she claimed would assist Corinna in finding love with a "certain someone."

"Which will make my sister's life complete," she added with a smile, handing the basket to a maid so the cups could be taken down to the basement kitchen and put on ice, "because her new portrait, which I have had the pleasure of seeing, is going to be the sensation of the Summer Exhibition."

"I cannot wait to see it," Lady A declared, which made Corinna a little nervous. She was grateful when the talk turned to Belinda's first smile—which Alexandra claimed could be caused only by indigestion—and on to Juliana's burgeoning belly. Not that Juliana's belly was actually protruding yet, but she kept rubbing it as though she could feel the baby inside, which made Corinna pine once more for a baby of her own.

She wondered how long it would be before Griffin

talked to Sean, before she could broach the subject of their marriage. Her stomach fluttered at the thought, with both excitement and a touch of nerves.

Soon Rachael arrived with her sisters, the three of them chattering enthusiastically as they made their way through the foyer. Corinna wondered what could possibly have happened to make them babble like that, but at the drawing room's doorway they all fell silent. She saw the three of them exchange significant glances before Lady A exchanged significant glances with *her* sisters. . . .

And even distracted by all her excited and nervous thoughts, Corinna couldn't help thinking something mysterious must be happening under her very nose.

"Good afternoon," Rachael said, breaking the silence.

"Good afternoon," Corinna returned. She watched Claire and Elizabeth make their way to two chairs and sit down, clucking over the new baby. And then she watched Rachael choose a seat on the sofa beside Lady Avonleigh.

Rachael paid no attention to the new baby. Instead she leaned close to Lady A, breathing in the kind lady's scent. She closed her eyes momentarily, and a faint smile curved her lips as she sighed a contented sigh, even though that odd mixture of camphor and gardenias couldn't possibly be pleasing.

And then something happened that was odder still: Lady A smiled a matching faint smile and sighed a matching contented sigh. And then she leaned so close to Corinna's cousin that the two of them were all but mashed together.

Lady C pulled out a handkerchief and dabbed at her eyes and nose. "Oh, dear. I seem to be coming down with the sniffles."

"So do I," Lady B said, although she looked perfectly fine. In fact, she and Lady C were both smiling. And so were Claire and Elizabeth. And they were not faint smiles. They were smiles a mile wide.

"Would anyone care for some orange custard?" Juliana asked, rising from her seat. "Corinna, could you come with me to the kitchen to fetch it? And Claire and Elizabeth? I cannot carry ten cups all by myself, and James said that I shouldn't overexert myself in my delicate condition."

Juliana could certainly carry all ten cups in the same basket she'd brought them in, Corinna thought, and she hadn't seemed to overexert herself doing so earlier. But she rose and followed her sister, anyway. With a decided lack of regard for her delicate condition, Juliana hurried Corinna and their cousins from the drawing room and through the foyer. Halfway down the steps to the basement, she turned to them. "What in heaven's name is going on here? What on earth am I missing? Something has happened between Rachael and Lady Avonleigh. Something significant. I can tell."

A blind and deaf woman would be able to tell, Corinna thought.

Elizabeth coughed a little sniffly cough. "Lady A is Rachael's grandmother."

"What?" Juliana and Corinna burst out together.

Claire elbowed her sister in the ribs and sighed. "Rachael is Lady Avonleigh's granddaughter. And we're her granddaughters, too. It seems our mother was Lady A's younger daughter—the one who jumped off the London Bridge. Only she didn't, not really. She married our father and moved to Greystone instead. And never went back to London, because she was afraid someone there would recognize her, and her family would know she was alive."

This was what had happened to make the two sets of sisters babble like that, Corinna realized. And no wonder—the six of them turning out to be related was a positively amazing coincidence. Even more amazing than everyone's being too busy to accompany her to Somerset House at the same time.

"That's why everyone was busy yesterday," Juliana

marveled. "You two and Rachael and Ladies A, B, and C were all together, discovering all of this."

"Brilliant deduction," Corinna muttered sarcastically before turning to her cousins. "Your mother didn't have asthma, then."

"No, she didn't. That was just an excuse." Claire pulled a handkerchief out of her sleeve and blew her nose—because she was overcome with emotion, *not* because she was coming down with the sniffles. "Please don't tell Rachael you know. She'd be mortified."

"Why?" Corinna asked. "None of this is any fault of hers. Does she think so little of us that she believes Aunt Georgiana's deception would change our feelings toward her?"

"I fear she's not thinking at all right now." Claire crossed her arms over her amethyst bodice and leveled a familiar stare at her sister. "Much like Elizabeth. Again."

Elizabeth sniffled, too. "I'm sorry."

"We promise not to tell a soul." Corinna turned to Juliana. "Don't we?"

Juliana reached to touch both her cousins' arms reassuringly. "We love Rachael, and we're thrilled that she's found more family to love."

Juliana *sounded* sincere, but Corinna couldn't help noticing that she hadn't actually promised. She suspected her sister had her fingers mentally crossed. There was something in her tone, a frisson of glee, perhaps, that made Corinna sure she was already plotting her next move.

Juliana was a born meddler, after all, and no doubt she thought this news wonderful for all concerned. For their cousins, of course, and also for Lady A, who'd sorely missed her younger daughter and now had grandchildren at long last. But mostly for Griffin and Rachael, because Rachael's newfound happiness put Juliana that much closer to her goal of seeing the two of them together as a couple.

Corinna had no doubt Juliana would accomplish that goal, because her sister was not only a born meddler; she was an annoyingly good one—and anyone with two eyes in her head could see that Rachael and Griffin *did* belong together. Just like she, Corinna, belonged with Sean. Sean, of course, was the "certain someone," because Juliana believed they belonged together, too. She'd made orange custard to bring them love. Regardless of the fact that it would be ineffective, that was a meddlesome thing, and Corinna was certain Juliana had plenty more meddling planned. But for the very first time in her life, she found herself hoping Juliana's meddling would work.

Juliana would be smug beyond belief, of course, but it would save Corinna from having to reveal that Sean had posed for her, which would be totally worth putting up with a slew of smugness.

Chapter Forty-seven

An earl's funeral bore little resemblance to the simple ceremonies performed by a country vicar like Sean's father. Lord Lincolnshire was to be buried in Westminster Abbey on Friday, and Sean had also arranged for a reception at Lincolnshire House afterward. Getting everything in place took the better part of the day, and it was late afternoon by the time he trudged up the steps to the garret studio, hoping Corinna wasn't already waiting. A small part of him couldn't wait to see her, but most of him dreaded her arrival. He wanted a few minutes to prepare himself, to steel himself for what lay ahead.

He didn't have to do this, he knew. There were other, easier ways out. Soon the truth would be revealed, as Hamilton was due in town for the judging and would waste no time claiming his new title. Once that happened, society would make it clear to Corinna that Sean was unacceptable. Or he could allow her brother to explain the facts. But he wasn't a man who expected others to do his dirty work. He still picked up a hammer if he saw the need on a construction site, and he wouldn't leave this task to others, either.

And he had to say good-bye. He needed to tell Corinna just how much he wished things were different. He'd brought something to give her to remember him by, and he'd do that first, while she was still clearheaded enough to be capable of understanding what it meant.

He wanted one last kiss, and he wanted, one last time, to hear her sweet, feminine voice.

Reaching the top of the stairway, he opened the door to the garret and heard a harsh, masculine voice instead. "Go away."

"I beg your pardon?" Thinking for a moment that he must have entered the wrong building, Sean took a step back. Then he blinked as the man turned to face him, paintbrush in hand. "Hamilton? What are you doing here?"

"Working. I'd planned to lease this space, if you'll remember, so I consider it mine." He gestured to a large canvas on the easel, where the essentials of a scene were already taking form. "The falls, with the Lady of the Waterfall visible in the towering gush. Inspired, is it not? What do you think?"

Sean shut the door behind him. "I think you were due back weeks ago."

Hamilton merely shrugged. "I arrived earlier today, in time to vote on the submissions for the Summer Exhibition." He turned back to his canvas and began adding mist rising at the bottom of the falls. "I told you I would."

"You also told me your uncle would die within days."

"He didn't?"

"Not until this morning."

Unsurprisingly, Hamilton displayed no emotion at the news of his uncle's passing. But he wouldn't stay calm for long—not once he heard what had transpired since he left the country. Having long since resigned himself to the fact that this entire exercise had been for naught, Sean's main regret was that he'd been unaware of Hamilton's arrival—that he'd failed to speak with the man before the Summer Exhibition selection. He hadn't realized it would take place the very day after the submissions were due.

"Did you vote for Lady Corinna Chase's painting?" he asked with a sigh.

"Who the hell is Corinna Chase?"

"The woman we met in the British Museum. The one who said she wanted to paint portraits."

"I don't remember her. And I haven't the slightest idea. As usual, I voted for my favorites without looking at any artists' names." He added more mist. "The entire proceeding proved very tedious. No less than fourteen rounds before the final selection was decided on, and all the while all I wanted was to work on this picture."

"It was a portrait of Lincolnshire. Seated on a bench in Berkeley Square, holding a book—"

"I don't recall anything like that. Not that I would have recognized the old bastard in any case. I've not set eyes on him since I was a babe—"

"Sweet Jesus, he was your father's identical twin. And she painted him looking younger, probably very much as you remember your own father."

"I didn't see any portraits of my father, Delaney. And I voted for very few portraits overall—you know I prefer landscapes." Having finished adding the mist, he deftly painted some water spraying back up. "My favorite canvas, however," he mused contemplatively, "did turn out to be a portrait. I'm not sure whether it made the final cut—it may not have, because it was very unusual. A sensual study of a golden-haired man, rather scandalously undressed and bathed in candlelight. Henry Fuseli was quite taken with it as well."

That certainly wasn't Corinna's. Which meant Sean was finished with this discussion. "Nothing went the way you said it would, Hamilton. Nothing went as planned."

The man cocked his head, then added a wee smidge of white to a brown blob on his palette. "What could possibly have gone so wrong?" he asked, mixing the colors together idly.

"Everything," Sean said in clipped tones. "To begin with, all of London believes I'm you."

"What?" His attention finally snagged, Hamilton whirled to face him. "How the devil did that happen?"

"Lincolnshire asked me to take him to a ball, promising to keep my identity a secret. My identity as you, you understand. Once there, however . . ."

It took a good five minutes to explain everything—five minutes during which Hamilton put down his palette, dropped heavily to the threadbare sofa, and finally, inevitably, exploded.

"You bloody son of a bitch! You were instructed to keep the old man happy and stay out of society entirely! Given that you didn't keep your end of the bargain, I'll be damned if I'll keep mine. Deirdre will never see her divorce. She'll bear the next Lincolnshire earl if it's the last thing she does—and with any luck, she'll die in childbirth, so it will be."

Sean had expected no less. Neither was he surprised when Hamilton stalked out of the studio.

Resigned, he drew off his coat and cravat, unfastened the top button on his shirt, and slowly lowered himself to the sofa to wait for Corinna to arrive.

Chapter Forty-eight

"Corinna," Sean said when she walked in.

Just *Corinna*. Nothing else. He rose from the battered sofa and walked toward her, and she could see the sadness etched in his face, the weariness in his eyes. He looked battered himself, his coat off, his shirt negligently unbuttoned, his hair disheveled as though he'd run his hands through it over and over.

"Lord Lincolnshire is gone, isn't he?" she said quietly, but it wasn't really a question. "Did you stay up all night with him before he passed?"

Sean's answer was physical, not verbal. He stepped closer and gathered her into his arms. They stood there like that for a very long while, Corinna's eyes closed, her ear pressed to his chest where his heart beat steadily through the thin fabric of his shirt.

"I don't know what happened with your painting," he finally said in a bleak tone of voice.

"Something happened?" she asked, confused.

She felt rather than saw him shake his head. "Hamilton returned and voted before I could speak to him, so he didn't speak to any of the other committee members about you, either. And he said he mostly voted for landscapes."

She opened her eyes, her gaze falling on a large canvas propped on the easel, a scene of a waterfall. Proof of Hamilton's return. Unfinished though it was, the painting was impressive . . . but the selfishness of its creator made it ugly to her.

And she couldn't care how the vote had turned out, not now. Maybe tomorrow it would matter to her, but right now all that mattered was here in her arms. The man she loved was hurting.

"It's not important, Sean. Whatever happened will be." She sighed and pulled away. "It's all over. I know you're sad that Lord Lincolnshire is gone, and I am, too. But you can reclaim your life now, and that's good, isn't it? The sadness will pass, and you'll be able to return to what needs to be done, and . . ."

She couldn't bring herself to say that now they could take steps to be together. Sure as she was that he wanted her, he hadn't asked her to marry him yet.

"Corinna. *Críona.* I need to talk to you. But first I want to give you something," he said, reaching into a pocket. He pulled out a fine link chain with a pendant attached, but she hadn't time to see what it looked like before he took her hand and put the necklace in her palm, folding her fingers around it. "It's only silver. My family could never afford anything made of gold. I've the money now to have bought you something more suited to your own family's position—gold and diamonds, rubies or pearls—but I wanted you to have this."

He still held her hand with both of his wrapped tightly around it. He felt warm, and whatever was inside her fist felt hard but delicate. "This belongs to your family?"

"For a hundred years or more." His lyrical words came slower than usual, and his voice was a bit rough, the sound of it making her heart hitch. "It was my mother's, and my grandmother's before her, and so on going back for generations."

"Oh, then it should be Deirdre's now, should it not?"

"I want you to have it," he repeated, releasing her. "Have a look at it, Corinna."

Slowly she opened her hand and drew out the necklace, raising it by the chain so the pendant dangled at the bottom. A symbol. Two hands holding a stone heart, surmounted by a crown studded with a few tiny gems.

"They're not diamonds," he told her, "only marcasite. I cannot tell you what the heart is made from, because I don't know."

"It's green," she said with a soft smile. "Like your eyes."

"Is it? I never knew that. But I can assure you it isn't an emerald."

"No, it wouldn't be, because it's opaque. And I care not what it's made from, anyway. It's beautiful. And it's from you." Anything Sean had given her would have been beautiful to her, of course, but it really was a very pretty thing. "Has it meaning? Beyond the fact that it's been passed down?"

"It does, aye. It's called a claddagh. The hands signify friendship, the crown loyalty, and the heart love. All the things I feel for you, *a rún*, all the things in my own heart."

A rún meant *my love*—she remembered that—and he'd said *love* in English, too. "Oh, Sean. It's perfect." Tears welled in her eyes. "So much better than diamonds or gold." He loved her. She'd known for some time in her heart, but hearing the words made it more real. "I love you, too. I love you so much I feel like I might burst, like I cannot hold it all inside me. Will you put this on me?"

She turned around, and he clasped it around her neck, his warm fingers brushing her nape. When she turned back, he cradled her face in his hands and lowered his lips to meet hers. It was a long kiss but a gentle one, heartfelt and deep, the tenderest kiss she'd ever received, and she didn't push it to be anything more, because she knew he was hurting.

When he drew back, his eyes burned into hers so intently she caught her breath in reaction. "We need to talk now," he said. "Let's sit down."

"All right." Suddenly feeling apprehensive, she

walked the few feet to the sofa and sat. He sank down beside her, angling himself so he could see her. "What is it?" she asked.

He took both her hands. "Corinna. *Críona.*" His voice broke on the Irish word, and she watched him swallow hard. "Lincolnshire told me a story last Friday. That seems so long ago, doesn't it?"

She nodded, her heart pounding with love or apprehension, or maybe a mixture. Today was only Tuesday, yet Friday night, the night she'd spent in his arms, seemed such a long time ago.

"It was a story about his twin brother, Hamilton's father, and why he sent him to Ireland," he started.

And then it all poured out.

She listened, silent, taking it all in, until he finished. Until his hands squeezed hers hard, so hard her own hands hurt. "Corinna. That will happen to me now. Having impersonated Hamilton, there is no chance I will ever be accepted in society."

"Oh, God." She knew he was right. The *ton* wouldn't look kindly upon a man who had tricked Lord Lincolnshire. "Why didn't I think of that?"

"I didn't think of it, either. I knew all along that, by perpetrating this hoax, Hamilton was risking his reputation as an artist. I even warned him of that, and I feared that if it happened he'd retaliate by refusing to release Deirdre. But I never considered how it would affect me personally. Maybe because I didn't think it would matter. Not being part of society, I cared nothing for what they thought of me—not until I fell in love with you."

"Oh, Sean." She leapt the small distance between them, wrapping her arms around him, burrowing her nose into the crook of his neck where she could inhale his warm male scent. "I love you, too," she told him, the words muffled against his skin. "I was waiting to tell you. Everything was so complicated. But now it's over, and we'll work this out. It will be difficult, but—"

"Corinna. You don't understand." He unwrapped her

arms and set her away, far enough to meet her eyes, to capture them with his intense green gaze. "I cannot marry you. There isn't anything I want more in the world, but it's impossible."

"No." That couldn't be. "This wasn't your fault. You didn't even want to do it. You did it for your sister, and for Lincolnshire—you made him happy. You shouldn't have to suffer—*we* shouldn't have to suffer—because you did the right thing."

"I'm not saying I did the wrong thing. I did the only thing I could. But no one ever promised life would be fair. The people in your social circle aren't going to countenance my lying to such a well-respected man; nor will they ever forgive me for fooling them."

"I don't care. I don't need the people in my social circle. I love you. I want to be with you. If they won't forgive you, if they make our life here too uncomfortable, we'll go to Ireland—"

"Your art would be shunned no matter where you made it. You'd never be admitted to the Royal Academy."

"Sharing my life with you is more important than the Royal Academy. I don't care about that, either."

"*I* care." He caught her close again, captured her gaze once more. "And should you marry me, Corinna, you and I aren't the only ones who would be shut out of society. Your family will be ostracized as well."

A hole opened up inside her, robbing her of breath.

Alexandra and Juliana, Griffin and Rachael, Frances and the cousins . . . Should she stay with Sean and bear the consequences, they, too, would be rejected by all of society.

She couldn't do that to them.

She was willing to give up her personal dreams in trade for Sean, to condemn herself to a life apart from all she'd known. That would be artistic . . . wild, passionate, romantic. But she couldn't take her family with her.

She'd be more selfish than Hamilton should she do that.

Her heart cracked, and she could see in Sean's eyes that he felt the same. His overwhelming sadness, his staggering weariness, his battered appearance . . . understanding all of that now, feeling it herself, she moved into his arms.

They clutched each other, held each other close for a long, long time, wrapped in a cocoon of anguish while sobs racked her body and despair claimed her soul.

And then, when she'd cried herself dry, when there was nothing left inside her but a vast, aching emptiness, he walked her home in silence.

Chapter Forty-nine

As Friday afternoon slid into evening, Corinna stood alone in Lincolnshire House's yellow drawing room, wearing a black dress that matched her mood. Excited voices drifted from the crowded salon, where a reception was being held following Lord Lincolnshire's burial. More babbling came from the entrance hall, where the crowd spilled out.

Ladies very rarely attended funerals, so Sean had arranged the reception to allow the women in the earl's social circle a chance to pay their respects. She'd wager he hadn't anticipated such a crush. He wasn't part of the crush, of course, and she'd been told he hadn't attended the ceremony, either.

The reception should have been a polite gathering, the guests soft-spoken and sober rather than excited. But tongues had been wagging ever since this morning, when John Hamilton had shown up at Westminster Abbey and announced he was the next Earl of Lincolnshire. As she was female, Corinna hadn't been present to witness that, but she'd heard all about it. The men at the funeral had been astonished, to say the least. The new Lord Lincolnshire had informed them that his impostor's name was Sean Delaney, and Sean's reputation had been torn to threads before the reception even started.

Just as he'd predicted, she thought now with a heavy-hearted sigh.

For the past two days, lines had run through her head annoyingly, unceasingly. Pamela thinking *life is no life without you*, and Ethelinde deciding *hope seemed to be excluded from her heart*, and how, in *Children of the Abbey*, Amanda had cried, *the hand of fate is against our union, and we must part, never, never more to meet!*

But although she'd known Sean was right and there was no way they could be together, some small part of her must have been holding out hope, because somehow she'd managed to get through those two days without completely falling apart. She'd buried herself in her art, locked herself in her room, and fixed Lord Lincolnshire's portrait. That had kept her from thinking too much and from facing her brother or anyone else. The picture was finished, and she'd brought it over this morning while Griffin was away at the funeral.

Lord Lincolnshire's house steward, Mr. Higginbotham, had praised the portrait mightily and promised to find somewhere to hang it immediately. Unaware at the time of the trouble brewing in Westminster Abbey, he'd also praised "Mr. Hamilton," telling her each of the staff had received letters that morning with details of their new assignments, to begin Monday.

After she'd left, Mr. Higginbotham had hung the portrait in the yellow drawing room, on the wall behind the armchair where Lord Lincolnshire had been sitting when Corinna first offered to paint it. She stared at it now, thinking it seemed the right place for it. Above the chair like that, it almost seemed as though the dear earl were still sitting there. The portrait was mounted beside a Rembrandt, and it should have been a thrill to see one of her own paintings next to an old master.

But she hadn't the capacity to feel thrilled when everything else had gone so very wrong.

Even Mr. Higginbotham was scandalized now. A few minutes earlier, when she'd asked him where to find the painting, he'd been sputtering with indignation. From this day forward, Sean would be shunned by society, and that meant she could never see him again without ruining her family. That seemed the only thing that mattered. She didn't know yet whether her picture had been accepted for the Summer Exhibition, but she couldn't bring herself to care.

"Corinna?"

Hearing footsteps behind her, she turned to see Griffin enter the room, holding a glass of liquor the color of raw sienna pigment.

"What are you doing in here all alone?" He came to a stop before her, his gaze drifting up to the painting over her head. "Isn't that the portrait you did of Lord Lincolnshire?" When she didn't answer, he looked back down to her. "I thought you submitted it for the Summer Exhibition."

"Obviously I didn't. I submitted something else."

"Really?" Sipping, he looked curious. "What?"

A picture of the man she loved, the man she'd lost. That thought brought a flood of pain. As she couldn't tell her brother she loved Sean, instead she lashed out at him. "Why should you care what I submitted? All you're concerned with is getting me married off!"

"That's not true, Corinna. All I'm concerned with is your happiness. I want to see you happy."

He looked hurt, and that made her hurt even more. "Well, you have an odd way of showing it," she cried, tears flooding her eyes. She couldn't take this anymore.

Not any of it.

Pushing past him, she ran from the room, out into the entrance hall. The grand, pillared area was crowded with people dressed in black—people gossiping—people drinking up the contents of Lord Lincolnshire's liquor cabinet while vilifying the man she loved.

Their faces blurred as she headed for the front door, her brother at her heels.

"Griffin!" Rachael said as he shoved a glass at her. "Where are you going?"

"After my sister!" Having passed Rachael already, he wove through the mass of guests. "I'm going home," he called back.

Rachael watched him follow Corinna at a run, then just stood there for a moment, feeling a bit dazed. She raised the glass to her lips and took a sip, hoping whatever was in it would be bracing.

Brandy. It burned a path down her throat, felt warm in her stomach. She sipped again.

Juliana walked up. "Where did Griffin go off to?"

"He went after Corinna. I believe he was concerned for her well-being. He seems more responsible than I remember."

Her cousin smiled. "You seem to like him much more than you used to."

Rachael shrugged a shoulder—casually, she hoped. "I guess he's changed over the years."

"Yes, he has. He would make an excellent husband now, don't you think?"

"For someone else," she said warily.

"For you. I think you two would rub along wonderfully together."

"He's my cousin. You know I won't marry a cousin."

"Rachael . . ."

Juliana glanced away, her gaze sweeping the thronged entrance hall. Her husband was talking to Alexandra and Tristan, and Rachael's sisters and Noah were in the salon. Apparently satisfied that no one important was watching, she took Rachael's arm and drew her into the room Griffin and Corinna had vacated.

"I know your secret," she said in a low voice.

Feeling blindsided, Rachael struggled to look normal while she sipped more brandy. "What secret?"

"I know John Chase wasn't your father," Juliana said gently. "And I know you're Lady A's granddaughter."

Rachael relaxed a little, and not just due to the brandy. Apparently her cousin *didn't* know her real father had committed treason, or surely she would have mentioned that, too, because if there was one thing Juliana loved, it was a juicy secret like that.

And she supposed it wasn't all that dreadful for people to know the rest. Her mother had been married when Rachael was conceived, after all—it wasn't as though Georgiana had been carrying a bastard child when she married the Earl of Greystone. And while not being John Chase's blood daughter was a disappointment, being Lady A's granddaughter was a joy.

Still and all, it *had* been a secret. "Who told you?" she asked.

"It doesn't signify. It was an accident, not intentional, and the person I learned it from wished you no harm. But, Rachael, I . . . well, I realize you wanted it kept secret, but I thought it best to reveal I know, because there's something you apparently *don't* know. Or haven't realized yet."

Juliana paused for effect, or maybe to give Rachael a moment to absorb what she'd already said. Because what she said next seemed somewhat confusing.

"You're not Griffin's cousin."

Rachael hadn't thought much about that, but it was true, of course. "I know we're not blood related, since I'm not really a Chase, but . . ."

"But what?"

"He's still family. Griffin is Griffin. My cousin. We grew up together."

"Why should that matter? There would be no risk of you two conceiving a damaged child like your cousin Edmund, and that was your issue, was it not? You wouldn't have to worry about having a child like that with Griffin."

She'd never thought about that, either. Two years ago, when Griffin had first come home from the cavalry, she'd found herself stunned by how much he had changed. *Handsome as sin personified,* she recalled thinking. The reckless, gangly youth she'd remembered had grown tall, dark, and sleekly muscled, and she'd been shaken by the sudden force of attraction she'd felt. But she'd told herself he was her cousin—not knowing any different at the time—and that had been that.

That *wasn't* that, though, was it?

"Oh, damn," she finally said softly. "I've been such a bloody idiot."

"We all are sometimes," Juliana soothed.

But Rachael wasn't listening. She'd shoved the glass at Juliana, her black skirts rustling as she ran from the room.

Chapter Fifty

"Can I not just be sad over the loss of Lord Lincolnshire?"

"Not this sad. You've been hiding in this room since Tuesday." Griffin gazed down at his sister lying on her bed, her back to him. Her knees were hugged to her chest. He couldn't see her face, but she didn't strike him as sad.

More like devastated.

"I'll miss the old man, too," he added, "but it has to be more than that."

She heaved a sigh so pathetic it broke his heart. "All right, it's more than that," she admitted, tears in her voice. "The Summer Exhibition committee did the judging on Tuesday, and my painting wasn't accepted."

"Did you receive a letter saying so?"

"No. Not yet. The Exhibition won't open until the first Monday in June, and until the Hanging Committee has finished arranging all the selections on the walls, a few pieces may be in question. So I wouldn't expect a letter yet."

"That's good news, then," he told her, trying to cheer her. "Acceptance must at least be a possibility. Surely they'd have sent a letter by now if the answer were a definite no."

"You don't know that. And I've heard that Mr. Hamilton—I mean, *Lord Lincolnshire*"—this pronounced with a plethora of disgust—"didn't vote for any portraits."

"He's not the only man on the committee."

"No, there are eight others, two of whom abhor women painters. Another three didn't like my portrait of Lord Lincolnshire, and two more gave me no opinion at all."

"So you'll try again next year." Griffin sat on the edge of the bed and rubbed her back. "Maybe you should sign a man's name next time."

She rolled over, and the glare she gave him convinced him it had been a poor time to jest.

"I'm sorry," he muttered quickly.

Now that he could see it, her tear-streaked face made him feel like a complete failure as a brother. He'd known her art was important to her, but he honestly hadn't known it meant so much that she'd be so crushed by a temporary setback. He couldn't remember her ever being this distressed before, not even the two times he'd taken short leaves and come home when their parents had died.

"I know this is important to you," he said carefully, "and I'm sorry if you've felt I've discounted your art while trying to find you a husband. That wasn't my intention. I've just been a little . . . focused. Apparently *too* focused. I promise not to do that from now on, all right? I won't push suitors on you. When you see a man you're interested in, just let me know, and—"

"Leave me alone, Griffin," she growled.

"But—"

"Now."

"Very well." He rose and backed away, his hands held out defensively. "I'm sorry, Corinna, truly I am. But I wish you would believe me when I say I want to see you happy."

Rolling to face away from him again, she said, "I know that," in a wan little voice.

He supposed it was the best he could expect for now.

He'd done all he could, he told himself as he left, softly closing the door between them. Too bad it wasn't good enough. Turning to face the door, he banged his forehead against the polished wood, pressing hard.

He would never understand women, never figure out what made them tick. Never be able to decipher their moods. He felt bad that he'd made light of Corinna's art, and he would pay more attention in the future. Make more of an effort to show her he cared and help advance her career, if he could find a way to do that. But he was also certain finding her a husband to love would improve her disposition.

Or at the very least, make someone else responsible for dealing with it.

He banged his head against the wood again.

"Griffin," he heard nearby. "Are you all right?"

A low, sultry voice that was all too familiar.

He straightened and turned to see its owner, finding her standing there in a black dress that should have made her look drab, or at least less alluring than usual. But it didn't. It had a wide neckline, revealing a good deal of her shoulders, and it rustled as she moved closer, the bodice hugging her seductive curves. Her hair had been done up formally for the reception at Lincolnshire House, leaving just a few loose chestnut tendrils that fell in soft waves around her face.

He swallowed hard and took an uneasy step back, bumping against Corinna's door.

"May I have a word with you?" Rachael glanced around the open corridor. "In private?"

He nodded shortly and led the way to his study, aware all the while of her come-hither scent following behind him. Would this torture never end? He'd found her grandmother, hadn't he? He'd tracked her mysterious origins, learned what had become of her father. What more did she want from him? Why wasn't she with Lady Avonleigh over at Lincolnshire House, with her happy new family?

After ushering her into the study, he shut the door and turned to her. "What do you want, Rachael?"

She blinked, no doubt taken aback by his unintended harshness. But she recovered her composure quickly. And when she answered him, it was in a tone that made a ball of heat smack him in the gut and spread down.

"I want you to kiss me."

His pulse hammering, he hesitated . . . until she licked her lips.

"Corinna?

A knock sounded on her closed door.

"Are you all right?" Juliana called.

Corinna might have ignored anyone else, but there was no putting off Juliana. "I'll live," she muttered, rolling over and levering herself to sit on the edge of the bed. She shoved the claddagh necklace she'd been clutching under her pillow, and, with the back of a hand, mopped the last of her tears off her face. "Come on in."

Juliana did, holding up a piece of heavy, cream-colored paper with a large, broken red seal. "A letter came for you."

Just what she needed now, the news of her rejection. Well, at least the suspense would be over. "From the Royal Academy?"

"From the former Lord Lincolnshire's solicitor. Addressed to 'The Marquess of Cainewood.' And then inside it says, 'My Lord Marquess and Lady Corinna Chase.' "

"What does the solicitor want?" Not that Corinna really cared.

"You're requested to attend the reading of the late earl's will at Mr. Lawless's Queen Street offices on Monday at noon."

Corinna shrugged. "Lord Lincolnshire probably left us a trinket. One of his four hundred Ming vases or some such. For being kind through his last few days."

"I don't think he'd leave you and Griffin *one* vase.

Two, maybe." Juliana smiled, a transparent effort to raise Corinna's spirits. "I'm famished. The reception at Lincolnshire House is winding down, so I walked over here to ask the staff to serve a family dinner before the rest of us go home. Will you come down and join us? And where is Griffin?"

"How should I know?" Corinna paused. "And how did you come to read a letter addressed to Griffin if you haven't seen him?"

"Well, obviously," Juliana said airily, "I opened it."

Chapter Fifty-one

Griffin had kissed Rachael in his study. He'd kissed her *across* his study. He'd kissed her as he'd eased her down to a long leather sofa, and now, a good thirty minutes later, he was lying half on top of her, still kissing her.

She'd been kissed before, but not by anyone who kissed anything like Griffin. He put his entire heart and soul into a kiss. When Griffin was kissing her, she was wholly convinced his mind was on nothing but that. On nothing but her. Which made it difficult to think about anything but him, either.

In fact, he made it difficult to think at all.

His kisses went from sweet to warm to burning and back again. From gentle to deep, from rushed to unhurried to frantic. Her senses were reeling, and her mouth seemed filled with the taste of him—hot male and brandy. Her blood seemed filled with him, too, coursing through her veins and beating a seductive rhythm in her ears.

When he finally drew away, when he struggled to his elbows and gazed down at her, she still found it hard to think. His eyes were so very intense, his dazed smile a little crooked, looking delicious. Placing a hand behind his neck, she pulled his mouth back down to hers and kissed him again.

A long while later he drew away once more, and her head finally cleared.

A little.

"You're not my cousin," she murmured.

"I know."

"That means we can marry."

He was off her like a shot. "Oh, no."

"Oh, no?" Shoving herself to a sitting position, she decided she'd probably shocked herself as much as him by saying that. But it was true.

She wanted to marry Griffin.

She loved him.

She wasn't sure when she'd fallen in love, because she'd never admitted that to herself before—she hadn't been able to, having never overcome thinking of him as a cousin. But she knew she could lean on Griffin; she knew she could depend on him. He'd always be there for her—he'd shown her that, hadn't he? And wasn't that the most important quality for a husband?

And it didn't hurt that he was so handsome he made her breath catch. So tall and lean, so virile and masculine, so well built. His eyes such a pure leaf green, his jaw so strong and square, that slightly crooked smile so engaging.

"Oh, yes," she said, "I want to marry you."

"You *don't* want to marry me," he returned flatly, a hint of panic in those green eyes. "You think I'm an irresponsible scapegrace."

"Not anymore." Or not exactly. Yes, he said stupid things, and he did stupid things sometimes, too. He had his flaws. But what man didn't? At least she knew Griffin's flaws—she knew what she was getting into with him.

And she'd never felt that powerful force of attraction with any man but Griffin.

She loved him just as he was, flaws and all.

"I do want to marry you," she disagreed, "and, really, how can you refuse me? You've been kissing me for half an hour."

He shifted on his feet, glancing away from her. "They were only kisses, Rachael. And you invited them. You cannot expect a man to turn down an offer like that."

He hadn't kissed her only because she'd invited him. She might be a bloody idiot for not realizing there was no reason she couldn't marry him, but she wasn't so bird-witted she didn't know when a man wanted her.

Griffin had been wanting her for two years, at the very least. A man didn't look at a woman the way he looked at her—or kiss her the way he just had—unless he wanted her. And he loved her, too. She was sure of it. Look at all the trouble he'd gone to in order to find her family. A man didn't go to such trouble for a woman he didn't love.

She couldn't let him get away with saying the time they'd just spent in each other's arms had been *only kisses*. "Are you telling me all those kisses meant nothing?"

He looked back to her. "That's what I just said, isn't it?"

Oh, that had come too easily. She'd asked the wrong question. "You didn't enjoy them, then? Not at all?"

He hadn't an answer for that, which didn't surprise her. He'd be lying if he claimed he hadn't enjoyed himself.

"Tell me, Griffin," she drawled, rather amused by his increasing discomfort, "would you approve of a man kissing Corinna for half an hour if he had no intention of marrying her?"

He couldn't deny that without lying, either, of course. To his credit, he didn't. "No, I wouldn't approve. But she's my sister."

"Well, I think I deserve the same respect as your sister." Rising from the sofa, she reached for her reticule. "So unless you change your mind and declare your intentions, I trust you won't ever kiss me again."

Her lips still felt tender from their previous kisses, and she wanted more. But she wasn't worried she wouldn't get them. Another of his flaws was resisting change, but he'd come around eventually.

She figured he'd be kissing her inside of a week.

He jumped to avoid her as she headed for the door. Reaching it, she placed her hand on the knob and glanced over her shoulder. "Will you be attending Lady Hammersmithe's ball tomorrow night?"

"I'm planning to bring Corinna."

Deliberately she licked her lips, watching for a reaction, hiding a smile when she saw that reaction in his eyes. "I'll see you there, then," she practically purred as she opened the door and waltzed out.

Chapter Fifty-two

The atmosphere in Hampstead was very thick that Friday evening. So thick it seemed an effort to breathe. Just drawing air in and out of his lungs seemed to take everything Sean had.

Sitting across from Deirdre in his dining room, he shoved his plate across the mahogany table. "I'm not hungry. I've not eaten in three days, and I'm not hungry."

His sister knew what he'd lost. When he'd asked her where he could find the claddagh necklace, she hadn't asked why. " 'Tis sorry I am for you, Sean," she said softly, her eyes flooded with sympathy.

He didn't want sympathy—he wanted the calendar flipped back to April, to before he'd received that damned letter from Hamilton. Shifting his gaze away, he stared at a blue wall. "I'm not the one who has to go back to a husband I despise."

"At least the man I love isn't forbidden to me entirely, as Corinna is to you. I'll give John a son and *then* I'll move in with Daniel."

Skeptical, he looked back to her. "You'd leave your child?"

Her chin in the air was so familiar. "Rather than stay with John, yes."

"If you say so," he murmured. But he knew she wouldn't. Once she had a son or a daughter, she'd change her mind. Hamilton would banish Deirdre and their offspring to the countryside, and she'd live there, bored out of her mind, for the rest of her life.

And even should she find the will to leave her child, would Daniel Raleigh wait a year or two or more while she made a son with Hamilton?

He doubted that as well.

"Two letters, sir." A footman walked in, holding them out. "One for you and one for the lady."

With its large red seal, Sean's letter looked important. As the servant left, he cracked the wax and unfolded the paper.

"Who is it from?" Deirdre asked.

"A solicitor on Queen Street in Cheapside. A Mr. Peregrine Peabody. He's wishing to meet with me Monday at noon."

"Regarding what?"

"He doesn't say." Whatever it was, it couldn't be good. "I assume I will finally learn who's been poking around in my business, and what he's managed to trump up to ruin me or put me in prison. And what it's going to take to prove him wrong." He glanced at the folded paper Deirdre held, recognizing the scrawl on the outside as the same on the damned letter he'd received back in April. "What does your husband want now? His uncle isn't in the grave even half a day. Is the rotter summoning you to his bed already?"

She broke the seal and scanned it. "He isn't, no. Not yet. He says I'm to attend the reading of the late Lord Lincolnshire's will on Monday. He's sending a carriage to fetch me at eleven o'clock."

"Where is the reading being held?"

"John doesn't say. Just that the carriage will come in the morning." She glanced up from the paper, looking nervous. "Remember that ball Lord Lincolnshire took us to? What if someone who was there recognizes me as the woman introduced as your wife?"

Sean reached to lay his hand over hers on the table.

"I don't expect the Billingsgates' guests will be at the reading, Deirdre. It will likely be just you and Hamilton and that lawyer named Lawless."

"I'm not sure that lawyer ever got a good look at me. We were never formally introduced."

"You've nothing to worry yourself about, then." He patted her hand. "Even should Lawless recall seeing you at Lincolnshire House, you *are* Hamilton's wife. Lincolnshire's niece by marriage. It's not unbelievable you'd be at the man's deathbed."

"That's right." He saw her relax a little. "I wish you could come with me, though."

"I wish I could, too," he said dryly. "I also wasn't formally introduced, but I've no doubt Lawless saw me. And should he not remember me, I'm certain Hamilton would be happy to remind him. And in any case, I cannot go with you because I'll be busy Monday at that time."

Feeling yet more incapable of breathing than earlier, he heaved a sigh. The atmosphere seemed to be getting even thicker.

"The way my luck has been going lately, I'll probably be busy getting arrested."

When Rachael and her siblings returned home from the reception at Lincolnshire House, their butler handed a folded paper to her brother. "A letter, my lord."

With its large red seal, it looked important. "What does it say?" Rachael asked as the butler closed the door.

Pausing in the foyer, Noah raised the letter to his forehead. "Hmm. I'm getting a vision. I think it says—"

"Noah." She whacked him with her reticule, feeling giddy. She was in love, and she was going to get married. Griffin was going to be kissing her inside of a week. Maybe tomorrow night. "Open it, you fool."

"If you insist." He broke the seal and scanned down the page. "It's from a solicitor in Cheapside, Mr. Lawrence Lawless. He wants us to attend the reading of Lord Lincolnshire's will Monday at noon."

"Us?" Elizabeth slid off her pelisse. "What do you mean by 'us'?"

"All of us." Shrugging, Noah looked up. "It's addressed to all four of us."

Chapter Fifty-three

"You're late," Juliana said when Griffin arrived at Lady Hammersmithe's ball Saturday night.

"*Fashionably* late," he corrected, spotting Rachael talking to her sisters. She was wearing another clingy dress, a sapphire blue one with a wide, low neckline and tiny sleeves that left her shoulders and most of her arms bare.

"Where is Corinna?"

"Still in the doldrums." He looked back to Juliana. "You can blame her for making me fashionable. She refused to leave the house."

"Yet you came anyway," she said, appearing speculative. "Why is that?"

He wasn't about to tell her he'd come to see Rachael. Juliana meddled enough without him encouraging her. "Am I not allowed to socialize without an agenda?" Since she looked even more speculative, he changed the subject. "I expect tonight's buzz is still all about yesterday's revelations?"

"Mr. Delaney, you mean? Actually, no. The chitchat tonight is about how everyone's been invited to the reading of Lord Lincolnshire's will on Monday."

"Everyone?"

"When James and I arrived home last night, there was a letter waiting. Alexandra and Tristan got one, too. As did every other household in Mayfair, if one can believe the talk."

"I've never heard of such a thing."

"The reading is going to be a shocking squeeze." Juliana sounded thrilled at the prospect. "Lord Lincolnshire cannot have left bequests to everyone, so I wonder what could be the reason."

"You'll know soon enough." He looked over toward Rachael, but she was gone. "Have you seen Noah or any of his sisters?"

"Last I noticed, Rachael was talking to Claire and Elizabeth." She glanced around. "Oh, Rachael's dancing now. And Noah just walked into the refreshment room." That speculative look came into her eyes again. "Why do you ask?"

"I was just wondering if they received a letter, too," he said casually. "I'll go ask Noah."

He left her and ambled toward the refreshment room—then went right past it. And around to the far side of the ballroom, where Juliana couldn't see him. He couldn't care less whether his cousins had received a letter.

But Rachael dancing . . . well, that was another matter altogether.

He shifted uneasily, watching the rake Rachael was dancing with pull her closer, watching him run a hand slowly down the back of her clingy dress. When the music ended and she curtsied to the rake, Griffin moved quickly to block her path off the dance floor.

"What are you doing, Rachael?"

"What do you mean, what am I doing?"

"Why are you dancing?"

"I'm at a ball, if you haven't noticed. What else should I be doing but dancing?"

"I don't recollect you dancing at a ball in the last two Seasons, except with me. You told me you didn't like men pawing you."

"Well, I thought I didn't, at the time." Watching him, she licked her lips. "But a certain experience last night changed my mind."

"I didn't paw you last night," he protested, fighting an urge to paw her now. He'd wanted to paw her last night as well, but he'd managed to control himself then, too. She was Rachael, for God's sake. He'd known her since she was in the cradle. She'd asked only for him to kiss her, and he wouldn't have presumed to do anything more.

"Maybe I wanted you to paw me," she suggested. "It crossed my mind that might have been enjoyable."

Clenching his jaw, he looked away. Bloody hell, she'd accused him of disrespecting her and all he'd done was kiss her for half an hour. After she'd asked. Now he wasn't allowed to kiss her again unless he proposed first, but it was all right if another man pawed her?

In the distance, Juliana caught his eye. Standing in a clutch of jabbering chatterboxes, she glanced between him and Rachael and raised a speculative brow.

"Instead of dancing," he gritted out, "why don't you just gossip like every other female?"

Rachael followed his gaze. "I'm not Juliana, if you haven't noticed."

Now, *that* he'd noticed. He'd never once been tempted to stick his tongue in his sister's mouth.

"I prefer dancing to gossiping," Rachael informed him archly. "Especially now, since I'm looking for a husband."

"You're doing what?"

"You heard me. Since you don't want to marry me, I've decided to find another husband." The lips he'd kissed last night curved into a satisfied smile. "Stop gaping, Griffin. You look better with your mouth closed. Not that I care what you look like anymore," she added, and sailed off.

Three minutes later Griffin was still standing there, and Rachael was dancing with another man. Another rake. This one seemed to be whispering secrets in her ear.

Ten minutes later, another rake was holding her too close.

Ten minutes after that, another rake was making her laugh. Had Griffin ever made her laugh? *With* him, that was, not at him?

It stuck in his gizzard, seeing her in the arms of other men. When she came off the dance floor for the third time, he pulled her aside again. "Why all of a sudden do you want to get married?"

"I'm twenty-four years old, Griffin, and I wasted two Seasons chasing down my father. I'll be on the shelf if I don't marry soon. That was what decided me."

"You don't just *decide* to find a husband, Rachael."

"Odd statement, coming from you. Is that not what you've decided for Corinna?"

"I've changed my mind. I'm thinking now it would be better to wait until she falls in love. I'd suggest you do the same yourself."

"I *have* fallen in love," she informed him. "But since it took twenty-four years to happen, I don't think I can afford to wait for it to happen another time. Your mouth is open again," she added before she turned in a swish of clingy skirts and walked away.

Not a minute later, she was dancing once more.

Griffin's mouth remained open for quite a while.

She loved him? Hardly a word passed her lips that didn't disparage him. And if she loved him, why the devil was she dancing with yet another rake? One with the gall to put a hand on her luscious derriere, no less? Just for a split second, but Griffin had seen it. He wanted to strangle the man.

Juliana sauntered by. "Close your mouth, Griffin," she said as she passed, her voice filled with speculation. She turned to walk backward, a smug smile emerging as she studied him. "You look jealous," she said before turning again and walking away.

Now he wanted to strangle *her*.

Was he jealous? Could he possibly love Rachael back? He'd thought what he felt for her was just lust, but mere lust shouldn't incite jealousy. It was easy enough to find someone to satisfy lust, after all. Women did tend to throw themselves at him.

And if this was what jealousy felt like, he didn't care for the emotion one bit.

By the time Rachael curtsied to the rake who'd touched her luscious derriere, Griffin was standing next to her. "You must have misunderstood me yesterday, Rachael."

She turned to him. "How is that?"

"It isn't that I don't want to marry you. I just don't want to marry you *now*. I'm not ready to take on a wife. At the moment, I've too many other responsibilities. I'm quite concerned about Corinna. Before I even think about settling down myself, I need to concentrate on getting her married. To a man she *loves*."

"I'll tell you what you need to concentrate on, Griffin, and that's growing up. You're thirty years old. For God's sake, Noah's growing up, and he's only twenty-two. If I wait until you're ready, I'll be waiting forever."

"I'm not asking for forever, Rachael. Just until Corinna's married."

"Corinna won't be married for another year at least. The Season's more than half over, and she hasn't shown interest in any man yet. In fact, your sister may not *ever* marry. Have you considered that?"

He hadn't, and the thought struck terror in his heart.

And Rachael wasn't finished. "If I agree to wait until she's married, I could end up a shriveled old lady, and you'll still be asking for time." She shook her beautiful head. "Thank you for the offer, but no."

"But I love you."

He couldn't believe those words had come out of his mouth, but even more than that, he couldn't believe her response.

"I know that, Griffin. But I want children. I'm going to find someone who's willing to marry me while I can still bear them." She rose to her toes and kissed him on the cheek. "I'll see you at Lincolnshire's solicitor's office on Monday."

Chapter Fifty-four

When Sean arrived in Queen Street on Monday at noon, he found it clogged with traffic and pedestrians. Having never seen any street in Cheapside so busy, he considered himself lucky to find a place to leave his curricle in a mews only two blocks away. Walking back, he mentally rehearsed what he might say in the meeting. At the bottom of the three steps that led to the solicitor's office, he stopped to check the plaque mounted by the building's door to make sure he was in the right place.

88 QUEEN STREET
PEABODY & LAWLESS
ATTORNEYS-AT-LAW

Mr. Peregrine Peabody being the solicitor he was supposed to meet, he nodded to himself and started up.

Then stopped again, ignoring a steady stream of people pushing past him up the steps.

Peabody and *Lawless*?

Lincolnshire's solicitor?

His first thought was to slink away. A summons issued by Lincolnshire's solicitor was potentially much worse than being summoned to discuss supposedly nefarious business dealings. He knew all his business dealings were on the up-and-up, after all. No matter who accused him of what, he ought to be able to prove his innocence, even if doing so might prove a grand piece of work. When he'd told Deirdre he might be busy getting arrested today, he hadn't really *meant* it.

But had impersonating Lincolnshire been an actual crime?

Had he been summoned here to be arrested?

"Sean!" Coming up the steps, Deirdre looked astonished to see him. "What are you doing here?"

"I wish I knew." He gestured toward the plaque. "These are Peregrine Peabody's offices, too."

Another woman mounting the steps did a double take, then turned to face him. "Mr. Delaney, isn't it? You have quite the nerve showing up here. Hmmph," she added, pushing through the door, no doubt to spread the news that he'd arrived.

There was nothing for it. There would be no slinking away. "Come along," he muttered, taking Deirdre's arm and steeling himself to face the fire.

But instead he came face-to-face with Corinna.

At first, Corinna thought Sean was a figment of her imagination. She wasn't ever supposed to see him again, and he especially didn't belong here. But then their gazes met and held, convincing her he was real, and something disturbing shuddered through her.

A mixture of love and anguish and regret.

Seeing him made her happy and sad, excited and apprehensive, all in a single instant. Her hand went up to touch her necklace, but it wasn't there, of course. She could wear it only in her room at night, where no one would see it and ask questions.

She started toward him.

"You need to come inside now, Corinna." Griffin appeared, giving her no choice as he took her arm and began weaving her through the crowded corridor. "Mr. Lawless is about to begin, and you've been commanded to sit in the front."

She looked back, but Sean was already lost in the crowd. She could only hope he was following.

Griffin had told her that everyone they knew had been asked to attend the reading, but she'd figured he'd been exaggerating. She'd had no concept of just how many people would show up. They crammed the large chamber where the reading was to be held and spilled out into the corridor, filling the building all the way back to the front door. With all the bodies in the way, she and Griffin barely managed to squeeze into the room.

Mr. Lawless was a very tall, very serious-looking man. Over a sea of chattering heads, Corinna could see him from where she was stuck in the back. "Ladies and gentlemen," he called. "I beg your attention! Will the following individuals please make their way to the front row. John Hamilton, the ninth Earl of Lincolnshire. His wife, Deirdre, the ninth Countess of Lincolnshire. Lady Corinna Chase. And Mr. Sean Delaney."

The crowd suddenly parted like the Red Sea, letting Corinna through. Griffin followed and went to stand at the left end of the front row, against the wall. Corinna noticed that the rest of her family already waited there. Four chairs at the front sat empty save for small signs set upon them that said, RESERVED. Corinna dropped gratefully onto one of them, and a moment later Mr. Hamilton—Lord Lincolnshire—lowered himself to the chair on her left, and Sean took the seat to her right.

Deirdre sat beside Sean rather than her husband.

"Why were you asked here?" Corinna whispered to Sean.

He looked pale. "I wish I knew. I assumed—"

"Ladies and gentlemen," the solicitor interrupted. "Although the eighth Lord Lincolnshire requested your presence, I feel compelled to inform you at the outset that you did not all receive bequests. Alas, while he was well-known for his generosity, Lord Lincolnshire's largesse did not extend quite that far." He paused while an amused titter ran through the room. "Rather, Lord

Lincolnshire asked you here to stand as witnesses to his final wishes."

Now a speculative murmur circulated the room instead. Mr. Lawless waited for that to die down before continuing.

"Let us begin." An expectant hush fell as he raised a large document. " 'I, Samuel Hamilton, eighth Earl of Lincolnshire, being of sound mind and failing body, declare that this is my last will and testament. I revoke all prior wills and codicils. I wish to thank everyone who has assembled to bear witness to my wishes. I have instructed Mr. Lawrence Lawless not to schedule the reading of this will until my nephew, John Hamilton, has arrived in London and presented himself as my heir, which I hope will prove to be sooner rather than later. I assume that doubtless scandalous event has by now taken place.' "

Shocked whispers buzzed around the room, accompanied by a few more titters. Corinna and Sean exchanged wary glances.

" 'I imagine it came as a surprise that an impostor has been posing as my nephew. It certainly came as a surprise to me. What may come as a larger surprise indeed is that I also discovered my true nephew, John Hamilton, was responsible for the deceit. He demanded another man impersonate him and made certain said man did so by means of blackmail.' "

Gasps filled the room, and John Hamilton jumped from his seat. "I object to that slander!"

Griffin stepped forward. "This is not a trial. You have no right to object to anything." He shoved the man back down. "Stay, Lincolnshire," he ordered as though the new Lord Lincolnshire were a misbehaving dog.

Which he was, of a sort.

Mr. Lawless cleared his throat and continued. " 'Needless to say, I was disappointed to learn my nephew is as immoral as the reputation that precedes him. For him I wish all the censure he deserves. Contrarily, I wish everyone to know that his impostor, whom I am now identifying as Mr. Sean Delaney, proved one of the best men I've ever had the privilege to meet. He treated me better than an uncle—indeed, better than a father—and were I to be granted one impossible wish, it would be to have had such a man for my son.' "

Corinna's heart had stuttered when Sean's name was read off, and it was racing now. An expectant silence filled the room as Mr. Lawless lowered the document and looked around as though making sure everyone had heard his words. He nodded slowly before raising the will once more.

" 'And so, my dear friends, I have summoned you to this event in order to beseech you to treat Mr. Delaney as I believe he deserves to be treated. Rather than persecuting the man, I beg you to accept him into our circle. I will remind you that you've all claimed numerous times that you'd do anything for me, and *this* is my most fervent request.' "

The solicitor glanced up again, this time looking directly at Corinna and Sean.

" 'In addition . . .' "

At the significant pause, everyone sat up straighter.

" 'In addition, although I will not put any conditions in this will stipulating the matter, as I believe such decisions are best left to those whose hearts are involved, I wish to publicly convey my hopes that Mr. Delaney will propose marriage to Lady Corinna Chase.' "

If Corinna thought everyone's gasps were loud before, the ones they emitted now sounded nothing less than a roar. And the loudest gasps of all came from her family. Meeting Griffin's eyes first and then those of her sisters, she reached for Sean's hand.

"And now, for the bequests . . ."

She hardly heard what came next, at least not at first. She felt faint. Her blood was thundering in her ears. Sean's hand felt warm in hers, and when she squeezed it and he squeezed back, she feared her heart might burst.

She glanced back to her family. Griffin's mouth was open in shock, Alexandra nodded approvingly, and Juliana's grin was smug beyond belief.

The last, at least, was no surprise.

And the reading wasn't yet finished.

" '. . . only my title as required by law and the small amount of entailed property that goes along with it,' " Mr. Lawless was saying. Given the indignant huff to Corinna's left, she guessed that was the new Lord Lincolnshire's punishment. " 'The balance of my fortune will be held in trust, the income to go to charity. I name Mr. Sean Delaney as trustee to oversee all investments and distribution, because I know him to be a man who has no need for the income himself, a man with an excellent head for business, and most important, a man who is eminently fair and makes decisions for the right reasons.' " The solicitor paused for effect. " 'Unless . . .' "

Skirts rustled and shoes shuffled. Everyone sat on the edge of their seats.

" 'Unless,' " he repeated, " 'my errant nephew, John Hamilton, grants Deirdre Hamilton a divorce, in which case he shall receive half the income of the trust in perpetuity.' "

John Hamilton stalked out of the room as Deirdre collapsed in a swoon.

Chapter Fifty-five

Still holding Corinna's hand, Sean walked with her and Deirdre toward Mr. Lawless, who stood by the door, where he'd been busy ushering everyone out. Although Sean's little party was the last to leave the chamber, excited chatter could be heard from the corridor. The reading of Lord Lincolnshire's will would doubtless be talked about for weeks.

"I'll be setting up the trust in the next few days," the solicitor said. "I'll need to meet with you to go over the details. Shall we say next Monday, at the same time?"

Sean nodded. "Agreed. But I've one question I'd like answered today."

"I have *lots* of questions," Corinna said.

"I'm thinking your brother can answer most of them," Sean told her, and looked back to Lawless. "Why did the letter I received requesting my presence here come from your partner rather than you?"

"Those were Lord Lincolnshire's instructions. He didn't want my name on the letter. He thought you might not show, fearing arrest."

"Lincolnshire was a clever man," Sean said, as arrest was exactly what he'd feared on seeing Lawless's name. "My thanks." He held out his free hand, and the solicitor gave it a firm shake. "I shall return a week from today."

The chatter ceased as they stepped into the corridor.

Apparently a nosy lot, most of the people followed them outside, where Corinna's family waited, bunched together on the pavement. Sean tried to drop Corinna's hand as they approached, but she tightened her grip.

Lady Stafford, Corinna's middle sister, elbowed their brother when she noticed the two of them walk up. Cainewood turned. "Ah, there you are, Corinna. Due to the atmosphere here on Queen Street"—he waved a hand, indicating all the busybodies—"we've decided to discuss these developments at home." He looked to Sean. "I would appreciate your participation in the discussion."

"I'm riding home with Sean," Corinna announced.

"*Sean?* Since when do you call the man Sean?" Glancing down to their clasped hands, her brother's eyes widened. "It's not proper for you to ride alone with an unmarried man."

"Sean has an open curricle, so I can assure you nothing improper will happen."

Snickers came from all around them, this sort of exchange being exactly what nosy busybodies loved to overhear. Cainewood's jaw seemed to be clenched. Suspecting none of this boded well for the man's approval of his suit, Sean turned to Corinna. "I need to take Deirdre with me, *a rún*," he told her apologetically. "The curricle seats only two."

"Your sister is welcome to ride with my husband and me," Lady Stafford piped up at the same time Cainewood said, "*What* did you just call my sister?"

Deirdre smiled. "*A rún*. It means 'my love.' " She didn't seem to notice Cainewood's reaction as she turned to his middle sister. "And I would be pleased to ride with you, Lady Stafford. Thank you for the offer."

"I think you should call me Juliana," Lady Stafford told her. "I've a feeling we'll be related soon."

The buzz around their little group was getting deafening. Cainewood's next words came from between his teeth. "I think—"

"Oh, let them ride together, Griffin," Corinna's eldest sister interrupted, wheeling a squeaky perambulator back and forth. "My goodness, what do you think could happen in an open curricle? There's my carriage now." A large vehicle crept to a stop in the snarl of traffic. "Let's all go," she said, pushing the perambulator toward it.

Her husband followed. Lady Stafford took her own husband's arm and smiled at Deirdre. "Our carriage is this way, Lady Lincolnshire."

"Call me Deirdre," Deirdre said. "I won't be Lady Lincolnshire for long."

As the three of them walked off, a lovely young woman moved to stand squarely before Corinna's fuming brother. "It seems your sister may be getting married a lot sooner than you expected, hmm?" she all but purred.

"Good God," Cainewood said, and walked off, too.

A delighted smile on her face, the woman joined three other young adults. "I want you to drop me off at Griffin's house," she said as they all departed.

Leaving Sean and Corinna alone.

Well, except for the dozens of buzzing busybodies.

"Who was that?" Sean asked.

"My cousin Rachael. I think Juliana is about to get even more smug. Where is your curricle?"

"In a mews about two blocks from here." Still holding her hand, he drew her in the right direction. The crowd parted to let them through, but Sean felt at least a hundred eyes on his back.

"Am I dreaming?" Corinna asked, seemingly oblivious to all the curious gazes. "Just an hour ago, all was lost. Now suddenly your reputation is restored—no, more than that, it's golden—and we can get . . ."

Her voice trailed off, as though she were afraid to say what came next.

"Married?" Sean supplied.

"You never actually asked me." They turned a corner, and she threw herself into his arms. "Oh, Sean, I've never been so happy!"

He held her tight, risking a short kiss, since they'd escaped the prying eyes. She tasted better than forbidden sin, and she felt divine pressed against him. But he couldn't bring himself to quite share in her happiness.

"Let us not count our chickens before they are hatched," he advised, remembering Cainewood's clenched jaw. "Lincolnshire's endorsement notwithstanding, your brother may not approve."

"Oh, don't worry about Griffin," she said gaily, rising to her toes for another quick kiss. He obliged her, of course. "I have a plan to persuade him."

"What do you mean?"

"Never mind." A bounce in her step, she turned and resumed walking. "We're all going to live happily ever after, just like in Minerva Press novels."

"Not all of us," he pointed out. "Not Hamilton."

"No one will buy his paintings now, will they? He's going to *need* half the income from his uncle's trust."

"Very clever, that stipulation." They turned into the mews where his curricle was waiting. "Lincolnshire knew it would get him to free Deirdre."

"She looked so happy, Sean."

"Believe me, she is." Digging a coin from his pocket, he handed it to one groom as another helped Corinna climb up. Sean walked around to the driver's side and swung up beside her, lifting the reins. "And I'm relieved to know she won't be living in sin. Or at least, not for long."

As the horses clip-clopped out of the mews, Corinna snuggled up against him. "What do you mean?"

"Deirdre won't be waiting for the divorce to come through before she moves in with Raleigh," he said with a sigh, turning onto the street. "That will take a long while, and she'll not be patient. Impulsive, my sister is, not to mention a wee bit wild."

"I guess that wildness runs in your family," Corinna said, grinning up at him. "Her brother posed naked for an artist."

Chapter Fifty-six

A short time later, Griffin found himself seated on a sofa in his drawing room, surrounded by members of his family and a couple of near strangers with Irish accents. And each and every one of them—except for the baby—wanted something.

His two brothers-in-law wanted to go home. *That* he could understand. If he weren't already home, he would want to go home now, too.

Alexandra wanted to know how Lincolnshire had come to learn everything his will had revealed. He couldn't blame her for that, as he'd be clamoring for the information himself if he didn't already have it.

Juliana wanted Corinna to marry Delaney. Corinna wanted to marry Delaney. Delaney's sister wanted Delaney to marry Corinna. And Delaney wanted to marry Corinna.

These four people were responsible for half of the new cracks in his teeth.

And then there was Rachael, sitting beside him on the sofa, enveloping him in her come-hither scent. *She* wanted to marry *him*.

Which made her responsible for the rest of the cracks.

The beginnings of a headache pulsed in his temples. Alexandra wasn't seated. Holding little Harry, she was bouncing him unceasingly in a rather frantic, rhythmic fashion. It worked to keep the baby from crying, but Griffin's headache escalated just watching her.

"How on earth did Lord Lincolnshire learn everything?" she asked for the third time.

He decided to give her what she wanted first.

But before he could unclench his jaw to do so, Delaney answered. "I'm thinking Lincolnshire got the facts from your brother," the man told her. "A mere two days before he died." Sitting on a sofa across the drawing room, with Corinna beside him—*right* beside him—he looked to Griffin for confirmation. "That morning he summoned you . . . it wasn't to say good-bye, was it?"

"No, it wasn't," Griffin said. "He wanted information. I take it he asked you to find future employment for all of his staff?"

"He asked me to continue employing them all at Lincolnshire House, which I knew Hamilton wouldn't do. So I offered to find alternative employment for them instead."

"Well, you did too good a job of it, raising his suspicions. He subsequently requested that Mr. Lawless hire someone to investigate the various concerns where his servants would eventually work, to make certain they all existed and his people would be treated well. In the process, Lawless discovered all of the concerns were owned by a single man, a certain Mr. Sean Delaney." Griffin paused, feeling rather awed despite his suspicions that this man had kissed his sister. "You own a *lot* of property, Delaney."

"Among other things. You needn't worry that your sister might ever want for anything."

Griffin snorted. "You'll keep her in dresses, I expect—should I agree to let you have her." When Corinna opened her mouth to protest, he forged ahead. "From there, Lawless made further inquiries and learned you were posing as Hamilton, and furthermore, that Hamilton was your brother-in-law. Feeling you were a good man"—this uttered with more than a little irony—

"Lincolnshire summoned me to ask if I knew why you might have done such a thing."

"And you confirmed his suspicions?" Corinna asked.

"He was close enough to confirming them for himself. I told him Delaney agreed to the hoax for his sister's sake and attested that Hamilton was quite deserving of his less-than-stellar reputation. Lincolnshire seemed especially incensed that his nephew had refused Mrs. Hamilton the divorce she sought." He looked to Delaney's sister. "He was quite taken with you, if you didn't know."

"I loved him, too," she whispered, tears in her eyes.

"He considered your brother a saint, and he compared you to the angels. He wanted you happy. And he requested that I not reveal what he knew. He wanted to settle everything his own way. I expect his will was rewritten that very afternoon."

"Didn't you think we'd have wanted to know?" Corinna asked rather indignantly. "I was devastated, and Sean thought he was being set up to take a fall—"

"I agreed to keep Lincolnshire's secret in order to make the old man happy. The exact reason you kept secrets, if you'll recall. I followed through after his death because I like to think I'm a man of my word. I felt Lincolnshire deserved to resolve the matter as he wished. And furthermore"—he glared daggers at her—"I had no knowledge the two of you were involved, so I had no reason to worry for your happiness should Delaney be discredited. You denied any interest in him, and you told me you were saddened over the loss of Lord Lincolnshire and because your painting isn't likely to be accepted for the Summer Exhibition."

That tirade rendered his youngest sister speechless, a rare state for Corinna. Griffin found a measure of satisfaction in that.

He was going to allow her to marry Delaney, of course. He was thinking a late summer wedding at Cainewood Castle, after the Season ended, would be perfect. While he wished he knew Delaney better, he liked what he'd learned of the man thus far. Lincolnshire had judged him worthy, and Griffin trusted the earl's judgment. Most important, Corinna was in love, and Griffin wanted to see her happy.

But he was sick and tired of being manipulated by all the people he loved.

Before he granted his permission, he was planning to make everyone else squirm for a change. And he planned to enjoy it.

"Do you not *like* Sean?" Corinna finally asked.

"I would *like* to have his skill for investing," Griffin said dryly, leaving it at that for now. He shifted to look at the man in question. "Given Lincolnshire's attitude, I suspected he wasn't planning to make you pay for your deception. But I felt no responsibility either way. As far as I was concerned, you had dug your own grave."

Slowly Delaney nodded. "And now I expect I have to lie in it."

"No, you don't," Corinna disagreed heatedly. "Griffin will allow us to marry. I have a secret that will ensure it."

Suddenly Griffin wasn't finding this so enjoyable. His headache was getting worse. "Another secret? What the hell sort of secret?"

"Maybe he kissed her for half an hour," Rachael suggested sweetly.

Griffin cracked another tooth.

"Open your eyes, Griffin," Juliana put in. "A blind man could see they belong together."

"I see they seem to be *glued* together," he said darkly.

Delaney immediately put space between himself and Corinna, and Corinna immediately scooted right back against him. Griffin found that slightly amusing, which worked to calm him down a bit.

Delaney's pretty blond sister cleared her throat. "Lord Cainewood, you admired Lord Lincolnshire, did you not? I'm thinking you should trust his judgment regarding my brother."

"I'm thinking this is none of your concern," he said, thinking she was the only one with an intelligent argument.

Unsurprisingly, Juliana wasn't ready to give up. "What do *you* think, James?"

Her husband looked at her as though flowers had just sprouted from her ears. "I think I'm staying out of this."

"Alexandra, Tristan?"

They both shook their heads, Alexandra doing so while still maniacally bouncing the baby.

Crossing her arms, Juliana looked back to Griffin. "You have to let them marry."

"I don't *have* to do anything."

"She's over twenty-one," she pointed out with more than a little smugness. "They can elope to Gretna Green."

"I won't do that," Delaney put in quickly. "I won't go behind her brother's back."

"I *knew* you'd say that," Corinna said. "That's why I'm prepared to use the secret."

Griffin swung back to her. "*What* secret?"

"Maybe he kissed her for *more* than half an hour," Rachael suggested.

Which made Griffin wonder if maybe things had gone beyond kissing. "Did he paw you, Corinna?"

She looked confused. "Did he what?"

An awful thought occurred to him. "You aren't in the family way, are you?"

"No, I'm not in the family way! He didn't do anything that could get me in the family way. Sean's much too honorable to even consider such a thing. He's the son of a vicar, if you didn't know."

Griffin hadn't known, and he was rather pleased to hear it. "So, then, what's the secret? What *did* he do?"

She hesitated, her gaze darting about the room. She

appeared to be holding her breath. Beside her, Delaney looked like he wished the floor would open up and swallow him. Alexandra stopped bouncing, and the baby started crying.

Griffin saw Corinna's breath rush out, saw her suck in another one—a single, shuddering, ragged breath—and then she opened her mouth—

"You know what? I don't want to hear it." Suddenly, he didn't. He was absolutely certain it was something that would make him furious, something that would make him demand Delaney marry his sister immediately.

In fact, he was going to do just that, just in case.

So much for a late-summer wedding at Cainewood.

"You two will be married tomorrow."

Corinna finally left Delaney's side, rushing over to smother Griffin in a hug. "Oh, thank you, thank you, thank you for not making me use my secret. You won't be sorry."

"I'm sorry already," he muttered. "It's a miracle I have any teeth left in my mouth."

"They cannot marry tomorrow," Juliana said. Smugly. "They'll need a special license. And she'll need a dress."

"She has dozens of dresses. I know, because I paid for all of them." Griffin disentangled himself from his sister and set her away. "Very well, then, you have until Friday to get a license and pick a dress. Not a day later. And you and the vicar's son will not be alone together until then." The baby was still bawling, a racket loud enough to rattle his aching teeth. He had a raging headache. "Leave, all of you, please. Except for Corinna. Now."

Most of the family shuffled out. Mercifully, the baby's cries faded away with them, and as they left the house, the noise ceased altogether.

"I'm going to walk Sean and Deirdre to the door," Corinna said quietly. "I'm not leaving." The three of them walked into the foyer.

Rachael had stayed put, naturally. Now she moved

closer, enveloping Griffin in her damned come-hither scent again. Against his better judgment, he shifted to face her.

"I've reconsidered your offer," she said in her low, sultry voice.

"What do you mean?" he asked, fearing he knew what she meant.

"I said I wouldn't wait until your sister married. But as I can wait until Friday without becoming a shriveled old lady, I've changed my mind."

She moved closer, so close her mouth was a whisper from his.

And she licked her lips.

"Do you want to kiss me, Griffin?"

His head hurt. He felt beaten down. And he was being manipulated again, damn it.

But he very much wanted to kiss her.

He loved Rachael. She was so open and refreshing, so competent and levelheaded. Having run an earldom for a number of years, she would be a fine helpmate. He didn't want to lose her to a rake with the gall to touch her luscious derriere.

The next man to touch her luscious derriere was going to be *him*.

Her sweet breath washed over him, tantalizing him, making his own breath catch. Her mouth was so close he could taste her already. Struggling for control, his heart pounding double time, he leaned in. She met him halfway and nipped at his bottom lip, and he yanked her close, feeling his control snap, crushing his mouth against hers.

A bloodcurdling scream came from the foyer.

His heart pounding triple time, he leapt to his feet and rushed out to see who was being murdered.

No one was dead. But it was difficult to be thankful for that when he saw the way Corinna was wrapped around Delaney. No man should ever see his sister in such an embrace. She was literally hanging on the fellow, her arms around his neck, her legs all but around his waist.

She was sobbing, and she clutched a crumpled letter. Delaney's sister plucked it out of her hand and brought it to Griffin.

Somerset House, Monday 26 May

Lady Corinna Chase:

The Royal Academy's Summer Exhibition Committee is pleased to inform you that your painting has been accepted for our 1817 Exhibition. Please be advised that Varnishing Day will take place Friday 30 May in preparation for the Exhibition's opening on Monday 2 June.

Congratulations,

Benjamin West, President

"I cannot believe it," Corinna choked out through a sob.

"I'm not at all surprised," Griffin said.

She slid off Delaney, thank God, and dashed the tears off her face. "You're not?"

"You're very talented, Corinna." He was pleased as punch for her. "Since Varnishing Day is Friday, we'll move the wedding to Saturday."

"And make it a double wedding," a sultry voice added from behind him.

Chapter Fifty-seven

The Great Room, which housed the Summer Exhibition, had been built at the very top of Somerset House so it could be illuminated by skylights. It was accessed by a wide, winding staircase that seemed endless. Corinna's knees trembled as she climbed up it Friday afternoon, gripping her paint box like a life preserver.

"Are you getting tired?" Sean asked, taking her arm to steady her.

"A little," she said.

She was glad Griffin had relented and allowed Sean to accompany her. But unfortunately, he'd done so only after extracting a solemn promise from the "vicar's son" that he would bring her there and straight back, and she knew Sean was so honorable he'd stick to that promise.

Which meant this would be another day without kisses.

The four days since Griffin had agreed to their marriage seemed the longest four days of her life. Two special licenses had been procured, and the minister booked, and nothing much more had happened. The double wedding tomorrow was going to be a very quiet affair, even smaller than Lady Cavanaugh's. Besides the two brides and grooms, only Corinna's family and Deirdre, Rachael's siblings, and the ABC sisters would be attending. Aunt Frances couldn't come, as she was still in confinement—new mothers stayed at home for the first month.

The wedding would take place in the afternoon in the Berkeley Square house's drawing room, and then they'd have a little dinner, and then everyone would go home.

Juliana was very disappointed. She'd wanted more of a fuss made about everything. But Corinna didn't care about the wedding, just like she didn't care that she didn't have a new dress to wear for it. The wedding was only something to get past.

The wedding *night*, however . . .

"I'm a little tired *and* a little nervous," she admitted, still climbing.

"About our wedding night?"

"No." The thought of that was just exciting. "What if my painting is hung up very high? Or down near the floor?"

"Why should it matter where it's hung? It's an honor just to be in the Exhibition, isn't it?"

"The room is designed with a line going around it, a strip of molding mounted eight feet above the floor. The pictures placed with the bottom edges of their frames along the line are considered the best. It's an extra honor to be hung not high or low, but right there in the middle. I'm afraid to look."

"Well, I don't see how not looking is going to change anything. But if you want, I'll look for you and let you know."

"You can't." On the landing, she stopped before the Great Room's open door to catch her breath. "You won't recognize my painting." That was another thing she was nervous about. "It's not Lord Lincolnshire's portrait."

"It's not?" He looked totally nonplussed. "Well, what is it, then?"

"My secret," she said, and stepped in, hurrying to the center of the room.

Varnishing Day seemed to be chaos. Artists were everywhere, on chairs and ladders and their knees, blocking Corinna's view of all the pictures on the soaring walls. They hung frame-to-frame, fitted like puzzle pieces floor to ceiling. She turned in circles, frantically searching for her own.

"Sweet Jesus," Sean burst out.

"Where? Where is it?"

He took her by the shoulders and swung her around. "There. And it's quite some secret."

She stared at it, feeling breathless, and not because she'd climbed a hundred stairs. "They liked it."

"They wouldn't have accepted it had they not liked it, *críona*."

"But it's on the line. In the place of honor. They *really* liked it."

"Hamilton loved it," he said dryly. "He described his favorite submission to me precisely. 'A sensual study of a golden-haired man, rather scandalously undressed and bathed in candlelight.' I had no idea the scandalously undressed man was *me*."

"And neither did he, a man who's known you since childhood. No one will recognize you, Sean." Tearing her gaze from her picture, she turned to him. "I changed your coloring."

"But Deirdre will want to come see it, and your brother—"

"I didn't end up telling Griffin my secret," she reminded him, thanking God she hadn't needed to. "It won't occur to them it could be you. You're not angry with me, are you? No one here is recognizing you, either. And it's not because they haven't noticed the painting." Indeed, several artists not involved in their own work stood before it, discussing it, a sight that made her heart sing. "Why didn't you tell me Hamilton liked it so much?"

"When he described it, I was certain it wasn't yours. I saw no point in mentioning he loved someone else's work."

He shook his head in apparent disbelief, but she was thankful he didn't seem angry. Her hand went up to touch her necklace. She was so lucky to have found such a tolerant man.

"Are you going to varnish it now, then?" he asked.

"In a minute." She wanted to let it all sink in for a while first. She shifted her paint box to her other hand, looking around. "Sean," she whispered, thrilled. "It's J. M. W. Turner. There, in the top hat and tails. I've heard he always dresses like that."

"His painting doesn't look finished."

The artist had hung an all but monochrome canvas. "You're color-blind. How can you tell?"

"It's a landscape, and the sky isn't even blue. How the devil did it get accepted?"

"Academicians are allowed to hang six paintings each without going through the selection process," Corinna explained in an undertone. "And Varnishing Day isn't just for varnishing; it's also for fixing little things. Turner is rather famous for this trick. While his fellow artists—"

"That's you," Sean interrupted.

"Oh, God, it is, isn't it?" She felt her heart might burst. "While the rest of us struggle to fix some tiny mistake, he practically paints an entire picture."

"Thus proving his technical virtuosity?"

"And awing everyone else in the process." She watched the dull painting blaze to life as Turner swiftly transformed it with glorious chrome and brilliant vermilion and costly ultramarine. He stood so close to his canvas he appeared to paint with his eyes and nose as well as his hands. "He's legendary," she whispered. "They call him the painter of light. He first exhibited here at the age of fifteen."

"While you're an ancient twenty-two?"

"I suppose I should feel lucky you're willing to marry such an old hag."

"We'd best wed quickly, *a rún*, before you get any older."

"Is tomorrow soon enough?"

"An hour from now wouldn't be soon enough."

She laughed, a joyous sound that warmed Sean's heart. "I don't know how Turner does it. He's been known to produce two hundred fifty pictures in a single year. It takes me at least two weeks to complete a painting."

"Not *that* one." Sean gestured to his image on the wall.

"That one just flowed out of me," she admitted. "I guess I'll varnish it now."

She looked nervous as she walked toward it, paint box in hand. Sean followed, moving a step stool so that she could reach it.

"Is that yours?" someone asked as she climbed up, setting off a volley of comments.

"She's unknown!"

"A female painted that?"

"A genius."

"I think it's shameful," a disgruntled man disagreed.

Through it all, Corinna held her head high, nerves notwithstanding. She made her own way in the world, just like Sean did. That was why he loved her.

Well, that and because she made his blood surge with just a look.

Only one more day until he made her his forever. Standing back, he smiled as she dipped her brush in varnish and began swiping it over his bare chest.

Chapter Fifty-eight

"Well," Griffin said. "That's it." Upstairs in the Berkeley Square town house, he shut the bedroom door and leaned his hands against it. "Corinna is on her way to Hampstead, to a house I've never even seen."

"You'll see it soon," Rachael said behind him, where he knew she was slipping off her shoes.

He heard the soft give of the mattress as she sat on the bed across the room, and he imagined her rolling down her stockings. To torture himself just a bit, he remained facing away, the sound of swishing silk making his body stir, making his blood heat.

"And I'm sure it's a fine house," she continued, her sultry voice sliding into him. "Deirdre told me it's enormous, and set in acres of gardens and woodland, and it was built by Robert Adams. She said her brother has more money than a pot of gold at the end of a rainbow."

"That man could eat a pot of gold for breakfast and never notice it was missing. I swear, Rachael, I didn't know it was possible for one man to have so much. It boggles the mind. But it doesn't matter. He has Corinna now, and that's all that counts. Corinna wanted him, and I wanted her happy."

"You did the right thing, Griffin. She loves him, and he loves her. And I love you."

"I love you, too." He straightened and turned, feasting his eyes on her. She rose and took a few steps toward him, barefooted and gorgeous. Hopping on one foot and then the other, he pulled off his own shoes and stockings, ripped off his tailcoat and waistcoat, leaving it all littering the floor as he started toward her.

He couldn't believe he'd wed Rachael. He couldn't believe anything that had happened this week, all the incredible events that had led to him marrying his sister to a man he hardly knew and to getting married himself.

And he couldn't believe he still hadn't touched his wife.

She was beautiful inside and out, the most beautiful thing in his life. And all he'd ever done was kiss her. For just half of one hour. For all his bluster about men keeping their hands off his sisters, he'd never imagined marrying a woman he'd barely kissed and never really touched.

"You're wearing your mother's wedding dress," he said, walking toward her, remembering her pulling it out of the heavy oak trunk, and how he'd thought it looked lacy and beautiful. It fit her perfectly, as he'd known it would. Rachael was all willowy, graceful curves, and the sight of her in his bedroom, in the white dress, made his throat ache. It made his palms itch.

He couldn't believe she was his and he still hadn't touched her.

"You look lovely," he told her, walking closer.

"You look better." He was standing before her now, so close they were only a breath apart. "I'm a Chase now."

Her come-hither scent was overwhelming him, making him dizzy. "Is that why you wanted to marry me? So you could think of yourself as a Chase again?"

"No, that's just a bonus. I wanted to marry you because I love you. I want to make children with you."

Hearing that spiked his lust, kicked his pulse up a notch or two or three. He very much wanted to make children with her.

And he still hadn't touched her.

Her face was raised, her cerulean eyes fastened on his. Her breath washed over him from between her parted lips. Slowly, very slowly, she licked them. "Do you want to kiss me, Griffin?"

"I do," he said.

But first he wanted to put his hands on her luscious derriere.

He did that, and then he used his hands to yank her against him, and after that a fever seized him, raging in his blood. Now that he'd touched her, he had to touch her everywhere. His hands skimmed her hips, her sides, her breasts, and he was kissing her. Kissing her mouth and nipping at it, claiming her with lips and teeth and tongue. He was mad for her. He'd always been mad for her, it seemed, but now she was his, and he was going to have all of her.

Somehow they made it to the bed and rolled there together. Somehow the wedding dress came off, and Rachael was tearing at Griffin's clothes, frantic to get her hands on bare flesh. She'd thought she'd been in control of this relationship, but something had been unleashed in the man she loved, unleashing a wildness in her, too. She wasn't surrendering herself to him, not exactly. Maybe they were surrendering to each other. It didn't signify, and she didn't care.

She ran her hands all over him, feeling his muscles jump beneath her fingers. Then her lips and her tongue, tasting his skin, savoring warm male with a hint of salt. He dragged his own mouth over every inch of her, her neck and shoulders, her breasts and belly, taking what she was furious to give.

She'd always been destined to be with him. Realizing that now, she cursed herself for all the wasted time, all the months she'd spent suppressing her feelings, thinking of him as a cousin or a brother and concentrating on things that didn't really matter. Happy as she was to have discovered new family, the person most important to her had been by her side all that time, and she was grateful beyond belief that she'd seen the truth before it was too late.

He was poised above her now, his intense green gaze burning into hers. What she saw there made her heart squeeze. Passion and desire, yes, but also devotion and understanding. And bountiful, beautiful love.

"This might hurt," he whispered.

"I don't care," she said, and she didn't. She wanted to join with him. She wanted to belong to him, and she wanted him to belong to her, pain be damned.

She wrapped her legs around his lean, bare hips, pressing herself closer, feeling an incredible urgency where he was ready to enter her. Slowly he lowered his head, and when he kissed her, she tasted her future. A future filled with possibility and wonderful days and endless, blissful nights.

She felt glorious, and he felt hot against her hands, against her body. His mouth felt feverish and sent a matching fever singing through her. Her world narrowed to one of pleasure and give and take, and when he finally slid home she held tight and knew she would never let go.

Although Sean's house was but a few minutes' walk from Hampstead Heath and the High Street, Corinna found herself amazed when the curricle started up the long, serpentine drive. The property seemed in a different world, the setting idyllic, a picturesque, pastoral landscape. As they approached the classical villa, the sun was setting low on the horizon, its last rays glinting off many glossy arched windows in the creamy white building.

"Oh," she breathed, "it's beautiful."

" 'Tis glad I am it pleases you, *a rún*."

Sean's melodic Irish lilt went right through her, and her veins thrummed with anticipation. She snuggled against him with a happy sigh. "We're almost there. You'll be able to touch me."

His arm tightened around her shoulders. "I'm touching you now," he pointed out.

"Not where I want."

"My straightforward Corinna." His low laugh rang into the night as he slid his hand down her arm, stopping at her elbow. "Here? Is this where you want me to touch you?"

"Not quite," she breathed on a frustrated sigh.

He slid down to her hand, rubbing the pad of his thumb on her sensitive palm. "Here, then?"

"Sean . . ."

His fingers brushed along her side and down her hip to the outside of her leg. Liquid heat pooled in her middle. "Closer?"

"Oh, yes." He shifted to rest his hand atop her thigh. "You're getting closer." His palm felt warm through her thin dress, and at the teasing sensation, her stomach did a flip-flop. "I feel like I've been waiting forever."

His hand went to the reins as he pulled the curricle to a halt. "Well, you're going to be waiting a lot longer, *críona.*"

"What?" She watched him agilely leap down and come around to her side.

"I want this night to be perfect," he said, reaching up for her. "I won't be touching you anywhere more intimate for quite a while."

It sounded like a promise or a threat, but he had to be fooling. Knowing he wanted her as much as she wanted him, she laughed when he scooped her into his arms rather than setting her on her feet. "Put me down, Sean."

"Oh, no," he said, striding toward the house. "They say the husband must carry the bride over the threshold to protect her from evil spirits."

She marveled that he carried her so easily. He was so strong, so masculine, so muscular. Feeling the heat radiating from his body, she linked her arms about his neck. "Do you believe in evil spirits, Sean?"

"I believe they're a good excuse to carry you." He pressed a warm kiss to her mouth as the door opened, revealing a portly, gray-haired servant. "Good evening to you, Simpson," Sean said, stepping inside. "This is your new mistress, Lady Corinna Delaney."

Simpson kept an admirably straight face as he shut the door. "Welcome, my lady."

"I'm pleased to meet you." Corinna glanced around the entrance hall, a square room with a polished wooden floor and pale blue walls trimmed in white. "Put me down, Sean."

He didn't. "If the bedroom is ready, Simpson, I'll thank you to make yourself scarce and see that everyone else does as well." While the man walked off in one direction, he carried Corinna in another. "You'll meet the rest of the staff tomorrow, *mo chroí*."

She wondered what he meant by the bedroom being ready. "We're inside now, so you can put me down."

"I think not." Holding her close, he carried her through a dining room with blue walls and a crystal chandelier. "I'm finding I rather like carrying you."

In truth, she rather liked being carried. No one had carried her since she was a child, and the pure romance of it made her head swim. It made her heart sing. Sean swept her through a drawing room carpeted in blue with blue sofas. "I don't want a tour," she said breathlessly. "Just take me to your bedroom."

"*Our* bedroom," he corrected in a tone deep with meaning. He carried her past a library with white columns and plush, ultramarine blue velvet chairs, and on into a small, cobalt blue lobby. "There's another wing and two more levels you can see tomorrow."

"I expect all of those rooms are blue, too?"

"Except for Deirdre's. I don't know what color it is. Maybe you can tell me."

"Not tonight," she said, thankful his sister had gone to Daniel Raleigh's house.

"I haven't any paintings," he said apologetically as he

started up a grand staircase with a blue runner. "You can buy any paintings you want and hang them wherever you'd like."

She turned her face into his neck, inhaling his clean, soapy scent. "I don't care about paintings, Sean."

"And everything doesn't have to stay blue. You can have the rooms repainted any colors you'd like, have the furniture reupholstered or buy new."

"I don't care what color the rooms are." She was melting. His heat seemed to penetrate her skin, making her liquefy in his arms. "All I care about is you," she told him as they finally reached the bedroom.

Set before a huge blue-toned tapestry, the bed was covered with a plush, sapphire blue counterpane and piled with lighter blue pillows. He walked to it, laying her upon it so gently, so reverently, every bone in her body seemed to dissolve.

When he stepped back, her breath caught. He was so very male, so strong and toned, so darkly handsome. He looked better than a Greek god, but even better than that, he was the best man she'd ever known.

And she saw what he meant by *ready*. Candles flickered everywhere—on the windowsill, along the marble mantel, atop every piece of furniture—bathing the room in shadows and dancing light. He must have set them about before leaving to marry her, must have instructed a servant to light them when they arrived. Like a Minerva Press hero, she thought, her heart doing a slow roll in her chest.

"Oh, Sean," she breathed. "It's a wonderland."

"Every bride should have a wonderland, *mo chroí*."

Sean thought she was a wonder herself, a vision in a simple white dress, those brilliant blue eyes hazy with desire. His necklace glimmered silver against her skin, and he found himself staggered by the raw possessiveness he felt at the sight. He couldn't believe everything had worked out so he could have her—it seemed a miracle, and much more than he deserved. He planned to go slowly and savor every moment. Before he touched her where she wanted, he intended to drive them both completely senseless.

He wanted this night to be perfect.

He slipped off her shoes, untied her garters, drew her stockings down, a sensual slide of silk. Slowly, watching her watch him, he removed his own clothes. Slowly he lowered himself to meet her; slowly he cradled her face in his hands; slowly he kissed her. Just a taste, a slow brush of mouths before it deepened and became long and slow and languid.

Slowly, slowly, he reminded himself, maneuvering his hands to unbutton her dress. Slowly he nudged it off a shoulder. Slowly he tasted her there, nuzzled her warm skin, breathed in her fragrance, heady and overwhelming.

He had such a need for her, a terrible hunger that made it hard to stay gentle. Through her dress he felt every tantalizing curve. He felt her quickening, felt her trembling, flooding his senses. He would never get over the wonder that a man like him had been gifted with such perfection.

I won't be touching you anywhere more intimate for quite a while, he'd said, and Corinna's husband was a man of his word. In his quest to make this night perfect, it was a very, very long time before he touched her where she wanted.

For forever, it seemed, he just kissed her. Kissed her mouth and her cheeks and her chin, trailing down to her throat. His utter lack of urgency proved transfixing. Feeling dreamy, feeling his slow pace drizzle into her, she tilted her head back in surrender and allowed him to take her where he would.

Sweet torture it was, sweet torment. Sliding her dress off, he teased through her chemise, rolling her over, rolling her back, searing heat following his fingers. He drew her chemise off and explored her bare skin, his hands and his mouth and his tongue everywhere but where she wanted them most.

Everywhere he touched her she felt a glow, a swath of sensation that claimed her body and robbed her mind. Murmured endearments tumbling off his tongue, his hands went between her thighs, stroking and caressing everywhere but where she wanted.

Candlelight danced as pleasure mounted, becoming unbearable, unendurable, unbelievable. Trembling with need, she reached down to give him the same. Stroking gently, she felt steel sheathed in silk, learning the length of him and the breadth of him and imagining him inside her. A glimmer of excitement darted through her, and her hands grew bolder.

Slow down, Sean mentally ordered as she drove him to distraction, threatening to shatter his resolve. Wanting to make this night perfect, he struggled to center himself, tried to pull back, pressing his mouth to the delicious curve where her neck met her shoulder in an effort to find calm. But the rising need raged out of his control. It had always been this way between them, and he knew it always would be, and he thought perhaps he should be thankful for that . . . and then he ceased thinking at all.

The world slipped away, leaving nothing but sensation and the passion that raged between them, powerful, fierce, and violent.

And he touched her as she'd wanted.

A slide of fingers, a slick caress, and she was arching helplessly against him. "Here?" he whispered. "Or . . . here?"

"Oh, there!" she cried as he found a spot so exquisite a skittering of heat flashed through her. "Now, Sean," she breathed, arching again. "Take me now."

She was shimmering, she was throbbing, and he was moving over her, nudging her entrance. Wrapping her legs around him instinctively, she sucked in a breath as he slipped inside her. A tiny burst of pain went as quickly as it arrived, leaving her astonished at the wonder of being filled, of being possessed, of being utterly one with the man she loved.

He was hers, and she was his, and nothing had ever been so right.

And then he moved in her, and nothing had ever been so sublime.

She raised her hips, straining to be closer to him, and together they sought a rhythm. Together they were lost; together they found oblivion; together they soared. They caught cries of pleasure in each other's mouths and, washed in candlelight, stayed locked together while the world slid back into place.

And it was perfect.

Author's Note

Dear Readers,

During the Regency, a female artist like Corinna might have had her picture accepted for the Summer Exhibition—but it's a sad truth that she'd probably never have been elected to the Royal Academy of Arts. In 1768, the founding membership did include two women, Angelica Kauffmann and Mary Moser. However, ladies weren't admitted to the Royal Academy schools until 1861, and the next female Academician, Dame Laura Knight, wasn't elected until 1936.

Although we think of art from Corinna's era as classic, it was the contemporary art of its time, and the Royal Academy's Summer Exhibition is the largest contemporary art show in the world. Held every year since 1769, the Exhibition is and always has been the place to see a wide range of new work by both established and unknown living artists. Admission cost one shilling in the nineteenth century, and the exhibit has been extraordinarily popular all along. Attendance grew from 60,000 in 1780 to 390,000 by 1879. In 2006, the show drew over 150,000 visitors (including me and my family!), and more than 1200 works were included.

The Summer Exhibition Selection Committee members who attended Lady A's reception were the actual committee members in 1817, with the exception of Thomas Phillips. I removed him to make room for the fictional John Hamilton. I do apologize to Mr. Phillips, but I had to choose someone, and he was the man with the least biographical information to draw on.

It's been said that the modern novel was born in 1740, when Samuel Richardson wrote *Pamela or Virtue and Reward*. A tale of frustrated sexuality, it sparked controversy that created a thirst for more of the same. As a result, reading Gothic and romance fiction became a decades-long craze. Or maybe it still is a craze . . . as a romance reader, what do you think?

In about 1790, an Englishman named William Lane saw an opportunity and established Minerva Press. For a number of years, Lane dominated the novel publishing industry. Over half the popular books were printed by Minerva Press, and Lane reportedly made a fortune. According to the poet Samuel Rogers, Lane was often seen tooling around London in a splendid carriage, attended by footmen with cockades and gold-headed canes. All of the lines from books that Corinna recalls in *The Art of Temptation* are real quotes from Minerva Press novels.

Most of the homes in my books are inspired by real places. I modeled Lincolnshire House on Devonshire House, which was designed by William Kent and served as the London residence of the Dukes of Devonshire for almost two hundred years. Because I wanted Lord Lincolnshire to live in Berkeley Square, I turned this house around—in reality, the house fronted on Piccadilly Street and its gardens backed up to the square. Devonshire House is no longer standing, but before it was demolished in the 1920s, many of the interior furnishings were moved to Chatsworth, the duke's residence in the countryside. You can still see some of them there.

Sean's house was inspired by Kenwood House in Hampstead. Set in an idyllic landscape beside Hampstead Heath, the house was expanded by Robert Adam between 1764 and 1779. Although Sean didn't have any paintings, the real house is a veritable gallery. Edward Cecil Guinness, brewing magnate and first Earl of

Iveagh, bought Kenwood House in 1925, and when he died in 1927, he bequeathed the estate and part of his art collection to Britain. The house is open daily all year round, and if you visit you will see important paintings by many great artists including Rembrandt, Vermeer, Constable, Turner, Reynolds, and Gainsborough. I like to imagine that Corinna might have put together such a collection!

The Chases' town house at 44 Berkeley Square has been described as "the finest terrace house of London." It was designed in 1742 by William Kent for Lady Isabella Finch. Unfortunately, you cannot visit, because the building is currently being used as a private club, but if you go to Berkeley Square, you can see it from the outside. Look for the blue door.

Stafford House, Juliana's home in St. James's Place, is based on Spencer House, one of the great architectural landmarks of London. Built in the eighteenth century by John, 1st Earl Spencer (an ancestor of Diana, Princess of Wales), it was immediately recognized as a building of major importance. Should you ever find yourself in London, I highly recommend a visit. Spencer House is open to the public every Sunday except during January and August.

To see pictures and learn more about the real places featured in *The Art of Temptation*, please visit my Web site at www.LaurenRoyal.com, where you can also read about the real people in the story, find modern versions of all the recipes, sign up for my newsletter, and enter a contest to win Corinna's claddagh necklace. If you try any of the recipes, I hope you'll e-mail me at Lauren@LaurenRoyal.com and tell me whether you enjoyed them.

If you missed Alexandra's story, you can find it in *Lost in Temptation*, the first book in my Sweet Temptations trilogy. Juliana's story was told in the second book, *Tempting Juliana*. If you've read any of my books, I'd love to hear from you! To send a "real" letter rather than e-mail (I answer both!), write to P.O. Box 52932, Irvine, CA 92619, and please enclose a self-addressed, stamped envelope, especially if you'd like me to send you an autographed bookmark and/or bookplate.

'Til next time,

Lauren

ENTER FOR A CHANCE TO WIN
the sterling silver claddagh necklace,
pictured on the back cover of this book!

You are eligible to enter the sweepstakes if you correctly answer this question:

How much money does Sean inherit?

(Hint: Read the prologue of *The Art of Temptation*, or go to www.LaurenRoyal.com to read an excerpt.)

A total of six winners will be selected from among eligible entries in six random drawings (one per month beginning November 2007 and ending in April 2008). There will be one winner per drawing. Submitting one eligible entry will make you eligible for all drawings, so enter early! However, please do not enter more than once; duplicate entries will be discarded.

To enter, either visit Lauren Royal's Web site at www.LaurenRoyal.com or submit your name, address, e-mail address, and your answer to the question to:

Lauren Royal
P.O. Box 52932
Irvine, CA
92619

All entries must be received by March 31, 2008. Limit one entry per person. Claddagh necklace approximately valued at $50. **No Purchase Necessary. See complete rules on reverse.**

Official Rules for
***The Art of Temptation* Sweepstakes**

NO PURCHASE NECESSARY.
A PURCHASE WILL NOT ENHANCE YOUR CHANCES OF WINNING.

Open only to U.S. residents ages 18 and up.

How to Enter:

To enter the *The Art of Temptation* Sweepstakes ("Sweepstakes"), either visit www.LaurenRoyal.com and follow the entry instructions posted online or type your full name, mailing address, e-mail address (if any), along with the answer to the question listed in the back of this book and mail it to the Sponsor at the address listed at the end of these rules. (Hint: Read the prologue of *The Art of Temptation* or the online excerpt for the answer to the entry question.) The entry must contain the correct answer to the question to be eligible. Limit one entry per person. Entries must be received by 11:59 p.m. (PST) on the entry deadline date indicated in the chart below to be eligible for that month's drawing and any or all subsequent drawings. Limit one entry per person/e-mail address for the duration of the sweepstakes.

Winners:

Six winners (one per drawing) will receive a sterling silver claddagh necklace—Approximate Retail Value ("ARV") $50 per necklace.

Monthly Drawing #	Drawing Date On or About:	From among all eligible entries received by 11:59 p.m. (PST) on:
1	11/10/07	10/31/07
2	12/10/07	11/30/07
3	1/10/08	12/31/07
4	2/10/08	1/31/08
5	3/10/08	2/28/08
6	4/10/08	3/31/08

General:

Entries are void if they are in whole or in part illegible, incomplete, or damaged. No responsibility is assumed for late, lost, damaged, incomplete, inaccurate, illegible, postage due, or misdirected entries. Winners will be chosen randomly by the Sponsor, whose decisions concerning all matters related to this Sweepstakes are final and binding. Winners will be notified by mail or e-mail. The odds of winning depend on the number of entries received. Employees, and their immediate family members living in the same household, of Sponsor or Penguin Group (USA) Inc., their parents, subsidiaries or affiliated companies, or the agencies of any of them, are not eligible for this Sweepstakes. Void where prohibited by law. All expenses, including taxes (if any) on receipt and use of prize are the sole responsibility of the winners. Any dispute arising from this Sweepstakes will be determined according to the laws of the State of New York, without reference to its conflict of law principles, and the entrants consent to the personal jurisdiction of the state and federal courts located in New York County and agree that such courts have exclusive jurisdiction over all such disputes.

Winners List:

To receive a copy of the winners list, please send a self-addressed, stamped envelope by October 10, 2008, to the Sponsor listed below, Attn: *The Art of Temptation* Sweepstakes Winners List.

Sponsor:

Lauren Royal
P.O. Box 52932
Irvine, CA 92619